PRAISE FOR KELLEY ARMSTRONG:

FROSTBITTEN

"Gripping."—*Publishers Weekly*

"Armstrong writes page-turning prose, none more throbbingly than when the werewolves enjoy romping, kinky sex."

—*Booklist*

MEN OF THE OTHERWORLD

"The intriguing tales, originally published as serials on Armstrong's Web site, unfold so fluidly that they read almost like a novel, providing a good introduction to new readers and a real treat for fans."   —*Publishers Weekly*

"It truly is a treat, even for those not familiar with Armstrong's previous work. . . . No matter which man is narrating . . . Armstrong creates a distinct and engaging voice and depth of character while maintaining her own sophisticated style."

—*Winnipeg Free Press*

LIVING WITH THE DEAD

"As Armstrong readers have come to expect, this book is balanced between likable characters and the creepy evil that they fight, all wrapped together with nonstop, edge-of-your-seat action."   —*Library Journal*

"Rarely is the ninth book in a series as fresh and entertaining as the first, but this Women of the Otherworld volume defies the odds."   —*Booklist*

PERSONAL DEMON

"A page-turning thriller. Fans of the paranormal will delight in the eighth Women of the Otherworld yarn, with its ass-kicking, Bollywood-beautiful, former-socialite heroine and full complement of sorcerers, witches, werewolves, and other paranormal beings." —*Booklist*

"Better than sex and chocolate, Kelley Armstrong draws readers back into the Otherworld with a slam-dunk new story. . . . Non-stop action with just the right amount of romance and, without a doubt, a winner! Five blue ribbons."

—Dark Angel Reviews

"Exciting for readers looking for page-turning action . . . This is another series that manages to stay fresh even as the characters change and grow from book to book." —SFRevu

"Another winner from the pen of Kelley Armstrong . . . *Personal Demon* continues the high level of suspense, romance, and paranormal excitement as the previous books in the Women of the Otherworld series and is sure not to disappoint." —Romance Reviews Today

"Armstrong is a master of combining romance, mystery and the paranormal in one addictive package. And this latest addition to her series is no exception. Armstrong keeps providing new, fresh, and interesting characters who inhabit a dangerous world filled with shades of gray."

—*The Parkersburg News and Sentinel*

NO HUMANS INVOLVED

"Paranormal and show-business power struggles make for hard-to-put-down entertainment." —*Booklist*

"Armstrong deftly juggles such creatures as werewolves, witches, demons and ghosts with real-life issues." —*Publishers Weekly*

"Armstrong brings a new twist to the necromancer mythology [and] romance fans will be delighted with the inclusion of a quiet but meaningful romance. . . . [The] books, at their best, are about more than just a really cool supernatural world and this one delivers with action, emotion, sexiness and suspense."

—*USA Today*

"Armstrong doesn't do anything in small measures. . . . Another great story you won't want to miss!"—Romance Reviews Today

"I don't think any author other than Armstrong could blend dark horror, celebrity back-biting politics, and endearing romance elements together in one book, and oftentimes in the same scene. . . . Armstrong's intensity and talent never quit. This book will make you laugh, cry, sigh, scream, and beg for more."

—*The Parkersburg News and Sentinel*

BROKEN

"This is a book we've all been waiting for, and let me tell you, Kelley Armstrong does not disappoint. . . . Sit back and enjoy a howling good time with Elena and the Pack."

—Romance Reviews Today

"Action abounds as old characters and new ones run with a plot full of twists, turns and enough red herrings to keep the most persnickety of readers entertained. A vastly entertaining read!"

—Fresh Fiction

HAUNTED

"Kelley Armstrong is an author to be lauded. Instead of cranking out another adventure using werewolves, witches, or sorcerers, she has created an entire mythologically inspired afterlife that exists as another layer to the series."

—*Midwest Book Review*

INDUSTRIAL MAGIC

"Set in a supernatural but credible underworld of industrial-baron sorcerers and psychologically crippled witches . . . Breakneck action is tempered by deep psychological insights, intense sensuality and considerable humor." —*Publishers Weekly*

"Dark, snappy and consistently entertaining . . . Armstrong never loses the balance between Paige's sardonic narration, the wonderfully absurd supporting characters and the nicely girlie touches that add a little lightness to the murder and mayhem. . . . The series, in general, is developing into something more interesting and less predictable with every installment."
—SFCrowsnest.com

"Armstrong's world is dangerous and fun, her voice crisp and funny. . . . A solidly engaging novel." —*Contra Costa Times*

"A book not to be missed. The action is fantastic and the drama is very intense. Kelley Armstrong creates such fun characters that really jump off the pages. The book is fast paced, with lots of unexpected turns." —SF Site

"One of Armstrong's strengths is the creation of plausible characters, which is a real bonus in a series based on the premise that there are supernatural creatures walking and working beside us in our contemporary world. . . . *Industrial Magic* is a page-turner and is very hard to put down." —Bookslut

DIME STORE MAGIC

"[A] sexy supernatural romance [whose] special strength lies in its seamless incorporation of the supernatural into the real world. A convincing small-town setting, clever contemporary dialogue, compelling characterizations and a touch of cool humor make the tale's occasional vivid violence palatable and its fantasy elements both gripping and believable."
—*Publishers Weekly*

"Kelley Armstrong is one of my favorite writers."
—KARIN SLAUGHTER, *New York Times* bestselling author

"Magic, mayhem and romance all combine to create a novel that pleases on every level. The pace is fast, the dialogue witty, and the characters totally unique and enjoyable. . . . First-rate suspense, action-packed, and an all-round terrific read, I highly recommend *Dime Store Magic* and proudly award it RRT's Perfect 10!" —Romance Reviews Today

"After only three books, Kelley Armstrong has proven her talent in creating a truly imaginative and trendy realm. If you're into supernatural stories with a fresh twist, *Dime Store Magic* is just what you're looking for." —BookLoons

"The best book in this series that has been excellent since Book 1. Light humor makes the dramatic ending stand out in sharp contrast. Most laudable is the fact that each book in this series stands alone and complete, so that you can enter it at any point; and though eager for the next book, readers are not left dangling in midair." —Huntress Book Reviews

STOLEN

"Kelley Armstrong delivers a taut, sensual thriller that grips from the first page. Elena Michaels is at once sublime and sympathetic, a modern heroine who shows that real women bite back."
—KARIN SLAUGHTER, *New York Times* bestselling author

"Armstrong has created a persuasive, finely detailed otherworldly cosmology—featuring sorcery, astral projection, spells, telepathy and teleportation—that meshes perfectly with the more humdrum world of interstate highways and cable news bulletins. . . . More than just a thriller with extra teeth, *Stolen* is for anyone who has ever longed to leap over an SUV in a single bound, or to rip an evil security force to shreds, or even just to growl convincingly." —*Quill & Quire*

"*Stolen* is a delicious cocktail of testosterone and wicked humour. . . . Too earnest to attempt parody, [Armstrong's] take on the well-traveled world of supernatural beings is witty and original. She's at her best when examining the all-too-human dilemmas of being superhuman. . . . [*Stolen*] bubbles with the kind of dramatic invention that bodes well for a long and engrossing series. . . . This can only be good news for the growing Michaels fan club." —*The Globe and Mail*

"Mesmerizing . . . The 'otherworldly' atmosphere conjured up by Armstrong begins to seem strangely real. Armstrong is a talented and original writer whose inventiveness and sense of the bizarre is arresting." —*The London Free Press*

"A prison-break story spiffed up with magic . . . Armstrong leavens the narrative with brisk action and intriguing dollops of werewolf culture that suggest a complex and richly imagined anthropologic backstory. The sassy, pumped-up Elena makes a perfect hard-boiled horror." —*Publishers Weekly*

BITTEN

"Frisky . . . Tells a rather sweet love story, and suggests that being a wolf may be more comfortable for a strong, smart young woman than being human." —*The New York Times Book Review*

"Modernizes and humanizes an age-old tale." —New York *Daily News*

"Graphic and sensual, an exciting page-turner . . . [Does] much the same thing for werewolves that Anne Rice did for vampires in her *Interview with the Vampire*." —*Rocky Mountain News*

FROSTBITTEN

KELLEY ARMSTRONG

BANTAM BOOKS
NEW YORK

2010 Bantam Books Mass Market Edition
Copyright © 2009 by KLA Fricke, Inc.
All rights reserved.
Published in the United States by Bantam Books, an imprint of
The Random House Publishing Group, a division of
Random House, Inc., New York.

BANTAM BOOKS and the rooster colophon are registered
trademarks of Random House, Inc.

Originally published in hardcover in the United States by Bantam Books,
a division of Random House, Inc., in 2009.

ISBN: 978-0-553-58962-7

Cover design: Jamie S. Warren
Cover illustration: Craig White
Text design: Sarah Smith

Printed in the United States of America

www.bantamdell.com

2 4 6 8 9 7 5 3 1

To Jeff, who still believes I can,
even on the days when I'm not so sure

ACKNOWLEDGMENTS

Yet another thank-you to the same amazing team who helps me get these stories out there: my agent, Helen Heller, and my editors, Anne Groell of Bantam, Anne Collins of Random House Canada, and Antonia Hodgson of Little, Brown & Co. UK.

Big thanks as always to my beta readers. This time around, I had Ang Yan Ming, Xaviere Daumarie, Terri Giesbrecht, Laura Stutts, Raina Toomey, Lesley W., and Danielle Wegner. Yes, the list grows as the stories do—more eyes to make sure I don't screw up!

FROSTBITTEN

PROLOGUE

AS TOM WATCHED the moonlight reflect off the ice-covered lake, he had a reflection of his own: the world really needed more snow.

Sure, people paid lip service to the threat of global warming, tsking and tutting and pointing at the glaciers receding right over in Kenai Fjords. But in their hearts, they weren't convinced that a warmer climate was such a bad thing, especially at this time of year, late March, with harsh months of Alaskan winter behind them, and weeks more to go.

But Tom liked snow. God's Ajax, he called it. Divine cleansing powder. When spring thaw came, this lake and field would be one big swamp, nothing but mud and mosquitoes and the decaying corpses of every beast that hadn't survived the winter. For these few months, though, it was as pristine a wilderness as any poet might imagine.

A field of unbroken white glittered under a half-moon. The air was so crisp it was like sucking breath mints, and the night so silent Tom could hear mice tunneling under the drifts and the howling of wolves ten miles off.

Tom liked wolves even more than he liked snow. Beautiful, proud creatures. Perfect hunters, gliding through the night, silent as ghosts.

The first animal he'd ever trapped had been a wolf cub. He still remembered it, lying in a halo of blood on the newly fallen snow, lips drawn back in a final snarl of defiance, its leg half chewed off as it had tried to escape. Even as a boy, Tom had respected that defiance, that will to survive. When his dad had said the pelt was too damaged to sell, Tom had asked his mother to make him mitts out of it.

He still had those mitts. He'd planned to pass them on to his son but . . . well, forty-six wasn't too old yet, but there just weren't enough women to go around up here. Anchorage wasn't as bad as Fairbanks, but when you were a trapper with an eighth-grade education, living in a cabin thirty miles from town, you'd better look like Brad Pitt if you hoped to get yourself a wife.

Another wolf pack's song joined the first, and as Tom listened, he wondered whether one of those was *his* pack, the one that used to run in this field. For twenty years, he'd been able to count on pelts from them. Not many—he didn't trap wolves anymore, only shot them, being careful to target the old and sick, like a proper scavenger should.

He'd hear them when he came to empty his traps, their howls so close he'd grip his rifle a little tighter. They never bothered him, though—just let him go about his business.

He'd see their tracks, crisscrossing through the snow, and he'd find their kills picked clean to the last bone. Now and then, he'd even catch a glimpse of them, silently slipping through the trees. Once, on a winter's night just like this, he'd watched them playing out on the ice, even the old ones tumbling and sliding like puppies.

But then, a few months back they'd left this little valley.

Now those distant wolf howls stopped, and when they did, Tom realized how quiet it was. Unnaturally quiet. Folks talked about the silence of the Alaskan wilderness, yet anyone who spent any time there knew it was anything but silent, with the constant rush of wind and running water, the scampering of feet over and under the snow, the call of predators and the cries of prey. Right now, though, Tom could swear even the wind had stopped.

And if you've been out here long enough, you know this, too—that true silence means only one thing: trouble.

Tom lowered his pack to the ground and lifted his rifle, gripping it with both hands like a samurai with his sword. Not that Tom fooled himself into thinking a gun made him a warrior. Out here he was just another predator, and a pitiful one at that.

When a shadow rippled between the trees, he held perfectly still and tracked it by pivoting slowly, his rifle rising a few more inches.

The two worst mistakes you could make in the forest were complacency and panic. As hard as he looked, though, he caught only a glimpse of a big shape, hunched onto all fours. Then it was gone.

A bear? They rarely bothered with humans outside of cub season. And when bears took off, they made a helluva racket, especially when they had just come out of hibernation. Tom hadn't heard a thing.

The hair on his neck rose as old stories and legends crept

through his mind. Some native hunters wouldn't set foot in parts of this forest. This was Ijiraat territory, they'd say, the hunting grounds of shape-shifters who took the form of wolf and bear, and protected their land against all comers. Tales for children, Tom told himself. Old men trying to frighten the young.

He took a step, his boots crunching in the snow. A shape moved in the trees, closer now, and Tom brought his rifle all the way to his shoulder, gloved finger to the trigger.

Clouds slid over the moon and the forest went black. A twig cracked to his left and Tom swore he felt hot breath on the back of his neck. When he spun, nothing was there.

He took one hand off the rifle and fumbled in his pocket for the flashlight. It caught in the folds and when he wrenched, it flew out and sailed into the surrounding darkness.

The brush crackled to his right now. He spun again, finger still on the trigger, and this time he saw a faint shape. He was about to fire when he thought of Danny Royce. Another trapper, Danny had been spooked by shadows in this same valley just last summer and he'd fired his gun, only to find that he'd shot some kid, a wild-haired teen, probably a hiker or camper. Danny had buried the body and no one ever found it, but Danny hadn't been the same since—not sleeping, drinking too much and talking too much, blabbing his story to Tom like a sinner at confession, swearing the boy's ghost was stalking him. Tom knew the only thing stalking Danny Royce was guilt, but still, the story kept him from pulling the trigger.

The shape had vanished. Tom held his breath, scanning

the woods for any change in the shadows. Then he saw it, at least twenty feet away now, a huge shape between two trees. The cloud cover thinned enough for the moon to glimmer through and he could see the shape, too pale for a bear.

Tom hunkered down as slowly as he could, and with his free hand, he began feeling around for the flashlight. He allowed himself one glance at the ground and saw it there, dark against the snow. He scooped it up. His finger found the switch. The click sounded harsh against the silence. Nothing happened. He whacked the flashlight against his thigh and tried again. Nothing.

Something landed on his back, hitting him so hard that at first he thought he'd been shot. He lost his grip on the rifle. A blast of hot breath seared his neck, and a weight pinned him to the snow.

As the thing flipped him over, the flashlight bounced off a tree and flicked on just when fangs tore into his throat. Tom caught a glimpse of light fur and glittering blue eyes, and his last thought was *That's not one of my wolves.*

MESSAGE

YOU CAN'T HELP someone who doesn't want to be helped. And you really can't help someone who runs the moment you get within shouting distance, making a beeline for the nearest train, plane or bus terminal, destination anywhere as long as it takes him hundreds of miles from you.

As I chased Reese Williams through the streets of Pittsburgh—the third city in two days—I had to admit I was starting to take this rejection personally. I don't usually have this problem with guys. Sure, at five foot ten, I'm a little taller than some like. My build is a little more athletic than most like. I don't always put as much care into my appearance as I should, usually forgoing makeup, tying my hair back with an elastic and favoring jeans and T-shirts. But I'm a blue-eyed blonde, so men usually decide that they can overlook my deficiencies and not run screaming the other way.

Sure, if they found out I was a werewolf, I could understand a little screaming and running. But Reese had no such excuse. He was a werewolf himself, and considering I'm the only known female of our species, when guys like him meet me, they're usually the ones doing the chasing...at least until they realize that's not such a good idea if they'd like to keep all their body parts intact.

I'd lost Reese when he'd cut through a throng of rowdy Penguins fans heading off to a game. I'd tried following him through the drunken mob, but the Pack frowns on me cold-cocking humans for grabbing my ass, so after enduring a few unimaginative sexual suggestions, I retreated and waited for them to move on.

By then Reese's trail was overlaid and interwoven with a score of human ones. And the air here already stunk, the city core entering construction season, the stink of machinery and diesel almost overwhelming the smell of the Ohio River a half mile over. There was no way I was picking up Reese's trail at this intersection. Not without changing into a wolf in downtown Pittsburgh...another thing the Pack frowns on.

When I caught up with him two blocks later, he was being sucked in by the glow of a Starbucks sign, presumably hoping for a populated place to rest. When he saw that all the seats inside were empty, he veered across the road.

Reese ran into one of those office-drone oases typical of big cities, where they carve out a store-size chunk of land and add interlocking brick, foliage and random pieces of art in hopes of convincing workers to relax there, enjoy the scenery, listen to the symphony of squealing tires and blaring horns and imbibe a little smog with their lattes.

After a dozen strides, Reese was through the tiny park and veering again, this time to a sidewalk beside the lot.

Headlights appeared, blinding me, then dipped down into an underground lot. Reese grabbed the barrier and vaulted into the lane. I raced over to see the automatic door below closing behind a van . . . with Reese running, hunched over, right behind it.

I did a vault of my own and ran down the incline, reaching the bottom, then dropping and rolling under the door just as it was about to close. I leapt to my feet and darted through the dimly lit garage, hiding behind the nearest post. Then I strained to hear footsteps. For almost a minute, the van engine rumbled on the far side of the garage. It quit with a shudder and a gasp. A door desperate for oil squeaked open, then slammed shut.

Hunched over, I hopscotched between the sparse parked cars. Ahead I could hear the van driver's heavy steps thudding as he walked the other way.

A door creaked and a distant rectangle of light appeared. The door hadn't even clicked shut when Reese darted out from his hiding space, his boots slapping the asphalt as he ran.

I kicked into high gear, no longer bothering to hide, but he was too close to the stairwell. I was almost at the closed door when it flew open again, and I narrowly missed barreling into a middle-aged man.

"Sorry," I said as I tried to brush past him. "I was just—"

"Running for the exit because you're afraid to walk through an underground lot at night?"

"Uh, yes."

"There are plenty of lots aboveground, miss. Much safer. Here, let me walk you up to your floor."

It was obvious there were only two ways I could get past this guy—let him play the gentleman or shove him out of the way. Clay would have done the latter—no question—and thrown in a snarl for good measure. But I haven't overcome my Canadian upbringing, which forbade being rude to anyone who hadn't done anything to deserve it.

So I let the guy escort me up the stairs, and thanked him at the top.

"I'm not saying you shouldn't park underground..." he began.

"I understa—"

"Hell, it's your right to park wherever you want. What you *shouldn't* do is need to be afraid. This will help."

He held out a paper-thin white rectangle, making me think they really had done a lot with personal alarms since I'd last seen one. But it was a business card.

"My wife runs Taser parties."

"Taser...?"

"You know, like Tupperware parties. A bunch of women get together, have a good time, share some potluck and get a demonstration of the latest in personal security devices."

I searched his face for some sign that he was joking. He wasn't. I thanked him again and hurried out of the stairwell.

Reese's trail led out the front door. As I went after him, I realized I was still holding the card, which featured a cute little red Taser that I'm sure fit into a purse and accessorized very nicely, for women who carried purses or accessorized.

From Tupperware parties to lingerie parties to Taser parties. I shook my head and stuffed the card into my pocket. Right now, I actually wouldn't mind a Taser. It might be the only way to stop Reese. Of course, I'd need to get close enough to use it, which wasn't looking very likely.

THREE BLOCKS LATER, I finally caught up with Reese on a rooftop. He'd climbed up the fire escape, probably thinking I wouldn't follow.

When I swung over the top, he broke into a run, heading for the opposite side, boots sliding on the gravel. When I realized he wasn't going to veer at the last second, I threw on the brakes, gravel crunching as I skidded to a stop.

"Okay," I called. "I'm not coming any closer. I just want to talk to you."

He was close enough to the edge to make my heart race. He slowly pivoted to face me.

Reese Williams, twenty years old, and recently emigrated from Australia. With broad shoulders, sun-streaked wavy blond hair and the remnants of a tan, he looked like the kind of kid who should be leading tour groups into the outback, all smiles and corny jokes. Only he wasn't joking or smiling now.

"My name is Elena—" I began.

"I know who you are," he said. "But where is *he*?"

"Not here, obviously." I gestured around me. "In two days, you haven't caught a whiff of any werewolf except me, which should be a sure sign that Clay's not around."

"So you're alone?" The sarcasm in his voice made that a statement. I was the only female werewolf. *Obviously*, I needed protection, which must be why I'd taken refuge with the Pack and, for a mate, had chosen the Alpha's second-in-command—the baddest, craziest werewolf around.

"He's teaching," I said. "Georgia State University, this week."

His glower said he didn't appreciate my joke. I wasn't kidding—that bad and crazy werewolf also had a Ph.D. in anthropology and was currently lecturing at a symposium on cult worship in ancient Egypt. But there was no way Reese would believe that.

"Fine," I said. "You think he's been lurking in the shadows, out of sight and downwind for two days. *Unobtrusive* is one word that's never been applied to Clay but, sure, let's go with that theory. Unless he's learned to fly, though, the only way up is that ladder behind me, so you're going to see him coming. Now, let's take a minute and chat. The reason I've been chasing you for two days is that I want to talk to you about—"

"South Carolina."

"Right."

"I didn't kill those humans."

"I know."

He allowed himself two seconds of surprise, and in those two seconds, he looked like a kid on his first day away at college—lonely, confused and hoping he'd found someone to help. Then his face hardened again. He might be no older than a college student, but he wasn't that naïve or that optimistic, not anymore.

I hurried on. "You emigrated last year and hooked up with a couple of morons named Liam Malloy and Ramon Santos. They promised to show you the ropes of werewolf

life in America. Then the half-eaten bodies started showing up—"

"I didn't do it."

"No, they did, and they're blaming you for it. We
know—"

He inched back toward the edge.

"Don't—" I began. "Just stop there. Better yet, take a
step toward me."

"Am I making you nervous?"

I met his gaze. "Yes."

"A jumper would be a real mess to clean up, wouldn't it?
Better to calm me down and get me into a nice stretch of
forest for easy burial."

"That's not—" An exasperated sigh hissed through my
teeth. "Fine. You're convinced I'm going to kill you. The
only question, then, is—"

He stepped back . . . and plummeted.

I lunged so fast I nearly did a face-plant in the gravel,
scrabbling to get to the edge, heart in my throat, cursing
myself for being so careless, so flippant—

Then I saw the second roof, two stories below, and Reese
running across it.

Clay would have taken a dramatic flying leap. I felt the
urge, but reminded myself I was the mother of two and
would turn forty in a few months. Even though I had the
body of a bionic thirty-year-old, I had responsibilities to my
family, to my Alpha and, most important right now, to this
dumbass kid who'd get killed if I broke my ankle and
couldn't warn him about Liam and Ramon.

So I crouched on the edge, checked my trajectory and

jumped carefully. I landed on my feet and took off after Reese. I was barely on the second rooftop before he was off it. It was a three-story drop this time, which was a bit much even for a twenty-year-old werewolf. The thump of a hard landing and a gasp of pain confirmed that.

I picked up speed, hoping I'd see him huddled below, hurt and unable to run. But the pavement was empty, as was the parking lot beyond. I caught a flash of movement in a recessed doorway, where he crouched, hidden in the shadows, waiting to ambush me. Good thing I *hadn't* pulled a Clay and charged headlong after my prey.

I walked to the adjoining edge, lowered myself over, then dropped. Twin shocks of pain blasted through my legs as I hit the asphalt. I was going to pay for that in the morning. For now, I rubbed it out, then snuck to the corner of the building.

The wind shifted and I caught a whiff of Reese, his scent heavy with fear. It wasn't me he should be afraid of, though, but his old traveling buddies.

Liam and Ramon had killed three humans in South Carolina and set up Reese to take the fall. Now they were hoping to find and kill him before I got his side of the story.

How was I so sure of this?

Because they'd done it before. Five years ago they'd befriended a twenty-three-year-old immigrant werewolf named Yuli Etxeberria. When evidence of man-killing pointed to Etxeberria, Clay had wanted to swoop in and grab him. I'd held back. I'd been suspicious, but not suspicious enough. Liam killed Etxeberria and mailed us his hand, as if expecting a commendation for taking care of this "man-eater."

That wouldn't happen this time. I strode down the grassy strip between the building and the parking lot, as if I was scanning that lot, giving Reese the perfect ambush target.

When I reached the recessed doorway, I dove. Reese's shadow passed over me, pouncing and catching only air. I leapt up, grabbed the back of his jacket and threw him onto the grass.

He landed with a thud. He tried to roll out of it and bounce up swinging, but a twenty-year-old with a were-wolf's strength and agility is like a twenty-year-old behind the wheel of a Lamborghini—all that power but not enough experience using it—and he fumbled the bounce back to his feet.

I tossed him face-first onto the grass again. This time he stayed where he landed.

"Where did we leave off?" I said. "Right. Liam and Ramon and their plot to end your existence."

"Kill me?" He slowly rose. "Why would they—?"

He charged, hoping to catch me off guard. I stepped aside and he smacked into the wall, then wheeled fast and came at me again. Again, I stepped aside, this time grabbing him and pitching him through the air.

As he hit the ground, he let out a stream of profanity.

I shook my head. "If I wanted to hurt you, I wouldn't be throwing you on the *grass*, would I?"

"Right, you're here to help me, after getting tipped off that I'm a man-eater. Do you really expect me to—"

He tried the dash-in-midsentence trick again, making a break for the alley. I tore after him. As I caught the back of his jacket, he spun and hit me with an upper cut that sent me sailing off my feet.

I kept my grip on his coat, and we both went down. I tried to scramble up, but he pinned me. It was then that his wolf brain kicked in. His pupils dilated, his breathing quickened, his erection pressed into my thigh, his wolf side telling him this wasn't a fight—it was foreplay, and damn, I smelled good.

He froze as the still-human part of his brain warned him that what the wolf wanted was a very bad idea. But his nostrils still flared, drinking in my scent.

I knew which side would win, and that's when things always got ugly.

So while he fought his inner battle, I heaved him off me.

"That's why I don't do hand-to-hand combat with mutts," I said.

He nodded as he got to his feet, rubbing his face briskly with his sleeve, gaze down, cheeks flaming. He pinched his nose and shook his head, trying to clear my scent.

It took a smart kid to back off that fast. And Reese *was* smart—that was the problem. If he'd been a dumb lunk who'd keep trying to hump my leg, then he'd have believed me when I said I was here to rescue him. Instead, he saw all the ways it could be a trick.

"Liam and Ramon *are* after you," I said. "You haven't noticed because they aren't nearly as good at tracking as I am. Give them a few weeks to catch up and—"

He charged, switching to the dash-while-your-*opponent-*

is-in-midspeech tactic. Again, I sidestepped. Only this time, he hooked the back of my knee. I stumbled, but came up swinging. Unfortunately, he was already ten feet away, running for the road.

I took off after him.

FLIGHT

I LOST HIM. The condensed version is that Reese Williams possessed an admirable blend of intelligence and humility, and I was accustomed to dealing with mutts who'd sooner cut off their balls than run from a woman.

Reese did exactly what I'd have done if pursued through a city core by a more experienced werewolf. He ran for the nearest populated place—a busy restaurant. While I waited at the back door, he must have darted out the front and swiped someone's cab. By the time I realized he was gone, it was too late to follow.

Now, an hour later, I was in a cab of my own, getting out at the Pittsburgh International Airport.

What led me here wasn't good old-fashioned legwork. Ever since the werewolves rejoined the supernatural council, our mutt tracking has gone high tech. We now have Paige Winterbourne, genius computer hacker, at our disposal.

We knew Reese had been using stolen credit cards, alternating between at least three. Paige had identified two and was tracking transactions.

I didn't even get a chance to tell her I'd lost him before she was calling to say he'd used a credit card at the airport. As for *where* he was going, that proved more problematic. Paige had access to all the major airline computers, but this was a small one she hadn't ever needed to crack. So I was back to leg and nose work.

"You're booked on a flight to Miami," Jeremy said as I got out of the cab, cell phone to my ear. "That will get you through security. But from the sounds of it, you've delivered your message. If he's refusing to listen, I'm not sure what you plan to do about that."

"I want to tell him what happened to Yuli Etxeberria. If that doesn't work, I'll hog-tie him and haul his ass someplace safe until he smartens up."

Silence as I walked through the doors. It lasted so long that with anyone else I'd have wondered if the line disconnected.

"You don't need to keep chasing him, Elena."

"Just one more day. The kids are okay, aren't they?"

"Yes, they're fine. Clay called an hour ago. His last meeting was canceled, so he can help with Reese."

"Great. He can catch up with me tomorrow, after he stops in there and sees the kids."

"While I'm sure he'd love to see them, right now he wants to get to you. As soon as you figure out where you're going, he'll meet up with you."

I didn't argue. It'd been two weeks since I'd seen Clay—longer than we'd been apart in years. I was so accustomed to having him around that for two weeks I'd been unbalanced and off-kilter. And when it came to hunting Reese without my partner, I'd definitely been off my game.

"Etxeberria wasn't your fault, Elena," Jeremy said.

Ah, right to the crux of the matter, as usual.

"One more day," I said. "Just give me—"

"I'll give you all the time you need. You know that. Then once you're done, take an extra night with Clay before you come back."

WE HADN'T INTENDED to be apart so long. For Clay, even separate day trips were too much. That's the wolf in him, wanting his mate nearby at all times. Most werewolves inherit the genes and don't transform until their late teens, but Clay was bitten as a child, and that makes him more wolf than human.

Our separation had begun with a work trip for me that lasted longer than expected. In the meantime, Clay had left for Atlanta. I was supposed to stop overnight at home, then follow. Only that night, our darling three-year-old twins thought I'd gone out back for a "walk in the forest" and decided to follow . . . by jumping out a second-floor window.

While adult werewolves have superhuman strength and reflexes, and could easily make that leap, we don't get those secondary powers until puberty. As for whether those rules apply to the offspring of two werewolves, let's just say we're starting to think they don't. The kids escaped with minor injuries: a twisted ankle for Logan and a sprained wrist for Kate, which meant no Atlanta trip for me.

Thus the two-week separation, now thankfully almost at an end.

SOME AIRPORTS ARE perfect for losing a tail. Take Minneapolis. With its endless corridors of shops and restaurants it rivals the nearby Mall of America as a hellhole for the directionally challenged. Pittsburgh was not one of those airports.

By the time I entered the terminal, Reese had checked in and headed for his gate, but there wasn't far for him to go. I picked up my ticket and got my boarding pass. Two sets of escalators deposited travelers in a tiny presecurity square, bounded by a few shops. Reese's trail headed straight for the security checkpoint.

Once I was inside and off yet another escalator, it got trickier. I was in a rotunda of shops and restaurants with four arms leading to boarding gates. Still, the tidy layout meant there were a limited number of places for him to go. Even if I couldn't find his trail, I just needed to check all four halls and—

"Paging Chris Parker. Chris Parker, please report to gate C56."

I smiled. Parker was one of the aliases Reese was using.

When I got to the gate, though, the waiting area was empty, the plane already loaded. Reese was at the counter, showing his boarding pass and ID to the attendant. She was taking a good look at them, and he was struggling to stay calm, shifting and glancing around.

I shouldered my way through a throng checking the departure screens, then broke into a fast walk. The attendant was saying something to Reese. Questioning his fake ID? It looked a little off, didn't it? Better hold him for another minute, get someone to come and check it . . .

With a smile, she handed back his ID and boarding pass. Reese started down the long hall to his plane. I picked up my pace, but by the time I neared the desk, he was gone.

Gone *where*?

I glanced at the screen behind the attendant. It seemed to be stuck on the flight number and departure time, so I asked where the plane was headed.

"Anchorage." She blinded me with a smile. "Anchorage, Alaska."

MULTITASKING

"SO I'VE HIT the end of the line," I said to Jeremy as I settled into a seat. "As badly as I want to warn this kid, I'm not flying to Alaska. Hopefully, Liam and Ramon feel the same way."

"I'm sure they will."

I expected to hear his usual deep timbre of reassurance. Instead, his words carried a note of hesitation.

"You think they'll track him to Alaska?" I asked.

"No, I'm quite certain they won't. However, a trip to Anchorage might not be a bad idea, if you and Clay are up to it."

"Whatever you need. What's up in Alas—?" I stopped. "Those reports of wolf kills, right?"

One of my Pack responsibilities was tracking potential werewolf activity. Jeremy monitored newspapers and I took the Internet. This case had shown up in both.

Two men had presumably been killed by wolves outside Anchorage. That was newsworthy because, despite their reputation as dangerous beasts, wolves don't kill people. In North America there have been no documented cases of healthy wild wolves killing humans in the last hundred years. So when it seemed to happen, people got nervous. And we got really nervous because the one thing far more common than wolf attacks was werewolf attacks.

Two reports weren't enough for the Pack to investigate. And there were other recent reports of equally rare wolf activity—wolves attacking dogs and people spotting wolves near the city. If the wolves near Anchorage were getting bolder, then it stood to reason they might actually be responsible for these deaths.

But if I had another reason to go to Alaska...

"I can check it out while I hunt down Reese," I said.

"I'll reroute Clay there." A pause. "There's something else, too. Dennis was supposed to call me last week. He wanted to discuss something that seemed important."

"And he didn't?"

"No, and he's not returning my calls either."

Dennis Stillwell and his son, Joey, were former Pack werewolves who'd left for western Canada when Jeremy and his father's battle for Alphahood had turned ugly. They'd later moved to Alaska. That was thirty years ago, before I joined the Pack, but Jeremy and Dennis had kept in touch, and this silence probably bothered Jeremy more than the wolf kills.

"I'm off to Alaska, then," I said. "Should I call Clay and let him know?"

"I'll do that, and I'll book you a flight. You get something to eat. Try to relax."

UNFORTUNATELY, THERE WASN'T a lot of demand for travel from Pittsburgh to Anchorage, and the flight Reese had taken was the only direct one for the next twenty-four hours. So I was transferring in Phoenix.

The flight and the brief layover gave me time to think—too much time. In the last week, I'd been hit with two things that I really wanted to talk to Clay about. Things that weren't suitable for a phone conversation. Things that preyed on my mind every time I slowed down long enough to relax, which was likely another reason I kept chasing Reese when common sense told me to give up.

The first thing... well, that worried me, but it didn't have the same effect as the second. The second was the kicker, the one that had me avoiding quiet moments like this. It happened the day before I started chasing Reese. After the kids went to bed, Jeremy and I had been in the study, relaxing in front of the fire. He'd been reading a novel; I'd been reading my mail, which tended to pile up, untouched, for days.

Had I known who sent the letter, I'd have pitched it into the fire unread. But it had gone through my alma mater, so it had arrived in a University of Toronto envelope. I hadn't noticed the second envelope inside, distractedly ripping through both.

It was a letter from one of the men who'd fostered me as a child. I don't call him my foster father. That would give him a place in my life he didn't deserve.

I'd gone through a lot of homes after my parents died. I think when potential mothers saw me—the quiet girl with big, haunted eyes—they saw not a temporary placement, but a child they could rescue and make their own, and when

I didn't open up to them, when I didn't become the perfect, sweet daughter they wanted, they gave me back.

Being blond and blue-eyed meant I also attracted attention of a less altruistic kind from a few foster "fathers" and "brothers." Most times it was no more than a peek in the bathroom or a hand that lingered too long on my leg. But sometimes it was worse, especially from the man who sent me the letter.

In it, he said he was going through therapy now for his *problem*. He was sorry for what he'd done to me and his therapist thought that as part of the healing process, he should let me know. Apologize and ask forgiveness.

I'd gotten up from the couch, walked to the fireplace and dropped the letter in. Jeremy had looked up from his book with a soft "Elena?" but I'd strode from the room before he could ask anything.

I wish I could say that was that. God, I wish I could say it. But it wasn't, and the one person I could have talked to wasn't there, so the letter—every damned word of it—festered in my brain. Before I read it, I'd been off-kilter with Clay gone. Afterward, I seemed to stumble half blind through my days, ferociously fixated on whatever goal I was pursuing, be it making breakfast for the kids or chasing Reese, not daring to rest, knowing rest only brought back memories and fears and rage I thought long since vanquished.

Not vanquished, it seems. Just shoved into willful forgetfulness. And now it was back, and I couldn't forget, no matter how hard I tried.

I was just settling into the second plane, about to turn off my cell phone when it rang.

"Morning, darling," came a familiar southern drawl.

I straightened. "Hey, you. I hear we're going to Alaska."

"We are. Looking forward to it?"

"I'm not arguing the order, that's for sure. Now we just need to get the business part of the trip out of the way, so we can take advantage of the locale. Miles and miles of unexplored wilderness. It'll definitely make up for two weeks of short, crappy runs alone."

"So that's what you want me back for? A running partner?"

"Of course. What else?"

"I can think of a few things." Clay's drawl turned to a low growl that set me shivering. "If you can work it into your busy run schedule."

"I'm sure I can. Before the runs. After the runs. Any other time we get a spare minute . . ."

He laughed. "You *do* miss me."

"I do."

A moment of silence. "Just a sec. I think we had a bad connection. I could have sworn you admitted—"

"I miss you. Horribly. I can't wait to see you."

"They're serving the booze already, aren't they?"

"Ha-ha. Keep that up and I'll never say it again."

"The question is whether you'd say it if I was there."

"No, because if you were here, I'd be in your lap, wondering how we could slip into the bathroom."

"Tease," he growled.

My head shot up. I could have sworn I heard that growl . . . and not just through my phone. I scoured the aisle, but there were only a few passengers still boarding, none of

them Clay. Still, I scanned the first-class section. No familiar blond curls peeked over any of the seats.

"Elena?"

"Sorry." I pushed back the stab of disappointment. "So
when does your flight get in?"

"Around eight."

"I'll wait at the terminal for you, then."

The attendants started making the preflight rounds. We
said good-bye and I turned off my phone. As I settled into
my seat, I fought off that lingering disappointment. It'd
been so good to hear his voice that I'd even felt that slow
wave of calm that comes whenever he enters a room, a deep
instinct telling me I could relax now, that my mate was
close.

As I tucked my bag under the seat, I caught that feeling
again and picked up a scent as familiar as my own. I twisted
to see Clay looming over the back of my seat.

"Can't fool you, can I?" he said.

I grabbed him by the shirtfront, nearly yanking him
over the seat as I pulled him into a kiss.

"I definitely need to go away more often," he said as I let
him go.

"Absolutely not, unless it's a trip for two."

"Agreed."

He came around and took the seat beside mine. I should
have wondered when Jeremy insisted on booking my flight,
then said he could only get me into first class. Clay hates
coach—can't stand being that close to strangers.

"I believe I heard something about sitting on my lap—"
he began.

I shot onto it and was kissing him before he finished the sentence. His eyes widened before he recovered enough to kiss me back.

To say I'm not one for public displays of affection is an understatement. But over the years I've come to care less about what strangers think, and Clay has made equal strides to care *more* . . . or at least learned to act as if he does. So I sat in his lap and kissed him, and he didn't snarl at the woman across the aisle when she started harrumphing and glowering, and all was good.

"Now, how about that bathroom trip," Clay said as I slid back into my seat.

I looked up at the first-class bathroom . . . past two flight attendants and six rows of passengers, all facing it.

"You know, it always looks so much easier in the movies."

He laughed and fastened his seat belt. "So this was a good surprise, I take it?"

"A great one."

He blinked, genuinely surprised, and I felt a prickle of guilt. Clay and I had our issues—huge ones that had kept us apart for ten years. I'd grown so accustomed to holding him at arm's length that even now, I suppose in some ways I still did. I was quick to say a casual "miss you" on the phone, but never a heartfelt "Hey, I really, really miss you."

He knew I'd really missed him. It just threw him to hear the words. Another thing I needed to work on.

As the plane lifted off, I brought Clay up to date on the possible wolf kills. Yes, our fellow passengers could hear us, but no one eavesdrops on a conversation like that and thinks, "Oh my God, they're talking about werewolves!"

There had been two deaths so far. Both had been men out alone traipsing through the Alaskan wilderness at night, which seems to be natural selection at work, as much as African tourists who decide to camp beside watering holes.

The first victim had been a New Age Vancouverite on a spirit quest, fasting in a teepee. The second was an ex-con stealing from traps. Really, could you blame the wolves for thinking these two would make a nice late-winter feast?

The authorities were blaming a single man-eating wolf. At the site of both killings, they'd found the tracks of a huge canine. Werewolves change into very large wolves, retaining their body mass. And outside the Pack, most are loners.

Still, that didn't mean it *was* a werewolf. It just bore looking into, as long as we were going to Alaska for other reasons.

By the time I finished my explanation, dinner was served. Given the hour, most passengers stuck to drinks and peanuts, but no werewolf turned down food, however strange the time. While we ate, Clay talked about the symposium. Then I gave him another update—this one on Reese Williams.

Again, our conversation might sound odd to anyone listening, but as long as we didn't mention the W word, they'd fluff off my talk of fights and chases as a movie plot discussion. Most people were asleep anyway, as was I after dinner and a glass of wine.

While I napped, Clay read the Alaskan tourism information I'd downloaded earlier. Surrounded by strangers, he couldn't relax his guard enough to shut his eyes.

When I woke, I looked down to see city lights below.

"Still night?" I said, yawning. "What time—?" I checked my watch. "It's past six. Where's the sun?"

"It's past *five* local time, and it's Alaska, darling."

"Shit. That's right. Duh. So when can we expect to see the sun?"

"It'll start rising around eight-thirty, but won't get over those mountains for a while. An earlier daylight saving time doesn't do them any favors here."

"No kidding."

I could make out the city below, nestled in a valley, surrounded on three sides by snowy mountains and the fourth by the ocean. Beyond those lights of civilization? Miles of wilderness.

I smiled. "Uncharted territory."

"The best kind." Clay shifted closer, hand resting on my thigh as he looked out the window. "Still too dark to get to work, checking out those kills or looking for Dennis. We'll have to find other things to do."

"We could go to the hotel and get some sleep..."

He snorted.

"Sex or a run?" I asked.

"Do I have to pick one?"

I grinned. "Never."

PLAYTIME

ONCE IN THE terminal, naturally we had to check for Reese, in case his flight had been delayed or he'd decided to hang out here rather than pay for an extra night's hotel room. We went in search of all the secluded, tucked-away places he could hide. Unfortunately, post-9/11 these places are increasingly hard to come by in airports.

"Goddamn it," Clay muttered after our third possibility proved to be staffed by a security camera. "Where the hell is a mutt supposed to hole up around here?"

Before he stormed down the car-rental hall, I caught his arm and pointed to a sign warning of construction ahead.

"About time," he grumbled.

He hurdled over the barrier, pushed back the tarp and disappeared. I waited for any indication that the coast wasn't clear—screams, shouts, foul language—then followed. When I caught up, Clay stood beside a pile of drywall, his head tilted, nose lifted, trying to catch the sound or smell of workers.

I turned down a side passage. It was short, ending at a

locked door. I was considering the wisdom of snapping the lock when Clay strode up behind. He caught me around the hips, flipping me around, mouth going to mine.

He kissed me hard. Lips crushing. Hands grabbing. Fingers digging in. The smell of him filling my nostrils, thick and heady as hashish smoke. Brain spinning. Body screaming. Hands pulling his shirt up. Fingers gripping his sides. Skin to skin, touching, stroking, making that connection I'd missed so much.

A growl vibrated up from his chest, coming out in a long, low moan. Fingers in my hair. Winding. Pulling. Kissing harder. Teeth scraping. Tongue tasting.

His hands dropped to my waist. Button flicking. Zipper whirring. The chill blast of air against hot skin. The rough rasp of jeans shoved down. Warm fingers moving under my panties. Tugging. Fabric catching, pulling, stretching. A growl. A rip. A laugh.

Hands on my thighs, pushing them apart, as if I needed the encouragement. Back against wall. Wriggling. Straddling. Legs over hips. Come on, come on! Then...

Oh, God, yes. God, I missed you. God, I love you. Yes, please, yes...

Clay pressed me against the wall, nuzzling my neck as I shuddered and gasped.

"Speed record?" he asked.

"For us? Probably not."

He chuckled and kept kissing my neck, inhaling deeply, telling me how good I smelled, how much he'd missed me, how much he loved me, until the distant clang of a door had us jumping apart.

"No sign of Reese here," I said as I pulled my jeans back on.

"You can tell Jeremy we checked every nook and cranny. Now time for that run."

FIRST WE HAD to get the luggage and rental car. As much as Clay disliked dealing with people, I sent him for the car, since Clay and crowded baggage claims really don't mix. If someone picks up one of our bags by accident, his territorial instinct kicks in. Usually one glower makes the offender drop it and scuttle away, but on our last trip, a guy tried to take off with my bag even after I politely suggested it might not be his, and Clay . . . well, it was really best for all if I got the luggage alone.

Having also seen a young woman at the car-rental booth made the task-splitting decision that much easier. Jeremy would have reserved us a decent vehicle, but we can always use a free upgrade . . . and Clay gets a lot of free upgrades—double butter on his popcorn, an extra-large coffee when he orders medium, high-test fuel for the price of regular. I think it has something to do with being drop-dead gorgeous. Muscular body, chiseled face, bright blue eyes, golden curls. At forty-seven he looks midthirties, which is no longer a "hot young thing," but apparently a "hot mature thing" is still serious catnip.

Clay hates attracting attention of any kind, and to him, when he has a wedding band on his finger, attention of *that* kind is an insult. He makes no secret of his feelings, which only seems to earn him more freebies and upgrades, as women try harder to coax a smile.

"They were out of Explorers," Clay said as he met me pulling the luggage. "We got an Expedition."

"Uh-huh."

"And this." He held up a navigation system. "It was some kind of monthly deal."

"Did they have any free T-shirts? Ball caps? Travel mugs?"

"Nah. Got some maps, though." He held up a handful. "Good ones."

"Monthly deal?"

"Guess so."

We found our vehicle—a massive SUV with tinted windows.

"We didn't need to find a quiet corner inside," I said. "We could have just crawled in the back of this."

"Huh." He opened the hatch and looked in. "Could try it out..."

"I'm sure we will. Later. Right now, I want my run, followed by my postrun romp. Once took the edge off. Twice would spoil my appetite."

"Wouldn't want that," he said, and heaved our bags in.

THE PRESUMED WOLF kills had both occurred about twenty miles south of Anchorage, so with my laptop open to a newspaper article's rough map, we headed out, planning to run in the same general area in hopes of picking up a wolf or werewolf scent.

Clay and I can play at being irresponsible—stopping

for sex at outrageously inappropriate times is one of our specialties—but it's just a game. Neither of us would be able to really relax and enjoy our run unless we felt, in some small way, we were still doing our job and fulfilling our Alpha's expectations.

The map in the article was very rough. It showed the highway, one side road and two X's to mark the kill sites, with no concept of scale. So until we talked to locals, we were guessing at the location. But neither of us realized how *much* we were guessing until the highway left Anchorage.

In daylight, I'm sure the scenery was spectacular. The highway weaved along between an inlet on one side and mountains and valleys on the other. In the predawn darkness, it was awe-inspiring—the endlessness of it all, the choppy water and the looming hills and the snowy fields and forests.

The road wasn't empty. Steady headlights streamed toward us, people making their way into Anchorage for work. As for where these commuters came from, I had no idea. There were certainly no suburbs I could see—just the occasional sign suggesting an unseen town down a long, dark road.

Finally we turned off onto one of those long, dark roads. Clay drove a mile, found what looked like a service road and parked along it.

I hopped out . . . and sunk knee-deep in the white stuff. The air, though, wasn't as bitterly cold as I'd feared. I'd been in Winnipeg earlier this winter, when the temperature hit minus twenty Fahrenheit, but this didn't feel any colder than Pittsburgh.

At least I was dressed for the season, having boots, a down-filled jacket, hat and mitts in my luggage. Clay—returning from Atlanta—wasn't so lucky. I'd grabbed him a toque in the airport, but he was only wearing it to humor me. Cold weather never bothered Clay. I always joked that he was like one of those werewolves from medieval legends, with his fur hidden under his skin.

We left our valuables—watches, wallets, wedding bands—in the locked glove compartment, then set out, tramping through the deep snow. If I *had* to walk through this I'd have been cursing with every step. But because I chose to, in pursuit of an activity I was giddily anticipating, I didn't mind at all—laughing and lurching, grabbing on to Clay and dragging him down as I fell, getting tossed face-first into a drift, returning the favor . . .

We didn't go far from the road to Change, but it took us a while to get there.

The area was wooded enough for us to find separate thickets. I was finally past the stage of insisting on that, though I do make Clay turn his back if we share. I don't consider myself particularly vain, but I'm not keen to have anyone see me mid-Change, even Clay.

I undressed and put my clothes in a plastic bag I'd grabbed at the airport. And then it got cold—"Holy shit, holy shit, holy shit!" cold. When I got down on all fours, and sunk in snow up to my breasts, I was gasping for breath.

It took a few moments for me to relax enough to begin the Change, but once it started, the cold was the last thing on my mind. My body is shifting from human to wolf; it's not going to tickle. As I learned when I had the twins, a

Change is a lot like giving birth, except you skip the labor pains and jump straight to the "what the hell was I thinking?" screams of agony. Once you accept that it's a natural process and nature will see you through, you grit your teeth and bear it because you know it'll be over soon, and when it is, the reward will be worthwhile.

So I suffered the body-ripping, bone-cracking agony of the Change with only a few grunts and whimpers, as I'd done at least once a week for the last twenty years. And when it was over, I collapsed onto my side, panting, muzzle buried in the snow to cool off.

Once I'd caught my breath, I rose slowly. The pain was only a memory now, but I still took my time, finding my footing on four legs, paws crunching through the snow crust, icy shards prickling between my foot pads. I blinked hard, adjusting to a gray world, giving my brain time to convert the shades to colors.

My ears and nose were already in action, ears swiveling to pick up every distant crackle of falling ice, nose wiggling to catch every molecule of prey scent, both senses urging me to hurry up, get on with it, get out there and start exploring. I ignored them and stretched. My eyes slitted in bliss as my muscles ached, endorphins shooting to my brain, sweet as champagne.

I swished my tail against the snow, then stepped forward and back, reestablishing my center of gravity. After twenty years, all this was completely unnecessary, but it was like foreplay—delicious on its own, even better as a way to whet the appetite, anticipation and frustration growing.

Speaking of frustration . . .

As I stretched, footfalls padded around my thicket. Gold fur flashed, glistening under the moonlight. Then Clay's smell wafted in—that glorious rich scent, starting a whimper deep in my throat. I swallowed it and braced my legs against the urge to bound out and greet him.

Clay circled again, faster now, impatience growing. I lowered myself to my belly and slunk forward, slow and silent, until my nose was at the thicket's edge. Then I bunched my muscles, hindquarters rising, wiggling, waiting, waiting...

Clay loped past and I shot out behind him. By the time I heard the crunch of his sharp turn, I was running full out, tearing across the open stretch, eyes half closed, wind sluicing through my fur, moving so fast my paws didn't break the crust.

Clay's heavier mass meant he *did* break that crust, and he fell farther behind with each stride, the huff of his labored breaths interspersed with growls as I pulled away. I crossed the clearing and dove into the forest, but as soon as I did, I realized my mistake—protected by the thick canopy, the ground had only a thin layer of snow, and I lost my advantage.

Soon Clay's huffing was right on my heels. Then a grunt and a whoosh, and I knew he'd leapt. I tried diving to the side, but as my hind paws flew up, he caught one and wrenched. My front feet skidded out and I belly flopped.

With a snort, I bounded up and spun around. He was twenty feet away, prancing away, tail waving. Every instinct said to chase, but I toppled back down into the snow and whined in pain. Now Clay knows better than to fall for that.

He really does. But he can never bring himself to run off, in case this is the one time I really *am* injured.

He circled me, wide and wary. I licked my foreleg. He came a little closer, staying out of lunging range. I struggled to my feet, paw raised, then gingerly touched it to the ground. He came closer, head lowered, nose working hard to catch the scent of blood. I lifted my paw and whimpered.

Closer, closer . . .

I sprang. He danced out of the way and took off. I hesitated, then started snuffling the ground. He stopped, head tilting. I kept sniffing, checking out all the prey trails. Vole, hare . . . is that lynx?

He dashed past so close I felt the draft.

I kept sniffing. Marten, porcupine, more hares . . .

Another dash, this time snagging my tail hairs in his teeth and tugging. I snapped and snarled, then went back to sniffing. More voles, more marten . . . Hey, what's that? I scratched off the top layer of snow, trying to uncover the scent.

Clay whipped past again, this time veering and sending a tidal wave of snow over me. I shook it off, nose still working, trying to pick up the mystery scent. When I glanced up, I caught a whiff of it in the air. I tracked it to an old tree with missing chunks of rough bark. There, caught on one loose piece six feet from the ground, was a tuft of brown fur.

Bear? Oooh. We'd crossed paths with black bears in northern Ontario, but never one of their big brown cousins. I scrambled up the trunk, nails digging in as I stretched to sniff—

Clay plowed into my side. I went flying. Then I bounced up, snarling, and tore after him.

He was smart enough to know that his advantage lay in the forest, so that's where he stayed, keeping only a few strides ahead, dropping back, then sprinting ahead, taunting and teasing.

When the forest opened into a clearing, I hit full speed, head down, paws sailing over the snow, closing the gap, the delicious smell of him filling my brain—

He swerved . . . right at the edge of a small embankment. I tried skidding to a stop, but tumbled over it, down the five-foot cliff onto the ice-covered creek below, each leg going its own way as I spun snout-first into the snowy embankment on the other side.

From behind me came the rough growl of Clay's wolf laugh. My answering growl was not nearly as amused. I got to my feet slowly, digging my claws into the ice for traction. Then, without turning to look at him, I gingerly picked my way along to a spot where a branch poked through the ice. I scratched at the thinner ice around it until I had a hole. Then I lowered my muzzle and drank.

I lapped the cold water, so clean and sweet that I closed my eyes to savor it. I could hear Clay pacing along the embankment, his panting getting louder, thirst growing. I bit off a chunk of ice, making the hole bigger, then shifted aside to give him room. He tore down the creek side, slowing as he reached the ice, testing each step under his weight.

When he got up beside me, the ice groaned, but held. He brushed against me, tail beating the back of my legs as he drank, droplets of icy water spraying my face. I shifted closer, rubbing against him. He made a deep-throated noise closer to a purr than to a growl. I quietly scraped at the ice with my far front paw. Then I reared up and slammed down, all my weight on my front legs. As I twisted and tore off the crack of the ice rang through the quiet forest.

Now it was my turn to stand on the embankment and laugh, as Clay scrambled like a lumberjack on a runaway log jam, jumping from piece to piece as they sank beneath him. He leapt for the shore, but didn't quite make it, splashing down to his dewclaws in icy water.

I tore off, but I'd stayed to enjoy the sight a few seconds too long. He caught me ten feet from the embankment, grabbing my back leg, yanking me down, then pouncing over me and shaking, water spraying everywhere. I tried to buck him off, but he bit the scruff of my neck and pinned me beneath his soaked underside.

I flipped him over and we tussled, fangs flashing, nipping and kicking and snarling, tone changing, the need for exercise and play fading fast, the need for something more primal taking over. The nips and growls grew rougher. I wriggled free, about to take off in a final chase before a quick Change back and—

A scent floated past and I went still. Clay's teeth clamped around my lower jaw, trying to get my attention. I shook him off and got to my feet. He tried one last time to grab me. I growled and stepped aside, nose lifting telling him however much I hated the interruption, what I smelled demanded my attention.

The distant murmur of a voice got him to his feet. He turned his nose into the breeze. His sense of smell wasn't as good as mine, but after a moment he caught it. His only re-action was a grunt, deep in his chest, the canine equivalent of a mildly curious "huh." When I started toward the source, he caught my hind leg in his jaws. Just a light tug, like catching my arm.

I looked back. He had his ears down, expression uncer-tain, cautious even. Normally, Clay's leading the charge and I'm holding back, but this was one situation where I was bolder than he.

I chuffed, getting his attention, then gave a slow shake of my head. I'd be careful, but I was going to investigate. He snorted, his jowls vibrating, huffed breaths hanging in the air. Fine, but he wasn't happy about it.

I took off at a lope, Clay at my heels. The sun was crest-ing the mountains now, the valley still gray and gloomy, with patches of snow glittering where the sun pierced the thick trees. It was a strangely eerie time of day, shadows playing with the light. More than once I thought I saw something and slowed, only to gaze out over empty forest.

We went a half mile before the distant murmur turned into three distinct male voices, and even then I couldn't make out what they were saying. For that, I'd need to con-centrate, and I was focused on getting closer.

As the voices grew loud enough for me to eavesdrop without effort, Clay nipped my heels, saying we were too close already. I could have safely gone another fifty feet, but I stopped before those nervous nips became anxious bites.

I couldn't see the men, but their voices seemed to come from a lighter patch ahead, presumably the forest's edge. I circled to the east, until I could see a frozen lake through a gap in the trees. I kept circling, wide enough to keep Clay's complaints down to a steady grumble.

When I drew close to the forest's edge, I hunkered down, sliding across the snow on my belly. Clay tried to follow, wanting to stay close, but I chuffed and shook my head. He grumbled a little louder, but knew I was right. Our fur matches our hair color and, against a snowy backdrop, his gold caught the eye far better than my silvery blond.

I stuck my muzzle out beyond the tree line and took a deep breath. Four men—three standing, one on the ground. The scents didn't betray their positions; their voices did. For the three, their voices above my head told me their position. The scent of the fourth told me where he was. His smell was the one I'd caught back by the creek. The stink of decomposing flesh.

The smell wasn't overwhelming, but I should have picked it up while we'd been goofing around. I suspected it was no coincidence, then, that I'd noticed the smell and the voices at the same time. The corpse must have been buried under a layer of snow, now found and uncovered.

I pushed forward a few more inches. When my eyes passed the tree line, I could still make out only shapes in the twilight.

I shuffled another few inches forward. Clay's grumbling turned to growls. I stopped as soon as I could see the three standing figures. They were all too bundled to guess age, but I could take a good stab at occupation, given that two had badges on their hats and the third was in camouflage gear with a glow-in-the-dark vest.

At their feet lay the body . . . or what was left of it. Most of the clothing had been torn away. What remained was dark with frozen blood. Even up close it didn't smell too bad—a human nose would barely detect it. Freezing had kept decomp at bay, but by the time it got warm enough to stink, there wouldn't be anything left to smell. Being buried under the snow was the only thing that had stopped the scavengers from finishing what they'd begun.

I could tell that the body had been eaten, but unless I could get close enough to sniff it, I had no idea what had done the eating—wolf, werewolf, mink or one of the dozens of other predators out here. Even knowing what ate the man wouldn't tell me what killed him. At the tail end of a long winter, even wolves won't turn down free meat. And that, I realized when I concentrated on the men's speech, was exactly what they were saying.

"Fresh snowfall yesterday means no tracks today," the shorter cop said. "No way to tell if it was canine, ursine or Homo sapiens."

"You think a person could have done this?" The taller cop's voice squeaked with surprise and youth.

"Eat poor Tom for dinner? I hope to hell not, but I wouldn't put it past some of the whack-jobs we get up here. I meant he could have been murdered, then eaten by scavengers. He's so chewed up, we might not ever know for sure."

"I always told Tom he was crazy," the hunter said. "Checking his traps at night. But it was his favorite time."

There was a moment of silence for the dead man.

The younger cop broke it first. "I saw some wolf tracks back there."

"Wolf?" the older cop said. "You sure about that?"

"I can tell canine from ursine, Reed."

"He means there's more than one kind of canine out here," the hunter said.

"And I mean don't go jumping to conclusions," the older cop said. "Folks hear about paw prints near a dead body and they start crying wolf."

"My money's on a wolf-dog," the hunter said. "City idiots think it's cool to own a dog that's half wolf . . . until it turns out there's some wild beast in their pet pooch. Fancy that. Then what do they do? Let them loose out here and tell themselves they've done the humane thing."

"That'd explain the big canine tracks people have been seeing since the pack moved on. A wolf-dog got dumped here, started harassing the pack, scaring off the prey, so they left. If an animal's been raised by people, it doesn't fear them. It gets hungry? That big hunk of meat on two legs looks damned tasty."

As I backed up, Clay huffed in relief and circled in front to herd me to safety. Even being raised near people had never erased that gut-level anxiety that said a human in the forest was a bad thing. In this case, his instinct was right. If these guys caught a glimpse of a big yellow wolf right now, we'd be picking shotgun pellets from our butts for weeks.

I started walking away, my nose to the ground, skimming it like a metal detector. Clay watched for a moment, then made that rumbling noise deep in his chest, one that said he'd rather get as far from these humans as possible, but I had a point. He put his nose down and joined my search.

DOWNTIME

WE FOUND TRACKS about a half mile from the kill site. It looked as if the trail went in that direction, but we didn't dare follow it any closer—not until the people had left. I supposed they were waiting for the coroner or crime-scene techs. But whoever was coming was taking his time and I could still hear the men talking.

The tracks were definitely canine, as the young officer had said. While they seemed too big to be wolf, I won't say *definitely* too big, because wolves have been found weighing up to two hundred pounds. The average, though, is just over half that. These tracks were the size of Clay's, but the scent already told me we were dealing with a werewolf.

The trail was a few days old, the prints remaining only because the tree canopy protected this patch from the freshly fallen snow. I had to pace along it before my brain really latched on to the smell. Then I sat on my haunches and mulled it over, like a wine expert with a cork, trying to place the vintage. When it didn't tweak a memory, I sniffed again. No match to anything in my mental file cabinet.

I glanced at Clay, who was sniffing another section of the trail. He lifted his muzzle from the ground and shook his head—no one he knew either. My dossiers document twenty-five werewolves currently living in the United States, but we weren't arrogant enough to believe that actually meant there *were* only twenty-five.

Mutts were always immigrating and emigrating, plus there were a handful that stayed under the radar. Keeping tabs on all of them was impossible. We really only tracked the troublemakers and the ones from the oldest werewolf families, like the Santoses and the Cains.

Still, in the Lower 48, we could say with some confidence that we knew most of the werewolves around—either by reputation or by scent. Up here in Alaska, though, we might as well be in another country. The only Alaskans we had in our dossiers were the Stillwells, and if Clay didn't recognize this scent, then it wasn't either of them.

We couldn't follow the trail back to the kill site, but we could take it the other way. We'd tracked it for almost a mile before it ended at a clearing. Inside, we found a piece of plywood and a wooden crate. A werewolf's winter locker—a place to Change in the mud and snow, and to store your gear. We had something similar, if more elegant, at Stonehaven.

This clearing reeked of scent and sweat, meaning someone was using it regularly. As I sniffed more, I realized it was more than some*one*. We had two distinct scents and possibly a third.

Shit.

Two or more werewolves, none the Stillwells. And as

soon as they set foot in this clearing, they'd know there were two werewolves in town, one of them female.

Double shit.

I started backing out of their change-room, but it was too late. The moment I got within ten feet of the spot I'd left a scent that was sure to get their attention. Upon consideration, though, I decided that wasn't necessarily a problem. With the size of Alaska, finding two or three werewolves would be needle-and-haystack work. Now they'd be looking for us, which would make things easier.

As long as we'd already left our scents, we might as well take a better sniff around. We covered every inch of that clearing searching for remnants of the man by the lake, and found not a speck of blood or shred of flesh. That didn't mean much—the long run through the snow would be enough to clean off their feet—but it bore keeping in mind. It could also suggest a deliberate cleaning before returning to this spot. Maybe one of the mutts was a man-eater trying to hide the habit from his buddies.

Once we were sure we'd gotten all the information we could and had committed their scents to memory, we left the clearing. As I stepped out, I caught a movement in the bushes. I froze, blocking Clay. He nudged my hindquarters. I edged backward, scanning the woods. The only noise was the wind rustling dead leaves overhead. It was too quiet. Clay went still, knowing something was wrong.

I kept looking, ears swiveled forward, nose working. Nothing to see. Nothing to hear. Nothing to smell. Yet the forest stayed deathly silent. Clay nudged me again—now he was worried and wanted to get moving.

I slid from the clearing. Clay followed. We stood in the dense, dimly lit forest, looking, listening, sniffing, catching nothing. Then a bird called. Another answered. A squirrel chirruped and scampered over a branch overhead, dead leaves raining down. I shook one off my head, and I rubbed against Clay, grunting an apology for overreacting. He licked my muzzle and waited for instructions, ready to cede the lead now that any danger had passed.

We found the scent from the werewolves in human form, and followed it. It didn't go more than twenty paces before ending at a trail thick with the stink of mixed gas and oil. Snowmobiles.

I turned around and loped back a quarter mile toward the kill site, but the men hadn't left yet. There was no reason for us to linger. By the time the crew removed the body, all their tracks would have erased the faint trail of the killer. We returned to our truck and Changed back.

AS DISAPPOINTED AS we were over the awkward end to our run, neither of us suggested we crawl into the back of the SUV and finish it properly. We'd already done the quick-and-dirty solution in the airport. Now we wanted more, and if we couldn't get it on our terms, we'd wait and build up an appetite.

Speaking of appetites, breakfast was long overdue. We drove back to Highway 1—the main route through Alaska...or the 5 percent of it that could be reached by car. It was a two-lane highway that didn't bear much resemblance to the interstates I was used to, and it didn't have the facilities I was used to either. Earlier we'd passed only one service center. We returned there now and found a gas station, bakery and pizza parlor.

I was surprised by the neon sign in the bakery window offering espressos—not the kind of thing one expects to find at a highway outpost. But I wasn't arguing. I'd always considered myself a straight coffee person, but when I'd been pregnant and nursing, I drank decaf lattes to up my dairy intake and developed a taste for them, especially if they came with caramel. These ones did, so I got a large, a coffee for Clay and a bag of pastries.

We headed outside to eat and couldn't find a single bench or picnic table. Given the view—snow-covered mountains with the sun cresting the ridge—I couldn't imagine why everyone chose to drink their coffee inside. I suppose the subfreezing temperatures had something to do with that.

But the chance to eat with a view like that was too tempting to ignore. And Clay was just as happy not to have to eat with strangers. So we settled onto the wooden ties of a raised flower bed. Then we phoned home.

Jeremy and his visiting girlfriend, Jaime, were getting ready to take the kids to swimming lessons, meaning our timing was perfect—Logan and Kate were too excited about swimming to ask when we were coming back. Clay, Jeremy and I work mostly from home, meaning the kids have grown up with us there all the time, so you'd think they wouldn't mind our occasional absence. But because we're always there, that's what they're used to, and when we take off, they raise a hell of a fuss.

Clay talked to Kate first, which would give me plenty of time to enjoy my latte and muffin. I listened in as she told Daddy everything that had happened since he'd called the day before. *Every*thing. In detail. And through the entire fifteen-minute recitation, Clay's attention never flagged.

When the subject of kids first came up years ago, I'd joked that the only thing I could imagine worse than me as a mother was Clay as a father. I couldn't have been more wrong. Clay was an amazing parent. The guy who couldn't spare a few minutes to hear a mutt's side of the story could listen to his kids talk all day. The guy who couldn't sit still through a brief council meeting could spend hours building Lego castles with his kids. The guy who solved problems with his fists never even raised his voice to his children. And if sometimes Clay was a little too indulgent, a little too slow to discipline, preferring to leave that to me, I was okay with it. He supported and enforced my decisions and we presented a unified front to our children, and that was all that mattered.

Finally, Jeremy interceded on the call—telling Kate they had to leave soon—and he gave the phone to Logan. That conversation was more two-sided. Clay had sent Logan a junior science set from Atlanta, and they discussed experiments Logan had done yesterday, under Jeremy's supervision. Science wasn't Clay's area of interest or expertise, but he was as fascinated by the working of his son's precocious mind as he'd been with his daughter's adventures.

As Clay and Logan talked, I could hear Kate in the background, telling Logan to hurry, that she *had* to talk to Mommy. He calmly continued his conversation, neither hurrying to please her nor stalling to annoy her. Even before they could walk, Kate—my boisterous little wolf cub—had tried establishing dominance over her brother and he'd made it clear that she might be bigger and stronger, but he wasn't putting up with that crap. They were equals and she'd best not forget it.

When he finally handed her the phone, I listened to a replay of her day, then Logan came on and informed me that he wanted to go to school in the fall. Apparently, he'd overheard a phone call Jeremy took from the school, inviting us to the prekindergarten registration session. The twins would be four in the fall and Clay and I were still debating whether to send them.

Clay wanted to hold off until kindergarten. Normally I'm all for any socialization opportunity, but here I was leaning toward agreeing with Clay—they just seemed so young for school, even half-days. But now, Logan was putting in his request to go, while in the background his sister howled her objections. She wanted to stay home with us. Splitting them up wouldn't be an option—they were inseparable. Luckily, at this moment, my plate was full with other tasks and I could safely postpone this one until we got home.

Finally I got Logan to hand the phone to Jeremy, but I could barely hear him over the kids bickering about school. Then I caught Jaime's voice, reminding them it was snack time, and the arguing was replaced by pounding footsteps, then silence.

"Food always works," I said.

"We'll be in trouble when it doesn't. So, how was your flight?"

I told him what we'd done so far. He was impressed by the progress we'd made. Jeremy knew we wouldn't have landed in Alaska and holed up in a hotel for eight hours, but like any good leader, he understands that the day he starts *expecting* his troops to perform above and beyond is the day when they'll start feeling underappreciated and drag their heels.

"Go check into the hotel and get some sleep," he said.

"Has Paige gotten a hit on Reese's cards?"

He paused.

"That means yes," I said. "I could call her myself, you know."

"He used one to book a motel, but after that expensive flight, he's not leaving Alaska anytime soon, so you can get some sleep—"

"I napped on the plane. If Clay's tired, I'll drop him off—"

"I'm fine," Clay said.

"I know Reese isn't the most urgent item on our agenda..." I said.

"There's *nothing* urgent on your agenda."

"Which is why I want to clear him off my slate."

"You're wasting your time, Jer," Clay called.

Jeremy heard and sighed, then gave me the information. "Go to the boy's motel, speak to him and then get some rest."

"Do we have an address for Dennis or Joey Stillwell? I was just thinking, if it's on the way..."

He sighed again, and gave me the address.

"DENNIS'S APARTMENT IS closer," I said as I got into the driver's seat. "We should probably stop there before Reese's motel."

"Yeah."

"And I'm guessing you'd *rather* we checked on Dennis first."

A pause, then a softer "Yeah."

I glanced over as I pulled from the lot. "I know you're worried about them—Dennis and Joey."

"I'm not sure *worried* is the right word. I feel..." He looked out the side window, fingers drumming the armrest. "I don't really know how I'll feel, seeing Joey again."

I waited. There's no sense prodding Clay to talk. He doesn't need to be encouraged to share his feelings. If he wants to, he will.

"I feel bad, I guess," he said after a moment. "Falling out of touch."

"You were friends."

He nodded. "I was closer to Nick. Joey was a few years older. But, yeah, we were friends. Pack mates. Pack brothers. I should have kept in contact. I just... I was pissed off about them leaving. They didn't have much status in the Pack and that made them afraid to cross Malcolm. I get that. But I would have protected them. Joey wasn't a kid. He didn't need to follow his father. He could have said it wasn't right, abandoning Jeremy after all he'd done for them."

"But he didn't. They ran."

Clay went silent, loyalty to old Pack mates warring against a deeper feeling of betrayal.

"Yeah, they ran," he said.

"And you couldn't forgive that."

"No. I couldn't." He looked at me. "It was their duty—their obligation—to stand by us. They ran, and things got worse. Their support may not have counted for much, but it would have tipped the balance. Jeremy would have won the Alpha race without bloodshed. He could have used their help and I would have protected them."

And that is what it came down to. In leaving, they'd abandoned Jeremy and hadn't trusted Clay. I used to think that Clay was incapable of seeing other points of view. He can see them though—he just can't feel them. Dennis and Joey hadn't fulfilled their duty to the Pack and that felt wrong, so it *was* wrong.

"If they came back after Jeremy ascended, I would have been pissed, and it wouldn't have been the same between Joey and me. But I would have gotten over it."

"Why didn't they return?"

"Jeremy said they were still worried about Malcolm, that he'd come back and take revenge against those who didn't support him. That's bullshit. Malcolm was a vicious, manipulative son of a bitch, but more than anything, he was a fighter. A fighter doesn't crawl back after a defeat, even for revenge. Once he's beaten, he moves on and picks a new battle. Later, when we heard Malcolm was dead, Jeremy told them. By then, though, they'd made a life for themselves here in Alaska."

"But now you're looking forward to seeing Joey. Having an excuse to get back in touch."

"It's been a lot of years, and whatever I felt then is gone. You'll like Joey. Lucas reminds me a bit of him, but Joey isn't as . . . He never had much confidence, much . . ." He trailed off again. I suspected the word he wanted was *backbone,* but he couldn't bring himself to say it. "He was a decent guy. Quiet, thoughtful. A good friend."

"And a nice change from Nick now and then?"

A short laugh. "Yeah."

I drove another mile, then Clay said, "Speaking of Alpha ascensions . . ."

My hands tightened on the steering wheel. "You know."

"Yeah, Jeremy said he finally told you." His voice went uncharacteristically soft. "You didn't need to wait for me to get home to discuss this."

"It wasn't something I wanted to discuss over the phone."

He swore under his breath. "Jeremy can have the worst timing . . ."

"No, he was being very careful about the timing. He told me the news just before I was supposed to meet you in Atlanta, thinking that would give us a chance to discuss it in private. Then our kids decided to play Superman out the window. Oh, and about that, Kate finally admitted—"

"Which you can tell me later," Clay said. "Right now, we should discuss this. You just found out Jeremy wants you to be Alpha. That's a big deal. We need to talk about it. *You* need to talk about it."

"Yes, but not now. It isn't something I want to discuss in the car. And it's not critical. I'm just..."

"Worried."

My hands death-gripped the wheel, breaths coming so fast my chest hurt.

"Elena..."

I didn't look at him. "I'm fine. We'll discuss it later."

"Pull over and—" My expression stopped him short. He rubbed his hand over his mouth. "Okay. We'll talk at the hotel. But I don't like thinking you've been this upset—"

"I'm not upset."

"*Concerned,* and waited a week to talk to me. No wonder you were so happy to see me."

I looked at him. "Yes, I want to talk, but I *did* miss you. A lot."

"Can I get that in writing?"

I managed a smile. "Not a chance."

GONE

COMING INTO ANCHORAGE now, I got my first daylight look at the city. Ignore the gorgeous backdrop of ocean and mountains, and it could pass for any medium-size city with strip malls and strip joints, Wal-Marts and Walgreens. What did stand out was the snow—or the lack of it. The streets were bare and a lot of yards were, too. According to the digital signs we passed, it was forty degrees, the same as we'd expect in upstate New York this time of year, and we definitely had more snow.

Dennis's apartment building was as normal and average as the city itself. Nothing sleazy or spectacular. Nothing historical or postmodern. Just an unassuming, well-kept building.

According to the tenant list, Dennis was using his real name. All Pack werewolves do. We have IDs with aliases, but part of the reason for joining the Pack is to settle into territory, and it's easiest to do that using your birth name.

I buzzed his apartment from the building vestibule. When no one answered after the second one, I was about to find another way in when a tenant held the door open for us. I thought she'd mistaken us for neighbors, but as we walked into the lobby she asked who we were there to visit. I said Dennis. She didn't know him, and seemed faintly embarrassed by that, as if she should.

Clay knocked on Dennis's door. At a second knock, a neighbor's door opened. An elderly woman with bushy white hair and huge glasses peered out, blinking like a wizen-faced snowy owl.

"Sorry," I said. "We didn't mean to disturb—"

"Are you looking for Dennis?"

"Yes, we're friends of—"

"He's not there, dear. Been gone awhile." She eased out the door, gripping her housecoat around her plump body. "Dennis isn't the sort to make his presence known, not like some people"—a glare at the door across the hall—"but I usually see him every day. He brings up my mail and asks if I need anything when he goes out."

"And he hasn't been by lately." I spoke slowly, waiting to be interrupted again, but when I finished, she only blinked at me.

"He's been away a few days?" I prompted.

"Oh, no, dear. More than that. He's always going off for a day or two. This time it's been close on a week."

I felt Clay shift behind me. He didn't like that answer.

"So Dennis doesn't usually—" I began.

"You should speak to Charles. He's worried about him, too."

"Charles?"

"The landlord. Here, I'll take you to his office."

I said that wasn't necessary—we'd find it—but she insisted, toddling down the hall in huge polar-bear-paw slippers. As we took the elevator, she asked me questions—where we were from, what we did for a living, did we have any children? I answered honestly. That's one rule of were-wolf life—tell the truth when you can and it'll make the lies easier to track.

Clay kept quiet as we walked, but he held the door for her and checked his pace to hers. That's the wolf again—indulge the young and respect the old. Not a bad philosophy in general. Now if I could just adjust his attitude toward the other 90 percent of the population.

The landlord wasn't in his office. We found him in the front foyer, changing one of the tenant names on the list. The old lady—Lila—introduced us, then got her mail and scuttled off to read her new copy of *People*.

Charles the landlord was younger than I would have guessed. He looked about midtwenties, Native, burly and a few inches shorter than me.

"Yep, been almost a week, like Lila said." He pasted the new tenant's name in place. "Place like this, we get mostly good folk. Dennis is one of the best. Pays his rent in advance, never calls me in the middle of the night for a plugged toilet, does his own repairs, even helped me paint last fall when the student I hired didn't show."

He ushered us back inside. "I don't see Dennis every day, like Lila, but we usually bump into each other a few times a week. We stop and chat, then he'll come over to my place, and the wife makes him coffee." Charles chuckled. "The wife hardly ever makes *me* coffee, so that's a sure sign she likes him."

"It's been quite a while since we've seen Dennis," I said as he peeled a SpongeBob sticker off the wall, "so we don't know him that well. He was a friend of my husband's dad when Dennis lived back east."

Charles picked at the glue left on the wall. "Whereabouts back east?"

"At the time, it was New York State," I said carefully, thinking I was being tested—and not knowing whether Dennis had told the truth.

Charles laughed, making me jump. "I knew it. I knew it. The wife and I have ten bucks riding on this, trying to guess by the accent. I said New York; she said New Jersey. I wanted to ask, but she thought that was prying." He glanced at Clay. "You friends with Joseph?"

It took a moment for Clay to connect Joseph to Joey. "When we were kids. We lost touch after they moved."

"So we don't have his address," I said. "Or we'd stop there and ask."

"Damn. I hoped you did."

"Does he come by often?"

Charles snorted and started picking at another sticker. "I've been here three years and I've seen him only a few times. It's not right. His dad's a great guy. He's always talking about his son, and the guy can't bother coming to visit? Not right."

So Dennis and Joey were still introducing themselves as father and son. I hadn't been sure. With slow aging, that's one relationship werewolves often fudge.

"Do you have any idea where Dennis might be?" I asked. "Lila said he takes off a lot."

"He's got a cabin about thirty miles south. Usually he goes there for a few days a month. Sometimes longer, but when it's that long, he tells me, so I can collect his mail. He could be there, though. That's what I figure. Got himself snowed in."

I must have looked alarmed, because Charles laughed. "That's not cause to call 911 out here. If you have a back-woods place like Dennis's, you're prepared. Weather turns bad, you just hole up and ride it out, enjoy the peace and quiet. There aren't any phones out there, but Dennis has a sled. He could get out if he needed to."

"Sled?" I pictured a dog team, which really wouldn't work for a werewolf.

"Snowmobile. But while I'm sure he's fine, I am getting a little worried. I wanted to run out there and check, but the wife said I should leave him be." He grinned at Clay. "The last time I went, I spent the day ice fishing with Dennis, had a few beers, stayed the night, couldn't call and tell her... Wives get a little funny about stuff like that."

"We could drive up and check on him, if you have an address," I said.

I expected him to refuse. After all, we were strangers. But he said, "I wouldn't quite call it an address. There's no mail delivery out there. The road stops about a half mile from the cabin. What I have are directions and coordinates. It's rough country, though. What are you driving?"

"An SUV with a GPS unit."

"Perfect. Let me give you—" He reached into his back

pocket, swore and shook his head. "The wife convinces me I need a PDA for work and where is it? With her, for her grocery list. Can I call you with it when she gets back?"

"Sure." I gave him my cell number.

NEXT STOP: REESE'S motel. You'd think a guy using stolen credit cards would be living large, but this place—like the last motel I found him in—was the kind you see advertised on the highway for thirty bucks a night, wonder how it can be so cheap, then decide you'd really rather not find out.

It was yet further proof that I wasn't dealing with a typical careless kid. He'd been using one card for big purchases, like plane tickets, but keeping the others small, as if hoping they wouldn't be noticed until the next bill came in.

The motel was in a part of town with a drunk on every corner. A big sign out front announced a prerace visitors' special for the Iditarod. This year's race had left Anchorage two weeks ago.

I told the clerk I was supposed to meet a friend, but didn't know his room number, and he gave it to me. He'd probably have given me the key, too, if I asked nicely. In a place like this, no one wants to know why you're looking for a guy—they just want you to leave them out of it.

While I went to Reese's door, Clay headed around back. He was supposed to guard the rear window, in case Reese bolted when I knocked, but he returned before I got the chance.

"Window's too small," he said.

I lifted my hand to knock. Clay shook his head, grabbed the door handle and gave a sharp twist. When he pushed it open, unencumbered by bolt or chain, I knew what we'd find—an empty room. Clay shouldered past me and strode into the bathroom.

"Gone," he said.

"Meaning we're stuck on stakeout duty until he comes back." When we'd approached the door, we'd left a scent trail that would have Reese bolting the second he got within sniffing distance.

"I saw a coffee shop across the road," he said. "I'll go stand watch from there, while you check the place out."

There was nothing to check out. Reese traveled ultralight—unscented deodorant, toothbrush and a single change of clothing.

I grabbed my laptop from the SUV and caught up with Clay inside the coffee shop. He looked at my computer case.

"As long as I'm sitting around, I can do some more research into those deaths."

"If you can get Internet service in here, I'll give you my snack."

"I'm an optimist."

He shook his head and went to get us some food while I booted up.

I WAS SHUTTING my laptop as Clay returned with coffees and bagels.

"Don't say it," I muttered.

He handed me a coffee and set both bagels on his side of the table.

I snatched one. "I didn't bet anything. You want two, I'll grab you another. We're going to be here awhile anyway."

"No need for both of us to hang around. You wanted to stop by the newspaper. Do that and I'll watch for the kid."

I didn't really want to leave. I was just starting to relax, the tension of the last week fading. But the more tasks I checked off my list now, the sooner we could take a break.

"I'll be back in an hour." I nodded at the cement-hard bagels. "I'll bring a better lunch."

PERKY

THE PROPER PROCEDURE for one journalist approaching another would be to stop at reception and ask to speak to her. Better yet, call or e-mail ahead and make an appointment, invite her out to coffee. Proper procedure would have had me waiting hours, even days, to ask a few simple questions.

One advantage to being a Canadian journalist is that Americans don't expect you to know the rules. You're like a small-town reporter in the big city—as long as you're polite and respectful, they'll excuse your charming ignorance.

When I walked into the newspaper office, the receptionist was on the phone. I sneaked around the potted plants and into the back hall. Then a guy with bristly red hair and a neon green tie stepped from an office, saw me and stopped. He gave me a once-over and straightened his tie.

"Can I help you?" he asked, with a look that said he hoped he could.

"Elena Michaels, Canadian Press." I showed my card. He didn't even glance at it. "I'm on vacation in Anchorage and someone mentioned the possible wolf attacks you've had. I was wondering if I might speak to Ms. Hirsch about her articles. It's a subject our readers would be very interested in."

He listened to my spiel and nodded appropriately, but I suspected I could say I was selling Tasers door-to-door and still he'd take me to Ms. Hirsch.

We walked. He asked where I was from, how long I was staying, what I'd seen of Alaska so far . . . I could have sworn we passed the same set of bathrooms three times before, on the fourth, we nearly collided with a man coming out.

My guide—Garth—stopped and introduced me to the editor, saying I was a visiting journalist. We were shaking hands when a woman came out of the ladies bathroom down the hall. She glanced our way. Garth called, "Mallory!" and waved her over as the editor left.

From the end of the hall, Mallory Hirsch could pass for late twenties, with short blond hair, a trim figure and stylish suit. But with each step our way, she gained a few years. By the time she reached us, I'd peg her at early forties, with a tight, expressionless face that suggested I could add another decade presurgery.

"Yes?" she said, her voice as tight as her skin. Her gaze slid over me, taking in my ski jacket, hiking boots and jeans with disapproval.

"This is Elena Michaels," Garth said. "She works for the Canadian press."

"*Canadian Press,*" I said. "It's like Associated Press, only much, much smaller."

Garth laughed, too loud for the mild joke. Mallory's expression didn't flicker.

I repeated my spiel, expanding it to explain that we'd had wolf activity in Algonquin Park in the last few years, and I wanted to tie this into that as an examination of the issues surrounding humans and wolves sharing an ever-shrinking world. I thought it sounded good, but from the expressionless way she stared at me, you'd think I'd accidentally switched to French.

When I finished, she said nothing, just looked at me as if waiting for the rest of the explanation.

"So, I told Elena you could probably spare her a few minutes—" Garth began.

Her look made him shrink back.

"It really is only a couple of questions," I said. "I know how busy you must be—"

"Garth? You can go now."

He fled.

I continued. "I would love to buy you coffee. Or lunch."

"I've eaten. So you're looking for someone to write your story for you, Ms. Michaels? Crib from my article? Save yourself the legwork?"

"Um, no . . . as I said, I only have a few questions, ones that will launch my own investigation. And, of course, anything I discover, I'll share with you."

"Your own investigation?"

I sensed her hackles rising. "For my own article. For my own newspapers. I've already been to the general area where the deaths occurred, but . . ." I forced a smile. "It's a lot bigger country than I'm used to. If I had a better idea where the—"

"Everything I can tell you is in my articles. I presume you've read them?"

"Yes." *Wanna quiz me?*

She stepped back and did an openly critical assessment of me. "How old are you, Ms. Michaels?"

"I'm not fresh out of college, if that's what—"

"Married, I see. Kids?"

"Two," I said carefully.

"Little ones, I suppose?"

"Yes, but—"

"An outdoors type?" she said, taking in my boots and jacket.

"You could say that."

"Anchorage is an outdoorsman's dream. A full-service city minutes away from a wilderness filled with lakes, rivers, mountains, glaciers..."

"It is pretty amazing," I said.

"Warmer than you thought, too, I bet. No mounds of snow or sub-zero temperatures..."

"Having experienced sub-zero, it's a very pleasant surprise."

I smiled, but her expression didn't change. What was with the tourism spiel? Was she going to try selling me time-shares?

She continued. "Good city. All the amenities. The great outdoors in its full glory at your doorstep. The perfect place for a young family to relocate."

"Relocate?"

"But first, you need a job."

"Job? I don't need—"

"You're not in the building five minutes and you're al-ready shaking hands with the editor. I bet you think that's all it takes, don't you? A backwater place like Anchorage, there can't be any *real* journalists here. Probably all housewives, churning out articles before the kiddies come home from school. You can just show up, the perky Canadian girl—"

"Perky?"

"—and you think a spot will open up for you. A good spot. Maybe *my* spot."

"Um, no. I'm sure Anchorage is a great place to live, but I've already got a life—someplace else. I'm here to talk about the wolf kills."

"I'm sure you are. And I have nothing to say about them that isn't in my articles."

She walked away.

GARTH HAILED ME as I reached the doors.

"Did Mallory give you anything useful?"

I made a noncommittal noise.

"I might have another story for you," he continued. "I've been covering the disappearances of young women."

"Oh?"

"We've had three vanish in the last few months. It might make an interesting article for your readers back home."

Sadly, even in Canada, three missing girls wasn't news. It should be. Believe me, I know that, and I can rail against it all I want, but unless they're three teens from good families, even the police pay little attention. When I'd been in Winnipeg this winter, enjoying their twenty-below temperatures, I'd been researching a series on missing and murdered local women. The police had almost twenty cases of unsolved sex-worker deaths in as many years. Many of the victims were young, many Native Canadians, and all prostitutes.

One of my reasons for doing the articles was that Jeremy had sent me there to check out potential werewolf activity. Young sex-trade workers and street girls were the preferred prey of werewolves, who know how little attention will be paid to the deaths. It turned out that a few of those deaths had been a mutt. But it would be odd to have a man-eater in Anchorage mixing vanished young women with men left lying in the open.

"Were the girls from Anchorage?" I asked.

"One was. Two were from Native communities farther inland. Why don't we go grab a bite to eat and discuss it?"

"I'd love to, but I'm supposed to meet my husband for lunch."

His gaze dropped to my hand. "Oh, right. Sure. Well, if you decide to run the story, call me."

He headed back into the offices without giving me his last name, card or any way to "call him." I reached the exterior doors this time before he hailed me again. He walked over, looking chagrined, as if realizing how it must look, taking off once he discovered I was married.

"About Mallory's story," he said. "The wolves. There's someone else you could talk to. A local woman who knows more about the case than anyone, including Mallory."

"Oh?"

He waved for me to step outside. It had started drizzling. We ducked under an overhang.

"Her name's Lynn Nygard," he continued. "She works

for the state police. Mallory used her as a source, but I know she didn't give Mallory everything." Garth lowered his voice. "Mallory can rub people the wrong way."

Really? Huh. "Will Ms. Nygard talk to me?"

"Oh, sure. There's just one thing. Lynn has this theory about the deaths and it would, uh, help if you didn't... discourage it."

"Theory?"

He waved to a coworker stepping out for a cigarette, then lowered his voice. "She thinks they were killed by some kind of Inuit shape-shifter. There's a name for them—I can't remember it. You don't have to say you believe in them, just..."

"Don't laugh when she mentions it?"

"Exactly. If she warms to you, you can also ask about the missing girls. She has a theory on that, too."

"Alien abductions?"

He laughed. "Met a few Lynns in your time, have you?"

"I have. You said she works for the police?"

"They tolerate her eccentricities because she's the best damned crime-scene photographer and sketch artist in Alaska. Of course, according to her, that's because she's the reincarnation of Leonardo da Vinci."

"Ah."

"Yes, she loves that paranormal shit, but obsession can be good if you're looking for the best source of detailed information. You'll find Lynn in the phone book." He spelled her last name as I wrote it down, then gave me his card and offered, genuinely it seemed, to help if he could.

• • •

I CALLED CLAY from the SUV.

"How'd it go at the paper?" he asked.

"She called me perky."

"Ouch."

I told him about Mallory Hirsch. After he said a few choice words about that, I explained the lead on Lynn Nygard. "I called her place. No answer. I'm going to swing by there on my way, then grab lunch."

I MADE IT three blocks before Clay called.

"Change course, darling," he said.

"Did Reese show up?"

"Yeah. And we've got a situation."

SITUATION

I WAS STILL ten feet from Reese's hotel room when I smelled blood. I slowed, my stomach giving a reflexive clench.

Yes, I hadn't wanted Reese hurt, but if he gave Clay any trouble, fists would fly and blood would flow. That was a given. There was a time when I'd convinced myself that Clay liked hurting people, because that fit the way I wanted to see him. But I'd always known it wasn't the truth. For Clay, beating a recalcitrant mutt was like brushing his teeth. It wasn't something he liked or disliked—he was just doing what needed to be done. A swift beating helped stop the spread of respect-decay, the kind that led to strikes against the Pack and its Alpha.

That's why Clay and I made such a good team. I played good cop and no one thought it a sign of weakness because, well, I was a woman, so naturally I'd be the soft touch. When a mutt wouldn't listen to me, he had to deal with Clay's fists. The mediator and the enforcer. It worked fine until half the team wasn't around.

So as I approached the door, I rubbed my face, erasing

any sign that said I regretted anything Clay had done to Reese.

"Door's open," Clay called.

I found him pacing inside, cell phone at his ear. Reese sat on the edge of the bed, with a bloody towel around his right hand.

"I didn't do it," Clay said.

I motioned to the phone.

"Jeremy," he said. Getting medical advice, I presumed.

"What happened?" I asked Reese.

He glanced down at his towel-wrapped hand, as if startled to see it. His pupils were dilated and he blinked hard, having trouble focusing on his hand, still holding it up and staring. I glanced at Clay, but he'd turned his back to me as Jeremy gave instructions.

When I took Reese's hand, he didn't resist. His skin above the towel was clammy, despite the warm room. I slowly unraveled the towel until I saw his hand, and winced. Two finger joints of his ring finger and the last joint of his pinkie had been cut off.

"I didn't do it," Clay said.

"Feel the need to make that perfectly clear, do you?" I said.

He grunted and tossed the phone onto the bed.

"What happened?" I asked.

"No idea. I haven't gotten that far. Jeremy says we need to get him stitched up. We can get the details after."

CLAY RETRIEVED MY bag—with my first-aid kit—from the car. He had one in his luggage, too. Jeremy would sooner let us travel without clothing than forget emergency medical supplies.

I got Reese's hand cleaned, stitched and bandaged while Clay played nurse, taking away the dirty cloths and getting new ones. As for how he lost his fingers, Reese was staying mum. It seemed more shock than reticence, though, so Clay and I tried to distract him by discussing the latest injuries in our lives—our kids' fall.

"Logan wouldn't talk," I said. "But I finally got Kate to admit what happened, which was exactly what we thought."

"They jumped because they'd seen us doing it."

I explained to Reese. "Our kids have realized that our days don't end after they go to bed. We go for walks in the forest, we talk by the fire, the food comes out..."

"Especially the food," Clay said.

"Naturally they felt left out and kept getting up. Rather than turn bedtime into a battleground, we started going to bed at the same time, then sneaking downstairs or outside."

"Only they heard us if we went downstairs," Clay said.

"Being so young, they shouldn't have secondary powers. We aren't even sure they're werewolves—one or both or... it's complicated. Anyway, at this age, we don't know whether they have enhanced hearing or we're just louder than we think we are. But we thought we were safe, avoiding the stairs and jumping out our bedroom window. Apparently not."

"They tried it?" Reese said, his first words since I'd come in. "Are they okay?"

"One sprained ankle, one sprained wrist and one very guilt-stricken parent."

"Two," Clay said. "We're going to have to come up with another solution."

"Other than tying them to their beds?"

"That'll be option two."

I cut off the bandage. "I know, we should probably just clamp down—bedtime is bedtime—but I was thinking of a compromise. We'll let them stay up until eleven two nights and we'll go to bed early, and the rest of the week, they're down at the normal time. If they don't settle, then we get tough—no special late nights."

"That might work."

"I hope so. Or it'll be time to invest in bars for the windows."

I stood and stretched my legs. Reese had followed our conversation with equal parts interest and bewilderment, and now he just looked confused. He'd heard stories about us—any mutt who's been in the United States more than a month has. Tales of Clayton Danvers, child werewolf turned vicious psychopath, who at seventeen chopped up a trespassing mutt and passed out photos of it. Then he bit some poor girl in Toronto, made her his mate, imprisoned her with him at Stonehaven, forced her to bear his children, and dragged her along on his assignments as Pack enforcer, so she could—I don't know—wash his socks and serve him breakfast in bed, I guess.

There were truths in this, as in all mythology. The child werewolf. The axe-job and photos. The bite. But it was all vastly more complicated than any mutt's urban-legend version allowed. Now, seeing us together, hearing us talking, we seemed like a normal couple . . . or as normal as any couple who knew how to field-dress severed fingers.

"So," Clay said as he repacked my medical bag. "Your hand. Mutt do that?"

Reese flinched at the word. Some do, taking it as derogatory. Others wear it as a badge of honor. Most don't care, the word having long since lost its bite, a label no different from "Pack wolf." But seeing Reese's reaction, I quickly said, "Another werewolf, I take it?"

He nodded. "I was in the museum this morning. The art and history one on Seventh Street."

He explained that he'd gone, pulled by a mild interest in history coupled with the conviction that if any werewolf had followed him to Alaska, a museum would be the last place we'd look.

For Liam and Ramon, I was sure that was true. These were two guys who'd have trouble *spelling* museum. For Clay, though, there was no city attraction he was *more* likely to be found at. But I didn't mention that.

Reese's logic, while sound, didn't help him. He was found there, by two mutts who'd introduced themselves as Travis and Dan. They'd crossed his trail a couple of blocks away and followed it to check him out, as any werewolf would upon scenting another in the same city.

They seemed relieved to find he was just a kid—in our world twenty years old is still "just a kid"—meaning he'd have little fighting experience and no reputation. They were fine with Reese being in Alaska—temporarily, they hoped. He was no threat to them and as long as he stayed out of trouble, he was welcome to visit. They even gave him some advice on cheap motels, good buffets, safe places to run...

Friendly enough without being overly hospitable, which struck the right balance for a kid who'd already been burned. In the course of the conversation, Travis noticed Reese's class ring. He asked about the insignia. Reese let him take a closer look.

"Travis was checking it out, holding the end of my fingers. That's when it happened, so fast I didn't see the knife until..." He paled at the memory. "If I hadn't yanked back right then, he would have taken both fingers right off. I ran. I shoved my hand in my pocket and I ran as fast as I could. I could hear them coming after me. So I raced past this guard—an old guy. By the time he got up and yelled at me, I was out the door, but it made Travis and Dan pull back. There was a cab right out front. I got in and came here. I— I guess they wanted the ring, but it wasn't anything special. Just a high school ring."

"It wasn't about the ring," Clay said. "It was a warning. Get off our territory."

"Then why not just tell me to? Why act all nice, then—" He lifted his hand. "Do this?"

"How do you feel?" Clay asked.

Reese's face darkened. "How the hell do you think I feel? I lost my fucking fingers."

"Scared? Confused?"

"Hell, yes."

"And what were you going to do after you got it cleaned up? Tell the desk clerk you'll be staying a few more days, extending your Alaskan vacation?"

"Fuck no. I would have been on the first plane—" He stopped and nodded. "That's the point, isn't it?"

"Strike hard and fast, catch you off guard and scare the crap out of you. Lot more effective than giving a friendly warning and hoping you don't stab them in the back."

I asked about the mutts. He gave me a description. Travis was "huge." At least six foot four and buff. The rest of him hadn't left much of an impression—brown hair, he thought, neither long nor short. No idea what color his eyes were. No distinguishing marks.

Travis's size had blinded Reese not only to what *he* looked like, but to his companion. All he could say about Dan was two things. First, he was smaller. Second, he was Russian—he'd spoken little, but when he did, it was with a heavy accent. Oh, and while Travis's English was perfect and had an American accent, he'd had a few exchanges with Dan in Russian.

They didn't match anyone from my dossiers. Between Dan's accent and Travis's Russian, I guessed they'd been living abroad.

"We'll go back to the museum," I said to Clay. "I doubt they're hanging around, but I want to check the scents. Chances are these are the same guys we smelled in the woods."

"Hope so," Clay said.

I agreed. Multiple groups of werewolves in the Anchorage area was more than I cared to contemplate. Our simple trip had already become far too complicated.

"I'll take you there," Reese said. "I can show you where I was attacked."

"Just tell us where to look, and we'll pick up the scents. They're probably gone, but they could be staking it out, and you've already gotten hurt."

"And that's why I *want* to go back." He flushed. "I ran away."

"You'd just lost two fingers. Running away was the right thing to do."

Reese glanced at Clay. I knew better than to hope he'd back me up just to make the kid feel better. Reese probably knew that, too, which is why he ignored my reassurances and looked to Clay.

"If the guy's as big as you said, then, yeah, nothing wrong with running," he said. "But if you think you're going back now, hoping for payback? With us to watch your back and jump in if you can't handle it?"

Reese flushed again, deeper now. "I didn't mean—"

"No, I'm sure you didn't. But you didn't think it through either. If we meet up with these mutts, we can't be looking over our shoulders, keeping an eye on an injured kid itching for revenge. Elena came to Alaska to save your ass. I'm not letting you get killed now, making her feel bad."

I cleared my throat and shot him a look that said, really, this should not be the reason he didn't want Reese dead. But one glance at Reese told me that, if anything, he was relieved by Clay's honesty.

"All right then," Reese said. "I'll tell you whatever you need, then I'll hit the road."

I shook my head. "While Clay's right—you do need to leave Alaska—I'd like you to stay with a Pack member until we finish here."

"I appreciate the offer, but that's not necessary."

"Actually, it is. You're injured and you're still in danger—"

"I'll be fine," he said.

"As fine as Yuli Etxeberria?"

"Who?"

"The last guy Liam and Ramon blamed for their man-eating. He was a few years older than you and a recent immigrant. Lost some fingers, too. In his case, the whole hand—postmortem. Liam and Ramon mailed it to us. That's what I've been trying to tell you. They've done it before, and blamed another kid, and if you stick around, you'll be their next scapegoat."

"So you just wanted to warn me?"

"And see what you know about Liam and Ramon," Clay said. "Get your help finding them and proving they're maneaters."

I'd planned to keep that part quiet until I'd won the kid's confidence, but now that Clay said it, Reese looked relieved again.

"Why didn't you say so?" he asked me.

"Well, maybe because you kept taking off before I could explain, convinced Clay was lurking around the next corner."

"I don't lurk," Clay said.

"I'll tell you what I can about Liam and Ramon," Reese said. "Then I'll find someplace and lie low."

"If you're going anyplace on the continent, it's New York State," I said. "As a guest of the Pack."

Reese looked at Clay.

"If you die, she'll feel bad. I don't like it when she feels bad."

"Either that or I put you on the next plane back to Australia," I said.

"No," he said quickly. "I'm—I'm here for good."

That could mean he'd done something back home and couldn't return, but from the look in his eyes—determination mingled with dread—I knew it was more personal.

"All right then," I said. "You're staying with the Pack until Clay and I get back and take care of this business with Liam and Ramon."

"So where do you want me to stay? Syracuse?"

"That's where the Alpha lives," Clay said, as if this answered the question, which for him, it did.

"Another Pack family lives outside New York City," I said. "They have a big place, with lots of room. You'll stay with them."

"The Sorrentinos."

"That's right."

"And they'll just let me move in for a while?"

"Antonio will put you to work," Clay said.

Reese nodded, visibly relieved. In his world, this made sense—no one helps out of the goodness of his heart, and if he says he does, run the other way, as fast as you can.

Reese agreed and we made the arrangements. Nick would meet him at the airport. Tonight Jeremy would leave the twins with Jaime and drive to Antonio's place to check Reese's fingers.

We drove Reese to the airport. On the way, Clay gave him "the lecture," including all the do's and don'ts of meeting the Alpha, which was only slightly more complicated than an audience with the queen. Don't sit until you're invited to. Don't talk unless he asks you a question. Don't eat before he does. Don't make direct eye contact. Jeremy demanded none of this, but that wasn't the point.

Hierarchy is very important to wolves, and it's just as important to us. Give a werewolf the choice of two leaders—one who'll take him out for drinks and one who'll take his ear off if he drinks first—and he'll pick the latter every time. An Alpha is his master and protector. Pushovers, buddies and wimps need not apply.

Next Clay gave the house rules for living with the Sorrentinos, which sounded a lot like the Ten Commandments. Thou shall not lie, steal anything, kill anyone, disrespect your hosts or covet any of Nick's girlfriends. And if you break the rules, you'll get your ass kicked and handed to you in pieces—a part I suspect God left out.

Reese was fine with all this. It was a firm and clear language that a werewolf understood better than "Be a good houseguest."

After we left him at the airport, it was time to return to the scene of the crime: the museum.

WENDIGO

THE MUSEUM TURNED out to be only a few blocks from our hotel, which we hadn't checked in to yet. So we parked in the hotel lot and walked.

At the museum, we found the spot where Reese had been attacked. There was still blood spatter on the display, tucked back in a corner. It would be a while before people noticed it, and then they'd likely brush it off as a nosebleed.

The location made it easy to get down and sniff. I did that while Clay stood guard.

"And?" he asked when I stood.

"It's the same scents from the woods, which I suppose is something of a relief—at least we aren't dealing with more mutts."

Clay nodded, but I could tell he wasn't relieved. His gaze kept sweeping the room, never resting on any of the exhibits, which wasn't like him at all.

"You're worried about Dennis and Joey," I said.

"I'm sure they're okay. I just..." He glanced around, shook it off, then headed out. We took another route through the exhibits, and were almost at the front when Clay stopped.

"Dennis was here."

"Dennis? I hope he didn't follow those mutts in."

"He wouldn't."

I inhaled as he turned left and headed for a separate room.

"I don't smell anything," I said. "Are you sure?"

He was already in the next room. I followed him into a display of Native artifacts. Clay was crouched in the middle. Luckily, the room was empty—not that the presence of others would have stopped him from dropping down and sniffing.

When I moved into the room, I *did* smell Dennis—the same scent we'd picked up outside his apartment, and just as faint, meaning it was at least as old. As for how Clay had detected it from the lobby, it only proved that as hard as he was trying to keep his perspective on this, Dennis and Joey were front and center in his mind right now.

As he followed the trail, I looked around. It seemed to be a temporary exhibit focusing on local mythology and legends. If we did have time for sightseeing later, this room would top Clay's destination list. Even now, he kept glancing at the artifacts, reading the cards.

Myth and ritual was Clay's academic field. His specialty was anthropomorphism in religion—belief systems that included man-beast hybrids or shape-shifters.

"Was Dennis interested in this?" I asked.

"Not that I knew."

And he *would* have known. Clay's area of expertise

wasn't exactly a popular conversation topic among were-wolves. Before I'd come along, he'd had two choices if he wanted to talk about it—Jeremy, who'd struggle to feign interest, or Nick, who wouldn't even try. If Dennis had been even mildly intrigued, Clay would have pounced like a starving wolf spotting a lame doe.

I peeked out the door, making sure the coast was clear, then bent and sniffed the carpet. In a public place, this is definitely not pleasant, but I've done it often enough that I can mentally filter out the less savory smells and zoom in on what I'm searching for.

"No sign of the other mutts' trails," I said. "If Dennis ducked into the museum to hide from them, that would be incredibly coincidental, although I suppose he could have been following the same logic as Reese, thinking it's the last place a werewolf would follow. We're the exceptions. Well, if you don't count Karl, but his interest in artifacts is hardly academic."

Clay grumbled under his breath as he continued untangling Dennis's trail. Clay had a lot of problems with Karl Marsten joining the Pack, but when asked to add anything to the list of concerns, he'd said only "No more stealing from museums."

When Karl heard that, he'd been a bit taken aback, this probably being the last issue he'd expect Clay to raise, far behind the fact that Karl had once helped kidnap him. But Clay's priorities were never the expected ones. He didn't give a shit about the kidnapping—that was business. But stealing artifacts? That pissed him off. They'd eventually negotiated a compromise. Karl could still steal from museums, but only jewels and only the sort shown off as historical bling with no archaeological significance.

"Can you tell what Dennis was looking at in here?" I asked.

"Everything, it seems. His trail goes all through the room, several times. His scent's especially heavy right here, though."

I looked at the collection of drawings and newspaper accounts. "Wendigo psychosis? You did a paper on that a couple of years ago, didn't you?"

"Yeah."

"Maybe Jeremy mentioned it, then Dennis was visiting the museum, noticed this and slowed down for a look."

The Wendigo is one of the more popular and better known bits of Native North American folklore. During a particularly tough winter, it's believed that evil spirits possess people, transforming them into beasts craving human flesh. That sounds a lot like man-eating werewolves, which explains Clay's interest. It also, however, sounds like an explanation for cannibalism—during a very long and hard winter, the need to survive overcomes cultural taboos. Just ask the Donner Party.

That's why Wendigo *psychosis* interests Clay even more. It's a mental condition that apparently causes people to crave human flesh although other food sources are available. Again, the parallels with werewolves are obvious. The question is whether sufferers of Wendigo psychosis are werewolves, humans with an unrelated condition or humans with a weak strain of werewolf blood.

"I'll ask Jeremy if he mentioned my article," Clay said.

"If not, remember we've got three half-eaten human bodies in the woods. Dennis had to know about them and figured he and Joey were the only werewolves around. They sure as hell didn't do it."

"So he could have been looking for another explanation. Either way, Dennis was here at least a week ago, meaning his visit doesn't seem directly connected to those mutts."

Clay nodded.

"They may have had nothing to do with his disappearance."

Another nod.

"Or if they did, his disappearance probably means they pulled the same terror tactics they used on Reese. Dennis and Joey don't strike me as the type who'd stick around to defend their territory."

"They're not," Clay said as he waved for us to head out. "But they should have notified Jeremy. Sure, they're not Pack, so technically they can't hold territory. We'd still have helped, though."

"But *would* they have called? Or would they slip off to avoid any kind of confrontation?"

"Dennis would leave. He's..." He trailed off, and I knew he was trying to think of a milder word than *coward*. "Still, whether he likes confrontations or not, this was his home."

"Maybe he didn't run. Maybe he's snowed in at his cabin, like the landlord said."

As we stepped outside, I checked my cell phone for messages.

"He's not calling back," Clay said.

I'd begun to suspect the same thing. The young landlord had seemed helpful—refreshingly so when I was more accustomed to dealing with people like Mallory Hirsch. But, like Reese, I couldn't help questioning the kindness of strangers. Maybe in his own way, Charles was blocking us as much as Hirsch, promising us an address to get us out of his face.

We turned the corner and picked our way past museum expansion construction.

"We should try to find Joey," I said. "It won't be that hard if he's using his real name."

"First, we need to check into the hotel and rest."

A protest rose to my lips, but didn't make it out. I *was* tired. We'd accomplished a lot for our first day. Now it was time to take a couple of hours off to sleep, eat . . .

"Is that a yes?" Clay asked.

"It is."

"Good."

WE GRABBED OUR bags from the car. While I checked in, Clay prowled, getting the layout of the hotel, which was even more important now when we knew there were mutts in town.

After I checked in, I took a seat in one of the big lobby chairs and started an Internet search for Joey. Not surprisingly, there wasn't a listing in the phone directory. Jeremy said Joey worked for an advertising agency, so I angled my hunt that way. In a few minutes, I had a match—a Joseph Stillwell listed at Creative Marketing Solutions in Anchorage.

I called.

I was hanging up when Clay returned. "Good news. I found where Joey works. He's left for the day, but the receptionist confirmed he was in earlier, meaning he's alive and well."

Clay only nodded, but he was obviously relieved.

We took the bags up to our room. Clay barely got through the door before he was cursing. I passed him and walked to the other side of the room, which took about five paces.

"This *is* the Hilton, isn't it?" Clay asked.

"Yep."

The room was decently appointed, but showing its age, and was roughly the size of our en suite bathroom at home.

"Let's just hope we don't spend much time in here or we'll go stir-crazy."

Clay threw the bags onto the bed. "All this wide-open country and they can't afford to build decent-size hotel rooms?"

"Let me call down and see if they have a bigger—"

Clay caught me around the waist. "I'm sure Jeremy booked the best they had. It'll do."

"We could switch hotels. There must be—"

He cut me off with a kiss—a hungry, fingers-in-hair, leg-around-hips, who-needs-oxygen kiss, ending only when my cell phone chirped. His head whipped toward it, eyes narrowing, and I was glad I'd left it out of his reach or I'd have been picking pieces out of the plaster.

I untangled myself from him. "Normally, I'd say to hell with it, but considering we're waiting for a call . . ."

He strode over, snatched up the phone, then tossed it to me. "It's Dennis's landlord."

Charles had the GPS coordinates and directions ready to text to my cell. He apologized for taking so long. His wife had stopped at a friend's after shopping and, as he said, "You know how that goes." Actually, I didn't, but I understood the concept.

He warned us not to head out to Dennis's cabin tonight—it was already dark. I thanked him and promised to call back with any news.

When I hung up, Clay was already at the door.

"Eager to be off?" I said.

"Eager to be off before I decide it can wait five minutes, and five minutes wasn't what I had in mind."

"Me neither. Let's get this trip over with, then we can call it a night."

UNEASY

WE'D GONE ABOUT ten miles when I said, "So, how long have you known that Jeremy planned to make me the next Alpha?"

He looked over. "You want to talk about that now?"

"I think I need to."

"Good." He adjusted the rearview mirror. "I've known for just over a week. He's been giving you extra responsibilities since before the kids were born, but I only recently started thinking it might mean something. I asked him a couple of times, but he brushed me off. I was getting pissed, because I knew the one person who *hadn't* figured it out was you, and that's not right. I didn't like keeping my suspicions from you—it felt like a secret. So I called him on it. He admitted that he's planned to make you Alpha for years. The kids just slowed things down."

He whizzed past a truck. "Is that what's been bothering you? You thought I've known for a while and hadn't said anything?"

"Jeremy would have made you keep it a secret until he was ready. I'd understand that."

"You'd understand if I kept something that big from you? You *shouldn't*. Because I *wouldn't*. That's why Jeremy wouldn't confirm it. If there's a conflict between loyalty to mate and Alpha, Jeremy knows better than to test me on it."

And if that mate was also his Alpha? I turned to stare out at the dark waters of the inlet.

"You didn't suspect?" Clay asked after a moment.

"I noticed Jeremy's been asking my opinion more often, encouraging me to make decisions in the field, but that's been gradually happening for years. I thought that was just because I was getting more experienced and he felt more comfortable handing things off, knowing I wouldn't run off to Toronto again. Once he started seeing Jaime, it made sense that he wanted someone who could take over when he goes away for the weekend. But take over for good?" I took a deep breath. "No, I didn't see that coming."

I watched the rising moon skate across the waves and, for a second, thought I saw the white back of a beluga. I kept staring, telling myself I was just waiting for it to resurface.

"So how—" Clay began.

"Is Jeremy crazy?" I cut in, twisting to face him, seat belt digging into my neck. "I know, I shouldn't question his decisions. The Alpha's word is law and I should instinctively obey."

He laughed. "And since when have you done that? Plus in this case, I can safely say you're wrong. Sure, I had my doubts about Jeremy's sanity when he hooked up with Jaime, but I'm over that."

"You know what I mean. The ascension of a new Alpha

is supposed to prove to mutts that we're as strong as ever, and bolstering the leadership with fresh blood. What's a female Alpha going to tell them? That we've lost our collective minds."

"Which is why they won't believe it." He swooped past another vehicle daring to obey the speed limit. "They'll think it's a clever way to make me Alpha. If we announced that the crazy guy was in charge, they'd be arming themselves for Armageddon. By saying you're Alpha, it signals that we don't want to panic them. They'll be edgy for a while, but when they see it's business as usual, they'll relax."

"And then you'll take over?"

"Hell, no. You're Alpha."

"And you're okay with that?"

He turned off the highway. "No, I'm pissed. Fuming mad. Can't you tell?"

I gave him a look.

"Deep down, I'm furious. I'm just a master at controlling my emotions."

"Ha-ha."

"If I was fuming, you'd know it. If I was mildly annoyed, you'd know it. I'm not, because I'm not Alpha material. Mutt steps over the line? You and Jeremy say beat the crap out of him, and teach him a lesson. I say kill the bastard and save ourselves any future problems. Not Alpha material."

"But you're the best fighter. Everyone expects it will be you. Do you *want* to be Alpha?"

"No." He looked over, meeting my gaze and holding it. "I didn't expect to, and I wouldn't accept the post if he offered it. I like being second-in-command. If having you as

Alpha means I get to keep doing that, then I'm happy. All that political shit?" He snorted. "Can't be bothered."

"We could be co-Alphas. An Alpha pair, male and female, like wolves."

"What works for wolves doesn't always work for werewolves. To your average mutt, I'd be making you my co-Alpha for the sake of marital harmony, not martial strategy, which wouldn't reflect well on either of us. Werewolves have *an* Alpha. One wolf to rule them all. And that wolf will be you."

I stared out at a boglike area with skeletal trees, a wasteland surrounded by lush forest.

"But you'd be happier about the promotion if you had more competition."

I turned to him. "What?"

"It wasn't much of an Alpha race, and everyone knows it. Antonio would be good, but he's even older than Jeremy and he has a business to run. Nick and Karl are out of the question. I don't want the job. A victory by default isn't nearly so sweet."

"You think I'm put out by the lack of competition? Please. I—" At his look, I sighed and brushed my ponytail off my shoulder. "Okay, yes, it would be a lot more flattering if I wasn't the only choice."

"But that's not what's really bothering you, is it?" He glanced over, gaze boring into the side of my head, as if he could read my thoughts. "Is it another worry about becoming Alpha? Or something else?"

I shrugged. "It's nothing important."

"Never is. It's both, isn't it? Something to do with becoming Alpha and something separate. What else happened while I was gone?"

The words were on the tip of my tongue. *I got a letter from one of the men—*

Not now. Not yet.

"It's nothing— Wait. You missed the road."

He hit the brakes and reversed. "You were saying?"

"Later. We're almost there." I glanced over my shoulder at the narrow black trail that passed for a road. "And this is going to take some navigating."

WE SOON UNDERSTOOD why Charles had laughed when I asked for an address for Dennis's cabin. This was no lakeside cottage in Muskoka, down a pleasant winding lane lined with signs welcoming you to "The Grangers' Getaway."

We turned onto the trail, then onto another, then another, each one getting successively narrower until branches scraped both sides of the SUV. Then the road ended.

We got out and peered into the night. After a couple of minutes we found a trail. A dozen feet down it, there was a cinder-block shed with a wide door, massive padlock and Private sign. The area stank of mixed gas and oil. Boot marks led to the door, and snowmobile tracks led away.

"This must be where they leave their snowmobiles and ride in." I bent and sniffed. "Human, but I think I detect faint werewolf. An older trail."

Clay crouched and inhaled deeply. "Yeah, that's Dennis."

We followed the snowmobile tracks through knee-deep snow. As wolves, we'd move easier, but it wasn't worth the agony of the Change for a half-mile trek. Then there was the problem of showing up at Dennis's cabin naked.

The trail branched several times. The snowmobile tracks led down the second one, presumably to another cabin. I kept an eye on the GPS and took the first branch leading in the right direction.

The snow was thicker here, with no signs that anyone had passed this way since the last snowfall. We'd gone about fifty feet before I caught a smell that made me stop.

Clay inhaled. "Wolf."

Under my thick down jacket, goose bumps rose in a mix of excitement and trepidation. Wolves fascinate most werewolves. We feel the pull of kinship. Unfortunately, the wolves don't feel the same way.

Our blended smell of human and canine confuses them. They don't know what we are, so it's safest to assume we're a threat.

Clay and I had encountered wolves once before in Algonquin Park. They'd started to attack, then they'd decided we smelled too human for their liking, and run.

After that, if we went anyplace known as wolf territory, we steered clear of their trails. Here that wasn't possible.

"They're all over," I said as we walked. "It's a big pack, at least eight or nine wolves, I bet. The tracks are recent, too."

"I don't smell any on the wind, though."

"Me neither, which hopefully means they're far away." Not surprising—wolves tended to travel more in winter as they searched for food.

"Didn't those cops say a pack lived where they found that guy this morning?"

I rubbed my icy nose. "They said there'd been one, but it moved on. Maybe because of the mutts. We should find out when the pack left. That might give us some idea when our mutts arrived. I got the feeling it was recently."

We moved into a denser area of woods and the light all but disappeared. While our general vision was slightly better as humans, our night vision suffered. I slowed, paying more attention to where I put my feet. I still stumbled over a branch under the snow. Clay caught my arm.

"I should have brought a flashlight," I said.

"We're almost there. I see a light."

I followed his gaze to see several bluish lights twinkling through the trees.

I checked the GPS. "Either Charles got the coordinates wrong or that's another cabin. According to this, we have almost a quarter mile to go that way." I pointed.

"We'll check it out."

To head toward the lights, we had to leave the path. As we drew closer, the lights dimmed, but I could still see them, blue spots against the darkness just ahead.

We stepped from the trees.

"Huh," Clay said.

We stood at the edge of a clearing with no cabin . . . and no lights.

"Ghost lights? We should have brought Jaime."

I meant it lightly, but my voice wavered. As I looked around, every hair on my body rose.

"Do you feel that?" I asked.

"Yeah."

"Something's out there. Wolves?"

"Maybe."

It wasn't wolves. We both knew it. Both felt it. Clay's taut face turned my way, gaze scanning the trees.

"You sense trouble?" he asked.

"I don't think so." I rubbed the back of my neck. "Let's find that trail again."

UNNATURAL

THE MOON APPEARED then, lighting our way back to the trail. Even through the trees, it cast enough of a glow for us to follow. The wolf tracks continued as we drew closer to our destination. When I caught another whiff of scent, I stopped.

"Werewolf. Probably Dennis."

"Is he out here?"

I shook my head. "It's a trail."

Clay inhaled. "I'm not getting it."

I resumed walking. "It's faint. But a trail means he's been here recently. And that looks like a cabin just ahead."

Clay squinted at the black shape through the trees. "No lights on."

"Out here, off the grid, you don't use any more than you need to."

The moon against the snow lit the clearing to twilight. We looked across the yard.

"Shit, is that...?" Clay blinked, as if seeing things. He wasn't. The snow was crisscrossed with wolf tracks. Not a square foot in the clearing had been left untouched.

I walked a few feet, then bent. "Definitely wolf."

"That's..."

"Weird."

He gave a distracted nod, but we both knew that wasn't the right word. Looking out at that paw-print-covered snow, so close to a werewolf's cabin, the word that came to mind was *wrong*. More than weird. Downright unnatural.

If new wolves had entered the region and decided to challenge an occupying werewolf, they'd slink around his cabin for a closer look. The Alpha might mark it to make a statement. But here I saw paw prints of every size, right down to yearlings.

"Maybe it's sled dogs," I said.

Clay looked over.

"Dennis could have a neighbor with a team. He comes over, ties them up while he has a few drinks and they get bored, pace around."

"You smell dogs, darling?"

No. I smelled wolf.

I climbed onto the front deck. I walked to the window to peek in, but the drapes were drawn. More prints dotted the sill, as if the wolves had been doing the same thing I was.

The hair on my scalp prickled. I tugged my hat down, then rubbed my icy earlobes. As I turned, I caught a scent that made my breath catch. When I inhaled deeper, though, I couldn't find it again.

I glanced at Clay, crouched by the door, his fingers running down the lower panel, fingertips tracing rough grooves in the wood.

Claw marks. The deep scratches were ridged with splinters. *Fresh* claw marks.

Clay straightened and banged on the door. "Dennis? It's Clay." He paused, then added, "Clayton Danvers."

The cabin stayed silent. I moved to the window again, looking for any sign of light around the drawn drapes. There was none.

"Dennis?" Clay called. "Jeremy sent me to check on you."

He pounded harder now. The wood buckled under his fist, the door parting from the frame just enough to let out a puff of what I'd smelled earlier.

"Open it," I said.

"What?"

I grabbed the handle and rammed my shoulder into the door. The wood crackled and it flew open. The smell blasted out, sending me reeling back.

I caught a glimpse of what was inside. Then I hurried to the side railing, leaning over it, hands over my mouth, teeth clenched, gorge bobbing.

Clay's hand rested against my back.

"Sorry, I—" I turned. "I'm sorry."

He nodded, his gaze on the forest. I stepped toward him, uncertain. His hands went around my waist and I moved into his arms, my nose pressed against his warm neck. His arms tightened around me. After a moment, a shuddering sigh rippled through him.

"You stay here," I said. "I'll take care of—"

"I'm okay. It's been a lot of years."

We went inside. When I'd first smelled decomposition, I thought Dennis had been killed by wolves. The threat of a werewolf on their new territory might override whatever warning told them to stay away from people. The moment I'd looked through that door, though, I'd known it hadn't been wolves. Not the kind that walk on four legs, anyway.

Dennis Stillwell sat on a kitchen chair in the middle of the room, bound hand and foot with thick wire cables. It looked like he'd been tortured. How much was hard to tell. Despite the cold, he was starting to decompose. All I knew was that someone had tied him up, tried to get information from him, then killed him.

Clay looked at Dennis, his face unreadable.

"I'm going to find them," he said.

"I know."

WE BURIED DENNIS in the woods. We wanted to give him a burial, but more than that, we had to. If Charles or anyone else found him, there would be an investigation and an autopsy, and we couldn't risk either.

Werewolves rarely pass away in their sleep, so it's an unavoidable fact that sometimes there is an autopsy and an investigation, and our world hasn't crumbled yet. The anomalies in our blood and DNA probably left more than one lab tech scratching her head, and maybe a few had made notes of it, put it aside for a personal project, but nothing more. Still, we don't take chances, and even a mutt killing another mutt will dispose of the body. Only, apparently, these ones hadn't bothered. Did they not care? Or was this a message for someone? For Joey?

Clay and I had experience with body disposal. Too

much. We'd buried our own and we'd buried mutts, so we knew how to do it. Dennis Stillwell would simply disappear, like so many werewolves before him.

When we finished, we stood at the gravesite, the bitter wind whipping through the trees, freezing every inch of exposed skin and making our eyes water. Those tears were the only ones we'd shed. Nor would we say any words over the grave. That was the human way. Ours was quieter, more private, just a few minutes of silent respect and reflection.

When I felt a familiar prickle at the back of my neck, my head shot up.

"Wait," Clay said, his voice low. "Move slowly."

I turned my head and followed his gaze, sweeping across the forest.

"Oh my God," I whispered.

Reflections of at least a dozen pairs of eyes dotted the forest. I could make out gray shapes against the black forest. Wolves.

"We'll go back inside," Clay murmured. "Are there more behind me?"

"A few."

"Okay. Count to three. Then turn your back to me. We'll walk in that way. Keep your gaze up over their heads."

"Don't look them in the eye."

"Right. If one charges, then meet its gaze. It might back down."

I really hoped so. A dozen wolves against two werewolves? Even Clay wasn't itching to meet this challenge.

Back-to-back we walked into the cabin. As Clay bolted the door, I looked out. The wolves hadn't moved.

"Do you think they smelled the body?" I asked.

"Long winter. Food's getting scarce."

"That would explain the scratch marks on the door."

"Yeah."

Our eyes met, exchanging a look that said we were sticking to our story, even though we both knew it was bullshit. These wolves didn't look as if they were starving. They might take Dennis's body if they found it lying outside, but to trample the snow as if they'd been pacing around the cabin for hours and trying to scratch their way in? It was too much. Too unnatural.

Clay found a battery-operated lantern and an oil one, and we lit both and looked around.

"Well," I said. "I guess we have enough work here to keep us busy until the wolves move on. I'll clean up—"

"You look for clues. Get scents. You're better at that."

And he was better at cleanup—having had more experience, though neither of us pointed that out.

We set to work. As I soon discovered, finding scents under the stench of decomposition wasn't easy.

"I'm going to crack open the window."

I pulled the drape. Glowing green eyes peered in at me. I fell back. Clay grabbed me. With the lanterns reflecting off the glass, all I could see was the dark shape of a wolf leaping off the porch. I cupped my hands against the glass. A dark-colored wolf vanished into the trees.

Black wolf. Green eyes.

Clay moved beside me, squinting to see out. "Bold bastard, wasn't he?"

I rubbed my gloved hands over my arms, pushing down

the goose bumps. Black wolves weren't that unusual. Green eyes were, but I'd only seen their reflection against the light, and that often made animal eyes glint green. Besides, I could still see the gray wolves at the forest's edge and they'd never let a werewolf run past them like that.

"You okay?" Clay asked.

"He just spooked me."

Clay drew the drapes again. I walked as far as possible from the bloodstain in the middle of the cabin and got down on my hands and knees. A piercing wail sent me scrambling up.

"Wind in the chimney," Clay said.

I gave a shaky laugh. "A little jumpy tonight, aren't I?"

"With good reason."

He moved up behind me and rubbed my shoulders. When I tried to step away, he held me.

"Take a minute," he murmured. "It's only me."

I took a deep breath. It wasn't easy, being a woman in a werewolf's world, worrying that they're watching you for signs of weakness. It meant a lot to have someone in my life who didn't care if wolves at the door spooked me. If I became Alpha—*his* Alpha—would that change?

I leaned back against Clay and turned my head, cheek against his shoulder, inhaling. When my nerves were calm and the specter of Dennis Stillwell faded, I got back to work.

I didn't need to sniff around for long before saying, "I've got werewolf. And not just Dennis."

Clay nodded. No surprise there.

Another few minutes of sniffing. "It's the same two from the museum—the ones who attacked Reese."

Again, he nodded.

"I'm getting a third scent," I said.

"Werewolf?"

"Yep." I followed it, untangling the trail from the others. "He's related to one of the others—father, son, brother. That's why I wasn't sure I detected an older third trail in that clearing. Similar scents."

"Makes sense."

He meant both my explanation and the family relationship. It was unusual to find three werewolves together, but far more likely if at least two shared a family connection.

Clay had found a toolbox in the closet and was sanding the rough wooden floor. He couldn't buff out all the blood, but it would fade the stain, making it look like an old spill. As he did that, I walked to the dinette. The table was covered with papers and books.

"What did Dennis do for a living?" I asked.

"Electrician, I think. I remember Jeremy had him fix up the old wiring at Stonehaven."

I looked at the handwritten notes. They definitely weren't electrical diagrams.

"Hobbies?" I asked.

Clay shrugged. "Couldn't say. Jeremy would know. Why?"

I picked up a book in my gloved hand. "He seems to have been researching folklore and mythology. That must have been what he was doing at the museum."

Clay brought a lantern over and picked up a notebook as I thumbed through a sheaf of photocopied pages.

"Yeenaaldlooshii, Nagual, Wendigo..." I said. "Shape-shifter myths, particularly Native American. I'm surprised he didn't contact you."

He took the papers from my hand, reading them more closely.

"I'll find a bag and we'll take his work with us."

He nodded, his gaze still fixed on the papers. He didn't stop reading until I plucked them from his hand and added them to a canvas bag I'd already filled with the rest.

"What do you think he was doing?" I asked.

"No idea. Maybe a new hobby. Getting older and look-ing for answers." He took the bag from me. "We should get going."

I nodded and pulled back the curtain. The nightscape was empty. Behind me, Clay checked the other windows.

"All clear?" I asked.

"Seems so."

We stepped onto the porch. I inhaled. I could still smell the wolves, their thick scent hanging in the air, but the forest was still. We walked around the perimeter of the clearing.

"Vanished into the night," I murmured. "Just curious? They might be used to Dennis, so our scent doesn't spook them."

"Could be."

Clay surveyed the forest, but we heard only the whine of the wind.

"Let's go."

BEAST

WHEN WE REACHED the head of the trail, Clay turned and peered back at the cabin. Following his gaze, I saw a snowmobile parked at the far end of the deck.

"There wasn't a truck," I said.

He glanced over. "What?"

"I was just thinking. Dennis must have driven to the snowmobile shed in a truck, but there wasn't one on the road. Whoever killed him must have taken it, presumably so none of his neighbors would notice. Are you thinking we should do the same with the snowmobile? Put it back in the shed?"

"Good idea, but I was just looking for a faster way out of here. I don't want to be caught on a trail if those wolves come back."

On cue, a howl reverberated through the night. Another answered. I tracked the sound.

"At least a mile off," I said. "With luck they'll stay there. But if we can take the snowmobile and return it to the shed, we should."

We went back inside to find the keys. We didn't. Either the mutts took them for the truck or we'd buried them in Dennis's pocket.

Clay tried to hot-wire the snowmobile. Lucas had taught him how—for cars—but I don't think Clay had paid much attention. It wasn't a skill he'd ever needed, so he'd only listened to be respectful. Clay had taught Lucas a lot and if Lucas wanted to return a lesson, Clay wouldn't say he couldn't use it.

Only now he *could* use it, and could only vaguely recall the instructions.

After about twenty minutes, he settled back on his haunches and growled at the offending vehicle. "I remember how to do it with cars and the basic principles are the same but . . ." Another growl. "Machines. I'm a lot better at disabling them than starting them."

"Shocking." I hopped off the edge of the porch. "Forget it. By the time we get it going, we could have walked to the car and back."

He hated to admit the challenge had bested him, but after another moment of fiddling, he hefted the book bag, and we set out.

We could still hear the distant song of the wolves, so we relaxed, knowing they were far off. We talked about the kids and the school dilemma—a good distraction.

Clay moved into the lead as the moon slid behind cloud cover. "Kindergarten is a waste of time."

"Says the guy who got kicked out."

"I wasn't *kicked* out."

"No, they just strongly suggested that Jeremy reconsider

your readiness for school . . . and preferably find you another one to attend."

"Damned private schools. Elitist snobs."

"True. A public school would never get so worked up over a student dissecting the classroom guinea pig."

"It was already—"

"—dead. So I've heard. Which really wasn't the point."

"The point was that they failed to recognize my academic potential, and Logan is going to run into the same problems."

"We'll tell his teacher he's allergic to guinea pigs."

Clay let a branch fling back. I caught it before it hit my face.

"I'd agree," I said. "If Logan wasn't the one wanting to go to—"

Clay spun fast. I jumped, hands flying up, thinking he was goofing. Then I saw his face, rigid, as he stared out into the forest. A pair of eyes appeared from the darkness. Then another. And another.

"Shit," I said. "But we just heard them miles— That was another pack."

Clay stepped back toward me, my nylon coat whispering against his leather. I counted eleven pairs of eyes, and a couple more dark shapes farther back. A huge pack.

"Hear anything?" Clay asked.

He meant a growl or snarl, some warning of impending attack. But the wolves were silent, pale statues against the night, eyes glinting where the moonlight pierced the canopy.

"I think they'll leave us alone," Clay said.

"Just curious?"

He nodded and slipped behind me. "Keep walking. I'll keep a watch on the rear. No sudden moves or loud noises."

He knew I knew this—it was just his anxiety talking. For the first ten paces, the wolves stayed where they were. Then their eyes disappeared as they turned and started gliding along, still silent, keeping their distance, flanking us as we walked.

I'll never forget what that was like, the squeak of snow under my boots, adrenaline pumping so hard I didn't feel the cold, my breath coming in puffs, tiny clouds hanging in the air, the moonlight through the trees casting slices of light, the wolves gliding through them, then vanishing into the dark.

A wolf stopped in one of those moonlight slices. Its head swiveled as it looked the other way, deep into the forest. Another wolf stopped, then another, their gray shapes all turning.

One let out a low whine. Another growled. Clay tugged me back against him, his chin lifting, eyes searching, but the wolves paid us no attention. Then, on the wind, a scent whipped past, heavy and musky, the stink of it clinging to my throat.

Clay's face lifted, nostrils flaring. "What the hell is that?"

I took another sniff, but smelled only clean air now. The wolves hadn't budged. I swore I could feel their anxiety thrumming through the air.

The same wolf growled again. A bigger one twisted and snapped, like a grown-up telling a teenager to shut up. The younger wolf's ears lowered and his grumble vibrated across the air, but didn't rise to a growl again.

And then, as if in reaction to a command I couldn't hear, the wolves all turned and started to run, tearing back the way they'd come, paws pounding.

Only one remained—the wolf farthest from us, a dark shape I hadn't noticed hidden behind his lighter brethren. He stood his ground, hackles up, and even from here, I could hear the low warning growl.

The moon slid from behind wispy clouds, beaming light into the dark pockets between the trees, and I got a good look at him—not a black wolf but a dark red one, nearly twice the size of the others. It was the one I'd seen at the window. The wolf that I'd been sure, for a moment, wasn't a wolf at all.

Before I could say anything to Clay, a smaller gray wolf ran back, lunging and dancing in front of the dark wolf, then darting behind him and nipping at his heels. He looked out into the forest. The smaller wolf bumped him, whining. He snorted and turned toward us, green eyes meeting mine. Then he took off after the others.

"Did you see...?" I asked.

"Yeah."

"Was that...?"

"Think so."

A werewolf with a wolf pack? I took a step off the path, but Clay caught my arm.

"I want to check his scent," I said. "See whether he was one of the mutts who killed Dennis."

"We'll come back. Right now, we need to get to the truck before we find out what scared them off."

"Whatever it was, I think it's gone. I only caught that one whiff."

Clay kept his fingers on my arm, guiding me along the path.

"Did it smell like wolf to you?" I asked.

"Wolf?" He pursed his lips, considering it. "I thought it might, but I was picking up the wolves following us. With that stink, I was going wolverine. If it made the wolves run, though, I'm guessing bear."

"A pack that size running from a bear?"

He prodded me forward when I slowed. "Did you see that stuffed one in the hotel lobby? Damn near eight feet tall. I see anything that big, I'm running, too."

The moon passed behind thicker clouds and I slowed again, blinking hard as the path went dark.

"Get behind me," he said.

Clay's night vision beat mine, so he led the way, slowly but surefooted. As we walked, I swear it got darker, even the glow of the cloud-covered moon erased from the night sky.

I was about to say we definitely needed to invest in flashlights. Then a scent wafted past my nose, that awful musky smell coming from downwind meaning it was right beside—

Clay spun, his fist in flight, eyes widening as he realized he'd led with his bad arm. He checked himself, his left punching as I wheeled. Something plowed square into my back, knocking the wind from my lungs. My feet flew off the ground and I braced myself for a fall. Instead I jerked up short, legs windmilling, suspended in the air, that stench washing over me, held aloft by the back of my coat. As I twisted to see what had me, Clay pile-drove the beast. It grunted in surprise, and I went flying, my jacket ripping.

I slammed into a tree. Pain exploded. As I tumbled into a heap at the base, I blinked, barely able to see. Clay's face appeared over mine. He gave a whoosh of relief, seeing my eyes open.

Before I could speak, trees crackled, branches snapping. A snarl. Then a snort. Clay spun, fists sailing up. The crashing continued, growing distant. Clay waited, poised for a fight. When he was sure the beast was gone, he scooped me up. My head throbbed, hot blood trickling down my neck. Clay broke into a jog, carrying me.

When we reached the SUV, he bundled me inside and tried checking my injuries, but I pushed him away.

"Drive," I said. "Even the extra vehicle insurance isn't going to cover a bear attack."

He swung into the driver's seat and had the tires spinning before the door slammed shut. He tore to the end of the trail. When we reached the end of the next one, he pulled over.

"The blood is from my nose," I said, holding a handful of tissues to it. "It's not even broken."

He said nothing, just came around to my side to assess the damage for himself. He cleaned me up and when he was done, he checked for other cuts and found two scrapes.

"Jacket off."

I didn't argue. If he'd been the one thrown into a tree, I'd be doing the same. Maybe that's the wolf. Maybe it's just us.

He helped me out of my jacket. As he pulled it away, I

saw four long tears in the back, tiny feathers fluttering out like snowflakes.

"Shit."

I wanted to ask what had attacked me—a bear, I presumed—but the set of his jaw said he wasn't ready to talk yet, cheek muscles working, gaze hard as he checked my ribs and neck.

When he finished, he stood. His nostrils flared, breath puffing, then he wheeled, fist slamming into the nearest tree.

"Fuck!" He hit the tree again, so hard it groaned. "I used the wrong fucking arm. Stupid, stupid, stupid!"

I slid from the SUV and stepped in front of him, grabbing his fist as it flew again.

"That thing could have killed you," he said. "All because I led with the wrong fucking arm."

His fist drove toward the tree. I caught it, held both his hands tightly, then leaned in to kiss him. He didn't respond at first, his breath coming hard and fast, rage and frustration roiling in his eyes. I kissed him again and the watershed broke. He grabbed me in a fierce, bruising kiss that had none of the playful edge from earlier. I wrapped my hands in his hair and returned it, ignoring the pain in my nose, feeding on his rage and the frustration, feeling it slide away and, under it, the raw taste of fear—that terror that he wasn't as good a fighter anymore, not as good as he needed to be, not good enough to protect his Alpha and his family.

He pushed me up against the tree, then stopped as I winced.

"Your back," he said.

"My neck." I made a face. "I'd say it's okay, but on second thought, this is one escape we should probably complete *before* having sex."

He helped me into the car despite my protests that I was fine.

"So what was that?" I asked as he got in. "A bear?"

"All I saw was something big and hairy. I was busy watching you get tossed around by it."

"It was strong, whatever it was," I said, rubbing my sore neck.

"I tried to get a better look as it ran away, but it was too dark."

"I think it did that on purpose."

"What?" he said.

"It waited until the moon was completely behind the clouds, then stayed downwind so we wouldn't smell anything until it was right beside us. One very smart predator."

"A bear's not that smart."

"No. But a yeti might be."

He looked over sharply. Ten years ago, he'd have known I was joking, but with all we'd seen since then, the supernatural world unfolding before us, he wasn't sure until he caught my smile.

"The yeti is from the Himalayas, darling. That'd be a helluva swim. Around here, it'd have to be a Sasquatch or Bigfoot."

"I stand corrected, professor. But on that subject, I wonder if that thing has anything to do with Dennis's research. He saw it and was trying to figure out what it was."

"Yeah, that's what I was thinking. We need to go over

those notes. First, though, I want to find a grizzly—or at least a stuffed one. Get a good whiff of that."

I nodded. "Cross off the mundane possibilities before we start looking at the supernatural ones. And speaking of supernatural, what was up with that mutt? A werewolf running with a wolf pack?"

"There's stuff like that in the Legacy."

The Legacy was the Pack's bible—our combination of werewolf myth and genealogy. It did include a few stories of werewolves who'd embraced their wolf nature, choosing to immerse themselves in that side and that society. I'd always brushed them off as stories.

We reached the highway. It was so empty that I had to check the clock. Not even ten o'clock? Hard to believe.

As I ratcheted back my seat to rest, I noticed Clay gripping and ungripping the steering wheel with his right hand, flexing it.

Just before the twins were born, a zombie had scratched Clay. It'd broken the skin, but his arm got so badly infected that we'd been sure he'd lose it. Instead, he'd lost muscle and some function when the infected tissue had to be cut out to save the rest.

"It's as good as it's ever going to be," he said when he noticed me watching. "I can do all the physical therapy I want, but it's not getting any better."

"Even at less than perfect, it's a damned sight better than most."

No answer. *Better than most* wasn't good enough. Clay had to be the best.

I continued, "We've suspected for a while that you've hit

the limits of rehabilitation. Now we need to keep working on rerouting those neural pathways, teaching you to favor the left, which in most cases you do."

"Not tonight."

"Because you were surprised, so we need to work on your reactions when you're caught off guard. Jeremy can help—no one's better at sneaking up. And if we can't break you of the habit, you might be better to lead with your right and follow up with your left rather than pull back."

"Yeah." His shoulders relaxed. "That's an idea." He glanced at me. "I don't mean to brood."

"You're frustrated. As the queen of fretting, I'm certainly not going to complain."

He nodded, and I knew we were both thinking about the same thing: the latest object of my fretting, my ascension to Alphahood . . . yet another reason for Clay to worry about his bad arm.

BALANCE

WE WENT THROUGH a burger drive-through. That served as appetizers, gone before we reached the hotel where we ordered last-minute room service—a couple of decent Alaskan crab sandwiches and a big bowl of surprisingly good seafood chowder.

As Clay finished, he stretched out beside me on the bed. "So, are we going to finish our conversation about you becoming Alpha?"

"I thought we did."

"No, we stopped short of getting to the part where you tell me what's really bothering you. I've been putting together the pieces. First, you were eager for me to get home and discuss it, so whatever's bugging you must have something to do with me. But even after our talk, you're still worried."

I scraped the bottom of my bowl.

He shifted closer. "You're afraid that when you become Alpha, things between us will change."

Bull's-eye on the first shot. So why did my throat clench

when I tried to agree? Why did my brain fill with dozens of other things to say, ways to deflect, to tease, to make light?

I swallowed and forced the words out. "I'm happy."

"Hard to say, isn't it?" He shifted onto his side, his voice lowering.

"No, I . . . Obviously I'm happy. You know that."

"Feeling happy, acting happy, letting me know in little ways that you *are* happy? That's easy. But saying the words? It's like saying you miss me. An admission of complacency. After what I did, you don't feel you should be truly happy with me. At least you shouldn't admit it, not to me."

I tried to look at him, but my neck muscles still wouldn't obey, so I stared into my bowl. "I know you didn't mean to bite me. Not like that—without my permission." He'd thought Jeremy was going to separate us and he'd panicked.

"I put you through hell and then I only made it worse, all the mistakes I made trying to get you back."

"I've forgiven you."

"Forgive, yes. Understand, yes. Forget, no."

My stomach clenched. "I want to forget. I want to get past it. *Completely* past it."

"You can't. You won't. Maybe you shouldn't. But we're making little steps. Saying you love me. Saying you want to be with me. Saying you trust me. And now saying you miss me. The next big hurdle is saying you like your life the way it is."

"I *love* my life." I met his gaze.

"And you're afraid that'll change if you become Alpha. More specifically, you're afraid *we'll* change." He shifted closer. "I spent ten years dreaming of getting us here—

together, happy, kids—certain I'd fucked up too badly to even *hope*. If I honestly thought you becoming Alpha would ruin it, don't you think I'd kick up a fuss? Hell, I'd become Alpha myself if I had to."

I nodded.

"But you're still worried."

I sat up. "I'll get over it. Jeremy said he won't start the handover until the kids are in first grade, and even then we'll take it gradually. It's not like he's going anywhere. He's just...tired, I guess. Ready to train his successor."

"Are you ready to be that successor?"

I took a minute to think about it. "I'm...not sure. Right now, I'm most uncomfortable with being *your* Alpha. No matter how bad things got between us, that's one thing that always meant a lot to me—that you saw us as partners, as equals, that I never had to fight for that."

"Who takes the lead in the field now? You do. Have for years."

"That's not the same thing. Jeremy puts me in charge, but you feel free to give your advice or jump in if I screw up. Like with Reese. You knew he'd only accept help if he felt it came with strings attached—I missed that completely."

"Is there any reason I can't keep doing that if you're Alpha?"

I looked at him. "Will you?"

He laughed. "You think you can stop me from giving my opinion?" He twisted to face me. "Tell you what. It'll be a few years before you're officially Alpha, but why don't we start the handover now, between us. When we're on assignment like this, you're Alpha. You call the shots. You give the orders. I obey."

I smiled.

"I said *in the field*," Clay growled. "On *assignment*."

I eased back, pulling my feet up. "Oh, I don't know. Half measures could just get confusing. The only way this is going to work is total role immersion. As second-in-command, your job is to take care of me. Make me happy. Fulfill my every whim."

"You're ascending to Alphahood, not godhood."

"Close enough."

He grabbed my ankles as I tried to back up farther. "The only way this is going to work, *darling*, is through total role *balance*. In public, you call the shots. In private, I'm in charge."

"Pfft."

He leaned over. "You do want to make this work, don't you?"

"Not that badly."

I rocked back fast, wrenching my feet free and swinging out of bed. When he leapt up, I held out my hands, warding him off.

"And how long do you think that would work for you?" I asked. "Total control? A submissive wife means you don't get to *win* control anymore. No more chases. No more fights. Not much fun in dominance games if you're the winner by default."

"True . . ."

"You'd miss that, wouldn't you?"

He stepped toward me, eyes glittering.

"Uh-uh," I said, backing up. "It's a very small hotel room."

"But now that you've mentioned it, maybe I *am* feeling a little threatened by this whole Alpha business."

I stepped back, smacking into the dresser. "No..."

"I'm feeling the need to...I don't know. Reassert myself."

"Don't you—"

I dove out of his way, but didn't quite make it. He grabbed the front of my shirt. I yanked free, toppling a floor lamp. Clay grabbed it before it fell.

"Now, now, darling, you know how much Jeremy hates damage bills."

"Then you're going to have to stop chasing me."

"Then you're going to have to stop running, and start following orders."

I laughed my answer to that. He leapt at me. I jumped onto the bed, scampering across it. I stopped before hopping off. He'd stayed on the other side of the bed, still on the floor, slowly making his way to the end of the bed, ready to dart around and cut me off. I backed up. He backed up. I started forward. He started forward.

"This isn't going to work," I said. "The room's too small."

"Then stop running."

"Pfft."

"I'm getting older, you know. Keep running and I might decide I'm just not all that interested."

I glanced down at his crotch. "You sure look interested."

"But you're not?"

I bounced on the bed. "I can take it or leave it."

Now it was his turn to laugh. Then he started peeling off his shirt.

I stopped bouncing. "Hey, that's cheating."

"If you aren't interested, it shouldn't bother you."

He tugged the shirt off over his head, taking a little extra effort with the motion, making sure all those perfectly defined muscles got into the action. He tossed the shirt onto the bed and grinned.

"Your indicators might not be as obvious as mine, darling, but that sure as hell looks like interested to me."

"It's been a long two weeks."

He stepped back, eyeing the bed, considering a leap. "I'm sure you found ways to relieve the pressure."

"Actually, no. I waited."

"You...?"

"Waited. Isn't that what you always say? Get spoiled, and you only want the real thing? Better to build up an appetite? Well..." I met his gaze. "I guess I'm spoiled now, too."

He leapt onto the bed, coming at me so fast that I tripped trying to get off the other side. As I fell, he grabbed for my leg. I managed to jump up, standing on the bed again, sidestepping his grasp, then leaping over to the tiny desk. It groaned under my weight.

"If you break that, Jeremy won't be happy."

"I won't need to, if you stop chasing me."

He slid slowly off the bed, measuring the distance between us. "Always my fault, isn't it?"

"Always."

He lunged. I saw it coming and vaulted over his head for the bed again. As I jumped, my foot sent the desk lamp crashing into the wall.

"My fault, I suppose," Clay said.

"Naturally."

He started circling the bottom of the bed, then twisted, lunging and knocking my legs out, tackling me to the bed. This time, I couldn't get away. I tried . . . well, kind of. Within seconds, though, he had me pinned beneath him, face looming over mine.

"So what's this about waiting for me?" he said.

"Just like I said. I'm spoiled. I only want the good stuff."

That made him grin.

"It was a long two weeks," I said again. "Why did you think I missed you so much?"

He growled, pulling my hands over my head and holding them in one of his. I struggled . . . well, kind of.

"I could make you miss it a lot more . . . even being in the same room as me," he said.

"Think so?"

"Know so."

Maneuvering carefully, he managed to get my shirt and bra pushed up, then switched hands to get them off without releasing my wrists. He grabbed the pillow with his free hand, took the case between his teeth and ripped a strip off the end.

"Hey, *damage* bills," I said. "How are you going to explain that one to Jeremy?"

"Weak fabric."

He tied it around my wrists, binding them to the head-board. I gave a few experimental tugs.

He mock-frowned. "Hmm, maybe not so weak after all. My mistake."

He pulled off my pants, followed by my underwear. I arched, feeling the whisper of warm air from the heating vents tickle across my skin. Clay unbuttoned his jeans. I watched. He slid them over his hips. I watched. He kicked them across the room, then peeled off his boxers. I watched. I enjoyed. Then he slid his hand down his stomach, ending at the inevitable barrier. He wrapped his fingers around it and stroked. I watched. I enjoyed. I continued to enjoy until about a minute passed when I began to feel a little left out.

I cleared my throat. He stopped.

"Yes," he said.

"Ahem."

He arched his brows.

"Me..." I said.

"What about you?"

I kicked him for that, bucking under him, knee flying up and smacking against his back with an *oomph*. He grinned. I glared.

"You want something, darling?"

"Yes. Do you need instructions? Or directions?"

He stroked himself again, fingers tight, eyes narrowing in pleasure. "Nope, I think I'm doing just fine."

I kneed his back again. "I believe your mandate was to make me want you, and as hot as that is... it's not going to do the job all by itself."

"No, I believe the mandate was to make you *miss* sex,

not want it. Missing it would imply—" He leaned down. "—that you aren't going to get it."

I struggled against the tie. It was only a strip of fabric, laughably thin, but I couldn't get the leverage to yank hard enough. I tried, though, twisting and bucking under him.

"All right," Clay said with a sigh. "I suppose I could give you a little of this . . ."

His mouth moved to my nipple, biting and licking until I stopped fighting and arched up, eyes closed, hips straining for his. He moved on to the other, flicked his tongue across it, making me gasp and writhe.

"Or maybe a little of this . . ."

His tongue traced a path down my chest and over my stomach. I lifted my hips. He chuckled, and slowed down, tickling and teasing as I wiggled, trying to redirect him. Finally he made it, teeth grazing exactly the right place, nibbling and sucking, making me decide I could forgive him for toying with me, if only he'd keep toying with me *this way* just a little longer, driving me to that point where all it would take was—

He stopped. I growled. He chuckled.

"Sorry, darling, just thought maybe you were ready for a little of this . . ."

He slid into me. I moaned my appreciation. Foreplay is wonderful, but this was what it was all about, him inside me, slowly pushing deeper, building up to that moment when we couldn't hold back, that frantic, hard, desperate thrusting—

He pulled out.

"And I think that's enough of that, don't you?"

I snarled. I growled. I called him really, really nasty names.

"Now, now, darling," he said. "You just relax while I finish up here." He started stroking himself again. "If you want to watch, feel free. It won't take long."

I called him more names. I yanked and pulled and struggled so hard the headboard groaned.

"Hey, damage bills," he said. "You really don't want to explain that one to Jeremy."

"Then finish what you started and we won't have to."

His brows arched. "Is that an order? You know, I think this Alpha business is going to your head. Yet another reason why, if we're going to make this relationship work, we need balance. Outside the bedroom, you're in charge. But in it?" He leaned over me, teeth flashing as he grinned. "It's all about me."

I snapped the baluster from the headboard and leapt up, knocking him over backward and pouncing on him.

"Or maybe not . . ." he said.

I slid myself onto him. Just an inch. Then another inch. He grinned, eyes rolling up, a sigh hissing through his teeth. Another inch. I clenched him tight, and his hands slid up under my armpits, thumbs flicking my nipples. Another half inch. He groaned, eyes closing now, all but a slit, never completely closing, always watching me. Another half inch . . .

I jumped up, dancing backward on the bed.

He snarled and tried grabbing my legs. I backpedaled . . . right over the edge of the bed, grabbing the floor lamp as I went down. It toppled onto me. Clay sprang, pushing my knees apart, plunging into me. He knocked the lamp aside. I dimly heard it crash into something else. I didn't really care. I just arched up to meet his thrusts, bruisingly, wonderfully hard thrusts, his arms around me, mouth coming to mine, kissing me just as hard, growling deep in his throat, the growls getting ragged as my own breathing did, taking us closer and closer until... Bliss.

We lay there a moment, entwined around each other, panting. Then I lifted my head to look at the room. Two broken lamps. One ripped pillowcase. One damaged headboard. Not bad... Oh, shit. Was that a picture frame? *Two* picture frames. How the hell did we...?

I sighed.

"We'll snag the bill before Jeremy sees it," Clay said.

I sighed louder.

"Bigger room, darling. Like I said, we need a bigger room."

SNUBBED

WE WOKE BEFORE seven, which seemed plenty early given our long day and late night, but there were already two messages from Jeremy. I tried calling him back before checking the messages—usually one from Jeremy is a simple "call me when you get a chance." But no one answered at the house.

I added the four-hour time difference and figured he'd taken the kids for their usual play-at-the-park-then-go-out-for-lunch routine. By nature, we prefer to stick with our own kind, so we need to schedule socialization time for the kids.

Logan isn't keen on the socializing part, but he loves getting out and exploring the world. Kate, like her father, doesn't see the point. Once she's *at* the park, she's fine. She enjoys watching and following the older kids. I call it social interaction. Clay calls it stalking. Either way, she has fun, and when she starts getting bored, the promise of lunch perks her up again.

I retrieved the first message.

"Elena, it's Jeremy. No, I don't recall mentioning the Wendigo article to Dennis. More likely, Clay's—"

"Is that Mommy?" Kate's voice piped up in the background.

"Yes, but she's sleeping and I'm leaving a message—"

"Mommy! Mommy! Mommy!"

"Would you like to leave her a message for when she wakes up?"

"No. Want her home. Mommy?" Her voice rose, taking on that imperative tone I knew too well. "Come home."

"Kate, she's—"

"Now. Come home now. Tell Daddy. Come home. Mommy *and* Daddy. Come home *right now*."

"I'll call back."

The message ended. Parental guilt for breakfast. Yummy.

Message two.

"It's me again. I apologize for that. I thought she was downstairs. As I was saying, it's likely Clay was right—that Dennis was investigating whatever you two saw in the woods. As intriguing as that is, though, I'm more concerned with these apparent new immigrants. I decided to call—"

"Is that Mom?" Logan's voice sounded in the distance, then stockinged feet padded across the floor.

"Yes, I'm just leaving her a message. If you can wait a minute, you can say something."

"I want to talk to Mom. Not her voice mail."

There are times when it's nice having a preschooler who can communicate so well. This was not one of them. It's like when they were infants and we couldn't wait for them to walk . . . then we were running ourselves ragged chasing after them, wondering, *What the hell was I thinking?*

"You will talk to her," Jeremy said calmly. "Later, after she wakes up. Now can you sit on the bed and wait, please? We'll be leaving soon." He returned to the message. "I decided to call Roman."

Roman Novikov was the Alpha of the Russian Pack. He'd made contact with Jeremy last year, through the interracial council, wanting to ask about a new mutt they presumed was American.

This may seem perfectly natural. It's the twenty-first century, we have computers, telephones, a million ways to keep in touch long distance, so why wouldn't Alphas share information and resources? But it just doesn't happen, no more than wild wolf packs interact. We each have our own territory and most are content to pretend the others don't exist. Roman is one of the more progressive Alphas. We weren't the first Pack he'd reached out to, trying to open the lines of communication, but Jeremy was the first Alpha who'd welcomed the contact, and they'd talked a few times since.

"Roman thought—"

"When is Mom coming home?" Logan asked. His voice was far enough away to tell me he'd obeyed the command to sit on the bed. As for waiting quietly, well, the quiet part had been implied, as Clay would say. Since it hadn't been explicitly stated, it wasn't an actual order.

"In a couple of days."

"You said a couple of days two days ago. A couple is two. So she should be coming home now. Is she coming home?"

"Not yet. Now—"

"*When* is she coming home? Is Dad still with her? Why do they both need to be away?"

"I know you miss them, but they're very busy. They want to come home and they will as soon as they can."

"Kate!" Logan called.

The distant thump of answering footsteps.

"Jeremy's on the phone with Mom again, Kate."

"Mommy! Mommy! Mommy!"

I sighed. Why kick up a fuss and risk getting into trouble when you can get your sister to do it for you? Sneaky little beggar. We were going to have to have a chat about this. A firmly and carefully worded chat, so he couldn't find a loophole.

Besieged by Kate, Jeremy tried calling Jaime, but she was apparently out of earshot, so he quickly finished leaving his message. With Kate screeching in the background all I caught was something about a call, presumably that he'd phone later.

I tried calling him back. Still no answer. I had Jaime's cell phone number, but that wouldn't solve the problem, as the kids were with them. I left a message at home saying I would try again later.

"I miss them, too. But we'll get back as soon as we can."

I looked over to see Clay propped up on his elbow in bed, watching me. I nodded and said nothing, just put the phone down. He reached over and fingered a couple of bruises on my hip.

"You okay?" he said.

"That?" I managed a smile. "That's nothing. I'm sure I did worse to you."

"So you're okay? Not too battered and bruised?"

"I'm fine."

"Good." He scooped me up. "The water pressure in this place sucks. We're sharing a shower, and you're going to forget that phone call."

"Is that an order?"

"Nope, that's a challenge. For me. And one I will happily meet."

WE HAD BREAKFAST a few blocks down at the Snow City Café. A white chocolate and vanilla latte, pumpkin pancakes and side orders of smoked salmon and farmers sausage. Heaven.

On the way to the café and on the way back, Clay tried to bring up the subject of what else was bothering me. Again, I almost answered. Again, I chickened out. A letter from a former foster parent had nothing to do with our current situation, and even admitting that it was bothering me gave it too much power. We could talk about it later.

AT EIGHT-FORTY we were outside Joey's office waiting for him to arrive. We stood across the road, under the shadow of a crab shack awning. As Clay scanned the streets, his face was immobile, but I knew what he was feeling—dreading the horrible news he had to break to Joey, yet looking forward to seeing his old friend.

"He's coming," I said when I caught a werewolf scent on the breeze.

Clay pivoted, searching. "That's him. With the bald guy and the older lady."

If we hadn't been looking for Joey Stillwell, I would have never noticed him. He blended with everyone else on the street, one of those cookie-cutter businessmen who filled every American business core at this hour.

He was average height. Slender, though softening at the edges as he settled into middle age. I knew Joey was only a few years older than Clay, but he really *could* pass for fifty. He was bespectacled and serious, with frown lines that said serious was his usual expression. His brown hair was shot through with even more gray than Jeremy's, making me wonder if he dyed it trying to look his true age.

"Go on," I said to Clay.

"Come with me. We should—"

"Go. I'm in charge now, remember?"

He smiled and loped off. We'd decided earlier that Clay should approach Joey alone. It seemed right—he came from a part of Clay's life before me. Even if Dennis had told Joey about me, I didn't need to complicate the reunion.

"Joey!" Clay called as he jogged across the road.

Joey should have heard him, but he kept walking as if not recognizing the old diminutive.

"Joseph!"

Now even his companions heard, both turning, the older woman catching Joey's elbow as he kept walking. Her lips moved, telling him he was being hailed.

Joey glanced over his shoulder. He saw Clay. No sign of

recognition crossed his face. I'd met Clay a few years after Joey left the Pack, so I knew Clay hadn't changed much. Hell, other than aging, he hadn't changed at all, from his hairstyle—close-cropped gold curls—to his fashion sense— jeans, T-shirt and leather jacket.

Joey kept walking. I tensed. But Clay only broke into a jog again, not slowing until he was close enough for Joey to smell him. He laid a hand on his shoulder, in a quick squeeze.

"Joey," Clay said. "It's Clay. Clayton Danvers."

Still Joey's expression didn't change. In a voice so soft I could barely hear it from across the road, he said, "I'm afraid you have the wrong person."

Clay grinned. "Sorry. It's Joseph now, isn't it? A bit old for Joey. You never much liked it as a kid either."

"You've mistaken me for someone else."

Before Clay could respond, Joey gave a curtly polite nod and strode back to his coworkers.

"He seemed to know you," the man said as they approached the office doors.

"Does that accent sound like anyone I'd have grown up with?"

The woman laughed. "It's damned sexy, though." She glanced back, admiring Clay's rear view as he walked away. "You couldn't pretend to know him for my sake? Invite him to coffee? Make an old lady's day?"

The other man laughed and they headed inside.

ANOTHER DAY, ANOTHER cappuccino. And another unique and wonderful place to enjoy it. If we had more caffeine-fill-up locations like this back home, I'd become a total coffee-house nut.

This café doubled as a Russian Orthodox museum and was across the road from the museum where Reese had been attacked. We were the sole patrons that morning, the silence broken only by the occasional murmur of conversation between the clerk and a Russian Orthodox priest.

I had hoped the quiet surroundings and the religious artifacts would draw Clay out. But we were almost done with our coffees and he had yet to say a full sentence.

"Waylaying him like that might not have been wise," I said finally. "I wanted to tell him about his father—and warn him about the mutts—as quickly as possible, but we caught him off guard. He's used to hiding that part of his life, so he did it instinctively in front of his coworkers."

Clay said nothing.

After another minute of silence, he spoke. "I should have made contact years ago."

"He could have done the same."

Clay shook his head. "I was pissed off when he left and I didn't make any secret of it. It was up to me to make the first move."

"Which you just did."

"Too little too late." He sipped his coffee, his gaze disappearing into the cup's depths.

"Well, we still have to talk to him, whether he wants to chat or not. He needs to be warned about the mutts, if he doesn't already know they're here."

"He doesn't. Otherwise, he wouldn't be carrying on, business as usual. We'll talk to Jeremy later. Get his advice."

I was about to say I could handle this—if I was going to be Alpha, I had to make simple decisions like this—but as gung-ho as Clay had been about the transition last night, change didn't come easily for him. By nature, he deferred to Jeremy and right now, it was best to leave him in his comfort zone.

As we drank, I noticed a community bulletin board beside the counter. Prominently displayed was a mini-poster with pictures of three young women.

The clerk had vanished into the back rooms, so I excused myself and went over. If Clay noticed, he gave no sign.

As I suspected, the poster was for the three missing women the reporter had mentioned yesterday. They ranged in age from seventeen to twenty. Two were Native, one Caucasian. All three had gone missing from Anchorage on Saturday nights.

The poster listed the streets where they'd last been seen, but not the exact locations. I'd venture a guess and say they were in bars, despite being underage. The women's group that printed the poster had left that bit of information off because they knew it wouldn't rouse the right degree of sympathy. It shouldn't matter. At that age, what was wrong with visiting a bar on Saturday night? Yet it wouldn't invoke the same reaction as saying they'd gone missing from the library.

I looked at the three photos. All the girls were pretty, but in that average way that most young women are. Cute enough to catch a guy's eye. And they had caught *someone's* eye.

Did they leave the bar with the wrong man? Did someone follow them home? Did their disappearances have any-thing to do with the mutts? That was the million-dollar question.

The dates overlapped with the supposed wolf kills. I'd been ready to dismiss the connection earlier because the city disappearances were too different from the forest kills, but now I wondered.

Different, yes. But two distinct types of victims serving two distinct purposes: one for hunting and one for sex. Both would end up dead. In the forest, though, there was no need to hide the body—blame would fall on the wolves.

Yet if people found the same partially eaten victims within the city limits, concern would leap straight into panic, with every gun-owning citizen ready to shoot the first large canine he saw. Even the cockiest mutt wouldn't dirty his bed that badly.

"You think there's a connection?" Clay said as he came up beside me.

"I'm not ruling it out." I turned to him. "Ready to go?"

"Yeah. Got a lot of stops to make today. Better get moving."

"Let's start with an easy one." I leaned over the counter to get the attention of the clerk, who was counting stock in the next room.

Instead, the priest stepped from his office. "May I help you?"

"Sorry. We were just hoping for tourist information."

"Such as . . ."

"A museum of natural history maybe? Or a children's museum? Someplace we'd find wildlife displays."

"The Federal Building."

"The..."

He laughed. "Yes, not the first place you'd look, is it? As you can see..." He gestured from the café to the museum. "We Alaskans have eclectic tastes in our pairings. The Federal Building has an excellent collection of wildlife displays. It's free to the public and only a few blocks from here."

"Perfect. Thank you."

MUSEUMS AND TRUCK stops weren't the only places to find lattes in Alaska. In fact, I was beginning to wonder whether a city bylaw required all businesses to have an espresso machine.

"Oh, look," I said, pointing as we walked. "Faxes, copies, postal services...and espresso."

Clay jerked his chin toward a window across the road. "Hunting licenses, ulu knives..."

"And espresso. Just what you need when shooting and carving up big game. Do you get the feeling Alaskans like their coffee strong?"

"Long, dark winters, darling. They need something to keep them going."

We found the Federal Building a mere block from our hotel. At the foot of the steps, a young man was setting up a sausage stand, the meat already sizzling on the grill, the smell making my stomach growl. Then I saw the sign.

"Reindeer sausage?" I said.

"Works for me." Clay pulled out his wallet. "You want one?"

"Sure. We just won't tell the kids we ate Rudolph."

BACKTRACK

THE FEDERAL BUILDING did have an excellent display of stuffed beasties. We found wolverine and several subspecies of bear. Getting a scent from a taxidermy version is less than ideal, but we could smell enough to know that none of the creatures there had been the one that attacked me.

As for what *had* attacked me, we both suspected our best source would be the notes we'd taken from Dennis's cabin. So, exercising my new powers as Alpha-in-training, I sent Clay back to the hotel room to get a closer look at Dennis's work while I grabbed supplies—energy bars, fruit, water, brandy, all the little extras a werewolf needs to call a hotel room home.

When Clay hesitated, I reminded him that he'd been the one to suggest the shift in roles. "So that's what I'm doing," I said.

"And that's what I'm doing," he said. "There's one area with Jeremy where I get to argue a call. Personal security. We can both get the stuff, then both go to the hotel."

"A waste of time. As you said, we have a lot to do. I'm

heading that way." I pointed down the road. "I saw a shop a block away. The wind will be at my back. No one can sneak up on me."

He grumbled, but eventually gave in. I headed in the direction I'd indicated . . . and kept going to Joey's office. I'd planned to go inside and ask for him, but as I rounded the corner, I saw him ahead, a tray of coffees in his hand.

I jogged up behind him before he reached the doors.

"That was a shitty thing to do this morning," I said.

He jumped, sloshing coffee and cursing. I waited while he cleaned up with napkins from his pocket. He took his time and didn't so much as glance at me until he was done. He knew I was a woman and a werewolf—my scent would give that away—and I was pretty sure he knew who I was, but when he did look up, he still seemed startled. His nostrils flared as he drank in my scent. Then he rubbed the back of his sleeve over his nose, as if clearing away the smell.

"Normally I'd apologize for making you spill your coffee," I said. "But I shouldn't have been able to sneak up on you like that, not coming upwind."

"What do you want?"

I took the coffee tray, walked to a marble-topped raised flower bed and set it down, then sat beside it. Joey stayed standing.

"I'm Elena."

"I know who you are."

"And you know who Clay is, despite that stunt you pulled this morning."

His mouth tightened. There'd been a time I'd never have talked to a stranger like that. I could blame all those years with Clay, his attitude rubbing off on me, but the truth, as I've come to realize it, is that being with Clay just gives me an excuse. Years ago, I might not have talked to Joey this way, but I'd have wanted to.

I continued. "Maybe he caught you off guard, and we're sorry for that. But you could have come out after your coworkers were gone."

From Joey's expression, he wouldn't have done that even if Clay had suggested it.

"You need to speak to Clay," I said. "If only for a few minutes. He has something to tell you. Something important."

"Then you can tell me."

"Clay really should."

He picked up his coffee tray.

I caught his elbow. "Please. It *is* important."

"Then say it and go. I'm not interested in a reunion."

I moved in front of him. "Whatever Clay did or said twenty-five years ago—"

He looked up sharply, his frown cutting me short. It took a moment before he seemed to understand what I meant.

"That's over," he said.

"I know you didn't part on the best terms."

"The terms were fine. He was annoyed, but we worked it out, and we parted. The key word there is *parted*." He glanced at me. "Didn't Clay get all those birthday cards I sent?"

"No, he never—"

"Because I didn't send any." He adjusted the tray, holding it in both hands now, between us like a shield. "Clay thought I was running away from trouble with the Pack. I wasn't. I was running away *from* the Pack, from all that werewolf crap he's obsessed with—they're all obsessed with. I only stayed as long as I did for my father's sake. I was happy for the chance to leave and now I have no interest in resurrecting past ties. Whatever Clay came all this way to tell me, you can get it over with and go."

"Is that an order?"

He seemed to flinch at my tone, then squared his shoulders. "I know I can't hold territory, but as a favor to an old Pack brother, I'd like Clay to respect my wishes and leave Alaska."

"How about you tell him that?"

A definite flinch that time. He turned to go.

"And what about the other werewolves in Anchorage?" I called after him. "Are they supposed to respect your wishes, too? I don't think they're going to leave that easily."

A slow pivot. "What other werewolves?"

"Three mutts. We found their tracks near the latest wolf kill. They also attacked a young werewolf yesterday, about two blocks from here. So in the past twenty-four hours, you've had six werewolves trespass on your territory, and you never even noticed?"

"I must have missed them on my daily border patrols." He shifted the coffee tray to one hand. "You don't get it, do you? No, I didn't notice them, because I don't care. I don't want to live my life like that—constantly on alert, constantly watching, working out so I can meet the next challenger, knowing there's always going to be one right around the corner. That's exactly what I came to Alaska to escape."

"Which would be just fine, if you could convince other werewolves to respect your wishes. Live and let live is not the werewolf motto, no matter how hard you and I might wish otherwise."

He looked at me then. Really looked at me for the first time since I'd approached him.

"This isn't my world either," I said. "I was born human. Raised human. I like being a werewolf—I won't lie about that—but there are parts of it that I really *don't* like. I've spent two days chasing a twenty-year-old kid about to be framed and killed by a couple of mutts for man-eating. I follow him to Anchorage and what happens? Completely different mutts find him first and cut off two of his fingers. He didn't challenge them. He even said he wasn't sticking around. But they wanted him gone *now*. That's the world we live in. These mutts are going to find you and when they do, you won't be able to ask them nicely to leave you alone. They already kil—" I stopped short. "Clay needs to talk to you."

The shields fell again. "No."

"It's about your father."

Joey scowled. "Oh, hell. Let me guess. Dad whined to Jeremy about me, and sent Clay to have a little talk. My old buddy to set me straight."

"No, your father didn't say a word to Jeremy. But I did talk to your dad's landlord yesterday. I take it you two had a falling-out?"

"No, we just . . . We drifted apart."

From what the landlord said, it sounded like Joey had

done the drifting. Further separating himself from everything werewolf in his life, including his father.

"Look, about the mutts?" Joey continued. "Tell Clay I appreciate the warning. If you're having trouble tracking down my dad, I'll do it and I'll pass on the message. But Clay doesn't need to worry about me. I'm not a werewolf anymore—not like you two are, not like my father is. I'm a regular guy struggling with a disability that makes me disappear into the shed twice a month and change into a wolf. I don't run in Anchorage. I don't run in the forest. I don't even hike outside the city. These guys aren't likely to cross my path and if they do, I'll go the other way. Now if you'll excuse me..."

He started walking away.

"Joey."

He stopped, shoulders tightening. "It's Joseph."

"I'm sorry." I walked up behind him. "Joseph. About your father. I really wanted Clay to tell you, but we went to his cabin last night. We found him." I paused. "He's dead."

His head slumped forward. I stayed where I was, behind him, respectfully out of sight.

"Was it them?" he asked, turning toward me. "Those werewolves?"

I nodded.

His gaze moved to mine. "And you wonder why I don't want anything to do with this life? Because this is where it gets you. No matter how nice you are. No matter how hard you work to avoid trouble. This is your end. Murdered by mutts. Buried in the woods." He paused, glancing away. "I take it that's what you did. Pack protocol and all." The words carried a bitter twist.

"Yes. We had to."

"Exactly my point. A short, brutal life ending in an unmarked grave."

I waited a moment, then said carefully, "Your father seemed to be researching something."

"Oh, my father and his damned research. There was a time when we were on the same page, wanted the same thing—to be left alone. Then I decided that wasn't enough. But just when I'm backing out of the life, he's diving into it. Gets that cabin. Decides to rediscover his inner wolf. A damned midlife crisis."

"Do you know what he was—?"

"I know nothing about my father's life in the last couple of years. I didn't care to. Now, please tell Clay I'm sorry, but I don't wish to see him, and I would appreciate it if you'd both leave Alaska as soon as possible."

He started walking away quickly.

"Joseph, please. We just want—"

He disappeared into the building.

I waited, hoping he'd come back out. When he didn't, I made it to the corner before a familiar sensation washed over me. I didn't turn, just waited for Clay to fall in step beside me.

"Didn't go as well as you hoped, huh?" he said.

"No."

We crossed the street.

"Thanks," he said. "For trying to get him to see me."

We walked half a block before I asked, "So how's the research going?"

"Do you really think I'd go back to the room and read? While you're walking around with three killer mutts on the loose?"

"It was, I believe, an order."

"Not exactly. More of a firm suggestion. You need to work on your wording."

I shook my head. "So how much did you hear?"

"Most of it."

"I guess your friend has changed."

"Some. But of all of us, Joey was always the least into the wolf stuff. It doesn't surprise me that he's gone this way. I don't understand it, but it doesn't surprise me."

We walked another block in silence.

"I'm sorry I couldn't get him to talk to you. I really—"

"—tried, I know. You went back because you knew I was looking forward to seeing him again. I appreciate that. I really do."

"I wanted the news to come from you, but I couldn't walk away and not warn him, about the mutts and about his father."

"And that's all we can do. Warn him. Then leave him alone."

AS WE WALKED back to the hotel, I made two calls, the first to Lynn Nygard, the "paranormal enthusiast." She still wasn't home. I'd try again this evening. Thinking about that interview made me realize there might be an easy way to get it. So I placed the second call.

"Hope Adams," a young woman's voice answered. *"True News."*

"Hey, Hope. It's Elena. How are you doing?"

Clay rolled his eyes as I launched into small talk. He would have gotten straight to the point. I asked Hope what she was working on and told her what we were doing, and while part of that was civility, most was genuine interest.

I've never been what you'd call a social butterfly, but there had been a period in my life, after Clay bit me, when I didn't have any female friends. Even during the stretches when I wasn't living at Stonehaven, I couldn't seem to get past the acquaintance stage with other women. I felt too different. When the werewolves rejoined the supernatural world, I started to fill that void, first with Paige, then with Jaime and Hope. And while I'd never be one to chat on the phone for hours or set up shopping weekends in New York, it was nice having other women to talk to.

I liked Hope. In her I saw determination and a need for self-reliance undermined by shaky self-confidence, and I could relate to that. I'd been the same way at her age and some days I don't think I've come far since.

I'd met Hope through Karl Marsten. Their friendship moved to romance a couple of years ago. I'm still not sure how I feel about that. I worry that Hope will get hurt, but Karl seems committed enough . . . as committed as a werewolf jewel thief mutt-turned-reluctant-Pack-member can get.

"Anyway," I said. "I called to warn you that I'm now your assistant."

"Cool. I've been telling my editor for years I need one. When can I start forwarding all my alien abduction mail to you?"

"Whenever you want Logan and Kate to start answering it."

She laughed. "Actually, that's an idea. Reply in crayon scrawl and they'll spend weeks deciphering the coded message from E.T....weeks during which they won't pester *True News*'s beleaguered Weird Tales girl. So what's this assistant business about? You need a cover?"

"Exactly." I explained about Lynn Nygard. "I thought I'd buy myself some street cred by saying I work with you. I'll say I'm on vacation, not officially following a story."

"But intrigued by her theory, you're checking it out, with the unspoken hint that maybe, just maybe, she'll make it into our hallowed pages. Sure, go for it. Not like anyone here will deny it. When your job is investigating the paranormal, no one questions a phantom assistant, as long as they don't need to pay her salary."

"Speaking of paranormal..." I told her about our encounter with the mystery beast. "And no, I don't really think it was Bigfoot or a yeti or the Abominable Snowman, but if you have a spare moment to check your files, see if there are any reports on strange encounters in Alaska, I'd appreciate it."

"Consider it done."

I'D BARELY HUNG up when I got a call from a number I didn't recognize, one that looked like it came from overseas. A wrong number, I was sure, but I answered anyway.

"Elena Michaels?" an accented voice asked.

"Yes?"

"It is Roman Novikov. Jeremy said that I would be calling?"

Shit. That was the part of the message I'd missed—not that Jeremy would call back, but that Roman would. I gestured for Clay to stop walking and ducked into the mouth of an alley, getting away from the traffic noise.

"Yes, he did," I said. "Thank you. We appreciate this."

"It is not a problem." He chuckled. "Though it is different, speaking to a werewolf and hearing a woman's voice. A nice difference, though. You are well?"

"I am, and yourself?"

A brief exchange of pleasantries followed. My heart thumped throughout it. I'd never had any contact with Roman before, and now, talking to an Alpha, knowing I'd soon be Alpha myself, wondering whether that would put a sudden end to any international relations...Let's just say I knew I had to make a good impression.

He asked how Clay was and how the kids were, then about the weather in Alaska.

"That is weather for the beach!" he exclaimed. "I thought your Alaska was supposed to be like our Siberia. It is colder everywhere in Russia this time of the year. But I suppose you do not mind the cold. It is in your blood. Jeremy says your mother is from Russia. An Antonov. What city did she come from?"

I admitted that I didn't know. My mother died when I was five, and I wasn't sure whether she'd come to Canada as an immigrant or her parents had. While there'd never been

grandmas and grandpas and aunts and uncles at my childhood Christmases, I had a vague recollection that such people existed. To research my family tree, though, would mean
confirming the suspicion that I had family who, on the
death of my parents, turned their back on me and let me
spend my life in a succession of increasingly worse foster
homes. I don't care to face that truth, so all I know is that
my mother was of Russian ancestry. I explained that to
Roman.

"And there was no family to take you? That is not right."

"I survived." I thought of my foster families. Thought of
that letter and felt the rage boil, needing only the smallest
reminder to surge to the surface again. I squeezed my eyes
and forced it back.

He continued. "I ask only because, I have been thinking
after Jeremy mentioned it, that it is rare for a bitten werewolf to survive. We have one in my Pack. He was the grandson of a werewolf's daughter, and I have always thought that
is why he survived, because he had the blood. I have two
Antonovs in my Pack. It is an old family of werewolves." He
chuckled. "But it is also a common enough name, so I am
likely mistaken. I only thought it was interesting. I should
like to meet you someday, see if you look like our Antonovs,
if you would like to come. With your mate, of course, and
Jeremy."

"Sure. I'd love to." But would the offer evaporate when
he found out I was to be Alpha? Did Jeremy really know
what he was doing?

"Enough of my old man ramblings. I am calling about

this problem you are having. With the...I do not know what you call them. Stray dogs?"

"Mutts. It means a dog that isn't purebred."

"Ah, that is the same thing we call them. Interesting. But it would seem these 'mutts' of yours really are *ublyudokii* of ours, a group we thought we had gotten rid of. The leaders, though, are yours. Americans. Originally, that is, though it has been many years since they were on their home soil. They are a pair of brothers. The Teslers. Travis and Edward."

Travis—that was the name of the big guy who'd cut off Reese's fingers. "I have a Tesler in my records, but I think the last time he was seen was before I joined the Pack."

"That is not a surprise. It would seem this Tesler brought his young sons to Ukraine many years ago. We heard nothing of them until a few years ago, when the sons decided they wanted a pack of their own, a pack of criminals. Murderers. Rapists. Thieves." He spat something in Russian, and I was sure it wasn't complimentary.

"A gang of troublemakers, then?"

"No, that would have been easier to deal with. They are smart, organized criminals. Their specialty is guns—the buying and selling of them, not the using of them."

"Gun-runners."

"Yes. If they had stayed in Ukraine, perhaps we would have, how do you say it? Looked the other way. But they were not happy with that. They started to move around. First Romania, then Belarus, then Georgia."

"Circling your borders."

"Yes, as I said, they are smart. They did not dare trespass, but they caught our attention. We watched. Then they recruited two of my Pack, new members."

"Culling from the edges. They were getting brazen."

A humorless chuckle. "Brazen, yes. I sent my wolves after them. When they escaped, they only got more brazen, crossing our borders to do business. It was then, as we were tracking their activities, that I discovered the real reason they moved so often. When you hire rapists, you hire men with a habit they will not easily overcome."

I thought of the missing Alaskan girls. "They were raping locals."

"At least one was. Raping and killing. While I would like to take the credit for scaring them out of Russian lands, my wolves were only an added incentive, as you would say. The police got too close. That is why they fled and, it would appear, became your problem."

"Well, they're on our radar now, and it seems they're tired of running. They're taking a stand, killing off the local werewolves. With any luck, that means they'll stay still long enough for us to eliminate them."

"If you need help with that, I could send some of my wolves."

"I appreciate the offer, but for now, let us get a better look at what we're up against. Do you have any idea how many there were? We're only finding traces of three, but from what you say, there are more than that."

"My sources tell me they did not all leave with the Teslers. A falling-out, perhaps? Five or six went, including the brothers. Others stayed behind. Another four or five.

Of course that does not mean they intend to stay behind forever."

"Let the Teslers and a few others come over, scope out new territory and clear it before the others make the trip. In that case, it seems we've found them at just the right time. Our Pack can handle five or six. If we need help, though . . ."

"We are only a phone call away."

CLAY STOPPED IN the lobby to grab a snack from the coffee stand while I went up to our room. I stepped off to the sounds of a couple fighting so loudly that I backed into the elevator to give them privacy before I realized the foyer was empty. So was the hall. The voices came from a room at the end of the corridor. Even without werewolf hearing, I'd have caught every word. Small rooms *and* lousy sound-proofing. Great. I wondered how many guests we'd woken during our room-wrecking romp last night.

As I walked down the hall, the fight continued, the man giving the woman shit for flirting. If that was her perfume I smelled soaking the hall, I didn't blame him for being concerned. Or maybe her husband dumped the bottle in the hall. I hoped not—if we could smell it from our hotel room, we were definitely switching. The stench was already giving me a headache.

I opened our door, stepped in and took a deep breath of what I hoped was clean air. It wasn't. And what I smelled made me realize the perfume hadn't been spilled accidentally—someone had been covering an odor that might stop us from opening this door.

I backed up into the open doorway, still sniffing, trying to catch any scent in the air that would suggest a mutt was still in our room. Even when I didn't smell that, I eased in, my back to the wall, moving slow. I kicked open the bathroom door. Empty. The maids had left the shower curtain open, so I could see the tub was bare.

I ran into the main room and leapt onto the bed to check the other side. The room was empty. But it still stunk of werewolf—two of the ones who'd killed Dennis.

It stunk of something else, too. The scent wafted up from under me. I looked down at the sloppily made bed. Then I bent and yanked back the covers. The smell of semen rushed out. I swore and hopped off the bed.

As I leapt, I caught a glimpse of something floating in the water bottle I'd left on the nightstand. I picked it up. Inside were two partial fingers. Reese's.

At the whirr and click of Clay's card in the lock, I raced over. I grabbed the door, pushing my way out and pressing him back into the hall.

"The mutts were here," I said. "We'll find a new hotel."

He caught the door before I could close it.

"You don't want—" I began.

He shouldered his way inside. I strode after him. He stopped in the middle of the room, his back to me. He looked at the bed, and inhaled sharply. The tendons in his neck pulsed. Another sniff. He grabbed an open drawer I hadn't noticed earlier—the one I'd been stuffing my dirty clothes in.

He lifted a pair of blue cotton underwear. I could smell

the semen from here. He threw them down and strode past me to the door. I caught his arm. He shook me off.

"Clay, don't—"

The door banged open, hitting the wall.

"Clay—"

He was gone. I paused to get my own temper under control. Racing into the hall screaming at him wasn't going to help. When I did hurry out, the hall was empty. I could still hear the couple fighting, the woman now protesting that she hadn't been flirting, but simply trying to help the man find his friend's room—he obviously hadn't spoken good English.

Broken English? Looking for a "friend's room"? The mutts hadn't been here long ago, not if this couple was still arguing about it.

I raced into the stairwell after Clay. The door five floors below banged shut. I flew down and caught up with him outside. He stood on the sidewalk, nostrils flaring as he tried to catch the scent.

I walked up behind him.

"Don't," he growled, not turning.

Rage poured off him, his profile rock-hard, the pulse in his neck pounding.

"I'm not going to stop you," I said. "I just want to be sure you know you're walking into a trap."

His shoulders stiffened.

"They broke into our room in the middle of the day," I said. "They left Reese's fingers in my water bottle. They jerked off in our bed and in my dirty underwear. Do you think they're trying to scare you off?"

"No, they're trying to piss me off."

"As much as they possibly can. Invade and soil your territory. Insult your mate. Insult you. Then sit back and wait until you come charging after them, too enraged to see that you're walking into a trap."

He was breathing hard, condensation streaming through the cold air as he fought every instinct that insisted each moment he delayed was hesitation, a sign of weakness.

I reached to touch his back, then stopped myself.

I lowered my voice. "If you go after them now, you'll have no problem finding them. They'll have laid a clear trail leading straight to the perfect ambush spot."

He said nothing.

"We have to pull back," I said.

He shook his head. "I can't ignore this. I need to—"

"—meet the challenge or they'll think you've lost your edge, and they'll come after me."

A curt nod, his gaze still moving along the street.

"They're giving us the best chance we've had to get to them," I said. "Or at least to get a good look at them. Do you think I'd turn that down?"

His shoulders moved, barely more than a twitch, but enough to tell me I'd made my point. I laid my hand against his back for a moment. Then we set out.

BAIT

THE MUTTS HAD indeed left us a clear trail. And I didn't much like where it led. Our hotel window overlooked the northwest corner of the city, and while I'd marveled at the distant view—that thrilling triumvirate of mountain, forest and sea—the closer landscape had been less inspiring.

A couple of blocks past the hotel, the city seemed to end in a wasteland of scarred and scrubby fields crossed with train tracks and dotted with industrial buildings. A flat, open basin ran from the train station to the ocean, and this was where the mutts had gone.

When the sidewalk ended, we entered no-man's-land. The bitter wind lashed us and froze our ears until all we could hear was its howl. A faint icy drizzle rained down. The ground underfoot was slick and muddy on the surface, still frozen underneath.

"They're going to see us coming a mile away," I said.

"That's likely the idea."

"We need a plan."

"Yep, we do."

"And that's my department now, isn't it?"

He glanced over, face softening for the first time since he'd walked into our hotel room. "Yep, it is."

"Damn."

CLAY DIDN'T LIKE my plan. When I invited him to suggest an alternative, though, he just grumbled that I was the boss. In other words, the plan was fine. He just didn't like it.

West of the train station, we put on a performance for our hidden audience. Clay gestured for me to go wait inside the station. I argued that I wanted to stay with him. We bickered. He picked me up, set me down facing the station and gave me a slap on the ass, along with firm commands, including go, sit and stay. Being an obedient mate, I obeyed.

As Clay loped off to take care of those nasty mutts for me, I circled to the front of the station and took a seat on a raised monument displaying—according to the plaque— the first train engine used by Alaska Railroad. There I was, out in the open, where Clay couldn't see me—a perfect lure for the mutts. Clay would follow the trail for a while, then pretend to lose it. With him out of sight, at least one of the watching mutts was sure to break cover and come after me.

Clay hated the part about using me as bait. I had to admit that even I couldn't help thinking, *Gawd, not this old trick again.* But it worked, again and again.

Give mutts the choice between attacking Clay and attacking Clay's mate, and they'll pick me every time. It's not only easier; it's going to hurt him more. Even if they can rise above that cowardly temptation, there's one temptation they can't fight—the siren's allure of my incredible hotness. Okay, the siren's allure of my incredibly hot bitch-in-heat scent.

I'd been sitting there only about five minutes when a man walked around the train station and headed toward me. I inhaled, but the wind was going the wrong way. He fit Reese's description, though—early thirties, big and brawny, short brown hair and a square face.

My first thought was, *Oh, shit, Clay's supposed to grab him* before *he gets to me.* My second thought was, *No problem, I can take him.* My third, as he got closer, was, *Um, probably* . . . And my fourth, when he was near enough to smell, circled back to that initial *Oh, shit.* He was human.

Apparently, my incredible hotness proved alluring to more than just werewolves these days. Or Alaska had a shortage of single women.

"Hey there," he said. "You look cold sitting up there, all alone."

I smiled—civil, nothing more. "I'm waiting for someone."

"Come inside and wait. I'll buy you a coffee."

Espresso, I was sure. "Thanks, but my husband will be here in a minute."

His gaze dropped to my hand, covered in a glove. Then he studied me. Whatever look a married woman is supposed to have, apparently I lacked it, because he stepped closer.

"How about lunch? There's a great diner just up the hill. Nice and warm."

"I'm fine. Really. Where I come from, this is a pleasant spring day."

"And where's that?"

Damn, I'd walked right into that conversation-prolonger.

"Canada. Anyway, I'll just wait— Oh, hold on. My phone's vibrating."

I answered, talking to silence. "Sure, and where's that?" Pause. Laugh. "Okay, then." Pause. "Yep, I'll be right there."

As I hung up, I slid off the wall. "That was my husband. He needs me to check out something he wants to buy." I rolled my eyes. "Men."

"Where is he?" the man asked.

"Over there." I waved at a collection of buildings, and hoped one of them was a store. Then I started out.

"Why don't I give you a lift?"

"I'm fine."

"It's a long walk."

Clay's piercing whistle cut through the howling wind. That was his signal that the mutts had taken the bait and that he needed his backup in place.

"Sorry, I really have to—" I tried stepping around the man, but he blocked me.

"I'll give you a lift."

"Thanks, but I'm fine."

Another sidestep, another block, this one moving into my personal space, making the hair on my neck bristle. I shifted back.

"I'm fine," I said, my tone taking on an edge.

"No need to get snippy. I'm just being friendly."

"And I'm just saying 'Thanks, but no thanks.' "

Clay double-whistled. The BOLO signal—be on the

lookout . . . because these mutts have split up and one could be heading your way.

"I'm sorry," I said.

He smiled. "No need to apologize. We all get a little cranky now and then."

"No, I meant for this." I kicked his kneecap. As he twisted and crumpled, I slammed my foot into the back of his knee and he crashed to the ground, cursing me as I took off.

Clay whistled again. A locator beacon this time. He seemed to be behind the cluster of buildings I'd pointed out a moment ago. There were several routes there. I picked the one across open ground where I could keep an eye out for mutts.

The wind had whipped up again, buffeting me as I ran, making me slide in the mud, barely able to stay upright. The whine of the wind filled my ears. The stink of rotted fish filled my nose. I kept running, eyes slitted against the gale.

At a roar behind me, I spun to see a truck barreling across the open field. My eyes teared up from the wind and I couldn't see the driver—just that the truck was heading straight for me. I ran full out. It kept gaining. At the last second, I leapt aside and the truck skidded past, brakes squealing, veering as it spun into a sharp turn. It came at me again, tires spewing a hail of mud and rock. I dove away and it raced past like a charging bull.

When I glanced back, I could see a man in the driver's seat, but mud now dappled the windows. The truck roared at me again. As I darted out of the way, the window went down. Inside was the man from the train station.

"Did you think that was funny, you crazy bitch?" he shouted.

Crazy? I wasn't the one using my 4x4 as a weapon. I marched toward his side of the truck. He jerked back, this clearly not being the "fleeing in mortal terror" reaction he'd hoped for.

He rolled up the window and hit the gas. The tires spun, spitting mud. The truck rocked, but didn't budge.

I took a running leap. The truck shook as I landed in the bed. The man kept pumping the gas pedal, now jerking the wheel side to side, hoping to dislodge me, but the truck only spun in place.

I walked to the front corner nearest the passenger door. Then I leaned down, grabbed the door handle and wrenched, twisting it all the way around, the insides grinding and snapping. He lunged over to hold the door closed, but I'd already let go.

He slammed the truck into reverse. I stumbled, hands slapping the cab. I kept my balance, though, and when the tires started spinning again, I moved to the driver's side. He slapped down the lock. Again I leaned down. Again I wrenched the handle around, then retreated into the bed.

He tried to open the door.

"Hey . . ." he said, jangling it. Then "Fuck!"

I watched through the back window as he reached across and tried the passenger door, yanking and jiggling the handle until he realized I'd jammed them shut.

"What the fuck?" He twisted to glower at me.

I smiled, finger-waved and was turning to go when something slammed into my back, sending me flying against the cab. As I scrambled up from the truck bed, my nostrils filled with the smell of my attacker—one of the mutts from the hotel.

He stood in the middle of the truck bed. With sandy brown hair to his collar and dark blue eyes, he was a huge rectangle of a man and had the thick neck of one who hasn't been content to spend a mere hour at the gym each day. The slight yellow cast of his skin and the nasty glitter in his eyes suggested he hadn't been content with the extra boost of werewolf strength either. A steroid-pumped monster of a mutt. Travis Tesler, who'd cut off Reese's fingers—I didn't blame Reese for running. First chance I got, I was doing the same.

"Did I spoil your fun?" he asked, lips curving in what I supposed passed for a smile. "I thought Pack wolves didn't hunt humans."

I kept my expression wary, eyes not quite meeting his, shoulders lowered, feigning every sign of submissiveness.

"You got him pretty good." He snickered as he watched the man still vainly pumping on the door handles. "Bet you think you're clever."

I cast an anxious glance at the open land beside me.

"Your man's long gone," Tesler said. "It's just you and me."

He stepped closer. I feigned a flinch and drew back.

He took a deep breath. "Damn, you smell even better in person."

Behind us, the man banged on the rear window. We both ignored him. I inched along the cab toward the edge. Tesler stepped toward me again. I scuttled back.

"Not nearly as tough against your own kind, are you?" he said.

"I-I don't want any trouble."

"Well, see, that's not going to work, because I do."

I shook my head, my gaze fixed on the lower half of his face, so he couldn't see my eyes. "Please. Whatever you want, I'll do it. Just don't—"

He lunged and rammed me back against the cab. Pinning me there, he lowered his nose to my neck and inhaled.

"Fuck, that is something else."

"Pl-please don't—" I stammered, then I slammed my fist into his gut.

He stumbled back, doubled over. An uppercut to the jaw sent him sailing backward. A roundhouse kick toppled him over the side, and he hit the ground flat on his back, his gasp and curse swallowed by the gusting wind.

I jumped onto the edge of the bed, balancing on the back corner, waiting for him to get up so I could kick him back down, then make a run for it. Only he just lay there, looking up at me. Then he smiled.

"Now that's more like it. *Damn,* that's more like it."

He licked blood from his lips. His smile widened and blood gushed, streaming down his cheek. His smile changed, all amusement vanishing, replaced by something ugly that hit me in the pit of the stomach, prodding awake everything that horrible letter had unburied. The terrified little girl inside screamed for me to run, just run. Only I couldn't. I didn't run anymore, not from men like this.

He got up, slow, as if testing his muscles. I tensed and watched his thighs, waiting as they bunched and then—

He leapt up and grabbed for my ankles, but I was already in flight. I swung behind him and got in two lightning-fast hits before he turned and came at me, still moving slow as I danced back.

"You like this?" He licked the blood again. "Get the old adrenaline pumping. Land a few shots. Make a guy bleed." He smiled that ugly smile. "I bet you've made a lot of guys bleed for you."

He swung. I ducked, but he followed with a pile driver to the side of my jaw, holding none of that steroid-pumped superhuman strength back. The earth rushed up to meet me. I lay on the frozen ground, blinking hard, struggling to remain focused, knowing if I didn't . . .

Stay conscious. Stay conscious.

Tesler loomed over me. "If you hit me, honey, I'm going to hit back. I hit a lot harder, don't I?"

Stay conscious. Stay—

"Down for the count? I was hoping for a few more rounds." He grinned. "But I guess this will do."

As he reached for his belt buckle, any urge to drift off evaporated. Then the man in the truck hit the horn.

"Ah, fuck."

Tesler glanced over. The man blasted the horn again. I closed my eyes to slits. When Tesler looked back at me again, he frowned and prodded my leg, checking whether I'd passed out. The man banged on the window, his shouts muffled by the wind. The mutt cursed, gaze swinging between me and the truck. Then his belt whirred as he pulled it through the buckle. I tensed, ready to leap up, hit him with everything I had. Fight, bite, scream, kick . . .

The horn blared.

"Guess you'll keep a moment," he muttered. "Maybe you'll even wake up." A short laugh. "I'd like it a lot better if you woke up."

Belt undone, he strode to the driver's window and rapped. It squeaked as the man lowered it a few inches.

"I'm not going to let you do that." The man waved a cell phone. "I'm calling 911."

If he really intended to, he would have. He didn't want to get involved, but his conscience said he couldn't stand by and watch a woman get raped, so he had to at least make the threat and hope that was enough.

"Did you see what that bitch did to me?" Tesler pointed to his bloodied face. "And what she did to your truck? That's going to cost you. And for what? Because you were having a bit of fun with her?"

"Yes, but—"

"Tell you what . . ."

He leaned in, lowering his voice. I stayed where I was. He might have his back to me, but he was still paying attention, testing me, seeing whether I'd leap up and run when I had the chance. While everything in me screamed for me to do just that, I held myself still and waited.

"I could use some help," Tesler said. "She's a real firecracker. If she wakes up, I'm in trouble. So how about you help me." He chuckled. "There's enough to go around, if you don't mind seconds."

I waited for the man's cry of outrage. He only hesitated, then looked over at me.

"She'll be unconscious?" he said.

Tesler laughed. "Not if I have my way, but sure, I'll knock her out again if that's what you like."

I felt the man's gaze travel over me. My skin heated, red-hot fury burning through the old terror.

You coward. You goddamn, fucking, low-life coward.

I wanted to fly at both of them. Show them what they were dealing with. Show them I wasn't weak, wasn't a victim. Images flickered across my half-closed lids. That letter. That damned letter. The face of the man who sent it. The faces of other foster families, the men and boys I was supposed to call father and brother. Cowards every one. Preying on the helpless. Only I wasn't helpless anymore. I was—

I shoved the rage back, gritted my teeth and stayed where I was. Just another minute. Another few seconds . . .

"Let's get you out of there," Tesler said.

I listened as he yanked on the door and waited for the moment when he got it open, when the flurry of activity would distract—

"Shit. That bitch really did do a number on your doors. Put down the window and let me get it from the inside."

"I already tried."

"Just put down the fucking window before she comes to and runs away."

The window whirred. I tensed, ready to spring . . .

Tesler grabbed the man's shirtfront.

"Wha—?"

Tesler slammed his palm into the man's face, his nose flattening with a sickening crunch, head snapping back, neck breaking. The man went limp. Tesler checked his pulse.

"Did you really think I was going to share with a human?" he said as he threw him to the floor of the cab. "Now that's taken care of, time for the fun part." He turned. "What the—? Where—?"

A growl of rage sounded behind me as I raced across the open field.

LOCOMOTION

TESLER RECOVERED FAST and gave chase, his footfalls so heavy I swore I felt the ground shake. I searched the cluster of buildings ahead, hoping for some sign of Clay, but the landscape was empty and silent.

I whistled.

Silence.

I whistled again, and then it came, the faintest answer off to my right. I turned that way and ran so fast all I could hear was the pounding of my feet and heart. I hated myself for running, but I knew I faced more than bruised ribs and injured pride if I lost this fight.

I caught another whistle, louder and closer now, from behind the building to my right. Clay was coming for me. I glanced over my shoulder. Tesler was nowhere to be seen.

Shit. I sheared off in the direction of Clay's whistle and gave a double one to warn him to be on the lookout.

The building was a small factory of some sort, with machinery whirring inside. There was only one car in the lot. If there were any windows, I couldn't see them.

I slowed to listen for Clay and, yes, to try to sense him, reassure myself that he was close. When I didn't pick up that faint feeling I shook off the unease—relying on a sixth sense was Jeremy's realm; the rest of us had to make do with scent and sight and sound. Only I couldn't smell him either.

I jogged to the rear of the building and looked both ways. The lot remained empty and still.

I whistled. The answer came in seconds. A whistle. Not *Clay's* whistle. Then, on the end of it, *his* whistle farther away, in the direction I'd first heard him.

I swung my back to the wall and listened, but heard only the muffled machines inside. Then I caught the faint scuff of a shoe . . . overhead. I glanced up as a shadow edged over the roof.

Tesler jumped. I tried to twist out of the way, but he caught my shoulder and I spun, feet scrabbling against the gravel. His fingers whispered across my new ski jacket as I lunged out of reach.

I started to run, but kept slipping on gravel, losing my speed advantage fast. There was a small building ahead, some kind of storage for the factory. I ran for that.

Just keep ahead. One step ahead. That was all I needed to do until Clay arrived. He couldn't be far.

I made it to the building and raced around the front corner, then along the wall. Tesler's footfalls were at least a half-dozen paces back. Too far to lunge and grab me. Too close to sneak around the other way. Now I just had to keep him going around the building in circles until Clay showed up.

I zipped around the rear corner . . . and found a fence blocking my path. I skidded and swerved, my boots sliding.

He dove and caught the back of my jacket. I wrenched, but he had a firm grip. I yanked down my zipper, trying to get out of the coat. His foot caught mine and down I went.

I fought—kicking, clawing, writhing—but within seconds he had me pinned. He was a man who knew exactly how to pin a smaller opponent so she couldn't get away, couldn't fight back, couldn't do anything but scream. And I would scream. I didn't care how mortified I'd be later, because all that mattered was getting away before he did what he wanted to do.

I barely got the first note of my scream out before he jammed his forearm down on my throat, cutting me off, a move so deft it was almost instinct. I knew now who'd been responsible for those missing girls around Roman's territory, and who was responsible for the ones here. I knew what Tesler had done many times before and what he was about to do to me.

Even as I struggled, that voice inside told me to stop. *You can't fight. Just lie still and go someplace else. Find the old place, the one where he can't touch you. Just go there and wait until it's over.*

His hand pushed under my shirt, under my bra, fingers digging in, nails scraping. I snarled and twisted and tried to hit, to claw, but he had my shoulders pinned so I couldn't do more than lift my hands a few inches off the ground. I rocked and heaved so hard I thought I was going to dislocate my shoulder, but I didn't care. I bucked and squirmed until he had to shift his weight to keep me still, one arm at my throat, the other hand squeezing my breast. And when he shifted, I got the momentum I needed to wrench my arm free.

I grabbed a fistful of hair and yanked. His hand flew from under my shirt, catching my wrist and wrenching until it was at the breaking point. I kept pulling, but came away with a handful of hair, my grip lost.

He pinned me again. When his hand went back under my shirt, he twisted my breast hard enough to bring tears to my eyes. I rocked and bucked and flailed, but I couldn't get free. I just couldn't, no matter how many fights I'd won, no matter how many years I'd trained, no matter how strong I was and how many times I'd told myself that no one, *no one* would ever touch me like this again. It was happening and there was nothing I could do.

The more I struggled, the harder his forearm jammed down on my neck, until finally I couldn't breathe. I kept fighting. I heard myself gasping. I saw the world tilting and darkening. But all I could feel was his hand at my waist, ripping at my jeans as he clawed and grabbed and grunted.

Then he was flying off me, Clay's face behind him, twisted with rage. Clay spun, holding Tesler by the back of his jacket, his skull on crash course with the wall, and I knew that's where it was headed. Clay was going to kill him. And I didn't care.

No, I *did* care. I was glad of it. I would do it myself if I had the chance. I could say I was doing it for the girls he'd raped and killed, to make sure there wasn't another, and while that was part of it, I was really doing it for me—so he would never get the chance to come back and rape *me*.

It only took a split second for Clay to whip Tesler

around, for me to think I was glad of it, for Tesler's body to spasm in panic as he realized he was about to die. But in that moment, a second mutt flew around the corner.

I leapt to my feet to cut him off, but he was already in flight. He smacked into Clay's shoulder and threw him off balance. Clay didn't drop his prey, but that moment of reprieve was enough for Tesler. His feet found the ground and his fist headed for Clay's jaw. Clay ducked the blow, but in doing so, released him.

The second mutt was a smaller, wiry blond. I recognized his smell. He'd been in our hotel room, Dennis's cabin and the museum. Tesler's buddy, the one who'd introduced himself to Reese as "Dan." He grabbed Clay by the back of the coat, but I yanked him off his feet, breaking his grip on Clay.

And so we paired off. Dan gladly turned on me, leaving his bruiser of a friend to Clay. His first few strikes were halfhearted—if he dispatched me quickly, he'd have to leap into the fray with Clay.

When I dodged his blows and landed two of my own, Dan started fighting in earnest, still slow at first, like a pro with a full card ahead of him, trying to figure out the least amount of energy he can expend. But he soon figured out that a lower weight class doesn't necessarily mean an inferior fighter.

After a few hits Dan ducked a blow, danced to the side...and kept going, taking off across the parking lot. I chased him past two buildings, and then circled back to Clay.

Clay was having only moderately more trouble with his

match-up. Tesler might be an expert at overpowering women, yet his fight skills were little better than the average Saturday night brawler's. If he landed a blow, it sent Clay reeling, but Clay was faster and more agile and easily dodged most of them, and soon figured out the guy's routine.

When a solid right hook sent Tesler spinning, Clay eased back and looked over at me.

"You want to take over, darling? Finish him?"

"Fuck off," Tesler snarled, spitting blood.

He swung. Clay ducked.

I stepped forward. "I've got it."

"Good. Just watch your clothes. He's a bleeder."

Tesler charged with a roar. Clay deftly veered out of his path . . . and I veered into it, catching Tesler's arm, wrenching and flipping him over my shoulder. He landed on his back, winded and blinking.

Again, I watched his leg muscles and sure enough, they bunched, and as soon as I was within reach, he sprang. He tried to grab my leg and yank me to the ground, but I wasn't going down. Even if it meant taking a blow I could have dodged, I wasn't going to give him any chance to get me on the ground again.

It didn't matter that Clay was there to protect me. I needed to know that I could best him.

At first, as long as I stayed on my feet, it was an even match. But I had rage on my side, and the balance started to shift. I landed a few good blows—cracking ribs and knocking out a tooth. Not that it mattered. This was only an exercise—me needing to prove something to myself—because when it was over, he wasn't walking away.

I took a glancing blow off the chin and reeled back, concentrating on keeping my balance. As I shook it off, Clay spun. Dan had returned, sneaking up behind us. Then a shadow passed overhead. I looked up to see another mutt on the roof.

"Clay!"

It was a split-second distraction that my opponent took full advantage of, diving at me and grabbing me around the waist as he tried to take me down. I locked my knees. Pain shot through my legs as they tried to bend in a way they weren't supposed to. I twisted and stumbled, but kept my balance.

The mutt on the roof jumped. He knocked Clay's shoulder as Clay tried to dance out of the way, then both mutts went at him. The new one was smaller than Tesler—only a little bigger than Clay—but the family resemblance was clear. This was the relative I'd faintly smelled at Dennis's cabin, the younger brother. A kick and a right hook from Clay sent him sprawling, leaving Clay with the smaller blond mutt.

Tesler senior rushed me. A high kick caught him in the chest and he stumbled back, then caught himself. I waited for him to rebound, but he stood there, rubbing his jaw. Playing possum again. The guy had a very limited repertoire. I waited for his move. But he didn't run at me…he went the other way.

Only after I'd chased him about a kilometer did I realize my mistake. I glanced back and, sure enough, Clay was in hot pursuit, his prey abandoned. Any other time, he'd have waited for my signal saying I needed help, but he wasn't leaving me alone with this one.

Even on open ground, Tesler kept his advantage, and a stabbing pain in my left thigh slowed me down, no matter how hard I tried to ignore it.

When I heard the squeal of the train leaving the station, it gave me an idea. I waved my plan back to Clay. I didn't really need to. We've been together long enough that if he sees a runaway mutt and an oncoming train, he'll know what I'll have in mind.

I slowed. Clay changed direction, circling wide around Tesler. The mutt, hearing my pounding feet slow to a patter, glanced back and although I was a good ten meters away, I swore he smiled. I looked at him, then behind me, searching the empty horizon, as if looking for Clay.

I whistled. Then I whistled again, louder and more shrill, moving from "Hey, where are you?" to "Oh, shit, where *are* you?"

Tesler bent over, hands on his thighs, catching his breath. The wind had died down and I could hear him panting, almost in time with the chug of the approaching train. Behind him, Clay circled, unseen.

Still bent, Tesler studied me. He really wanted to finish it, but long fights and long runs weren't his forte and he was winded. He had to weigh the thrill of dominance against the smack-down of potential defeat at the hands of a woman, maybe his *last* defeat if Clay caught up. I could say the survival instinct won out, but I suspect it was ego—if he didn't choose to fight, I couldn't beat him. He straightened, then started turning to run.

I rushed at him before he noticed Clay. He wheeled, fists going up. I danced back. He swiped a fresh gush of blood from his lip and smiled. I was spoiling for a fight, but I was afraid—an irresistible combination. He turned his back square on Clay. I took one boxer's two-step forward, then back, going a little farther back than forward, as if inching away while trying to convince myself I was ready to take him on.

Finally Clay reached the point where Tesler smelled him. His nose jerked up and he spun so fast he almost lost his balance. Then he tore off south...just as the train started to pass—a solid wall of slow-moving cars blocking his escape route.

He turned almost full circle and realized he was trapped. I braced myself for him to charge the weakest obstacle—me—and he started to, then he feinted to the side and ran full out toward the train.

"Fuck no," Clay growled under his breath.

"Fuck yes," I said as Tesler grabbed a ladder between cars.

We followed. It always looks so easy in the movies. But even with a slow-moving train and werewolf agility and strength, getting on that ladder was a feat...particularly with a 250-pound mutt at the top of it, determined to keep you from catching his ride.

Clay was almost to the top when Tesler's foot shot out, aiming for his jaw. Clay grabbed him by the ankle and wrenched. Tesler went down, scrabbling and kicking to keep from being pulled over the edge, holding on with every ounce of strength in his overpumped arms. Meanwhile, I was hanging from the bottom rung, trying to keep my back from scraping along the tracks.

Tesler scrambled out of Clay's reach, got to his feet and took off across the tops of the cars. We gave chase.

At any moment, I expected the train to grind to a halt, throwing us through the air as someone spotted us and sounded the alarm. But it kept chugging along, picking up speed as we raced over the cars, bent forward, the metal vibrating under our feet, train rocking from side to side, every freezing-rain-filled dent enough to send us skating, the stink of diesel filling our nostrils, the whine and grind of metal setting our teeth on edge, drowning out every word Clay called back to me. Well, not every word . . . just the ones like "stay there" and "keep back" and "wait."

And of course every car had to end . . . in a fifteen-foot drop over ground whizzing past fast enough to make my stomach lurch. That leap between shaking cars set my stomach plummeting every time, no matter how much clearance I had. My first foot would land and it always slid a little, just enough to rip an "oh shit" from my lips before I found my balance.

Finally Tesler reached a flatcar loaded with timber, took one look and decided that jumping onto those logs was one feat he didn't care to attempt.

He feinted left, then right, then took a running leap toward the side of the car. Clay did the same, and leapt off . . . as Tesler checked himself at the last moment and stayed on board. With me.

He turned to face me, that ugly smile twisting his lips—then disappearing as it met my fist. It took him a second to recover from the shock, not of the hit, but of finding me standing my ground when surely I should be running as fast as I could. I hit him again, knocking him over. Predictably, he tried to grab my legs and bring me down with him. I stomped his hand hard enough to make him howl.

As he scrambled up, I kicked. He instinctively closed his legs, but I wasn't aiming there. When it works, it works, but if that move was as reliable as it looked in the movies, no man would ever get the best of a woman in a fight.

As he concentrated on protecting his valuables, he hunched over, his jaw coming into perfect alignment with my foot. I kicked him, and he fell back hard enough to make the roof twang.

I grabbed his shirtfront and hauled him up. Clay was back on board now four cars away, making his way toward us. He motioned for me to hold the mutt and wait for him. I pretended not to notice and dragged Tesler to the front of the car.

I held him over the edge, getting a good long look at his face, drinking in his fear as he realized he was about to drop head-first under a running train—

Tesler bucked. I braced, steadying myself, but when he rocked again, his bulk was too much and I lost my balance. He grabbed me and, for a second, I was the one looking down at the train tracks rushing below, hearing Clay's bellow, his pounding feet. Then I twisted and kicked, and we rolled onto the roof of the car.

Tesler caught me and tried to toss me over the side, but

I grabbed his wrist and flipped him over my shoulder. He managed to snag my leg at the last second, and dragged me over the edge as he fell. My fingers grazed the steel edge, found a hold and clung on. One solid back kick with my free leg struck Tesler square in the jaw and he let go, hitting the ground and rolling away from the train.

"Hold on," Clay shouted into the wind as he made his way toward me.

"That's what I'm trying to do!" I called back.

And *trying* was the operative word. I was barely clinging by my fingertips, legs knocking against the side of the train as it chugged along. I glanced back at Tesler, now up and running, and flexed my fingers.

"Don't you dare," Clay said, grabbing my wrists before I could drop and go after Tesler.

He was right, of course. Given the angle I was hanging at, letting go would run me a good chance of falling right under the train. That didn't keep me from watching with regret while Tesler disappeared into the distance as Clay hauled me onto the car.

"We have to go after—" I began, heading for the ladder.

Clay caught me and pulled me down into a crouching position to keep my balance. "Take a second."

"I don't need—"

"Yes, you do, and he's already too far away. Whether we leave now or in two minutes, his trail will still be there."

As I looked out over the now empty field, shame licked through me. How long had it been since I had done something so stupid? I always appreciated that Clay never tried to fight my battles, never interfered unless I was in serious danger. So when he'd warned me to stand down, I should have known he had good reason.

When I apologized for the bone-headed move, he said, "Circumstances." Nothing more, but it was all that needed to be said.

It *had* been the circumstances—Tesler plus that damned letter, coming too close together, those old fears resurrected. An explanation, but not an excuse. If I was going to be Alpha, I couldn't have weak spots. I had to overcome my ego and my fear and my rage, and trust my bodyguard.

I stayed on the train only long enough to catch my breath, then we climbed down, backtracked, found and followed Tesler's trail. A real warrior would have lain in wait and ambushed us. Tesler ran straight for a wide stream that, judging by the signs, was a popular fishing spot, and waded through the icy water to hide his trail.

We walked along the banks for about a hundred meters, then decided the smarter move would be to predict his destination—back to his brother and buddy. We took off that way.

QUESTIONS

WHEN CLAY CAME after me, the other two mutts had chased him only as far as the edge of the building, like dogs making a token effort to frighten a trespasser off the property while really hoping he doesn't turn around. Then they'd stayed there, waiting for Tesler. Unfortunately, he didn't return. We snuck up close to them just as he called his brother, apparently telling them to meet up someplace in the city.

"Follow?" Clay said.

I shook my head. "They'll catch on before we get to the rendezvous point, and we can't pull anything downtown in broad daylight. I say grab one and get some answers." I peeked around the building corner and sized the two up. "We've got the leader's little brother and a flunky."

"The brother," Clay said. "Interrogate, then hold him hostage."

"Where?"

Clay shrugged. "I don't care. Hog-tie him and leave him out here. Or kill him and pretend we've still got him, hope big brother takes the bait."

I shook my head. "He's family; he won't talk, and if Tesler decides he doesn't particularly want his baby brother back, we're screwed."

"You're the boss."

"You disagree?"

He leaned out to look at the two men. "I don't think it's a sure bet either way."

"We'll try the flunky, then."

CULLING ONE FROM a herd of two can be tough, presuming the other one wants to object to his Pack mate being taken. This one didn't. As soon as he saw we'd homed in on his companion, he took off to find his brother.

Then Clay held Dan while I found and secured the interrogation room—a storage unit for a business that rented boats and fishing equipment, seasonal rentals that were now out of season.

Clay brought the mutt in. When we put him into a chair, he started to fight in earnest until Clay clocked him, dazing him enough to get the bindings on.

"This scenario seem familiar?" Clay said as he booted the rolling chair into the middle of the room. "Remind you of what you did in a cabin up near here? To an old friend of mine?"

Dan's mouth opened, ready to spew some variation on "It wasn't me—I was just following orders." But before he got the first word out, he snapped his mouth shut and switched to a new tactic—babbling in his mother tongue.

"You can skip the 'I don't speak the language' shit," Clay

said. "It's only gonna piss me off, and it won't help you one bit. You know Roman Novikov, Alpha of the Russian Pack? He's offered to translate, make sure your civil rights aren't violated before I break your kneecaps."

"It's not Russian," I said.

Clay glanced at me.

"He's not speaking Russian. We can get Jeremy or Roman to confirm that, but I'm pretty sure of it."

To a unilingual ear like Clay's or Reese's, I'm sure it sounded like Russian—it did even to a bilingual one like mine. But my mother used to sing to me in Russian and taught me some words in language games, like the ones Jeremy and I play with the twins. So while I couldn't remember more than a half-dozen words, I knew Russian when I heard it—and this wasn't.

I told Clay it could be Polish or Ukrainian. Neither Jeremy nor Karl nor any of our other multilingual sources could help with those.

"That's that, then," I said. "If he can't answer our questions, he's of no use to us."

"Kill him?"

Dan's head jerked up fast enough to tell us his grasp of English was adequate.

"Should have grabbed the brother," Clay said. "Held him as a hostage. Think we can still catch up with him?"

"He's long gone. But we can use this one to send a message."

Clay nodded. "Have to make it a good one, though. Scare the shit out of them. Snapping his neck won't do."

I took out my hotel key card and lifted it, just out of the mutt's view. "How about this?"

"Shit." Clay rubbed his chin. "The last time we used that..."

"Messy, I know. But we need messy. The only problem is the screaming."

The mutt jerked around, moving the chair enough to see what horrific instrument of torture I held. When he did—and realized he'd outed himself—he let loose a stream of Anglo-Saxon profanity.

"Huh," Clay said. "Seems he knows some English after all. Let's see if we can expand his vocabulary."

He slammed his fist into Dan's jaw. The mutt gasped and snarled, then started to swear.

"Nope," Clay said. "Same words. Let's try—"

He grabbed an oar from the wall and swung it against Dan's kneecaps. Wood and bone crackled. Dan bit off a scream, his eyes rolling. Then he lifted those eyes to Clay.

"What do you want to know?" he said in perfectly serviceable English.

WE MIGHT HAVE removed the language barrier, but that didn't mean we were getting anything useful from him. We started with the most important issue: why had they killed Dennis? And the corollary questions: did they know about Joey and if so why were they leaving him alone? We weren't worried about tipping Dan off about Joey—it wasn't as if this mutt would ever see his buddies again to tell them. But Dan insisted he had no idea what we were talking about. Other werewolves in Anchorage? Never met them. His scent found at the site of a murdered former Pack member? Huh, we must be mistaken. Maybe our sense of smell wasn't as good as we thought.

On to Reese, then. Nope, he didn't cut the fingers off any young werewolf in a museum. Hated museums. No, he hadn't witnessed any finger-cutting either. As for why his scent was there, he had no idea. Maybe another werewolf in Anchorage had a similar scent. Maybe *that* was the one we'd smelled in Dennis's cabin, too. All werewolves did kind of smell alike, you know.

What about the invasion of our room and the "deposit" he'd left in our bed? Nope, not him. Tesler admitted they'd been there? Ah, that might explain things, then. Tesler was crazy. He wouldn't put it past the guy to kill the old man for kicks, cut off that kid's fingers and jerk off in my underwear.

But we hadn't mentioned that the dead werewolf was old. Or where we found the second deposit. No, we must have. How else would he know?

Dan wasn't too bright, but he was tenacious. Though he was quick to turn on his leader, there was no way he was admitting to having done anything himself. Still, as if to prove his usefulness, he did volunteer to give us full dossiers on the Teslers if we'd put him into protective custody like Reese. When we didn't say anything in response, he seemed to take that as agreement.

As Roman had suspected, the Tesler brothers—Travis and Eddie—spent most of their lives in Ukraine. That's where their father was from, before he emigrated to the United States and tried to make a life as a farmer. When that failed, he'd gone back home, taking his young sons with him, and years later they'd met this mutt—Danya Podrova.

The story Podrova gave came close enough to Roman's that we knew he was at least attempting to tell the truth. The Teslers ran a small gang that had moved around Eastern Europe, staying off the Russian Pack's territory. Of course, in Podrova's version, the Russians were a bunch of bullies who'd kept them on the run, when all they wanted to do was settle down and ply their trade. And the nature of that trade? Gun-running, he readily admitted; he even offered to help the American Pack set up its own enterprise.

"Very good money," he said. "Lots of places, they need guns. Pay a lot of money."

So the Tesler gang had jumped around Eastern Europe, picking up new members as it went. Then they'd run into a spot of trouble because of Travis Tesler's habit.

"He likes the girls. He likes the ones who do not always like him, if you understand."

Oh, I understood.

Podrova downplayed Tesler's problems with the law. They'd been planning to move anyway, he explained. Eddie had been researching Anchorage, thinking it might be a stable base of operations. A port city in the wild country, far enough from the American Pack that no one would pay them much attention.

Right now, it was just Podrova and the brothers, setting up in Anchorage. Two others were off on business, establishing trade routes in the Lower 48. And, as Roman suspected, more had been left behind, waiting for the brothers to get established here. Part of those efforts, it seemed, was clearing out all other werewolves.

That explained why they'd killed Dennis, but not why he'd been tortured. And what about Joey? Considering how quick these mutts were to pounce on Reese and now on us, it seemed unlikely that they'd been here for over a month and didn't know they still had another werewolf in town.

But here Podrova retreated into silence. He didn't know Dennis. And those men murdered in the woods? He didn't know them either. Wolves got them, he'd heard. As for the girls? Well, yes, Tesler did have a bad habit, but he didn't do that anymore, not after the trouble he caused back home.

So, Dennis had been killed by werewolves, three humans had been slaughtered by wolves and three girls were missing—all since this mini-pack had come into town. But they had nothing to do with any of it.

Clay took me aside.

"I need you to stand guard," he said.

"I know what you have to do, Clay."

"Yeah, but you don't need to see it."

"I think I do, if I'm going to be Alpha. Jeremy plays his part. He takes the lead and asks the questions."

"Maybe, but after all these years, I don't require supervision. I know what you want from him. I'll get it. If I have questions, I'll come out and ask."

"I need to see—"

"But *I* don't need you to see it."

I met his gaze and understood. It wasn't just about me. Alpha or not, I was still Clay's lover, and this wasn't a side of himself he cared to show me. As Beta and Alpha, Clay and I would never be like Clay and Jeremy. We shouldn't try. If we were going to make this work, I had to remember that.

So I stood guard. What Clay was doing took time—and right now it was time I didn't really want to spend by myself, lost in my thoughts, thinking about Travis Tesler and what he'd tried to do to me.

For twenty years I'd been the only female werewolf in a world of men who viewed women not as mothers and sisters and girlfriends and wives, but as receptacles for satisfying two basic drives: sex and reproduction. Some saw me and yearned for what they couldn't have—a partner, a mate, a woman who would understand and accept them and share their lives completely. Others felt a very different yearning—the drive to take revenge on Clay for enforcing Pack law or to step up on the hierarchy ladder by hurting the man one rung from the top.

After all those years, all those encounters, attempted rape should be par for the course. I should have dealt with it again and again, until I finally expunged the demons of my childhood and those old wounds scarred over, tough and impenetrable. But they hadn't.

There had been a few halfhearted attempts—mutts who weren't rapists, by nature, but thought it would be an easy way to hurt Clay. Property trespass more than sexual assault. It hadn't taken much of a fight to dissuade them, and I'd never felt seriously threatened.

For the rest, they'd dreamed of sex not rape, of sweaty hand-to-hand combat, bites turning to bruising kisses, punches to rough gropes and eager caresses. Mutual passionate sex—their egos would never accept anything less.

They wanted to show me that they'd be a better mate than Clay—a better lover, a better partner, certainly a saner one. When seduction failed, most backed off, leaving the delusional few who were convinced it was only a matter of time before I came around.

For twenty years, I'd shattered illusions. Illusions of revenge. Illusions of love. Illusions of sex. But not illusions of rape. These men had never felt inferior to a woman—a mere human—so they'd never felt the need to prove their superiority. Now I'd met a mutt who did and he was still out there, thwarted and waiting for his chance to try again.

I had only to think about it and somewhere inside me, I was twelve years old again, shivering under the covers, praying he wouldn't come tonight and knowing if he did, there was nothing I could do.

BLAME

WHEN THE WAREHOUSE door opened, I jumped. Clay closed it and paused, back to me, collecting himself before turning and fixing a neutral expression on his face. It was a struggle, and he soon gave up, lines deepening around his mouth and between his eyes, face pale and drawn. Blood flecked his shirt and neck. More speckled one cheek. I tried not to think about how it got there.

"Done?" I asked.

"Almost. He's out cold. I'm checking in before I finish."

"Did he give you anything?"

"A bit. Not enough."

Dan had admitted that Tesler killed Dennis in a territorial dispute. He said Dennis had found them and ordered them out of Alaska. He'd challenged Tesler, they'd fought, Dennis died and Tesler had tied his body up in the cabin to make it look like a break-and-enter gone bad.

Which was bullshit. Dennis might have gotten more "in touch with his inner werewolf," but that inner werewolf still would have taken one look at Tesler's hulking outer wolf and run the other way. What we'd seen on Dennis's body were the signs of torture, not a fair fight.

When asked about this, though, Podrova had laughed. Were we not torturing him for information? What, then, did we think Tesler wanted? As for that, Podrova got vague again, but he hazarded a few guesses—bank account details, keys to Dennis's truck... If Tesler was going to waste time killing the guy, he sure as hell was going to make sure he turned a profit. Sadly, given everything we'd seen and heard of Tesler, this made sense. Though it had been hard to gauge the extent of the torture, it had seemed the kind of thing thugs would do, tying up a homeowner and making him give PINs and passwords so they could empty his accounts.

Podrova also admitted they'd had contact with Joey. They left him alone because they had an agreement with him. As for what that agreement was, he had no idea—that was Eddie Tesler's area. Apparently, baby brother was the brains of the operation, which didn't surprise me—Roman said the gang was smart and Travis Tesler didn't strike me as a deep thinker. All Podrova knew was that for now, Joey was untouchable.

Podrova had also admitted that their pack was responsible for the wolf kills. Well, the first, at least. One of the other members had killed him, and that's why he'd been sent away on business—in punishment. Eddie didn't tolerate man-killing. Like the rapes, it wasn't conducive to a settled lifestyle.

As for the other two victims, Podrova knew nothing

about them. Yes, the last one had been found close to where they Changed and ran, at a spot away from their cabin, which Eddie insisted on. But none of them knew why a human would be killed, apparently by large canines, in that same spot.

Clay suspected Podrova himself was responsible for the two unclaimed killings, that he'd acted on his own and covered his ass so he wouldn't be sent away like his comrade. Now he continued covering it, afraid that being outed as a man-eater would seal his fate with us. But of all the issues and questions, this was least important. We knew they were responsible.

There was a limit to how far Clay could push, and how much pain he could inflict while keeping the subject conscious and lucid, so he'd moved to what he knew was another important issue for me: the missing young women. And here is where, driven to his limit, Podrova no longer bothered being cagey. Yes, he was sure Tesler had taken those girls. When their little pack moved to Alaska, Eddie insisted his older brother lose the habit. Law enforcement would be stricter and more advanced here, and if they were settling in for the long term, they had to be more careful.

So while Podrova had no proof of it, he was certain those girls hadn't just coincidentally vanished after they arrived. Just as he was sure there would be more.

"And that's all he said. But what you really want to know is: where the hell is that cabin so you can stop this bastard? He says he doesn't know where it is, and as stupid as that sounds, I believe him. The Teslers do all the driving. This guy just goes along for the ride. He knows it's south of the city. He knows it's about an hour's drive. He knows they pass that service center before they turn off because they like the pizza there, so they stop in on the way back. Then, after they get back on the highway, drive awhile, then turn. And turn. And turn..."

I groaned.

"Yeah, it's like getting to Dennis's place, only it seems even farther in the woods. It's the same deal, too, where you can't get there in the winter except by snowmobile."

"But they bought the cabin, so if we research real estate transactions in the right time period..." I saw his expression and stopped. "They didn't buy it, did they?"

"This guy has no fucking idea, darling. All he knows is they came to Anchorage and they moved into a big cottage that was already furnished. The Teslers might have bought it. Or they might have killed the owners. Or they might just be squatting in some out-of-towner's summer cabin. This mutt does as he's told and he doesn't clutter his brain with details. He's just happy to have an Alpha to tell him what to do." He swiped the blood from his cheek. "I'm not going to get anything more from him on that, but if there's something else..."

There was more I *wanted* to get, but nothing he *could* get. If the mutt was unconscious, he'd passed the breaking point. Even if Clay could rouse him, he'd had a taste of painless oblivion and he'd spout whatever lies Clay seemed to want to hear if it would take him back there.

"That's enough," I said. "I'll help with the rest."

"I've got it."

"You're going to need to bury—"

"It's a dirt floor and tools. I'll make do."

"But I can—"

"Got it."

He went back inside. When he came out later, he carried a bag, presumably holding any belongings that could identify the dead man. We walked to the shore where I helped him clean off the blood. By the time we'd finished, his mood had lifted. He wasn't ready for cracking jokes, but he'd returned to a quiet equilibrium.

I used to think that Clay didn't feel anything when he had to torture mutts. He does; he just doesn't let it linger. It's part of the job and part of the man he's chosen to be—the sadistic psycho that mutts use to scare their sons. With a reputation like that, no one dares cross him to get to the Alpha, which is the point. But the problem with being a legend is that you have to live up to it.

I might wish sometimes that it could be different, that we could rule by reason and justice instead of might and fear. But it won't happen. Not in my lifetime. Like Jeremy, I can rule *with* reason and justice, but no one will listen without that sharp end of the stick.

WE'D BARELY STARTED walking back to the hotel when I finally blurted it out.

"I got a letter last week. From one of my foster parents."

"One of the men?" he asked. He knew I didn't like calling them "foster fathers."

I nodded, then stuffed my hands in my pockets. "We can discuss it later. I know this isn't the time. I just—I should talk about it and I keep avoiding it, so now that you know, you can . . . I don't know. Just forget—"

"There's a damned good reason you mentioned it now."

He looked over, catching my gaze. He was right, of course. What happened to me with Travis Tesler resurrected an issue that hadn't been buried very deeply.

Clay asked who sent the letter. He wasn't asking for a name. He wouldn't recognize it. There'd been a time, back in the beginning, after he bit me and was frantically trying to make amends, that he'd asked for names. He hadn't been surprised when I wouldn't give them.

Years ago, I'd sent letters to the Children's Aid Society and warned them about the families I'd had trouble with. By then, most weren't fostering anymore. But for those that were, I was assured my concerns would be investigated, and in follow-ups, the remaining few had been removed from the list. So no other children were in danger, and that's all that had mattered to me. All that *should* matter.

Clay wouldn't necessarily agree. When we'd been dating, he'd gone after an old foster brother who'd been stalking me. Beat him brutally. I was there. I saw it. And I don't know what horrified me more—watching it or wishing I'd been the one delivering the blows.

That was the beginning of where things had gone wrong for us. In asking for the names of the men who'd abused me, Clay had only been grasping at straws, desperate to find a way to prove his love.

Even later, when I would talk to him about what had

happened, I think he felt that something should be done. By unspoken agreement, then, we never referred to them by name, so now, when he asked which one sent the letter, I said only, "Maple Street."

He swore. Slipped his arm around my waist. Pulled me closer as we walked up the hill to the hotel.

"He's going through therapy," I said.

"Electroshock?"

I couldn't suppress a smile. "Unfortunately, no. But as part of this therapy, he's supposed to contact his victims and ask—" I choked on the word. "Ask for forgiveness."

Clay's reaction to that was predictable. And, again, it made me smile, and wish I'd told him the day the letter arrived. It was like his reaction to Mallory Hirsch's bitchy treatment of me—there was a great deal of pleasure to be found in imagining unleashing him on those who wronged me, even if I knew I'd never actually do it, that the guilt would outweigh the pleasure.

"I hope you told him where to stuff it," he said finally.

"I don't forgive him," I said.

"Hell, no, you don't. And why should you? So he can feel better? Get on with his life? And what's he done to help you get on with yours?"

I didn't answer. I couldn't. I wished I'd kept the letter so I could fly to Ontario, march up to him and . . .

And I don't know what. Not hurt him. Just show him that I didn't need his apology, I guess. Show him that I was okay. Better than okay. I was happy, in spite of everything he'd done to me, and no, I didn't forgive him. God help me, I would not forgive him.

"Sending you that letter was wrong," Clay said. "I don't give a fuck how bad he feels. What kind of therapist rips open the past by making him send a letter like that?"

"I'm sure it helps some victims."

"Well, not all. And it's irresponsible to pull that shit."

I nodded. And, again, I wished I'd told him earlier, because this was exactly what I wanted to hear, vindication that I had a right to be pissed off, vindication that I had a right not to want to reopen those old wounds.

Maybe a therapist would tell me this proved I wasn't healed. How I'd reacted to Tesler also proved I wasn't healed. When I said as much to Clay, though, he shook his head.

"The reason Tesler freaked you out is *because* of that letter. It brought all that shit to the surface, and it was just fucking bad luck that Tesler came along and tapped in to it. But that's over. He's a coward and you know it now. Hopefully, you'll never have to deal with him again—not alone, anyway, but if you do, then just show him who's boss and he'll run like hell. You're a better fighter than him. Don't forget it."

I nodded, but this time, I wasn't so sure I agreed. When Clay seemed ready to pursue it, though, I gestured at the bag he was holding.

"You took the mutt's clothing?" I said. "We'll need to find a place to burn it."

"Nah. It was all generic stuff. I only wanted this." He handed me the bag. Inside was Dan's jacket, washed denim with leather trim and a shearling lining.

"Nice, but it looks a little small for you."

He rolled his eyes.

"Okay," I said. "I give up. What did you want with his jacket?"

"It's not his. It's Dennis's."

"Dennis?"

"I smelled him on it when I was checking Podrova for ID. So I took it. No mutt is being buried in Dennis's coat."

I pulled it from the bag. "This isn't Dennis's. First, I saw his coat in the cabin—a plain, Sears catalogue parka. All his clothing was department store and that—" I pointed to the jacket. "—might have come from a catalogue, but if so, it was from one of those fancy collegiate stores. It's a young man's jacket. Dennis was trying to recapture his wolf, not his youth."

"Well, it smells like Dennis. Like he wore it."

He motioned for me to sniff the inside. I did and Dennis's scent was indeed there, as if he'd pulled it on once or twice, but under the mutt's more recent smell was another, deeper one embedded in the fabric. The real owner. And when I caught a whiff of that, I swore.

A smile creased Clay's eyes. "Admitting you're wrong, darling?"

"Not about that. Something bigger. At Dennis's place, I smelled another werewolf. A family member. I presumed it was Joey, but having now smelled Joey and smelling this, I was wrong. This coat belonged to a werewolf and it belonged to a Stillwell. But not Dennis and not Joey."

It was Clay's turn to curse, taking the jacket, inhaling deeper and cursing again.

"We need to talk to Joey," I said.

• • •

WE'D ALREADY NEEDED to talk to him—about this "deal" with the mutts and his lie about not encountering them. And now this: the existence, or former existence, of a Stillwell that Jeremy knew nothing about.

But this wasn't the sort of conversation we could have in Joey's office. We'd need to waylay him as he left work, and hope he didn't decide to put in too much overtime.

It was only midafternoon, meaning we couldn't talk to Joey for a few hours. That was fine, because right now, neither of us was in the mood for that conversation. We were tired and hungry and sore, and all we wanted was to crash in our hotel room . . . which was a problem.

"Already taken care of," Clay said. "I called Jeremy when we first split up. He'll have something booked for us by now."

First, though, we had to retrieve our stuff. My steps slowed as we entered the lobby, certain I could pick up the faint smell of Travis Tesler, my stomach knotting at the thought of going up there, smelling him, smelling what he'd done.

"Take a seat," Clay said, waving at the armchairs in the middle of the lobby. "Call the kids."

I hesitated.

"Plenty of people around," he said. "It's safe."

"That's not what I meant. I should help—"

"Sit."

When he started walking away, I called him back and leaned in closer to whisper, "My clothes. The ones he . . ."

"In the nearest trash, along with anything he so much as touched."

"Thanks."

"Hey, if you have to walk around naked for a few days, I'm not complaining."

I managed a smile, then picked a seat with my back to the manned counter, facing the doors. I couldn't imagine Tesler sneaking up on me here, but I felt better being careful. Then I called home.

I talked to Kate first. I started by reassuring her that we were coming home as soon as possible, fending off the problems Jeremy had with her earlier. It worked.

She told me about her day, specifically dinner yesterday after Jeremy had left for New York, when Jaime made them pancakes, which were good, but she hadn't done it quite right, because it wasn't breakfast so they weren't in their pajamas and Jaime had forgotten the blueberries, but no, Kate didn't want me to tell Jaime where the blueberries were because she wanted to save them until we got home, and as soon as we got home, we had to have our special pancake breakfast with blueberries and ham, and we had to be in our pajamas, and we had to pretend there wouldn't be enough for Daddy and smack his hand when he tried to steal ham from the frying pan, and then he had to carry me out of the room and lock the door and ...

It was a silly little ritual. The kind three-year-olds love, one that keeps evolving and every step must be performed every time and it's just as hilarious the tenth time as the first.

When Clay came down, I started to stand, but he motioned that he'd check us out and I should keep talking. I still passed him the phone and hurried off before he could argue. I wasn't the only one who could use the grounding of our daughter's chatter. As I walked away, I heard her saying, "And Jaime made us pancakes, but she..." and I smiled.

PROFESSOR

"NOW THIS IS more like it," Clay said as we walked into our new hotel room.

I tossed my suitcase in the corner and headed for the room service menu. Clay snatched it first.

"Excuse me," I said. "You're supposed to be reading Dennis's notes, remember? I believe that was an order."

"My stomach exercises its power of veto. Food first, work later."

AN HOUR LATER, his stomach full, Clay was propped up at the head of the bed, reading Dennis's notes aloud and adding lecture bits as he went. I was curled up with the pillows beside him, eyes closed as I listened.

Dennis's notes were mostly about other shape-shifter myths, ones Clay already knew. There was the Bajang from Malaysia, a dwarfish human that can transform into a polecat. Or the Grecian Striga, a witch that shifts into a screech owl. Or West African leopard men, the offspring of humans and leopard gods, who can take on the form of a cat. Go to Bali and you'll find the Leyak, black-magic practitioners who change into animals at night. The Scots have their Selkies, seals who can change into humans. Brazilians have Encantado, humans who shift into animals, particularly dolphins. And that's only the beginning.

The most popular shape-shifting form, though, is canine. Maybe that's proof that humans are, in some way, aware of us. But canines are also the animal they're most familiar with, from the companion dog to the predatory wolf. Canines work beside humans, live with humans and have, for centuries, competed with them, for both food and territory. Is it any wonder that when people imagine the animal shape of their dreams and nightmares, it's the dog, the fox, the jackal, the wolf?

In almost any culture that has canines, you'll find tales of hybrids or shifters. The Flemish have the monstrous black doglike Kludde, the Japanese have the raccoon-dog shifting Tanuki and the fox shifting Kitsune, Ethiopia has the wolf-dog Crocotta, North American Natives have their coyote and wolf shifting skin-walkers.

Clay knew all of them, but as he read, he infused every scrap of well-trodden myth with the excitement and passion of a new discovery. This was another part of Clay. The father, the lover, the enforcer and the professor. Four sides entwining into a whole—simple yet complex, fascinating and infuriating.

I propped myself on one elbow and leaned over to look at him, my hair grazing the notes in his hand.

"I love you," I said.

He swiped my hair away. "You interrupted my lecture for that? Tell me something I don't already know."

"I hate you."

"Know that, too. Keeps things interesting. Now where was I?"

"Pompously expounding on the arcane minutiae of shape-shifting lore."

"Been doing that for the last hour. Question is: which bit of minutiae was I expounding on?"

I lifted the notes to his nose.

"Ah, the Tlahuelpuchi. Actually, more a vampire myth than shape-shifter—"

"Similar to the Nagual," I said, "but differing in both the variety of transformation and the transmission of the power. A Nagual shifts into recognizable animal form and is believed to learn the craft, while the Tlahuelpuchi curse is inherited and the cursed being shifts into a bestial form, often resembling a bird, such as a vulture or that overlooked horror movie possibility—the dreaded were-turkey."

"You know it so well? You give the lecture."

"God forbid. The podium is yours, Dr. Danvers."

He put an arm around me, pulled me against his side and carried on.

WE WATCHED JOEY head for his car, a baby Mercedes that I was sure had never ventured past the city limits. He had his head down, frowning as he searched his pocket for his keys. He pulled them out, pointed the fob and saw Clay and me blocking the way.

Joey stopped so suddenly his loafers squeaked on the damp asphalt. "I said I didn't want to—"

Clay threw the denim jacket on the car hood.

Joey winced as the buttons scraped the paint.

"Recognize it?" Clay said.

"Looks like something you'd wear, so I'm guessing—"

"It belongs to a Stillwell."

"My father? Not exactly his style."

"It's not your father's and it's not yours. But it smells like you. Your kin. Want to know where I got it?" Clay didn't wait for an answer. "Off a mutt. One of the three who killed your father. Can you tell me why he'd be wearing it? Or who it belonged to?"

"Why don't you ask the guy who had it?" Joey frowned. "No, I suppose you can't do that, since he's probably no longer among the living. That's the problem with torturing and killing mutts, isn't it? You work so hard to get your answers, and sometimes they die on you first."

Joey's eyes lit up like Jeremy's when he hit the bull's-eye on a seemingly impossible target. But Clay just stood there, as if waiting for the punch line.

After a moment of awkward silence, Joey said, "I'm right, aren't I? You tortured him. Killed him."

"Yeah."

Again, Joey waited for a reaction—chagrin, embarrassment, shame. Again, Clay waited for him to get to the point.

"Did you use a chainsaw?" Joey said. "I seem to recall you like chainsaws."

"There wasn't a power outlet." Clay turned to me.

"That's what I want for Father's Day, darling. A gas-powered chainsaw."

That flush crept across Joey's face, his eyes hardening. "You know what you are, Clay?"

"No idea, but I'm sure you'd love to tell me."

"Yes, we interrogated the mutt," I cut in. "We were trying to figure out what happened to your father, three dead men and three missing women. And yes, Clay tortured him until he admitted they'd tortured and killed your dad, killed at least one of the men, raped and presumably killed the girls. So what did you do with your day, Joseph? Write a catchy jingle?"

"You don't know anything about me."

"No," Clay said quietly. "I guess I don't."

Joey jiggled his keys, as if deciding whether to try shouldering past Clay. After a moment, he pocketed them. "What do you want?"

"I've already asked: who does this jacket belong to?"

"I have no idea."

"Can I guess?" I said. "You and your dad had a falling-out. Was that because another son showed up on his doorstep?"

"I'm a little old to be jealous of my daddy's attention."

"I didn't say you were, but you might be miffed with him for being careless and bringing another werewolf into the world, something I don't think you'd approve of."

"If my father did, I know nothing about it. Now, if you'll excuse me."

Clay moved aside to let him into the car. He waited until Joey's hand was on the door, then asked, his voice low again, "Did you call them this morning, Joey?"

"Call who?"

"The mutts. They paid a visit to our hotel after I talked to you."

Joey turned, meeting Clay's eyes. "I can't believe you'd ask me that."

"But you do have their number, right?" I said. "It's part of your deal with them."

"Deal?" He turned to me. "What deal?"

Clay told him what Dan Podrova said.

"Well, that mutt's a liar," Joey said. "Big shock there. That's another problem with torturing someone—eventually they hit the point where they'll say anything to make you stop. No, I don't have a deal with a pack of thugs and I didn't send them to your hotel room. Now take your wife, Clay, and go home."

"We'll leave as soon as I'm done talking to you."

"I mean, go *home*. Back to Stonehaven. There's nothing here you need to concern yourself with. Take your pretty wife, go back to your Alpha dad and your kids, whom I'm sure are just damned adorable. That's your life. This is mine. Now leave me alone."

WE LEFT HIM alone. For now. But we knew he was lying. Was he colluding with a gang of gun-runners, hoping to make us leave before we poked our noses in too deep? Clay didn't think so, but he had to consider the possibility, and we had to keep doing what Joey didn't seem to want us to do— digging for the truth.

FASCINATION

LYNN NYGARD LIVED in a neighborhood in west Anchorage, one with winding lanes and thick trees, sparsely dotted with eclectic homes that ranged from cottages to sprawling McMansions. Hers was one of the smallest homes—a tiny A-frame chalet. I'd called her again after we'd confronted Joey, and she'd said to come right over. Clay drove me, but stayed in the truck.

I must admit that when someone said "paranormal enthusiast," I pictured a tiny, dimly lit apartment, smelling of canned stew, the walls covered in yellowed newspaper articles. It could be a stereotype. Or it could just be that I've met too many who conform to it.

The neighborhood and the house were not what I expected. Neither was Lynn Nygard. She looked like a schoolteacher—small and slender with sleek white hair. She ushered me in as she tried to wrap up a phone conversation, mouthing an apology to me and rolling her eyes.

"I haven't forgotten. I'm getting old, not senile. Now I have a guest..." A pause. "Yes, dear, I'll make all the arrangements." She waved me into the living room. "But right now..."

The person on the other end kept talking. A male voice. Judging by her tone, I was guessing a son.

"I really have to let you go, dear. There's a young woman here who wants to talk to me about the wolf kills." She widened her eyes. "Well, no, I didn't plan to mention my theory on the Ijiraat, but now that you mention it..."

A pause.

"No, that is an *excellent* idea. I'm so glad you brought it up."

Her eyes sparkled with mischief as her son's protests grew louder.

"Yes, dear, I promise to behave myself. But if something goes wrong, you will come visit me at the psychiatric hospital, won't you? Loosen the bindings on my straitjacket? Wipe the drool off my chin?"

She laughed at his reply, signed off, then turned to me.

"Do you have kids, Ms. Michaels?"

"Two."

"Well, eventually you reach the point where they aren't sure whether they're the children or the parents. One minute my son needs Mommy to arrange his wife's surprise party, the next he's trying to make sure I don't embarrass myself in front of strangers." She set down the cordless phone. "Coffee? Green tea? Red wine?"

I noticed an almost full wine glass on the kitchen counter behind her and said I'd have wine.

"So you work with Hope Adams?" she asked as she got down a glass.

"When she needs me. Otherwise, I freelance. Do you know Hope's work?"

"I'd be a poor paranormal fanatic if I didn't. With *Weekly World News* stopping tabloid production last year, *True News*—and Ms. Adams's column—is the only game in town for those of us who like the occasional vampire story with our daily doom and gloom. Not that *Weekly World News* was much competition. I stopped reading it back when they added a disclaimer that it was for entertainment only. Seemed like a license to give up even *trying* to uncover any truth."

She handed me a glass of wine. "Now, Ms. Adams? She's a professional. She doesn't take herself too seriously. After all—" She winked. "—we are talking about the paranormal, not world politics. But you get the feeling she really is looking for the truth. She strikes me as a young woman I could have a coffee with." She raised her glass to me and smiled. "Or a glass of wine."

The phone rang again. "The machine can get it," she said.

"No, go ahead."

It stopped ringing.

"Good. Now you wanted to know—"

The phone started again. She sighed and said she'd be just a moment.

I sipped my wine and turned to survey my surroundings. What I saw made me sputter, clapping my hand to my mouth before I sprayed my shirt. There, almost over my head, was a picture of me.

"Do you like wolves?"

I jumped. Lynn stood in the doorway.

"I didn't mean to startle you," she said. "I just asked if you liked wolves."

She pointed to the painting. It was me...as a wolf, in one of Jeremy's paintings. *Nightfall,* if I remembered right. It had been years since I'd seen this one. The public preferred Jeremy's more atmospheric pictures of wolves in city streets. This was the more natural style he liked better.

"It's a print," she said, as she sat. "I'd love an original, but I could never afford one. I must confess, wolves fascinate me, as they do many people these days."

"They are popular."

"From demonized to romanticized. No, my view of wolves is somewhat more realistic, I hope. True, they aren't the big bad beast of lore. But if I met one in the wild, I'd back away very slowly and get out of there as fast as I could."

"Not try to pet it?"

She laughed. "Exactly. But they do intrigue me more than other animals, which is why when those killings started, I took an interest—"

The phone rang.

Lynn sighed. "This time, I *am* letting the machine pick up." The answering machine clicked on, and we could hear that the caller was a young man who said he was in town on a logging contract and looking for a place to let.

"I'm getting a lot of interest," Lynn said when the message ended. "But not the sort I was hoping for."

"You're renting out a room?"

"Or two. My husband died a couple of years ago and I'm ready for some company. I was thinking of a stripper."

I can imagine my expression because she laughed. "That didn't come out right, did it? I meant I was hoping to rent rooms to girls on the exotic dance circuit. We get a lot of them through here and their living accommodations are less than ideal. I thought I could offer something nicer, more secure. A safe place to stay is hard to come by in that field."

"I heard a few girls have gone missing lately. They weren't strippers, though. At least, I didn't get that impression."

"No, they weren't. Not officially, that is. The first one was a part-time prostitute, though you won't see that in the articles. And rightly so, in my opinion. One whiff that those girls were less than saintly..."

"And they're dismissed as doped-up whores who took off with the first guy who promised them a new life in Seattle."

"Precisely. The second girl, now she *was* the type who should make headlines. Joy Sataa. An A student. Came from a fly-in community to attend college. But it's that 'fly-in community' part that moves her down the priority list."

"Native, as was the third girl, I think."

"Right again. Adine Aariak. Seventeen and living on the streets. Maybe turned a trick now and then, though no one on the police force recalls picking her up. Grew up with the three A's: alcohol, abuse and abandonment. She came to Anchorage hoping for a break, but we all know how that works out."

I sipped my wine, waiting for her to go on. When she didn't, I prompted her with "And you think...I heard something about aliens."

She grinned. "Ah, yes, my alien abduction theory." She leaned closer and lowered her voice. "It's bullshit."

I laughed.

"I don't believe in aliens. Well, no, I do, but not in alien abduction. Can you really imagine a recognizable alien race traveling thousands of light-years to impregnate humans? I just like to get folks going. They expect me to come up with outlandish theories, so I do, then have a good chuckle as they humor me and pretend to play along. A monster did get those girls—but one with a very human face. Again, an old story, too often told." She drained half her glass of wine. "Enough of that. You came to talk about other crimes. The ones in the woods."

"You don't think wolves are responsible."

"I will admit it is possible, but I very strongly doubt it. I've taken photos of the sites and the bodies, and while there is evidence of wolf activity, there's no proof that a wolf actually killed or even participated in eating the corpses. A wolf in winter won't kill something and leave it for scavengers. They can't afford to. My guess is that they visited the site, took a look, and left it alone. Wolves don't kill people. They just don't."

"Wolf attacks are rare. Deaths are rare to the point of being unheard of."

She smiled. "Good, you've done your research, which means I can skip the lecture and jump straight to the good stuff. Do you know anything about Ijiraat?"

"Just that they're shape-shifters from Inuit mythology."

Lynn explained that Ijiraat were a lesser known type of shape-shifter, indigenous to the Arctic and the Inuit. They were believed to be spirits of the land who could take on the form of any creature native to that land, from raven to wolf, and even human. As with most such myths, the Ijiraat were commonly believed to be evil, hell-bent on deceiving and destroying humans. Another branch of the myth, though, claimed they weren't inherently evil—just wild creatures that would, if threatened, defend themselves. One common thread in the stories was that the Ijiraat could influence memory. If you saw one, you'd forget all about it if you didn't tell someone else right away, which coincidentally explains why they aren't seen more often.

"Now, as with most legends, there are regional variations. The Inuit say that the type living here can only shift between three forms—human, bear and wolf. There's a rich history of sightings dating back over a hundred years, from tourists to weekend warriors to folks who only leave the woods when they absolutely have to."

She reached onto the table behind her to grab a folder, then handed it to me. I opened it to find a thick sheaf of typed pages.

"Those are all the accounts I've been able to find, both written and oral sources. I typed them all up into a database. You'll see notations on each account—a color and a number. The color indicates the reporting party's credibility. Green would be a group of trustworthy locals all reporting the same thing. Red would be a kid who admitted he was out in the woods drinking. Yellow is in the middle, and you have all kinds of variations in between. There's a legend on the first page. The numbers show how I rank how close the accounts are to the most common core story. Ten means it's dead on the money. One means it's so far off I only included it to be thorough."

"You definitely *are* thorough."

She laughed. "I might be a nut, but I'm the best organized nut around."

"Would I be able to borrow . . . ?"

"Oh, that's a copy for you to take."

As I flipped through a few pages, I caught familiar phrases and felt a surreal sense of déjà vu. Or maybe not so much déjà vu as spooky coincidence. I'd seen some of these pages . . . just a couple of hours ago.

"Do you give out a lot of copies?" I asked.

"Not as often as I'm asked for them. I don't advertise my research—I bring my children enough grief as it is—but people find out about my interests, as you did. With most, I prefer not to encourage their fantasies. Give them these and they'd be scouring the countryside looking for proof and shooting anything that moves—and not with a camera."

"So this is the only copy?" I tried to say it casually, absently even, as I scanned the pages.

"I did give them to someone else recently. A friend of mine." She blushed. "I suppose *friend* is being a bit hopeful. An acquaintance really. He's interested in the Ijiraat myth and he knows someone on the police force. My name, and my theory, came up when they were discussing the deaths and he got in touch with me."

"He's interested in the myth? An academic?"

"No, no. He's an electrician. This is just a hobby, but he's quite serious about it. Not obsessive, mind you. Just a scholarly interest in a nonprofessional way. Like mine. We hit it off quite well."

She sipped her wine. "Which reminds me that I haven't heard from him in a while, and I found a book he was asking about. I should call him. Perhaps invite him to dinner." She glanced at me. "Does that seem too forward?"

I'd developed a good poker face over the years, but it was hard to keep it as I said she should do it . . . knowing that the date would never happen. I couldn't help thinking that it would have been nice for Dennis and Lynn to have that dinner.

"Do you know what got him interested?" I asked. "People who suddenly take a serious interest in the paranormal . . . Well, in my experience, it screams 'encounter.'"

I could tell by her expression that she was uncomfortable with the question.

I hurried on. "Sorry, I didn't mean for the article. Hope has a policy of never reporting anything that isn't a firsthand account. I was just being nosy. When you work with this stuff, you can't help . . . looking for proof, I guess."

"I can imagine. Well, Den—he seemed to have had a sighting, but he never told me about it. I've learned not to push. There are some who are eager to pour their tale in any sympathetic ear, and those who need to work it through themselves first. He did say he has a cabin in the region reputed to be Ijiraat territory. He asked about the Ijiraat's forms, specifically. Whether they shape-shifted into bears or wolves, or perhaps into something that simply resembled both, depending on the witness."

"Like two people seeing an animal in a city alley, one saying it was a cat and one a rat."

"Exactly. It's a fascinating idea that I hadn't considered.

If a human is going to change into an animal, a full shift into a bear or a wolf seems rather unlikely. It would be more logical to change into something bearlike or wolflike. A beast on two legs."

"Like those old Hollywood wolf men."

"Yes, exactly."

CLAY WAS HUNGRY. I told him what I'd learned as we picked up burgers at a drive-through.

"Maybe these creatures do exist," he said as he took the paper bag and drove away without waiting for his change. "But I don't see any evidence that they're shape-shifters. I finished going through those accounts while you were inside and there's not one mention of the usual signs of a shape-shifting human—footsteps go into a thicket and paw prints come out, shoot an animal and see a wounded man later. Not a credible mention anyway. I'd say it's more likely to be a single-form humanoid like Bigfoot."

"Good point."

"Whatever Dennis saw could have been this Ijiraat, either a humanoid creature or a shape-shifter. And whatever attacked you last night was definitely no bear. The Inuit say these Ijiraat have been here for generations and people have been reporting sightings for a hundred years. But only now does it start killing people? When a pack of mutt thugs rolls into town?"

"Well, I think Lynn was missing that bit of info."

"Dennis must have seen something, and I agree there might actually be something out there. What I'm not buying is that the two—this creature and the killings—are connected. Except that if such a beast exists and this is its traditional territory, it's not going to be too happy about werewolves turning it into a killing ground."

"True. That might also explain why it didn't like *us* being on its territory last night." I unwrapped my burger and glanced at him. "We need to go back."

CURIOSITY

JUST BECAUSE WE promptly agreed to do something danger-ous didn't mean we weren't aware of the danger. Waltzing into those woods hoping to lure the beast would be like strolling down to an African water hole dangling a steak and calling, "Here kitty, kitty."

We had some sense of what we were up against. It was bigger than us, stronger than us and maybe even a better hunter than us. The best way to fight an opponent with fangs and claws is to have your own. Either that, or bring along a really big gun.

To be honest, I couldn't see how a gun would be that much of an advantage. Biting or swiping is a natural exten-sion of fighting. A gun is big and unwieldy, and if you don't get it up in time or don't aim it right or it jams, you're screwed. So I was sticking with what I knew.

But as we drove, I remembered that guy in Pittsburgh handing out cards for his wife and decided a Taser might be perfect for backup when we weren't in wolf form.

Was I totally comfortable buying a weapon? No, but

that had less to do with my belief system than with pride. I was a werewolf, damn it. I didn't use weapons. But these days it wasn't all about me. I wanted to live to see my kids grow up. So I bought the Taser. I'll refrain from commenting on the process except to say that the leftist humanitarian in me was appalled, while the warrior in me, heading into battle, was happy that she didn't need to fill out paperwork and wait six weeks for a license.

If we were attacked by the beast from last night, the Taser might not stop it, but it could slow it down enough to even the odds.

AS IT TURNED out, we didn't need a weapon. The forest continued its night symphony the whole time we were Changing, with only the usual cushion of silence around us, meaning we were the only predators within earshot.

I'll admit I didn't mind the excuse to return to these woods, and it wasn't just the new species of birds and animals or the new expanses of land stretching to the horizon. This forest *felt* different. The moment I'd start to relax, I'd get that prickle at the back of my neck, warning me not to get too comfortable. Things here weren't what I was used to and I couldn't lower my guard.

It was different. And different is good.

WE'D CHANGED BESIDE the road where we'd parked the night before. Then we followed the trail toward Dennis's cabin.

On the way, we found the spot where I'd been attacked.

I'd hoped that in wolf form, with my better nose, I might be able to get more clues as to what exactly had ambushed us. But while I could still smell it, the musky odor was so overwhelming it was like trying to pick apart the components of cheap cologne. My nose and brain revolted and could only process the overall stink . . . and wanted nothing to do with it.

We managed to follow the beast's trail for almost a mile. Then it dipped into a shallow, fast-running stream, as if the creature knew we'd try tracking it. We ran along the sides for another half mile, but we found no sign of where it had exited, and we gave up. As interesting as this mystery was, we had a more pressing agenda tonight.

At Dennis's cabin, I Changed back while Clay stood guard. He'd offered to search instead, to save me the extra Changing. I won't say it's less painful for him—I have no way of judging that—but he's been doing them from the age most kids learn to ride a bike. I've never known him to skip an opportunity because he'd prefer not to go through it.

But I had more searching experience and he had more guarding experience, so we stuck to our roles. The first thing I did was look for any evidence that Dennis had encountered the beast—a photo, a journal, anything. But I found nothing and soon began the real work of the night—figuring out how close Dan's story of Dennis's death was to the reality, while learning all I could about this mysterious younger Stillwell.

Now that I'd encountered both Tesler brothers and Dan, I could pick out their individual scents and re-create that night in the cabin. All three had been here. Travis Tesler's and Podrova's scents blanketed the spot where we'd found Dennis, meaning they both had been actively involved in his torture.

The bystander was Eddie Tesler, who seemed to have planted himself in a chair across the cabin and stayed there. That might suggest he disagreed with the torture, but beside the chair were a puzzle book and a pen, both reeking of Eddie's scent. He'd used the time to do a couple of word-search puzzles instead.

I found evidence of another bystander. The chair beside Eddie's smelled of werewolf, too, and was spattered with drops of blood from the younger Stillwell, whose jacket Dan had been wearing.

I followed the trails outside. Three werewolves had arrived—the Tesler brothers and Dan. Four had left, including young Stillwell. So Eddie hadn't just been chilling out during the torture—he'd been guarding a hostage. Maybe this was why Joey pretended not to know who this younger relative was, and why he was so anxious for us to leave the mutts alone and go home.

I searched the cabin, looking for more signs of the young man. I found them in Dennis's dresser. The top drawer was stuffed with clothes that didn't belong to him. Most had been washed, but a few still bore the younger man's scent. Further investigation turned up a toothbrush, a stack of comic books and a handheld game, all permeated with his smell. The game player had been etched with a name: Noah Albright. A few of the comics bore the same initials.

As I hunted, a story formed. Noah was Dennis's late-in-life son, left with his mother until he reached puberty. Then Dennis had made contact, explaining the situation to the young man and guiding him through his early Changes, which from his smell hadn't been more than a year ago. The kid stayed with his mom but still spent time with his father, here at the cabin. Then, on one of those visits, the mutts had shown up.

Was that why Dennis was killed? The new pack came calling, his teenage son was here and the normally passive Dennis fought to defend him?

So where was the kid? Was he still alive? I hoped so, and I was sure Joey believed it—or was being led to believe it. But honestly? I doubted it.

I CHANGED BACK for the return trip. The evening was still quiet, but not unnaturally so. There'd been no sign of the beast. No sign of the werewolves. No sign of the wolves.

After three Changes in two days, my energy was flagging and my stomach was growling. I would have been fine waiting to grab something later, but as we passed an open field, Clay stopped me and swiveled his ears, telling me to listen.

The snow was deeper here, and I could hear scratching under it. Clay crouched, hindquarters waggling. He plunged through the snow, then swung back up, head and ruff piled with the white stuff and, in his jaws, a squealing mouse.

He tossed the mouse back to me. I caught it. By the time

I'd eaten it, Clay had another. That one he kept, throwing his head back to gulp it down.

I raced forward and joined in. We tore through the clearing, no attempt to stalk and hunt, just plowing through the snow, scooping up mice, giving them one life-ending crunch, then swallowing them whole.

The mice could have run for cover, but most froze in panic, like villagers accustomed to stealthy snipers suddenly beset by rampaging berserkers. That made for easy pickings and we had a blast, seeing who could get the most.

Once I'd eaten my fill, I collapsed where I stood, my stomach gurgling happily. Clay strolled over and plunked down on top of me. I flipped him off and we tussled, but halfheartedly, too full and too tired.

I curled up against him. As I was tucking my frozen nose under my tail, I caught a whiff of werewolf scent on the wind. I stiffened. Travis Tesler's image flashed through my mind and on its heels came a heart-gripping moment of panic before my brain processed the smell. It wasn't one of Tesler's pack.

Clay grunted and swung his muzzle to the left. I could see the faint outline of a dark wolf between the trees. I started to rise, but Clay butted my foreleg, telling me to lie back down. Obviously, he'd scented or spotted the werewolf already and decided he was no threat.

The mutt stayed where he was, just watching us, and when I peered at him, seeing the dark red fur and green eyes, I realized it was the one who'd been with the wolves the night before. Clay grunted again, telling me to relax. I curled into a ball against him. Soon the heat of his body and the steady beat of his heart lulled me toward dreamland.

I was drifting off when Clay tensed. Before I could open my eyes, he sprang to his feet, accidentally booting me in my bruised ribs as he scrambled up.

I twisted to see the mutt barreling toward us, his lips pulled back in a snarl. As he charged, Clay stood his ground, his fur bristling, ears back, growl rippling through the clearing. The mutt kept coming. Then, at the last second, he veered around Clay and ran at me.

I braced myself and growled, but he never heard it. Clay lunged at him, a whirlwind of fur and snapping teeth. The mutt sheared out of Clay's way and took off, snow flying in his wake as he plowed headlong across the clearing, cutting a wide circle, only to head right back.

As the mutt ran at me, I braced for the hit. As with Clay, though, he checked himself at the last moment, then he snapped, catching my foreleg in a sharp bite. I dove at him, but he was already tearing off.

Again he started that wide circle, running full out and low to the ground. I glanced at Clay. Did this guy want a fight? Or a game of tag?

Clay lowered his head and snorted. Play was a rule-bound behavior with wolves. In a pack, it says, "I trust you enough to let my guard down." Maybe this mutt had seen us playing and was like the lonely kid at the playground, asking to join in. Clay was having none of that. Play was for his Pack brothers, not strangers.

Clay growled, telling the guy he was pissing him off. When he lowered his hindquarters to the ground again, the mutt charged. Clay lunged. The mutt ducked and zoomed out of the way, then came at him again.

With a roar, Clay sprang. When the mutt fell back, Clay kept coming, ready to give him a good trouncing, and clear up any misconceptions. I flew after Clay, grabbed him by the ruff and yanked him back. He reared up, snarling and bucking to throw me off, but I held on and growled.

Once Clay realized I was serious, he stopped. As the mutt zoomed back and forth in front of us, I let go of Clay and surveyed the woods. He got the message—this guy was trying too hard to get us to chase him.

I hadn't considered the possibility that this werewolf was part of Travis's pack. A "not quite right in the head" mutt who fancied himself a wolf, preferring to run with them and leave the hard work to his buddies. But now he'd been called on to do his fair share.

As I paced to sample the night wind, I expected the mutt to distract us so we didn't get a whiff of his pals lying in wait. Instead, he snorted, as if in satisfaction.

My nose picked up the faint smell of musk and I understood. I nudged Clay and pantomimed sniffing north. It took a moment, but he caught the scent, his fur instinctively rising. The beast.

When I passed the mutt, a sigh rippled his flanks, as if to say, *Finally.* He tried to fall in step beside me, but Clay loped up and shouldered him back.

With the mutt at our heels, we headed deeper into the bush, moving south, away from the beast. Then I began circling in its direction.

When the mutt realized what I was doing, he nipped my

rear leg. I wheeled and snapped. He growled and flicked his muzzle in the other direction. I grunted, shook my head and continued north.

Clay jostled me, saying, "I know you want to get a closer look, but be careful, okay?" I slowed to reassure him.

That *didn't* reassure someone else, though. The mutt raced in front of me and spun in my path, snapping and snarling. I stopped and lowered my head, ears back, tail out, fur bristling as I matched him snarl for snarl.

Clay stepped aside to sample the air and peer into the darkness. Then he lunged at me, knocking me into a tree, his grunted apology cut short as he grabbed the loose ruff around my neck and yanked me the other way.

I hesitated only long enough to get my footing... and to hear the crashing in the undergrowth.

We ran. When the noise behind us stopped and I tried to slow, the mutt nipped my heels. Clay fell behind. Once the mutt realized he'd lost one of his charges, he wheeled.

The moon had passed under cloud cover, leaving the forest as black as it had been the night before, so it seemed to take a moment before the mutt saw Clay's pale form, stopped, nose lifted, ears up. Then, Clay's eyes went wide and he shot forward, plowing into my side. I hit the ground, Clay atop me, as a huge shape swung into the spot where I'd been standing.

Clay jumped off me and spun, snarling at the beast. I scrambled up, but all I could see was that dark form, clouds still blocking the moon and Clay now blocking my line of sight.

The beast was on all fours this time. It was at least twice

as wide as Clay, its back humped like a bear, sloping to smaller hindquarters.

The beast snarled, a guttural not-quite-natural sound that made my fur rise. Teeth flashed and I caught a whiff of its breath, my stomach churning at the stench.

Clay stood his ground, snarling. Then, without warning, he charged. The beast reared, like a bear, one massive front paw swiping at Clay, but catching only air. Clay had checked his charge at the last second, veering around the beast instead. It tried to spin, but too late, as Clay vaulted onto its back.

The beast clawed the air, trying in vain to reach Clay. I launched myself at its stomach. My jaws clamped onto sparse, coarse hair, then into nearly bald flesh. I clamped down, fangs scraping ribs, blood spurting into my mouth.

Out of the corner of my eye, I saw the dark form of the mutt racing in. He leapt... and bit down on my rear leg, yanking so hard that I fell back with a flap of the beast's skin in my teeth, blood spraying my face.

I scrabbled up and spun on the mutt, but he was gone, trying to get Clay off the beast's back. I flew after him.

Clay kept slashing at the beast's neck, going for its throat. It roared and bucked. Then, from deep in the woods came an answering roar.

I barked, an awkward sound for a wolf, but I did the best I could, desperate to get Clay's attention. But he'd heard the second beast, and his brain wasn't yet blood-fogged enough not to realize we couldn't take on two of them. He snarled, telling me to get moving, then dropped and hit the ground running.

I headed for the open ground of the clearing, where we could get up some speed, but the mutt took the lead and steered us deeper into the woods instead. As we darted around trees, the beast tried giving chase, but the forest was too dense for him and he quickly fell behind, roaring in frustration. We kept running until we couldn't hear him, then we headed for our clothes.

SLEEPLESS

I WAITED WHILE Clay Changed. Once he was done, and dressing, I walked over to where the mutt lay near the path. I growled and jerked my head, trying to tell him to Change back, that I needed to speak to him. He only looked at me, uncomprehending.

When I stepped closer, a wolf shot from the shadows. It was the small gray one I'd seen with the mutt the night before. I backed out of her way. She eyed me with a baleful glower, then snuffled him anxiously. He snorted and bumped her away, as if to say, *Enough of that.*

Then his muzzle jerked up. He looked over my shoulder and I turned to see Clay coming. The mutt grunted and started walking away, as if his job was done and he was eager to be off.

I started after him. The gray wolf lunged at me, snapping. I fell back. She kept snarling, fur bristling until he circled back and prodded her flank. She started to leave with him, but couldn't resist tossing one last glower and growl my way.

"I think she's warning you off." Clay walked up beside me. To the wolf, he said, "Don't worry, she's already taken."

The wolf chuffed, but still glared at me before turning away.

I raced into the thicket he'd vacated, trying for a quick Change so I could go after the mutt and get him to talk. There was no rushing the process, though, and by the time I finished, he was long gone.

"I tried to call him back," Clay said. "But I don't think he understood, and I wasn't going after him, leaving you alone. Anyway, I'm sure we'll see him again. Hopefully he'll be by himself. I don't think his mate likes you much."

"You really think that's his mate?"

He shrugged. "If that's the form a werewolf chooses, it's no different from another taking a human mate."

"Uh, yes it is. If you'd been a zoo employee instead of a professor, would you have chosen a wolf mate instead of me?"

"Depends on how cute she was."

When I looked at him, he laughed. "I'm kidding, darling. The answer is no because, as much as I like being a wolf, it's not the form I choose. It's too limiting. You can't speak. Can't read. Can't write. The communication of intellectually stimulating ideas is nearly impossible." He grinned at me. "As for stimulation of other kinds? Serious limitations there, too. No hands." He slid his under my shirt. "No fingers." His tickled my sides and brushed my breasts. "No lips." He lowered his to my neck.

"Limiting."

"Very."

His mouth moved to mine, kissing me hard.

"Maybe this time we should complete our escape first?" I murmured.

A low growl, not exactly disagreement, just annoyance that I'd brought it up. I glanced over his shoulder at the truck.

"A big metal box with a folding backseat should be safe enough, don't you think?"

He peered at the truck, as if measuring the distance. Then he scooped me up and carried me to it.

BACK AT THE hotel, the first thing I did was call Joey's office. He wouldn't be in, of course, but that was the point—I could leave a complete message without him hanging up on me.

Couching it in suitably cryptic terms—in case his voice mail was monitored—I let him know that we'd figured out what was going on. The mutts had taken Noah and now they were holding him hostage, demanding something from Joey for his release. Joey was dealing with that and proceeding with extreme caution... meaning he didn't want two Pack enforcers in town, throwing their weight around and endangering his half brother's life.

Now that we understood the situation, I assured him we'd proceed with equally extreme caution and that we could help resolve the situation. I didn't expect him to take us up on the offer. What I was really saying, as politely as possible, was, "We know why you want us to leave town, and we aren't going."

Next we tended to our injuries. Neither of us had any broken bones, and that was all that mattered. Being a werewolf meant a lifetime of fighting, and like those who spend their life in the boxing ring, we've learned to ignore the bumps and bruises and cuts. Check for broken bones, clean the cuts, get some rest and we'd be good to go tomorrow. We had to be—unlike professional boxers, we couldn't call off a match because we weren't up to it. Werewolf healing helped with that. Twenty-four hours later, the only remaining signs of my encounter with the beast were a tender spot on the back of my head and one on my ribs.

We went to bed after that. I fell asleep as soon as my head hit the pillow. I didn't stay that way, though. Although Clay remained perfectly still beside me, I could sense he was awake and after a quick, dreamless nap, I looked over to see him staring at the ceiling.

I lifted up onto my side. Too deep in thought to notice me, he kept staring. I glanced over him to see his right hand clenching rhythmically at his side, arm muscles pulsing under the pitted scar tissue.

"Is it bothering you?" I asked.

"Hmm?" He followed my gaze to his arm, and made a final fist, then stopped flexing. "Nah, I don't feel it anymore."

"I mean is it *bothering* you?"

He was silent a minute, then he brushed my hair back over my shoulder.

"I ran away tonight," he said after a moment. "When I first smelled that thing, I ran."

Protests and reassurances sprang to my lips, but I knew he wasn't looking for that.

He continued. "I remembered what it did to you the night before and all I could think about was getting you out of there."

"Which under the circumstances was the smart thing to do."

"Yeah. But the reason I ran instead of fighting?" He lifted his arm and flexed. "It doesn't affect my fighting in wolf form. It's just a slight weakness in one of my legs, easily compensated. My first instinct, though, was to second-guess myself and flee. That's not good."

"But—"

"Under the circumstances, it was the right choice, and that would be fine...if I could say I made an informed decision."

"Which is tough to do when a three-hundred-pound beast is bearing down on you." I caught his look. "Yes, I know you don't want excuses. The point is that you don't have the confidence you did four years ago. Personally, I don't think that's such a bad thing. If you're still jumping on the back of raging beasts, you have more than enough confidence for my tastes."

He went silent, his gaze returning to the ceiling.

"It's not running from that beast that's disturbing you. It's the possibility that you might do it with a mutt. If enough of them confront us, your first instinct will be to hustle me out of there. If I'm just your mate, that's not a problem—you're getting me out of harm's way. But if I'm Alpha, I shouldn't need to be shuffled off, and if it looks like you're doing that, then the implication is that there's a problem."

"Yeah."

He went quiet again. I waited, knowing I'd prodded enough.

"With my arm . . . it's ongoing," he said. "I'm still working it through. With you in line for Alpha, though, it highlights another issue, one I've been avoiding."

When he didn't go on, I did prompt him, but he only slid his arm under me and pulled me close.

"It's nothing. I'm tired and I'm rambling."

"If something's bugging you . . ."

"I'll deal with it."

I paused. "And I can't help?"

When he said nothing, the temperature in the room seemed to plummet. I shivered. He rubbed my back, but it didn't help.

Since when didn't Clay share his problems with me? Sure, we were notorious for keeping minor issues from one another, trying to solve them on our own. But now clearly something *was* bothering Clay and he didn't want to share it, and that only fanned the embers of my real worry—that this was what being Alpha would be like.

There was a lot Clay didn't share with Jeremy. There were aspects to protecting the Alpha and the Pack that bothered Jeremy. Like me, he wished they weren't necessary. So Clay did them without sharing the details and Jeremy never asked.

My Alphahood would not be a radical change from Jeremy's. I believed in every reform he'd instituted and I'd continue his work. Most of his leadership style I admired and would emulate. But I wanted to be more involved. I wanted to be on the front lines, as I was now, not giving orders from the rear. I wanted to know everything that went on, even the parts that bothered me.

"If it has to do with the Pack, then I need to know what the issue is and how you think it should be resolved."

He glanced over. "And if I disagree?"

"As my bodyguard? Or as my mate?"

"Both."

I waited ten seconds, resisting the urge to flip over or move away. I could say I was respecting Clay's space and didn't want to guilt-trip him into sharing. But the truth is that pride kept me from showing I was hurt. So I settled in as if I'd already forgotten it, which I'm sure would have completely fooled him if he hadn't spent almost twenty years learning to read my moods.

"Remember that mutt who stalked you on our honeymoon?" he asked after a minute.

"The Cain kid? Tough to forget, as hard as I might try."

"Do you know why he didn't run away when I first warned him off?"

"Uh, because he's a Cain? Big family sharing one allotment of brain cells?"

"Because he didn't believe my reputation. He'd seen the photos. He insisted they were Photoshopped."

"Over thirty years ago? Kinda proves my point about the brain cells, don't you think?"

"But he's not the only one. Things have been changing. When you and I started working together, mutts ran from us the minute they figured out who I was. Then they started sticking around a little longer, maybe throwing a punch or two, testing my reputation. These days, over half the mutts in the country are younger than those photos. I'm their dad's bogeyman, not theirs. Kids like Cain don't see any reason to run until I give them one. And that was fine... until this." He lifted his arm.

"So? Even with your arm, you can take on guys like that—half your age, twice your size—and the outcome's never in question."

"But ten years ago, I wouldn't have *had* to take them on. I wouldn't have had to worry about Cain stalking you. The second he realized I was with you he'd have been on the next bus out of town. Now, with you becoming Alpha, the kids getting older... I don't want to keep proving I still deserve my reputation. That was the point of..."

He trailed off. The point of what? I was about to ask, when I understood. That was the point of what Clay had done at seventeen, dissecting a mutt while he was still alive, then taking pictures. I knew it wasn't as horrible as it sounded—the mutt had been anesthetized and out cold the whole time, dying before he knew what had happened. The point hadn't been torturing this particular mutt, but convincing other mutts that Clay had tortured him and that if they trespassed on Jeremy's property, he'd do the same to them.

And when I understood what Clay meant, I *really* understood what he meant.

"You're thinking... you're thinking of doing it again."

I should have kept my mouth shut until I could properly modulate my tone. I'd just finished sulking because Clay had implied this wasn't something I could handle, and now I said those words in whispered horror, confirming it. I wanted to try again, stronger, matter-of-fact, proving him wrong. Only he wasn't wrong.

Rationally, I knew that in killing one mutt horribly, Clay had protected Jeremy for over thirty years and saved the lives of every mutt who otherwise would have come to Stonehaven to challenge him.

Emotionally, though, I reacted like a little kid, screwing up her face and sticking her fingers in her ears. I didn't want to see it, didn't want to hear about it, didn't want to think about it. And I sure as hell didn't want to think about Clay doing it again.

"It's not important," he said after a minute. "Not now. I shouldn't have brought it up."

"But it's bothering you."

"Bugging me, not driving me crazy. We've got lots to do tomorrow. We need to get some sleep."

He lay back down. When I didn't, he tugged me down beside him, then settled in, one hand resting on my waist, the other tucked up between us, thumb rubbing my collarbone.

"When you . . . did it," I said. "Jeremy didn't know in advance, did he?"

"Nah. No reason to tell him, and better if I didn't."

Better? Or just easier? We lay in silence for a moment, eyes still open.

"I—"

I was about to say, "I want to know," but did I? Really,

did I? What would I be saying? That I wanted all the details in advance? That I wanted to help him plan it? Help him carry it out? My stomach twisted.

Clay wouldn't want that either.

Did it make me a coward if I agreed I was better off not knowing? Worse, did it make me a hypocrite? I could acknowledge that Clay was capable of doing horrible things to protect the Pack, and I didn't disagree with the final result . . . but I didn't want to think about it too much?

"Go to sleep," he murmured. "I haven't decided anything. I don't plan to for a while."

"But . . . when you do. Don't—" I lifted my head, his hand falling from my chest. "Don't do anything behind my back, okay?"

His lips tightened.

"That came out wrong. I just meant . . . I want to know. I don't want to find out after the fact. I'm not Jeremy."

He nodded, kissed my shoulder, then pulled me down again. After another wide-eyed minute of lying there, neither of us bothering to fake sleep, he said, "Are you okay? With earlier today?"

He meant Tesler, the attempted rape.

"I'm . . . okay for now."

He knew that meant that I wasn't really okay, just temporarily so, having slapped a bandage on the wound to stanch the bleeding while I tended to other things.

When I'd smelled mutt tonight, I'd had a moment of panic, thinking it was Tesler. An Alpha could not run from a threat. An Alpha could not have weak spots a mutt could exploit. I thought I didn't. Now I realized I'd been wrong. At a serious threat of rape, there'd been a moment when my fight response shut down, flight instinct taking over. I couldn't let that happen again.

When I said I was okay for now, Clay didn't ask if I wanted to talk about it. He looked for the answer in my face, then said, "Later, then?"

I nodded, curled up against him and closed my eyes.

CONTROL

THE ALARM SOUNDED at seven. Our first call went to Jeremy, updating him on the situation, getting his opinion of my decisions, then talking to the kids. We had a few muffins to tide us over, then dealt with our anxieties in the way we knew best. We headed downstairs to the gym.

THE BEST THING about hotel gyms? They're almost always empty. I'm sure plenty of business travelers insist on booking a place with a gym, so they can spend twenty minutes in there, then congratulate themselves for sticking to their routine between cocktail parties and room-service binges.

When we arrived, there was one guy coming out of the pool change-room and heading for the weights. By the time I was dressed in my sweats, he was heading back in, not even having broken a sweat.

We started with the punching bag. I held it while Clay worked out his right arm. It didn't take long before he got bored of that and wanted a more active partner. We started slow, Clay throwing punches and me blocking them, working into it, not wanting to get too involved in case someone came in.

After about twenty minutes with no one even walking past the door, we swung into full sparring mode. I worked on Clay's reflexes now, feinting and lunging, trying to trick him into leading with his left. After four years of this, though, it's tough to catch him off guard in a structured environment. Finally, he grabbed my wrist and flipped me onto the mat, signaling rehab time was over.

When I rolled up, he danced away, grinning.

"Uh-uh," I said. "Someone comes in and we're wrestling, however innocently, it's going to draw attention to us, and we can never afford to draw—"

I wheeled, trying to kick his legs out from under him, but he spun out of my way. We faced off. I lunged, then feinted, managed to get hold of his arm and threw him over my shoulder.

He hit the mat with a *whoomph*, and lay there, winded, shaking his head. "And that wouldn't have called attention to us, darling?"

"You started it."

He dove for my legs. I pranced back out of the way and kicked. He caught my leg and down I went.

"Still tired from yesterday?" he said. "I could go easier on you."

I sprang up and we went a few rounds, throwing punches and kicks. Only a few connected, but not for lack of trying. We didn't "go easy" on each other, just avoided blows that would do serious damage. Bruises, though, we'd have. I didn't care. It's not like I'd be walking around Anchorage in shorts and a tank top.

Finally I had him pinned with his arms over his head, my knee on one thigh, keeping him down.

"Give up?" I asked.

He grinned. "Depends on the forfeit."

"Nothing."

"Nothing?"

I bent to the base of his throat and tasted it, hot and slick with sweat. He shivered. I grazed my teeth over his skin.

"You admit I beat you," I murmured between nibbles. "And we'll adjourn to the showers."

"*Beat me* is a little strong. You briefly got the upper hand. I'll admit to that."

"Nuh-uh. *Beat* you."

"Temporarily bested." He jerked his hands free.

I caught and pinned them again. "Beat." I tickled my tongue up to his ear, making him shiver again. "If you care to contest it, we could go a few more rounds." I leaned into him, rubbing against him. "Postpone the showers. Hope no one else shows up in the meantime."

He closed his eyes, hips lifting to grind into mine. When I pulled back, he growled deep in his throat and opened one eye.

"So to get sex, I need to concede defeat?" he said.

"Yep. Nasty and totally unfair, I know. But..." I slid my hand to his belly, tickling under his shirt. "Since I do seem to have the position of control..."

"Temporarily."

My hand slid under his waistband. "Ceding a fight is tough, I know." I wrapped my fingers around him and gave one firm stroke. His eyelids fluttered and he growled again, then he reared up, throwing me off. I tried to scrabble out of reach, but he grabbed my leg, yanking me facedown to the mat, then flipping me onto my back and pinning me.

"That's better," he said. "No need to choose when I can have it both ways."

I struggled, but he had the advantage of weight and strength.

He grinned.

"Like that, do you?" I said. "Well, there's one flaw in your plan. Unless you can get me into that change-room by force, the shower is out."

"No need to go at all, is there?" He glanced at the door, then pushed my shirt up over my stomach and tweaked my waistband. "Haven't seen anyone in almost an hour. And I'm nothing if not quick."

"You wouldn't dare."

A teeth-flashing smile. "Is that a challenge, darling?"

"No, it absolutely is *not*." I squirmed, but even with just one hand holding my wrists, he had me pinned better than I'd had him with two.

He pushed my T-shirt up my rib cage, stopping just below my breasts, then sliding his hand under, tweaking my nipples hard enough to make me gasp . . . and momentarily forget that I was opposed to this idea.

When I remembered to protest, he cut me off with a kiss. We broke off fast when footsteps sounded in the hall. They headed the other way.

"Going to the business center," Clay murmured. "No one's coming in here, so there's no reason I can't just..." He slid my sweatpants down over one hip and hooked a finger through my panties, giving a tug.

I tried to squirm away. "Don't you dare."

"Would you prefer the change-room? It's still an option." He nudged my knees apart. "Just say the word. You forfeit and we can take this someplace more—"

I leapt up. He hung on to my hands...until they swung up and clipped him in the chin. I scrambled out from under him. He lunged for my legs, but I backed out of his reach and shot to my feet. As he rose, I kicked his legs out. He went down, landing hard on the mat. I straddled his chest.

He sighed.

I victory punched the air. He shot up, grabbing me under the arms and tickling me. I squealed and caught his hands, and was about to pin him when I noticed a figure standing in the doorway.

It was Joey, watching us.

"You wanted to talk to me?" he said.

I scrambled off Clay, and stood, tugging my shirt down. It already covered me just fine, but I tugged it anyway, cheeks heating.

"Yeah, we did," Clay said. "You had breakfast?"

"Yes, but I suppose you haven't." A smile cracked Joey's composure. "And if I remember correctly, we'd better attend to that first or I can't expect to get a rational sentence from you."

"You two go on," I said. "I'll shower and catch up."

• • •

WHEN MY BLOOD stopped pounding, I switched the cold shower to warm, tilted my face up into the water and tried not to think of how much more fun this shower would have been if Joey hadn't shown up. I could still feel adrenaline slamming through my veins, the lingering euphoria better than any chemical buzz. And it was more than adrenaline. It was confidence, my anxiety over facing Travis Tesler again fading.

Given my background, my dominance play with Clay might seem odd. Disturbing even. One day I'm reduced to gibbering terror by a mutt pinning me to the ground and threatening rape. Less than twenty-four hours later, I'm letting my partner pin me, threatening public sex.

I'm sure I don't want to hear what a psychiatrist would say about that. But for me, it works. It makes sense. With Clay, it was different. When we'd first met, he'd taken his time. Friends first, then, very slowly, shifting to lovers. With Clay, I was always in control. I still am.

Dominance play is about control. For some, the thrill is giving it up. For me, it's about taking it back. I don't need "release words" with Clay. If I so much as tense, he stops. I choose to take the lead or I choose to give it to him. My choice. Always. That has healed me more than years of therapy ever could.

As strong as I felt right now, I knew my gut would seize with terror when I saw Tesler again. But for now I felt ready to handle it.

NOAH

CLAY AND JOEY were in the hotel restaurant, deep in conversation when I entered. Or, at least, Clay was deep in conversation, explaining something, his hands waving, a slice of toast in one, crumbs flying. I headed for the buffet, but a large table of businesspeople beat me to it. Clay caught my eye and waved me over. As I approached, he kicked out a chair for me, then moved his plate between us.

"Clayton sharing his food?" Joey said with a strained smile. "Must be love."

"No, he's just trying to make a good impression. Normally, he'd be stealing mine."

Clay started sliding the plate back his way, but I caught it and held it between us.

"Clay was just telling me about Nick," Joey said. "He said he's doing graphic design for his dad's company. I'm still trying to figure out if he's joking."

"He's not. Nick seems to like it. He's got a good eye for design."

"Now, that I can see. I remember how long it took the

guy to buy a shirt. I bet there are a lot of nice-looking young women working in graphic design, too."

We laughed. Five years ago, I'd have guessed that was indeed the reason for Nick's interest. But lately he'd been making changes in his life—finding a job he liked, actually showing up for it and taking a more active role in the family business.

Around the time I got pregnant, Nick had started getting restless. He'd even briefly flirted with the idea of having a child of his own, which lasted until the twins arrived and he decided babies were really a bigger plunge into the sea of domesticity than he cared to take.

Thinking of Nick reminded me that he'd left a message on my cell last night. Nothing urgent. Just touching base, looking for an update, and wanting to talk about Reese.

Clay and Joey chatted for a while longer, catching up. It wasn't the most comfortable conversation, but Joey was obviously making an effort, so Clay answered all his questions.

As the line for the buffet vanished, I went up for a plate. I came back to a silent table, as if the moment Clay finished updates, they'd hit a brick wall, the amiable mood dispersing as they realized how little they now had in common.

"So you got my message," I said as I sat.

Joey nodded and picked at his omelet, moving the mushroom pieces aside. I glanced at Clay. He shrugged and resumed eating.

Finally Joey said, "Noah isn't my brother. He's my son."

I tried not to look surprised. I shouldn't have been. It made more sense for Noah to be Joey's youthful indiscretion than Dennis's middle-aged one. It was hard, though, to imagine Joey ever being youthful enough to be indiscreet.

"Did you know about him?" I said when he didn't go on.

Joey shook his head. "I was with his mother for a few months, but I was very good about using condoms. Or so I thought. His mother...liked to drink. I'd join her sometimes, so I suppose it's not surprising that I might have forgotten a time or two. I ended the relationship because she wouldn't admit she had a problem, so nor am I surprised that she kept Noah from me. Dad was the one who found him, in a mall of all places. Noah was going to a movie. He was fifteen and starting to smell like a werewolf coming into his first Change. Dad followed him and we figured out who he was. Noah wasn't with his mom anymore. She'd sobered up and married a born-again Christian who didn't think 'love thy neighbor' extended to 'love thy new wife's son.'"

"So where was Noah living?"

Joey didn't answer for a moment, then said, "Noah has problems."

"Fetal alcohol syndrome?"

"More like FAE—fetal alcohol effects." A wan smile. "Yes, I've done my research. With Noah, it's mild symptoms. He's small for his age. He has some learning disabilities, some behavioral issues. Maybe it was the alcohol, maybe just his home situation and the whole—" A glance around at surrounding tables. "The werewolf instincts kicking in and his confusion over that. When we found him, he was in a juvenile detention center. He'd been living in foster care and got mixed up with the wrong crowd, robbing gas stations. The day Dad saw him at the mall was a field trip.

He still had a year left to serve, then another year in a halfway house."

Joey rubbed his hand over his mouth. "That was a tough time. Noah was coming into his powers, hormones going nuts, with no idea what was happening to him. He'd acted out a couple of times in the center. Got into some fights. Given his strength—and the fact that he had no history of violent behavior—they presumed drugs, and he had to go through testing... It was hell."

"Were you able to speak to him?"

"Eventually. His mom admitted I was his father—I think by that point she was happy to dump him onto someone else. We eased him into the truth, which, as it turned out, wasn't necessary. He jumped at the explanation. He was thrilled, even. Not a split second of disbelief."

"At that age, I suppose hearing 'you're a werewolf' is much cooler than 'you're having a mental breakdown,'" I said.

Joey nodded. "That was exactly it and I... I didn't understand, which is where the problem began." He paused while the server refilled our coffees. "As I've said, my dad and I had increasingly different views on the best way to handle our condition. It wasn't always like that. Yes, for years we'd been on opposite sides of the center, and not by much. As I got older, though, I started chafing more against the restrictions. I lead a normal life—career, friends, girlfriends. Having to worry about Changing while on business trips or hiding my strength from my buddies in racquetball or being gentle with my lovers so I don't bite..." His gaze slid my way and he colored, as if he'd just jammed his foot in his mouth.

"If you're trying to live as human, there are a lot more disadvantages than advantages to being a werewolf," I said. "I've tried it myself."

"Then you know what I mean. My father always embraced that side of himself more. He's not as involved with the world as I am. Self-employed, poker buddies rather than friends, short-term girlfriends only...As he got older, he started getting into the wolf part even more. He bought the cabin, took up hiking, joined a couple of wilderness appreciation groups, got interested in our origins and mythology. My dad is...was, I guess, I should say..."

Joey's eyes unfocused, grief etching furrows around his mouth. Then he cleared his throat and straightened. "We were different. But it wasn't a big issue until Noah came along."

"Which to teach him," I said. "Overcoming it versus embracing it."

"As his father, I thought it seemed natural to teach him my way. Dad wasn't happy with that, but he couldn't argue with my logic. If Noah was going to straighten out—finish high school, maybe go to college—then 'normal' was obviously the way to go. Only Noah..."

He trailed off, his gaze going distant again.

"He'd just found out he was something special," I said, "and he wasn't interested in being normal."

"I can tell you're a mother. You understand kids a lot better than I do."

"No, but I understand the point of view." I hooked a thumb at Clay.

He attempted a smile. "I guess so. And if I'd been Clay,

I'm sure I would have understood Noah's perspective better. I only wanted to make things easier for him. Instead I drove him to my father, which didn't help matters."

Joey sipped his coffee, gaze down. "I took it personally. My son was picking my father, and my father was happy to have him around. I felt left out. Silly for a man my age, but that's how it was. Everyone wants to belong, and that goes for Noah more than most. He wanted a place to belong. Dad gave him that. I should have backed off. Instead, I sulked like a teenager. In the last few months, I've hardly seen either of them."

"Was Noah living with Dennis?"

Joey shook his head. "He was going to, after he got his full release. There was no way his parole officer was turning a troubled seventeen-year-old kid over to a grandfather who'd just stepped into the picture."

Seventeen...I hadn't pictured him so young, but given everything that Joey had said, that made sense.

Joey continued. "For the last six months, Noah has been spending weekends with Dad. He'd just had his first Change, and Dad was trying to help him through it." He glanced at Clay. "He used all those lessons Jeremy did with Nick and me when we were that age. The rest of the time, Noah was in a group home. On Monday, Noah's parole officer phoned me and said he hadn't shown up Sunday night. I tried calling Dad. He didn't answer, which I figured meant he was still at the cabin. When Monday night came, I tried to drive up there but my car wouldn't make it. I wasn't worried yet. Just angry. I figured Dad had taken Noah into the backcountry and hadn't bothered coming out on time."

"Did he do that?"

Joey shook his head, frown lines deepening. "Dad was never irresponsible. I was just... In the mindset I was in, I *wanted* him to be irresponsible—proof I should be taking care of Noah. When Tuesday came, I started worrying. Then I got the call. From Tesler. They had Noah and started making demands."

"What did they say about your dad?" Clay asked.

"They said they had him, too. They only let me talk to Noah but... I believed them about Dad. I wanted to believe them. Then you showed up, made it to the cabin and found him."

There was more to this story, but Joey was clearly exhausted. We could wait for the rest. There was one possibility, though, that had to be raised. A difficult one. I floundered around, trying to figure out how to word it.

Then Clay jumped in and asked it for me. "Any chance Noah hooked up with these mutts himself?"

"What?" Joey's eyes went as round as his lenses.

I hurried to interject. "Not that he'd hurt Dennis himself or had any idea they were going to, but you said Noah was desperate to belong, and mutts like this will prey on the pack instinct."

"And if he's already a crim—" Clay began.

I stomped his toes. "If he's already been lured into trouble with the law, then the upheaval of the Change could lower his defenses against returning to that life, however much he may want to get out of it."

Joey's jaw worked.

I continued. "I'm not saying that's what happened or

that it's even likely. But if it was another teenager in his situation, that's the first thing we'd bring up."

"You're right," he said after a moment. "But the answer is no. If Noah was still with me, and Dad wasn't in the picture, then yes, I could see it. He would have been looking for that connection, that reaffirmation, and if those mutts showed up, they might have found a very willing recruit. But Noah is crazy about my dad. More important, he was happy with him. As angry as he is, what he really wants is family, security." He looked down at his hands. "It's so easy to see now, but at the time . . . I screwed up. If I'd supported his choices, I might have been there last weekend."

"And you would have been killed like your dad," Clay said. "These guys are ruthless. The only way to fight them is with someone who's just as ruthless."

"You."

"*Us,*" I said. "*Ruthless* might not be the first word anyone uses to describe me, but I have the experience and I can fight. So can we help you now?"

He paused. A long pause, gaze on his folded hands. "I'm still not convinced this is the right way to go about it, but I don't see that I have much choice. Yes, I need your help."

FOCUS

AND SO, OVER breakfast, the goal of our mission to Alaska shifted yet again. We came here to rescue a young werewolf from a pair of killer mutts. We stayed to investigate another killer. And now, while those deaths were still an issue, our focus had come full circle to rescuing another young werewolf from another pair of killer mutts.

And this one was . . . I hesitate to say "family," because it sounds so hokey. I suppose it's human nature to value personal ties, however tenuous, over anonymity. But this was about wolf nature. To me, rescuing Noah was more important than making sure more humans didn't die. I suppose that's a necessary instinct for a future Alpha to have, but it didn't keep me from feeling guilty.

WE SPENT THE rest of the morning in our room, where we could talk more openly with Joey and piece together our stories. He'd already taken us up to the point of getting the call from Tesler, who claimed to have both Noah and Dennis. That was the only time Joey had spoken to his son since his capture, and it had been a brief exchange, one Joey could recite verbatim.

Joey: Are you okay?
Noah: Yeah.
Joey: Did they hurt you? Are you—?
Noah: I'm okay, all right?
Joey: I'm going to get you out of there.
Noah: Think so?
Joey: I will. I promise. How's Dennis? Is he okay?

Joey wasn't sure whether Noah tried to say something or just made a noise, but before he could ask again, Tesler took the phone back.

Then Tesler laid out his demands. He didn't want much—just everything Joey had. He'd start by accepting fifty thousand dollars as a gesture of goodwill. Then Joey would use his local reputation and contacts to fix some un-specified "problems." Once that was cleared up, Joey would take his father and son and leave Alaska . . . after signing over his car, his condo and his dad's cabin to the Teslers.

Joey had scraped together a down payment on the fifty grand. The rest he'd get from liquidating his retirement funds. He was supposed to meet Tesler yesterday morning. That's when we'd intercepted him at work. His meeting with the Teslers hadn't been until lunch, but Joey feared they were watching, so he'd brushed Clay off. His instinct had been right and the gang had then followed our trail back to our hotel and had their fun there while we were out.

After our encounter with the Teslers, and Dan's presumed death, Eddie had called Joey back with a new demand. Get rid of us or all negotiations were off.

WE GOT EVERYTHING we could from Joey. It took a while, and by the end of it, he was exhausted by the constant questions. He took a rest while Clay headed outside to scout for any sign of the mutts, and I went to a quiet place downstairs and made phone calls.

I started with Jeremy, updating him and getting his opinion. Then I spoke to the kids. Their patience with their gallivanting parents was again growing thin. They wanted us home. And, talking to them, I wanted to *be* home. So I kept it short with promises that both Daddy and I would call again before bed and talk to them more.

Next I called Nick. Again, I began with an update.

"Sounds like you two might need some help," he said when I finished.

"We're considering it," I said. "Jaime is staying longer at Stonehaven, in case Jeremy needs to take off, and Jeremy's told Karl to be ready to fly. For now, though, just keep your schedule clear. We don't want to spook these guys by having the whole Pack descend on Anchorage."

"Or they might decide to cut their losses with their hostage."

"Exactly."

"So you think he's still alive? Joey's boy?"

"Joey hasn't heard from him in two days. I can only hope they want the ransom too badly to risk killing him."

"I'm still finding it hard to believe Joey has a teenage son. He's old enough—it's just hard to picture Joey as a middle-aged guy. I picture the kid who left our place twenty-five years ago. It sounds like he's changed, though—and not just his age."

"Clay says so."

A moment of silence.

"Speaking of young werewolves," I said. "How's Reese settling in?"

"Good so far. You were right about giving him chores. I didn't want to—with his hand and all—but Antonio figured you had a point, and gave him some work to do on the grounds, early spring cleanup. That really helped. Reese has stopped eyeing the door, ready to make a break for it."

"Paying his dues. He'll be happier with that. So how is it going otherwise? You seemed nervous about having him there."

"We're being careful. We're not about to give a stranger full run of the house, not when he could obviously use a few bucks. I've been working from home, so someone's always with him, but he hasn't given us any reason to worry. I even thought I'd take him out tonight. Got a party. He might like that. Get his mind off things."

"Next thing you know, you'll be lining up double dates."

"I've already got one for Saturday. Oh, did you mean give him one of my dates? I don't like the kid *that* much. But I'm hoping the party will cheer him up."

"Is he depressed about his hand?"

"He's not thrilled about it, but there's more. Have you got a dossier on him?"

"A very thin one. He only hit our radar after the problems with Liam and Ramon. All I know is that he's from Australia. Or New Zealand. I never did quite pin it down. Why?"

"I'm trying to figure the kid out. He's been asking me and Antonio about the rules for mutts—where they can live, whether they can get a job, how long they can stay in one city. If we mention the possibility of him going home, he shuts down."

"Something happened. I know that, but I have no idea what. It could be that he killed someone or came close. It seems more personal, though."

"No, I agree. He does mention his family, parents."

"His father, you mean?"

"No, I'm pretty sure both parents are in the picture."

Reese wasn't a bitten werewolf, so to hear that he may have grown up with both parents was a surprise. That's rare enough that I'd only heard of one case in the United States— a mutt with a wife and kids—but he stayed so far under our radar that I'd never been able to confirm the story.

"You think it has something to do with his family, then?" I asked.

"I have a hunch it does. I'll keep fishing."

"Be careful. He's skittish enough. Push and—"

"He'll bolt. I know. I'll take it slow, but I think it's important. The kid wants to open up. I'll work on it, at least until you need me there."

AFTER JOEY WOKE up, we spent the afternoon with maps spread over our hotel bed, marking the locations of Dennis's cabin and the kill sites, trying to narrow down where we might find the Teslers.

That was our best hope: corner them in their lair. We could let them come to us, and I'm sure they would, but for now they seemed to have gone to ground, maybe waiting to see whether Joey would get rid of us. If he didn't, they'd hurt Noah, to prove they would. We had to find them first.

JOEY SEEMED AMBIVALENT about joining us, but when we gave him the option of staying behind, he said he needed to come, though he might not be much help in a fight.

"An extra pair of eyes and ears," Clay said. "Still useful."

Joey picked up dinner. I'd suggested we go out, having been cooped up inside all day. But Joey knew Clay would be happier eating in his room. He'd brought back Malaysian. It was one ethnic food I wasn't familiar with, and it wasn't quite to my taste. I like spicy, but this was too spicy to enjoy. For Clay, food is fuel, and he made sure his tank was full for the night ahead.

"So Karl Marsten is a Pack member now?" Joey said. "How hard up are you guys for new blood?"

Clay rolled his eyes, and stuffed a curry-sauce-drenched boiled egg into his mouth.

"Not that I know the guy," Joey said. "But even when we left the Pack, he had a reputation, and he wasn't more than a couple of years older than me. A thief, wasn't he? And a ruthless SOB, if I remember right. Killed mutts who came on his territory, ignoring the fact that non-Pack werewolves can't *hold* territory."

"Which, ultimately, became an issue," I said. "He wanted territory and had to join the Pack to get it."

"And you let him in?"

I shrugged. "Ruthless is good if it's on your side. He's not the most committed Pack member, but he'll be here if Jeremy calls. And if he doesn't jump fast enough, his girl-friend will give him a shove. She thinks the Pack is good for him, and he gives us a hundred percent to please her."

"His girlfriend knows he's a werewolf?"

"She's a half-demon."

"Half... Shit." He shook his head. "Dad said the Pack had gotten involved with other supernaturals but..." Another shake of his head. "Dad wanted to know all about it. Fascinated. I'd rather just leave my world at werewolves. That was another issue we didn't agree on." He went quiet for a minute, then shook it off. "So Karl Marsten, huh? Didn't Malcolm kill his father?"

I glanced at Clay.

"Wouldn't surprise me," he said. "But I never heard that."

"I did, back when we were with the Pack. You and Nick had gone someplace, and I had to hang out with the Santos boys. Malcolm was there with their dad and uncle, and they were talking about it, how Malcolm had killed Josef Marsten. Raymond was razzing Malcolm because the boy got away on him."

"Karl?"

"I presume so."

I'd never heard that, certainly not from Karl. It might explain some of his reluctance to commit himself to the

Pack, taking orders from a man whose father had killed his own. I'd have to talk to him about it.

"So you've got two kids, right?" Joey said. "Twins?"

I nodded. "A boy and a girl. Three and a half."

"Planning to have more?"

"Right now, two is enough."

Clay nodded as he tore a bite off a giant prawn. "Got too much else going on. Two is good. We can give them all the at-att-enshun..." Clay stumbled over the word, slurring it.

I looked over sharply. He blinked hard, as if struggling to keep his eyes open.

"I guess I'm not the only one who should have had a nap this afternoon," Joey said.

Clay kept blinking, as if he hadn't heard Joey. He frowned, annoyed, and rubbed his hand over his face.

I touched his arm. "Are you okay?"

"He looks ready to crash," Joey said with a laugh. "Too little sleep and too much food. Guess I should have grabbed espresso instead of Cokes. Why don't you go lie—?"

"You, you bas—" The word fell away in a slurred jumble. Clay gripped the table, pushing himself up.

"Clay?" I said. "What—?"

He fell forward. I lunged for him, but he caught himself at the last second, holding the table, swaying, still trying to focus. Joey had stumbled back, out of his way.

"You son..." Clay slurred the rest. His head wobbled, eyes trying to find Joey. "If you hurt her, I swear, I'll hunt you down and—"

He collapsed into my arms. I lowered him to the floor,

frantically checking his pulse, finding it strong, then spinning on Joey.

"What did you—?"

Joey wasn't in his chair. As I turned, I felt a prick on the back of my arm.

I wheeled, fists flying up, hitting Joey's outstretched hand. A syringe fell to the floor. I stared at it, my brain swimming, knees buckling.

"I'm sorry," Joey said.

I crashed to the floor.

BARTER

I WOKE TO the slap of ice-cold air on my face. I tried to nestle under the covers, but couldn't find them. Clay moved behind me. I backed toward him, to snuggle up, keep warm, expecting his arm to go around me, spoon me against him, warm breath on my neck, familiar scent washing over me. But he moved away and shook my shoulder.

"Elena, wake up." His voice was distant, distorted.

He kept shaking me.

I pushed his hand off my shoulder. "Tired. 'S cold," I mumbled. "Window's open. Close..."

I stopped. I wasn't in bed. I wasn't even lying down. I opened my eyes, the lids gummy. A blast of bitter wind made me gasp, frigid air filling my lungs, knocking sleep from me.

I was looking at a car window, partly rolled down. Forest beyond. Deep, dark forest, the trees so close I could reach out and...

My hands were bound behind my back.

I twisted, looking for Clay. Joey sat in the driver's seat. I was in the passenger side. The backseat was empty.

"Where is he?" I snarled, struggling to get free, realizing I was bound hand and foot. "Where is he?"

"Back at the hotel. They didn't want him."

It took a moment for me to understand, but when I did, I thrashed wildly.

Joey shrank back against the door and waited until I'd figured out I wasn't getting free, and when I did, I said, slowly turning toward him, "You're exchanging me for Noah."

"I have to. That's what they demanded yesterday. I had until tonight to bring you or they'd kill him. That's why I tried to get you to leave. If you'd taken off, they couldn't expect me to do it." A whine crept into his voice, as if this was all my fault. "I tried to warn you off."

"No, you didn't. You made a halfhearted suggestion that we leave town, but you didn't really want us to go. You just wanted to be able to tell yourself you tried and—"

I stopped and scanned the forest. At any moment, Tesler was going to step from the darkness, and I was wasting any chance I had of escape by bickering.

"Did you hear the last thing Clay said to you?" I asked.

Joey didn't answer.

"Do you think that was an idle threat? Knowing Clay, do you really think it was an idle threat?"

No answer, but I swore he went a few shades paler, gaze darting away, lips tightening.

"You remember what Clay did to that mutt thirty years ago? You were there."

"I wasn't—"

"Not at the scene, but around at the time. His *friend* at the time." When I emphasized the word *friend,* his lips tightened more. "You know what he did and why he did it. But a whole generation of mutts has grown up since then, a generation that considers that ancient history, and isn't afraid anymore. You know Clay won't accept that. He can't. If they've forgotten, then he needs to remind them. He needs to prove he still deserves his reputation. What better way than to repeat it, only not using a mutt this time . . . but an old friend who betrayed him."

Joey went white. Then green. Then red, his jaw setting as he swiveled to face me. "You don't need to threaten me, Elena."

"No?"

His eyes met mine, hard now. "No. Why do you think we're just sitting here?"

"Because you're waiting for Travis Tesler to—"

"The meeting place is half a mile away, the meeting time a half-hour from now. I stopped here because I've changed my mind. I can't go through with it."

My gaze went as hard as his. "Bullshit."

"Bullshit? Do you see Tesler? Why would—?"

"You stopped a half mile from the meeting place. Then you woke me up. If you'd changed your mind, you'd have put the car in reverse and gotten the hell out of here, leaving me asleep as long as possible. Instead . . ."

I trailed off as I understood.

"I want my son back," Joey said. "I need him back. You're a mother. You should understand."

If my hands were free, I would have scratched his eyes out for that. His *son*? A kid he'd rejected by dumping him on *his* father? A kid who obviously needed something Joey refused to provide because it clashed with his own worldview?

He expected me to understand the depth of his feelings because I had children? He had no idea what it meant to be a parent. No fucking idea.

"You want me to barter myself voluntarily for your son," I said when I found my voice.

"You're strong. A fighter. Clay's *chosen* mate." He said this as if it was an honor I'd won in the gladiatorial ring. "I saw you and him this morning, play fighting. He wasn't *letting* you win. You're a better fighter than I've ever been or could ever hope to be."

"So you're saying I should walk into captivity and fight my way out."

"You're smart." Desperation edged his voice now. "Clay listens to you and he never used to listen to anyone but Jeremy. My dad said Jeremy was always talking about you, that he thinks you'll be Jeremy's choice for successor. A female werewolf as Alpha? For Jeremy to even consider that, you must be—"

"Freaking amazing. A werewolf Wonder Woman. Is that how you're going to play this? Yes, I'm smart...smart enough to know you don't give a rat's ass whether or not I can escape Tesler. You just want me to volunteer so you'll feel okay about this. If you turn me over, he'll kill me before I get a chance to fight."

Joey shook his head. "He doesn't want you dead. This

isn't about status or reputation. If it was, he'd have asked for Clay, not you."

"So what does that tell you?"

He looked at me as if he didn't understand the question.

"Tesler wants me. The female. Do you think he plans to woo me with roses and candlelight?"

"Well, no. I guess he..."

"You guess *what*?"

His gaze slunk to the side again, "It's my son's *life*, Elena. And if Tesler wants you, that means he won't kill you. You'll get a chance to escape. There will be time for Clay to get here."

I could only stare, blood pounding in my ears. "You're saying I should let him rape me, for as long as possible, because it will kill time until my white knight can arrive?"

"It wouldn't have to be rape," he mumbled.

The pounding blood filled my head. "Are you... are you asking me to seduce...?"

"Willing or not willing, Clay would understand. You did what you had to and he'd forgive you."

"For—forgive me? He'd *forgive* me if I got raped?"

"No, I meant it would be okay. He'd still—"

"Want me? Touch me?" My voice had taken on a note between rage and outrage. "Is that what you think I'm worried about? Whether he'd still want me if I've been raped?"

I yanked at my bonds so hard I felt blood trickle down my arms, but I kept pulling, struggling to get to him, to grab him by the hair and smash that self-absorbed—

A flicker of movement in the woods stopped me cold, my rage congealing into terror. I was still bound and helpless, having spent my time threatening and fighting the only person who could save me. Now Joey would shove me out the door and speed away without a backward glance and I'd—

A porcupine poked its head from the trees and looked quizzically at the car. Around it, the forest stayed motionless.

I still had time. *Now stop screwing around and use it!*

When I turned back to Joey, the fear and rage had frozen over, cold and hard now, my brain and my path now clear.

"Do you really think Tesler is going to give Noah to you? Ever? Why should he? You've proven you'll do anything he asks in the faint hope of getting him back."

"Which will keep him alive." His gaze lifted to mine. "Maybe they won't let him go today or tomorrow, but as long as it's to their advantage, he'll live."

"So you're willing to do whatever it takes to keep him alive? Including tossing them the wife of your old buddy, to be raped, tortured and possibly killed? Just so your son can live another day?"

To protect my own children, I'd go farther than I care to contemplate. But I would never do this—throw their captors another victim to buy time I had no intention of using.

Joey was like a fugitive, holed up and surrounded by police, shooting random passersby simply to buy more time, to keep the cops at bay while praying the hand of the Almighty would reach down from the heavens and save him, because he sure as hell didn't plan on doing it himself.

"And then what?" I asked.

He looked at me blankly.

"And then what?" I repeated. "I make this sacrifice and I distract them, and you will use that time to..."

"I-I'll figure something out."

"Of course you will. You may not be stronger than them, but you're definitely smarter. You'll outwit them."

He nodded, relieved that I understood.

"Bullshit. If you were smarter than them, we wouldn't be sitting here. We'd be up at that meeting point, and I'd be slumped in this seat, pretending I was doped up and out cold. Clay would be lurking downwind in the forest. Travis Tesler would arrive. You'd make the exchange. You'd take Noah. Tesler would grab me and I'd kill him while Clay killed his brother. The end."

Joey stared at me. He blinked. He swallowed. His lips formed an "oh," but all that emerged was a faint sound of pain. And with that, my hate evaporated, leaving only a thin film of disgust, even that bringing a stab of guilt.

It'd been twenty-five years since Joey had been a Pack wolf, and even then, he'd never been in the thick of it. Expecting him to know how to deal with his son's abduction was like plucking a random human off the street, kidnapping his kid and expecting him to make the right choices. I couldn't hate him for what he'd done, but still that veneer of disgust refused to disappear, turning my words brittle.

"You won't figure out how to free your son. They'll wring everything they can out of you, and then they'll kill you. The only way to rescue him is to trust us. Starting with untying me, so if they show up, I'm not completely helpless."

He hesitated only a split-second before giving a defeated nod, and doing it.

"It would have been easier if we'd skipped the whole 'drugging and kidnapping' scenario, but it's too late for that, so the first thing you need to do is get us out of here before they find us."

Headlights off, he restarted the car as I kept talking.

"Once we reach the highway, you'll call Tesler. You'll say your plan failed. You bought Malaysian food, hoping to hide the drugs in something spicy and unfamiliar, but Clay wanted plain American fare. You're going to try again when we go out for drinks later. You'll call him when it's done."

As I talked, Joey nodded constantly, first anxiously agreeing with anything I said, praying I had a clue what I was talking about, then nodding faster as he realized I did.

"Put the car in reverse...and let's get out of here."

He did. And we didn't.

The tires spun, the small car burrowing deeper into the snow-covered lane. I scanned the dark forest anxiously as the whine of the engine buzz-sawed through the silence. He put the car in drive, then reverse, but it only rocked back and forth, getting more entrenched.

"Keep it in reverse," I said as I swung open the door.

I stepped out. It was like putting my foot into a bucket of ice water. Apparently, dressing me for the weather hadn't been one of Joey's concerns. I still wore jeans, a long-sleeved jersey and sneakers.

"Here," he said. "Switch. I'll get out and—"

"No."

There was no time for that, not with the sound of our

escape attempt echoing through the forest. I tramped to the front of the car, cursing Joey under my breath, this time for his rotten choice of transportation. Selling a fancy little car like this in Alaska should be illegal. Did it even have snow tires?

I planted myself in front of the car, pushed . . . and felt it push back.

"Rev—!" I started to yell over the whine of the engine, before catching myself and mouthing and pantomiming "reverse."

Joey nodded frantically, reached for the gear shift and—

I smelled Travis Tesler before I saw him, and my body recognized the scent before my brain could process it. I whipped my head around to see him making his way through the trees.

"Need a hand, honey?" he called.

Another scent flitted past on a crosswind, and I wheeled as Eddie came up behind me. To my left was a distant third figure, closing in, the three surrounding me and cutting off my escape routes.

I turned to the car. Joey hadn't noticed the mutts yet. His hands still gripped the wheel, his head bobbing to tell me he had it in reverse now, so go ahead and push.

I looked at Tesler. The bubble of panic rose, then popped, evaporating as my muscles tensed, the fight-or-flight response kicking in, my brain veering wildly between the two.

Fight or flight. Fight wouldn't be easy, with my only ally as useless as a Pomeranian at a pit-bull match.

No, fighting wasn't an option. Flight was—leap onto the

car, race over the top and take the only unguarded route into the forest. Run and leave Joey to his fate, hope that distracted them. And why shouldn't I? It was no less than he'd planned for me.

I put my hands on the hood, braced myself . . . and gave a tremendous heave. The car jumped up and out of the rut, accelerating backward a dozen feet before Joey hit the brakes.

That's when he saw Eddie coming up behind me, and Tesler, just beyond his driver's side door. Joey waved frantically for me to get into the car, but I knew I couldn't make it, had known it when I gave that shove.

So I waved just as frantically as Joey, mouthing "Get Clay!" then spun and raced toward the one figure who hadn't yet emerged from the shadows. I heard the brothers coming after me . . . then the roar of Joey's car as he sped off.

CAPRICIOUS

AS I BARRELED through the trees, I saw the third werewolf ahead. The figure was as slight as a woman and no more than five foot six. The gait, though, was masculine. His head stayed down as he tramped through the snow, in no hurry to get to the clearing and see what waited there.

When he heard us, he lifted his head. I knew who he was—had known it from the moment I'd spotted his figure in the distance.

His face was young and smooth, with light brown hair hanging into dark eyes. He reached up and impatiently swiped his hair back as he squinted at me, his night vision still poor, his first Change barely behind him.

Noah Stillwell. Joey's captive son—not bound and forced forward at gunpoint, but on his own, ready to help his pack mates take down their prey.

When he realized who was running straight at him, his hands flew up awkwardly, as if he hadn't yet decided whether to stop me, attack me or fend me off.

With scarcely a falter in my stride, I grabbed the front of

his jacket, yanked him off his feet and flung him to the side. I couldn't imagine either brother stopping to help the fallen boy, and they didn't, but the path was narrow and as Noah scrambled up, he got in their way, a chorus of grunts and curses echoing behind me. I hunched over, picking a path where the snow lay thinnest over the ground and running full out.

Running has always been my strong point. I'm particularly skilled at running away from things. I've been doing it my whole life, and not just metaphorically.

I've spent the last decade learning to stand firm and face my problems . . . or at least batter them until they're unrecognizable. So now, when I ran from the Teslers, it hurt—a mental pain so acute it was like running across a bed of nails, the spikes driving into my soles with every stride.

I told myself I wasn't running away, that this was just part of a plan that would eventually end in a standoff, a challenge and, of course, victory. The only part missing? The actual plan.

I darted through the trees, steering for the thickest part to hide my pale shirt and hair. Gradually, the sounds of pursuit faded, then stopped altogether.

I didn't kid myself. I hadn't lost them—they could easily follow my scent trail. They'd just stopped chasing me. I was miles from any populated place, running through the frozen Alaska wilderness dressed in a shirt and sneakers. They would regroup and come up with a plan to track and capture me. And I'd use this time to change into something a little warmer.

I just needed to get a little farther from them, so I could

relax enough for the Change. I'd gone about twenty more feet when bobbing lights ahead had me plunging into the undergrowth. Once I was hidden, I peered out.

I could see a cluster of three distant lights, bobbing at waist level. Flashlights? A fourth joined the group, then a fifth and as I squinted, I heard the faint rumble of engines. Snowmobiles.

I remembered what Dan had said—that the Teslers had two other mutts in their group, currently in the Lower 48 setting up trade routes. Could the Teslers have recalled them when we killed Dan? Possible, but if they had, they would have accompanied Noah and the brothers to the exchange. Far more likely, this was a group of humans. And if it was, then I'd run to them for help. My pride could withstand that indignity better than what was in store for me if the Teslers caught up.

Still, the small chance it was the mutts meant I slid cautiously from the bushes. The headlights bounced along like giant fireflies, the engines a low and steady rumble.

As I walked, the lights moved farther away. Did snowmobiles have rear lights? I had no idea, but they were clearly heading in the opposite direction. I broke into a slow jog.

The lights kept moving, no faster than me. Yet the engine rumble seemed to get louder, as if I was catching up.

I stopped. The hairs on my neck prickled as I looked around. The forest shimmered under the moon, a dusting of new snow glimmering on every branch. Quiet had fallen— not the unnatural silence that preceded the appearance of the beast, just an odd hush, as if even the night animals were careful not to make too much noise.

The lights stayed exactly where they were when I stopped. As if they were waiting for me...

Whoever was out there couldn't see me from here. Surely they'd stopped coincidentally.

I stepped forward. The lights didn't move. I took another step. Still they only bobbed in place. I could hear the engines, also seeming neither closer nor farther, but the rumble oddly muffled.

I didn't hear any sound of pursuit, though, and that was the important thing. I carefully moved toward what seemed to be a break in the forest. I could see the lights flickering through the last curtain of trees.

I stepped to the edge. A laugh came from the other direction. I wheeled. No one was there. The clearing stretched as far as I could see—a ribbon of white bordered by trees. Not a clearing, but a road. Perfect. I grinned. The skin over my cheeks pulled sharply with the sudden movement, as if my face had been mere seconds from freezing solid.

I turned back toward the headlights...and found myself staring down an equally long expanse of winding empty road, with no sign of the lights.

The rumbling of engines continued. I started following the road, looking for a place the snowmobiles could have turned off. Then I spotted the lights again, moving deeper into the woods on the other side.

I glanced each way, assuring myself no one was around, then I started across. A crack ripped through the night, loud as gunfire, and I spun, realizing I was in the middle of the road, too far to dive for cover on either side.

A long, bubbling laugh sounded off to my right, barely

audible over the dull roar of the engines. I peered into the night.

Another crack came. Not from my left or my right...

I looked down. The laugh sounded again, the bubbling burble of water flowing over rocks. With a third crack, a spider web of fissures shot through the "snow" at my feet.

This wasn't a road. It was a river. And I stood in the middle of it.

I looked around, keeping the rest of me perfectly still. The "engines" continued to rumble, water, running fast and free somewhere in front of me. I could see those lights dancing in the forest, and the babble of water still sounded like laughter—taunting laughter now.

I told myself it was Tesler and his buddies with flashlights, but that creeping feeling down my back said otherwise, recalled the lights leading us through the forest two nights ago. There were no humans here. No werewolves. No mysterious beasts. Just something...else. Something primitive, capricious and cruel. Some magic, deep in the forest, that cared little for my survival.

The lights danced for a moment, then winked out.

The ice beneath my feet groaned. I took a careful step. Then slid my other foot forward as slowly and carefully as I could, shifting my weight—

With a tremendous crack, the ice under me gave way and my legs plunged into the water, the cold so unbelievable that my brain shorted out, my gasp ringing in my ears. Then I felt ice under my fingers and under my cheek and I snapped to. I lay half on the ice, blessedly solid—

Without even a warning crack, the piece broke away and

dropped into the river, me still clinging to it. I felt the water surge over me, so cold it was an ice pick to my brain. And then, nothing.

I came to hurtling downstream underwater, caught in the current. I fought, twisting and writhing, but it was like tumbling through space. I had no idea which way was up. The agony of the cold was indescribable and my barely functional brain could only stutter through half-remembered statistics.

It took twenty minutes to die in icy water. Or was that two minutes? No, it had to be ten. At least ten. Please let it be ten.

I finally got my eyes open enough to see the way up— faintly lighter than the other directions. I propelled myself toward it. Up, up—

My fists bashed against solid ice.

I kept bashing, so close to freedom, those statistics circling my head like vultures. But it was like trying to break a window with a feather. My superstrength didn't matter. The water kept me from getting up enough momentum to break the ice.

I was trapped and there wasn't a damn thing I could do about it. All my strength, all my powers, all my instinct to survive—all useless.

When we die, we're supposed to see the faces of our loved ones flashing before our eyes. I wanted that. I so desperately wanted that. Everyone I cared about—Clay, my children, Jeremy, my Pack, my friends.

But my brain wouldn't let me picture them. It just kept

screaming that I was going to die and I had to do something.

I opened my eyes a slit again and saw one patch of ice overhead that was lighter than the rest, as if I could see the snow through it. I swam toward it, fighting the current, barely moving but keeping at it, inch by inch. I knew that patch was probably an illusion—the reflection of a star through the thick ice. I knew I probably wasn't even going to make it that far.

And then I saw my family's faces, not a serene, smiling final portrait of my loved ones, but Kate's blue eyes wide with panic, Logan's dark with worry, Clay's blazing, furious as he snarled at me to stop thinking I wouldn't make it, stop thinking it wouldn't be a hole, just swim, goddamn it, swim!

I reached up. My hands broke the water's surface, then came down on an edge as sharp as a steel blade. I gripped it, but the ice shattered under my fingers.

I pushed my head up, out of the water, gasping. The air felt like red-hot pokers shoved down my throat, the pain nearly making me black out. But I lifted my head above the water until I caught my breath, then felt along the edge of the icy hole. I found the thickest spot and managed to get my chest up onto the ice, but when I tried to push out farther, the ice groaned and cracked.

"Hold still!" a voice shouted.

I turned my head to see a figure running along the river's edge. It was Noah, stripping off his jacket as he ran. I tried to wriggle farther onto the ice.

"Hold still!" he yelled. "If it breaks, you're going under and you aren't coming back up."

He stopped parallel to me, then shimmied out on the ice until he got as far as he deemed safe. He tested it, rocking back and forth, then crouched. Holding one cuff of his jacket, he tossed it toward me. The other sleeve sailed out like a life-rope . . . and fell six inches short of my hand.

I wiggled, trying to reach it, but he yanked the jacket back with an angry "Stay *still*."

Moving on his stomach, he inched farther out, then threw it again. This time, it brushed my fingers. I caught the edge of the cuff, something I could tell by sight alone, my fingers too numb to feel the fabric between them.

I managed to get enough of a grip to tug myself nearer, then wrap it around my wrist. Noah pulled. I kicked, wriggling onto the ice, hearing it crack behind me. Noah kept pulling, carefully, then he heaved. The ice cracked and fell away as I shot toward him.

Noah backed up, still pulling, still telling me not to move, his face taut with concentration, tendons bulging as he dragged me to the riverbank.

"Okay," he said as I came to rest, huddled at the edge. "We need to—"

"What'd you pull out of the river, boy?" a voice echoed from the forest. "Is that my girl?"

Tesler stepped from the woods, his brother at his heels. Noah straightened. He turned from me, and there was my chance to escape. Leap up, knock Noah down and run . . . and I was no more capable of doing that than if I'd been bound hand and foot.

I huddled there, shaking violently. I tried to concentrate, but it was like standing on the precipice to oblivion—it took everything I had just to stay conscious and breathe.

"She fell in," Noah called back. His voice had changed, concern falling away, the timbre deepening, like a teen boy with his buddies. "Stupid city bitch. She ran out onto the river and fell through. If you want her alive, you're going to need to get her back to the cabin, pronto. She needs to get out of those wet clothes."

Tesler bent over me, teeth and eyes glittering. "Well, then, that's what we'll have to do. I wasn't planning to keep her in them for long anyway."

PRIZE

I WISH I could say I fought every step of the way. But even as that primitive part of me went wild with fear and panic, the rational part leapt in.

I could feel my body shutting down, hypothermia like a sedative creeping through my veins, whispering for me to go to sleep, just go to sleep. The only fighting I could do now was to struggle to stay alive. And staying alive at this moment meant letting Tesler sling me over his shoulder and carry me to their cabin.

THEIR "CABIN" WAS a big vacation house. The thick layer of dust over the knickknacks told me it didn't get much use, so I presumed they were squatting here, knowing there was little danger of the owner showing up. The security system had been ripped from the wall. Pizza boxes were piled by the door. Stains covered the carpets. The place reeked like a frat house—of spilled beer and sweaty bodies.

"You need to get her undressed," Noah said, dogging Tesler's heels as he entered the living room.

"Oh, believe me, I'm getting to it."

"Now, Travis. I'm not kidding."

I tried to look at Noah, but he'd turned away. Tesler dumped me on the bearskin rug in front of a smoldering fireplace.

"Strip."

"I'll grab her some—" Noah began.

Tesler wheeled on him. "You'll get her nothing, boy." To me, he said, "Strip. Unless you'd prefer I did it for you."

I pulled off my shirt. It took a few tries—my fingers refused to clamp on the fabric. I finally pushed my hands under and shoved it up over my head.

The cabin was already warm, with the fireplace still going and a woodstove blasting across the room. Tesler threw another log on the fire, then added tinder—pages ripped from books stacked by the fireplace. He looked over sharply as Noah reappeared in the living room, a towel in hand.

"Didn't I tell you—?"

"It's one towel. She needs to dry off." He walked over to me, and lowered his voice. "Don't rub too hard. Just pat your skin. You need to warm up slowly. Don't get close to the fire."

"You're a regular Boy Scout, aren't you?" Tesler said.

Noah shot a glower Tesler's way. "Do you want her *with* her fingers and toes or without?"

I was fumbling with the button on my jeans as Noah approached. He slung the towel over his shoulder and grunted

"Here." He undid the button for me, as circumspectly as he could. His knuckles brushed my belly, but I couldn't feel it. He pulled the zipper down, then hesitated.

"Got it," I said as I wedged my hands under my waistband.

I pushed my jeans down over my hips. He didn't move, staying so close I could hear his breath picking up speed.

"Oh, he's a Boy Scout all right," Eddie said. "Never seen a naked woman before, Noah?"

"Only on his computer screen," Tesler said.

They laughed as Noah muttered, "Fuck off," handed me the towel and started backing up, gaze still on me.

"Better get that bra, too, boy," Tesler said. "I don't want *those* freezing and falling off."

"I can manage." I slipped my hands under the straps. I got them down over my arms, but no farther, the chest band still tightly fastened, cups hanging, fingers too numb to work the front clasp.

"Come on, Noah," Eddie said. "Be a gentleman. Help the lady."

Noah slid forward and stopped in front of me, eyeing the clasp. He unhooked it, hands trembling, fingers grazing the bottom of my breasts as the Teslers laughed at him.

I doubt it was the first time the seventeen-year-old had unfastened a bra, but it was more than that making his breath speed up. His nostrils flared as he drank in my scent.

He took the bra off, wrapped it around his hands and stood there, looking down at me in my panties, his own pants tenting furiously.

"Thanks," I murmured, gaze averted as I took my bra from him.

He backed away slowly, still staring. I tried to wrap the towel around me, but it was only a hand towel—I'm sure Tesler would have taken it away if it covered more. I could feel all three of them staring now. I resisted the urge to cover myself or turn away. If Travis wanted me to cower in shame, I wasn't giving him that satisfaction.

"You forgot something." He pointed at my panties. "Noah, give the lady a hand."

I pushed them down to my ankles and kicked them aside.

"You owe me twenty bucks, bro," Eddie said. "I told you she was a natural blonde."

I moved a little closer to the fire. Not too close, heeding Noah's warning about warming up too fast and knowing it was true—I'd had frostbite before.

A few feet from the fire, I bent and sat cross-legged, then started drying my hair. They continued to stare as if *none* of them had ever seen a naked woman before.

"You know, you look even better without your clothes," Tesler said. "And you looked damned fine in them."

I ignored him and squeezed water out of my hair.

He continued. "I heard you have a couple of kids. Can't tell. You didn't lose your figure, that's for sure."

Actually, any "figure" I had these days came courtesy of my kids. I'd always been thin—athletic and boyish. But now there was some swell to my hips and I'd graduated to a B cup. Not that Clay cared—if he even noticed. Things like that weren't important to him.

At that moment, though, I would have preferred my old body. Maybe it would make Tesler change his mind. Wishful thinking, I know. He didn't care what I looked like. His interest had nothing to do with sex and attraction. It was all about dominance and control.

"I want her," Noah said, making my head whip around. He turned so I couldn't see his face, then said again, "I want her."

"I'm sure you do," Tesler chuckled. "And if you're a very good boy, I'll let you take a ride, just as soon as I've had my fill."

"I want to go first."

Tesler sputtered. "Excuse me?"

Noah turned toward him, face still averted from me. "Without me, you'd be humping a frozen corpse. I saved her. I risked my own life to do it. I deserve the first go."

"And I'm supposed to take seconds?" An edge crept into Tesler's voice.

"Just once. After that, she's all yours."

"Is she?" Tesler advanced on the boy. "How generous of you."

Eddie stepped between them. "Come on. Let the kid lose his cherry with a female werewolf. How many guys get that chance?"

"I'm not a—" Noah stopped, realizing it wouldn't help his cause to say he wasn't a virgin.

He still wouldn't look my way. He couldn't. As I stared at him, the anger rose. He'd been nice to me. Even when he'd been gawking, he'd seemed embarrassed. Faced with three antagonists, I'd looked for a friendly face and been too eager to see it, unconsciously shifting Noah into the role of potential ally.

I'd forgotten what he really was—a punk who'd let his grandfather be murdered by his new pals. Part of me had hoped that there was an explanation. Now I realized there wasn't. Dennis had taken Noah in and given him a chance to start over. Noah had repaid him by hooking up with these murdering bastards. That blood of Noah's I'd found in the cabin? It could have come from a fight with Dennis, not defending him.

Noah was studiously avoiding my gaze; he might not have a rapist's heart, but he still saw me as an object. He wanted me, and what I thought of that didn't matter. The only person whose opinion counted was Tesler.

"Fine," Tesler said. "He'll get a werewolf for his first time . . . just as soon as I'm finished."

"You're a little rough with the ladies, bro," Eddie said. "Let the kid go first. He's been good. He deserves a reward."

Tesler glanced over and fixed his brother with a look that made Noah flinch. Eddie didn't even blink.

"It's just a girl, Travis," he said, his voice low. "No big deal."

"She's not just—"

"Just a girl." Eddie met his brother's gaze. "No big deal, right?"

I remembered what Dan had said, how Tesler had promised his brother he'd stop raping girls. The two stared each other down for a minute, then Tesler turned that stare on Noah, as if hoping he'd get the kid to back down. Noah blinked, but nothing more.

"All right," Tesler said after a minute. "Here's the deal. Blondie here is indeed a proper prize, so let's do this properly. If you want her, you have to win her...by challenging me."

"Oh, for fuck's sake, Travis. The kid can't—"

"No, that's fine." Noah's chin lifted. "I accept."

"Great." Tesler headed for the kitchen, thumping Noah on the back as he passed. "Give me a minute to grab a beer, then we'll get started."

"In the meantime," Eddie said to Noah. "Take a look out front, make sure we aren't about to entertain any unwanted guests."

I hoped that meant I'd be left alone while Noah and Eddie went outside, but I knew better. Noah got on his gear and left. Eddie just walked to the window to look out. I could probably take him, but not without alerting his brother.

Noah had no hope of beating Tesler. I don't know why he'd even agreed to try—teenage ego, I suppose. But the more I thought about it, the more I wanted Noah to win that match. Not that I'd prefer Noah. When it comes to rape, there is no "prefer."

But if Noah won, he'd get time alone with me, time in which Tesler could expect to hear noises, even sounds of struggle. And that would give me the perfect opportunity to escape. Tesler wasn't the only one who could easily take on a boy like Noah.

But there was the rub—Tesler could take the kid, no question, meaning there was no chance Noah would win the challenge. Unless...

Tesler sauntered back into the living room, chugging his beer.

"So what's the handicap?" I asked.

He raised his brows, not lowering the can.

"It's going to take a lot of those to make it a fair fight," I said.

He sputtered beer. "Fair fight?"

"Foreign concept?"

Eddie chuckled. Tesler only snorted and continued drinking.

I walked over to him. "Why tell the kid he can fight for me when he doesn't have a hope of winning? Either tell him no or make it a fair fight by handicapping yourself."

"How? Tie both hands behind my back?"

"What are you worried about?"

His smirk froze, eyes icing over. "Worried?"

Noah came inside, cold air blasting down the hall.

"I guess there's no way you want him winning," I said. "If he gets first dibs, he might show you up."

He hit me so fast I didn't see it coming.

As I lay on the floor, Eddie shook his head, as if to say, *What did you expect?*

Noah had his coat off, boots still on, hair salted with snow. "What's going on?"

No one answered. I got up, swiped away blood trickling from a scrape on my elbow, grabbed my discarded towel and cleaned my fingers. Then I walked up to Tesler.

"Struck a sore spot, did I?" I said.

When he raised his hand to hit me again, I didn't flinch.

Dismay flashed in his eyes before he tossed the empty can aside and stalked back to the kitchen.

I started to follow.

Noah caught my elbow. "Don't bait—"

I shook him off and walked into the kitchen. Tesler was rooting through the fridge.

"I can see why you'd be worried," I said. "He's seventeen. What he lacks in finesse, he'll make up for in vigor. He's in his sexual prime... And how old are you?"

He popped open a beer.

"About forty-five, I'd guess. Getting a little harder to, well, get harder, I bet."

He kept his gaze fixed on the fascinating contents of the refrigerator. To get angry would be to confirm it.

"That's about the same age as your hubby, isn't it?" he said. "Got some experience with little blue pills?"

I laughed. "Definitely not. Clay doesn't need pills—or rape—to get it up."

The look he turned on me was pure hatred. And I knew that I'd just sealed my fate. Blow this, and I wouldn't just be raped, I'd be raped, beaten and killed—and no swift painless death either. A cold ball of panic congealed in my stomach, the little-girl voice screaming at me, demanding to know what the hell I was doing. I stifled it.

The key to not getting killed was not to blow this chance. Push, push and push until I got what I wanted, consequences be damned.

"No offense," I said, "but I'd prefer the kid."

He smiled, teeth bared. "I'm sure you would."

He guzzled the beer. I walked closer, making no attempt to cover my nakedness, and stopped a foot from him.

"How about you fight me instead?" I said.

He stopped with the can at his lips, then lowered it. "What?"

"Let me fight in the kid's place. That will make it fair. Same deal applies. I win, he gets me. You win..." I looked him in the eye. "I'm all yours."

He looked back at me and for the first time since we'd met, I wasn't afraid. Clay had been right—stand my ground and Tesler wouldn't stand his. His face darkened with fury, and I knew there was only one thing he could think about, only one thing he wanted: to regain control.

There was no logical reason to grant my request. Better to let Noah challenge him, beat the crap out of the kid and teach him a lesson. Take on me, and he could open himself up to the unbearable humiliation of losing to a woman.

But if he won, he would truly win, and the spark of defiance in my eyes would be doused forever. He could regain control, beat the crap out of me and even Eddie couldn't complain about it. Take me in a fair fight, then take his prize when it would taste the sweetest.

When Tesler opened his lips, I knew what was going to come out. Two words.

"You're on."

COMBAT

ONCE THE INITIAL thrill of success passed, I realized I was in deep shit. I might not have any external injuries from my plunge into icy water, but I felt like I'd swum across the English Channel. Every muscle ached and I was dead tired.

If I didn't fight, though, I could skip the "tired" part of that cliché. I'd just be plain old dead. And that's what I had to remember. Physical injuries were one thing, but I would not lose a fight for lack of will power. I just had to work past it. I could rest all I wanted later.

My odds of beating Tesler were about fifty-fifty. I could swing them a little more my way because I had seen him fight before, but I didn't want to get cocky.

If I lost, I'd be raped, beaten and killed . . . not necessarily in that order. There was still a chance Joey and Clay would find me in time, but my optimism on that front had faded the moment I sent Joey on his way. I'd led him to believe Clay would kill him horribly for his betrayal. And now I expected him to run back and tell Clay I was in the enemy's hands . . . and that he'd put me there?

I wouldn't be surprised if he'd hit the highway and kept going. In fact, I'd be shocked if he hadn't.

So I could only pray that fighting for my life would give me all the extra adrenaline I needed.

TESLER SEEMED PERFECTLY happy to make me fight naked—go figure. It was Eddie and Noah who argued—Noah protesting and Eddie acting as if his brother was obviously joking, which eventually forced Tesler to play along and say, sure, he was kidding and of course I could get dressed . . . as long as I wore my own clothes. What he didn't realize is that I'd draped them by the fireplace, so they were warm and partially dry.

Noah and Eddie cleared the living room, shoving the furniture against the walls. Then Tesler and I moved into the center of the room and faced off like boxers. He even bounced on his toes for good effect.

"Last chance to change your mind," he said. "Don't expect me to hold anything back just because you're a woman."

"I don't."

"You're going to come out of this feeling a helluva lot worse than you do right now."

"I expect to. And I appreciate you giving me the option, but I'm fine. I'll extend you the same courtesy, though, if you want to back out."

His expression sent a chill through me, and deep inside, that child's voice started screaming at me not to fight, never fight, I couldn't win, I'd only get hurt.

But I wasn't twelve years old anymore. I could beat this son of a bitch.

"You think you're tough, don't you?" Tesler said.

"No, not particul—"

He sprang, palms smacking into my shoulders. The floor disappeared under my feet and my head struck it with a crack that sent consciousness on a split-second holiday. I came to with Tesler towering over me, his hand wrapped in the front of my shirt. Before I could register what was happening, I was sailing through the air again. This time I slammed into the wall.

As I wobbled to my feet, the little-girl voice in me screamed and sobbed.

Why did you have to fight him? You know how that goes. Never, ever fight. You'll only get hurt and it all ends up the same, no matter what you do. You can't fight them. You can't.

Tesler strode over. "Want to change your mind? My offer's still open."

Yes, oh God yes! It's not too late. Tell him you'll be good. Then let him do what he wants. Just go to the place where he can't hurt you and everything will be okay.

Only it *wouldn't* be okay. My childhood self had faced many monsters, but none like this. For Tesler, regaining control wouldn't be enough. Complete destruction of the threat was required. There was no secret place that would save me from that.

I rose halfway, then pretended to collapse, wincing.

He bent over me. "Giving up? Good, because—"

My feet smacked him square in the chest and sent him reeling. I jumped up and hit him twice, then kicked and he went down. I'd aimed for the stone fireplace, and his head struck with a very satisfying crunch.

I walked over as he lay on the ground, shaking his head.

"If you want to quit, just say so," I said.

He leapt up with a growl. I feinted out of his way. We danced for a while before I landed a blow, then he blocked the second and got in a hard jab . . . and so it went.

It didn't take me long to reevaluate those odds and slant them in Tesler's favor. We had equal experience. But he was so much stronger that each blow sent me flying. He was also mad as hell and determined to put this bitch in her place. I was equally determined not to let him do that. But while his rage fueled his fists, mine fogged my brain—my best fighting tool.

Every time he landed a blow, my old fears surfaced, occupying the part of my mind that should be analyzing his moves and strategizing mine. I kept trying to pull myself back on track, focusing on his style and learning from it. It didn't work. I was losing and Tesler knew it. I saw it in his eyes as his fist connected and I went down. I felt it, too, as he pinned me, his erection grinding into my thigh.

When I felt that, the little girl in me went wild, gibbering with fear. I squeezed my eyes shut, struggling to quiet her. And then . . . and then I opened them and released her. I let that base terror shine.

And, oh, how he loved that, lust clouding his eyes. He pinned me harder, his crotch moving on mine, grinding until it hurt. Blood dripped from his lips onto mine. Sweat plinked into my eyes. The hated smell of him filled my nostrils.

I shrank back. "I-if I surrender . . ." I swallowed.

"Yes?"

I licked my lip, tasting his blood. "If I do what you want . . ."

"Yes?"

"Will you let me go afterward?"

"You'll do what I want? Everything I want?"

I nodded.

"And you'll behave? Be a good girl?"

I nodded.

He lowered his lips to my ear and whispered. "Then you aren't going to *want* me to let you go. But yes, when we've both had our fill, you're welcome to leave."

He moved his lips over mine again and hovered there. I lifted my head from the ground, and I kissed him—and it was just as nauseating as I'd imagined. I concentrated on the taste of his blood, nipping his lip, drawing more. He mistook my biting for passion and kissed me harder.

I closed my eyes so he wouldn't see my revulsion, but I don't think he would have noticed anyway. When he broke the kiss, his eyes were unfocused, dark with lust, his body relaxing against mine.

His lips moved back to my ear. "See, it isn't so bad, is—?"

I smashed my elbow into his throat so hard he fell back, gargling. I rolled and slammed my palm into his nose. Blood spurted. He gave a strangled cry, but recovered fast. I was already on my feet and he didn't make it past a crouch before my foot connected with his jaw, toppling him backward. A second kick and he spun, his forehead smacking the fireplace as he fell.

As I watched him lying there, on his stomach, blood pooling, I realized I didn't need an elaborate escape plan. Just kill the bastard. Kill him and—

A hand grabbed my ponytail and wrenched me back. I sailed off my feet, but twisted, finding my footing and coming up swinging. But Eddie still had my ponytail wrapped around his hand and yanked me like a dog on a leash, keeping me from hitting him.

"Enough," he said. "He's down. You win."

"The hell she does." Out of the corner of my eye, I saw Tesler wobble to his feet.

"She wins," Eddie said.

The brothers faced off in silence. I expected Tesler to argue. I prayed he'd argue. Blood streamed into his eyes and he could barely stand upright. Just give me a few minutes more, and I'd never have to worry about Travis Tesler again. He had no chance of winning, not now, after I'd tasted victory—could still taste it, his blood on my lips.

But apparently his confidence had taken a bruising, too, enough to sink under the weight of his survival instinct. "Fine," he said. Then he turned to Noah and snapped, "Get her out of my sight. You have twenty minutes. Then she's mine."

ESCAPE

NOAH HUSTLED ME to what was obviously "his" room, judging by the clothing on the floor and on every piece of furniture. He got me inside, then closed the door. At this point, the ideal strategy would be seduction. Lower his defenses, as I had with Tesler, then take him out and escape.

But as repugnant as the thought of kissing Tesler had been, faking attraction to a teenage boy was out of the question.

I managed to sit woodenly on the edge of the bed, then steeled myself to pull off my shirt, praying that would be all the distraction needed to get in a good, incapacitating blow. But I wasn't the only one who was nervous. Noah locked and double-checked the door, then moved to the window. He peered out, not pulling the blind, just squinting into the darkness as if expecting Tesler or Eddie to pop up like drunken guests on his wedding night.

And while he was engrossed in the view, with his back to me, I crept up behind him. Too late, I noticed my reflection in the window glass. He wheeled, his hands going up as they had in the woods, unsure whether to fight back or just ward me off.

At the last second, he went for option three—get the hell out of the way. I managed to catch his shirt collar as he dove past me. I whipped him off his feet again. Unlike in the woods, I couldn't throw him aside—the Tesler brothers would hear the crash and know it wasn't just rough sex . . . at least, not after only two minutes in the bedroom.

So I threw Noah facedown on the bed. As I pressed his face into the pillow, he kicked and flailed. I gritted my teeth against the blows, grabbed a discarded shirt and made a gag of it, tying the sleeves behind his head.

He relaxed then, realizing I'd been trying to silence him . . . but not permanently. When I grabbed a belt, though, and yanked his hands behind his back, he wrenched hard, and the sudden movement freed one of his hands. A well-placed jab to my throat freed the other.

I dove after him, but he danced back, moving not toward the door, but to the window. Still gagged, he gestured at it emphatically.

Was someone out there? Was that what had caught his attention earlier? Tesler spying on us? Or—my heart leapt—Clay?

I still grabbed Noah by the collar, but only to keep a hold on him as I peered out, trying to see what he'd seen. He yanked down the gag but said nothing, just shook his head, eyes rolling at the dense woman who couldn't understand his wild gestures.

He pointed at the window, then at me. The window. Me. Telling me . . . to escape?

I couldn't risk talking—the Teslers might overhear, so I pantomimed opening the window and climbing out, and he nodded. Then he pointed at himself and the window, gesturing that this was an escape plan for two.

So he hadn't been after sex at all. What Noah wanted, it seemed, was the same thing I had—a chance to run away. But that begged one question. Why? He could have made a run for it back in the forest.

It was a trap. It had to be.

But to what end? Thwart my escape to impress Tesler? He'd only mock and punish Noah for letting me almost get away in the first place. There had to be a motive, but I wasn't getting it—and the longer I pondered, the faster my chance slipped away. Get out and deal with him later.

I eased open the window. The screen was already off. I crawled out, sucking in a gasp as my stockinged feet hit the snow. Ignoring the cold, I dashed behind the nearest bushes. Then I watched as Noah came out. As he ran toward me, I tensed, ready to throw the first punch.

"Coats and boots are around the side," he whispered. "I snuck them out when Eddie sent me on patrol."

He pointed. When I took a step in that direction, he caught my arm and I spun, fists going up. He fell back, releasing me.

"No, I just— You're going to take me with you, right? I saved you, so now you'll take me along."

I looked into his eye for some sign of a trick, but saw only panic.

"Please," he said. "I had nothing to do with—" His voice caught. "With Dennis. I didn't even know they'd—I thought—" He swallowed. "I thought I was protecting him, but—" He swallowed. "After they killed him, they told me Joseph was next if I didn't— Only they were telling Joseph the same thing."

"They said they'd kill your dad if you ran off, while telling *him* they'd kill *you*." Easier than actually holding him hostage, especially when they were shorthanded. A kid with Noah's problems wouldn't be quick to figure out the scam . . . or a good solution.

He nodded. "When I found you in the river, I thought we could take off together. Only—"

"Only they showed up, so this was the backup plan. All right. We'll get out of here and I'll take you to your dad."

He shook his head. "No. I want you to take me back to the Pack. That's what he—" Grief filled his eyes. He blinked it back. "That's what Dennis wanted. He kept trying to talk me into it, but I wouldn't listen, wouldn't even let him ask you guys. If I had—if I'd made him come with me . . ."

"I'll take you back to the Pack. Now, let's get—"

"Looking for these?"

Tesler stepped into the moonlight, holding two coats and pairs of boots. He tossed them into the snow.

"I-I wanted to do it outside," Noah said.

"In stocking feet?"

"I-I thought we'd Change and, you know, do it as wolves."

"Quit while you're ahead, kid. So what happened? Let me guess, you fell in love at first poke and decided to run off together? No, for that you'd need to be all grown up. You don't want a girlfriend. You want a mommy, someone who will rescue you from the big, nasty wolves and take you back to the Pack. Am I close?"

"Only because you overheard us," I said.

He ignored me, gaze still on Noah. "You think they're going to take you, boy? Sure, blondie here might feel sorry for you. But the minute her hubby lays eyes on you will be the last minute you lay eyes on anything...if you're lucky. Do you know what Clayton Danvers does to mutts?" He pantomimed a chainsaw pull. "Bye-bye body parts."

As he talked, I took stock of my surroundings. No convenient stones to whip at his head. No convenient cliff to throw him off. No convenient jagged tree stump to impale him on. Damn. I was going to have to do this the hard way.

While he yapped, I sidled closer. He didn't seem to notice—bullying Noah was so much more fun.

I was about to take another step when Eddie came around the side of the house. *That* Tesler noticed.

"I've got it," Tesler said. "Go back inside."

"Let me grab the kid," Eddie said. "You can deal with—"

"I said, I've got it." Tesler's voice lowered to a growl.

His ego had taken a beating earlier. Now he was going to redeem it by proving he could handle a woman and a kid without his brother's help. And if that's what he wanted, I wasn't about to argue. Eddie hesitated, then retreated. I listened for the door, but didn't hear it. He hadn't gone back inside. Damn.

"So what sob story did the kid tell you?" Tesler asked with only a flickering glance my way. "How we killed his granddaddy and he had nothing to do with it?"

"I didn't," Noah said, lip curling in a snarl.

"Sure you did. You led us right to the cabin."

"You followed me!"

"No, I do believe you followed us first." Again, Tesler glanced my way, but fleetingly, as if he couldn't quite make full eye contact yet. "Did he tell you that? He found us in Anchorage. Gotta hand it to the kid—he's got balls. Too bad he lacks brains. Takes after his granddaddy."

Noah rushed at Tesler. I grabbed his shirt and hauled him back, murmuring, "That's what he wants."

"Oh, come on. He just wants to shut me up before I tell you why he came to us. Why he gave us all kinds of intel on the local wildlife—drug dealers, gun-runners, smugglers. A choirboy he ain't, no matter how sweet he might look."

I eased away from Noah, circling Tesler, who kept his gaze on his target.

Noah's chin lifted. "I wanted money, so I sold them information, but only about that stuff. I would never have led them to Dennis. They followed me and I tried to fight—"

"You're a little thug," Tesler said. "Hick town white trash who thinks he's cool because he's grown fangs and claws. But when things get ugly, he wants his mommy...or the nearest substitute."

I charged Tesler. He braced for a blow, but instead I launched myself at him, hitting him hard, knocking him off his feet. I flipped him onto his stomach before he landed, then crushed his face into the snowy ground, stifling any cries that would bring his brother running.

As Tesler struggled, I waved for Noah to go. When he didn't, I snarled a silent "Run!" Still he hesitated. I smacked

Tesler into the ground, then surreptitiously pinned him with my knee, and released him, making it look as if I'd knocked him unconscious. I gestured for Noah to go, that I was right behind him. He took off, motioning for me to grab the extra coat and boots as he took his.

Noah was barely out of sight before Tesler threw me off. We fought. I might have had a chance, if Eddie hadn't heard and come ripping around the corner. Some of the fight went out of me then.

As hard as I tried to ignore Eddie, I knew that the minute his brother was in serious danger, he'd leap in, and I couldn't take them both. Realizing that was like pinching off the adrenaline pump that had kept me going. Every bruise from our earlier fight flared, every joint screamed, my head throbbed and the exhaustion of fighting my way back from hypothermia seeped into every muscle of my body.

Finally, Tesler had me pinned by the throat. I found my strength again, wildly fighting as his hand crushed my windpipe. I gasped and gurgled, then blacked out. When I recovered, he'd eased off, but was looming over me, his expression warning I had only to twitch and he'd choke me again.

I lashed out, trying to jab his eye, unable to reach, his hands tightening around my throat again, smiling, elated for the excuse. As I fought, that little-girl voice screamed for me to stop. I couldn't. I blacked out again. When I came to, I saw flashes of my family—no serene last portrait, but their anger, their confusion.

Was I going to die to avoid being raped? Did I think that was somehow noble, defiant? No, it would mean letting

Tesler win in a far worse way—proving that he'd found the thing that scared me more than any other.

I stopped struggling. But as hard as that voice screamed, I wouldn't retreat into my safe place. I wouldn't look away. Travis Tesler might have won the battle for physical domination, but that was all he was getting. I promised myself that any satisfaction he gained from the next few minutes would be short lived. He would die for this. And I would be the one to kill him.

He grabbed my breasts. Grabbed, rubbed, squeezed until it hurt. I wouldn't look away. When he ground his hips against mine...there was nothing to grind. He was limp. He forced my hand down and made me rub him. Nothing happened.

"It's too cold," Eddie said. "Get her inside."

Tesler ignored him. He ground against me, pawed me, hurt me. I kept staring at him, and that was all it took.

He smacked my face. Once, twice. My nose bled into the snow, but still I turned back to him and met his gaze.

"Come on, Travis," Eddie said. "It's fucking freezing out here. Get her inside and you can—"

"Shut up."

He hit me again. Consciousness threatened another holiday, but I blinked it back and kept staring.

Eddie stepped toward us, hands out as if to pull his brother off me. Tesler swung at him, catching him in the thigh, making his leg buckle.

"I said back off," Tesler snarled.

"Or what? You'll choke me, too? Christ, Travis. It's a girl. Just a fucking girl. She's not worth this."

Tesler paused, then slowly nodded. "You're right. She's not." He turned to me, lip curled, teeth bared. "You think you're too good for me, bitch? You think I'm the worst thing that can happen to you? My brother's right. You've taken up too much of my time already. Eddie? Grab me some rope."

STAKED

I FOUGHT AGAIN, but it was too late. Even with the specter of a lynching dangling before me, I didn't have what it took to escape. I cursed my weakness. I hated myself for not finding some hidden well of strength. But I just didn't have anything left.

As I quickly discovered, lynching wasn't what he had in mind. He bound my ankles, then tied my wrists behind my back, as Eddie held me still. Once I was secured, Tesler ordered Eddie back inside. Eddie went—I was no danger to his brother now, and that was all that mattered.

Tesler started pulling me by the long end of the rope. He dragged me over every buried limb and rock, through every bush. Very satisfying, I'm sure, but he wasn't in the best of shape himself, and apparently my stifled yelps weren't worth the effort of dragging me over and through obstacles. So he threw me over his shoulder, and settled for verbal bullying.

"Do you know what's out here?" he said. "Something a lot worse than me. You've been running around these woods, you and your hubby. Have you seen our beast? I bet you have. It's curious, always sniffing around. It doesn't give us any trouble though. Know why? Because I figured out what it likes. The same thing I do."

"The missing girls," I whispered before I could stop myself.

"You saw the posters? Bet you figured I was responsible, didn't you?"

"You were."

"Just for taking them up on their offer. No one made them have a drink with me. No one forced them into my truck. They came along willingly. But as you may have guessed, I don't much like willing women."

"Where are they?"

"Here and there. Bits of them anyway. When I was done, I left them for our beast friend. You know how some werewolves have a reputation for eating after fucking? Well, they've got nothing on this bastard. I swear he was chowing down before he finished. Should have heard those girls scream."

I gritted my teeth and tried to block his words, to visualize something else. I managed to miss whatever he said next, then he dumped me onto the ground, jarring me back to the present.

I tried to stand up, but I could only twist and writhe. He grabbed the rope dangling from my hands and dragged me to a tree. I fought harder then, but it was no good. Even if I managed to get a limb free, he'd only truss me up again. So I waited as he tied the rope to the tree.

Then he stepped back and smiled. "Scared now?"

I said nothing. Did nothing. Just stood there and stared

at him. He lifted a hand to cuff me, then pulled back, pasting on that smile again.

"Oh, you're scared. And you'll be a helluva lot more scared when you see what's coming for you." He surveyed me. "You know what we really need? A video camera. Now that would be a home movie to pass along, make every mutt on the continent forget those faded photos of your hubby's work. Maybe I'll send them as a package deal. See what happens when you piss off Clayton Danvers? Well, here's what happens when you piss off Travis Tesler." He strolled over and lowered his face to mine—as close as he could get and stay out of biting range. "Mine would be much more popular viewing, don't you think? The Pack Beta's mate raped and eaten by a wild beast. Werewolf snuff at its finest. Hell, forget cementing my reputation. I'll sell copies and make a fortune."

When I didn't react, he pulled his gaze away and backed off, then cocked his head, as if thinking. "You know, I'm sure I saw a video camera in the cabin. I'll go grab that. Don't start without me, okay?"

I watched him saunter away. And I was left alone...in the Alaskan wilderness, dressed only in a shirt, jeans and socks, tied to a tree and reeking of blood. That's when the panic began to seep in.

I pushed it back and concentrated on getting free. I didn't have a hope in hell of breaking the rope or the tree—both were too sturdy even for werewolf strength. As for undoing the knot, a smart captor—one with some experience at this—knows how to tie his victim's hands so she can't undo them. Tesler had bound my wrists with the backs of my hands together, meaning I couldn't get to the knots. Even if I could, my fingers were too numb to work properly.

I peered into the night. It was as dark and still as ever. When the panic flared again, I berated myself for it. Whatever Tesler had done with the girls, it hadn't been this. That much I knew. Animals have different sexual wiring than us, and while some humans may have an unhealthy interest in them, they don't return it.

Yes, if I died out here, there were plenty of things that would eat my corpse and scatter the parts, and I suspected that was exactly what had happened to those girls. Tesler killed them, then let something—maybe even our mystery beast—do the rest.

If he'd really staked me out to be raped and eaten alive, he'd have stayed to watch. No, he expected to saunter back in a half-hour and find me huddled against the tree, gibbering with terror, begging him to rescue me. Instead, he'd come back and find empty ropes.

I tried rubbing the rope against the tree, but the bark was too smooth. So I whistled as loudly as I could, hoping Noah was close by. Of course, he wasn't. Long gone, I was sure.

For the second time in one night, I'd sacrificed myself to let a Stillwell escape, and though I felt better about doing it for Noah, I was still kicking myself. Yet as foolish as it seemed right now, this was what it meant to be Alpha—the kind Jeremy was and the kind I expected myself to be. It meant being willing to sacrifice yourself for Pack brothers who'd jump in to do the same for you first. Unfortunately, that last part didn't apply with Joey and Noah. So I was on my own.

I still had one trick up my sleeve—my biggest and best.

I took one long look around the forest, assuring myself I was indeed alone. Then I pressed closer to the tree, slackening the rope. I closed my eyes and concentrated on Changing. To do that, though, I had to shift my focus to my body. That's when I realized how cold I was. I couldn't feel my hands, couldn't feel my feet, my ears, my nose, my chin. The wind whistled through my thin shirt and pants and I shivered until I couldn't do anything *except* shiver, my teeth chattering, their clicking filling the silence.

A low whimper bubbled up from my gut. It was so cold, so damned cold. Frostbite was setting in, and if I didn't get warm soon, if I couldn't at least thaw my fingers under my armpits...

Then Change, damn it. Stop whining and Change.

I stumbled on my bound, stockinged feet, trying to inch behind the tree out of the wind, but the rope didn't have enough slack, and an eight-inch-wide trunk was a piss-poor windbreak.

I focused on Changing, but it wouldn't come. I couldn't even relax. It was too cold, too goddamn cold.

And what if I Changed and couldn't get free? Were my wrists bigger than my forelegs? What if I cut off my circulation, the ropes digging through fur and skin?

Stop thinking and Change. If the rope is too tight, you can gnaw through it.

I concentrated, but no matter how hard I tried, I couldn't get started. I was battered, bruised and exhausted. I desperately needed to Change, and that very pressure made it impossible to relax enough to launch the process.

I tried retreating into a mental sanctuary and thought I'd managed it when the distant crack of a branch sent me flailing, too aware that there were things out there, winter-hungry things, and I was defenseless and reeking of blood.

But as hard as I strained to look and listen, I could detect nothing. I settled into my inner place again. Then the tree vibrated against my back and my eyes flew open.

The tree shuddered again. I'm sure the ground did, too—I just couldn't feel it through my numb feet.

Something was walking through the forest. Something big.

As I gulped air, I remembered Tesler's words: *It's curious, always sniffing around.* I already knew that—whatever was in these woods, it *was* curious and it *was* dangerous, and if it found another predator—one that had attacked it before—staked to a tree and helpless . . .

When I inhaled, I caught the faintest stink of wild animal. Then a huge form reared up in the distance. Its massive head swayed. A wet snuffling cut through the silence as it sampled the air before dropping to all fours with a shudder even my frozen feet could feel.

The beast disappeared behind a barrier of bushes. The vibrations began again as it continued forward, slow and steady.

Change, damn it! Change!

But there wasn't time for that. If the beast came upon me mid-Change, I'd be even more defenseless than I was now.

Well, do something then. Just—

The creature reared, so close now I could see the brown fur, the rounded ears, the tiny eyes and the snub snout.

I was staring into the face of a bear. An ordinary, hibernation-groggy bear.

The first whoosh of relief didn't even make it past my lips before my brain screeched into reverse.

Just a bear? Just an eight-foot-tall, thousand-pound bear?

The bear snuffled, its piggy eyes straining to see me better. It dropped back to all fours with another earth-shuddering *whoomph*. Then it lumbered toward me, its massive bulk swaying.

"Go!" I yelled. "Shoo! Scat!"

Scat?

I whistled, and that got its attention. It reared up and grunted, breath streaming into the cold night air. Even from twenty feet away, the stink was enough to make my stomach flip-flop.

"Go! Scram! Shoo!"

I yelled and whistled, but it only peered at me through half-lidded eyes, part drowsy curiosity, part disdain, as if amused by this puny thing making so much racket. I'd always heard that if confronted by a bear, you should make as much noise as possible. It worked just fine on the little black bears I'd encountered in northern Ontario. But I was sure this guy was laughing at me. He sure as hell wasn't turning tail and running.

The bear lumbered forward, rocking like a boat on rough water, its nose working furiously. Every few steps it would pause, head tilted, as if trying to figure out the mystery of my scent.

When I growled, it grunted in surprise. I snarled and bared my teeth. That gave it pause, but only for a moment, before it kept coming until it was close enough to warm my face with its rank breath. Then it reared up, all eight feet of it, towering over me, and if my knees weren't frozen solid, I'm sure they would have given way.

The bear stared nearsightedly at me, its head swaying as if a better angle would tell it what I was. Its face lowered to mine, the smell of its breath making me breathe through my mouth.

I was trying to meet its gaze when a sledgehammer blow to my shoulder sent me sailing off my feet. I hit the end of the rope, arms jerking hard, feet tangling, trying to find purchase. Another blow knocked me off them again. I fell to my knees, bound arms raised, joints screaming.

The bear reared up, its roar thundering through my head. It raised a paw to hit me again and I tried to scramble out of the way, but there was no place to go, and it hit me in the side, claws raking through my shirt.

As I fell, arms jerking over my head again, my scalp started to prickle. A patch of skin between my shoulders itched. I looked up at my bound hands to see hair sprouting.

Oh, no. Oh, God, no. Not now.

But there was nothing I could do to stop it. I was in mortal danger and my body was determined to meet the threat with its best defense.

The bear kept batting me, testing my reaction, realizing I was weak, and it was very, very hungry.

My blood spattered the tree and speckled the snow and

all I could do was whimper and twist, trying to get out of its way, to get myself into a better position for the transformation, every twitch of the Change agonizing. I was on my knees, hands bound with their backs together, and if that was uncomfortable as a human, it was impossible as a wolf, but that didn't stop the Change. It kept ripping through me, clothing twisting, binding me.

My whimpers turned to screams, then unearthly yelping howls that only infuriated the bear. The second the Change was far enough along, I had to pull out of the ropes and run. But the thought of making that happen—of having that degree of control over my body, as the Change and the bear buffeted it—was laughable. I might as well be in a straitjacket, dangling from a crane.

Then, as my Change came close to a finish, the bear pulled back and delivered a blow that sent me flying up ... and knocked one of my hind legs free from the rope. That was all the incentive I needed. I landed on my back, forelegs in the air, and started twisting, wrenching and writhing. My shoulders screamed with the agony of having my paws bound back to back, but I kept struggling until one came out. I pulled the other, but the rope snagged above my dewclaw and wouldn't budge.

I found a precarious foothold, two paws firmly on the ground, the third skimming it, the fourth dangling in the air. I lunged, snapping at the bear, teeth sinking into its flank. It hit me and I flew backward with a chunk of bear meat in my jaws.

The bear roared and dropped to all fours. It charged. Being still half tied to a tree didn't leave much room for getting out of its way, but I did the best I could and it struck me only a glancing blow before careening off balance and sliding through the snow.

The bear recovered and turned on me. I snarled and leapt at it, dancing in an awkward sideways hop that probably wasn't nearly as menacing as I hoped. It did give the bear pause, though. Too much pause. Its head went up, body tensing. As it rose on its rear legs, I wasn't surprised to see it peering to see something in the distance—something more dangerous than me.

The bear snuffled, dropped and grunted. It shifted uneasily as it looked from me to the seemingly empty forest.

Was it Tesler? Hoping to find me sobbing and begging for my freedom? If so, he would run away the moment he saw the bear, coward that he was. With any luck, the bear would give chase . . . a vision so delicious I had to revel in it for a moment.

But the bear was looking away from the cabin, meaning whatever it smelled almost certainly wasn't Tesler. Noah? God, I hoped not. I tensed, straining to catch a glimpse or scent of the approaching figure, ready to distract the bear and growl for Noah to get up a tree.

The ground vibrated under my paws. My muzzle shot up, sniffing madly. I knew then what I'd smell, and it took only a moment more to catch a confirming whiff. The beast.

Bear forgotten, I yanked at the rope. My foreleg stayed caught at the dewclaw. The rear one was twisted awkwardly, making it impossible to yank hard enough. I fell on the rope, biting and pulling at it.

When the bear swatted my flank—a light, almost tentative tap—I wheeled, snapping as I hit the end of the rope. The bear stumbled back. It looked from me—a dervish of flying fur and flashing fangs—to the forest beyond, the vibrating steps now accompanied by the crackle of undergrowth. With a snort and a grumble, the bear ambled away, as if it wasn't fleeing, but had simply decided I wasn't worth its time.

I kept working at the rope, gnawing frantically. When I heard a snort right behind me, I turned, snarling. Then I stopped dead and stared.

IJIRAAT

WHAT STOOD BEFORE me was neither wolf nor bear, but a freakish mixture of the two. A foot shorter than the bear, it had the same wide skull, brown fur and massive body. But its pointed ears and long snout were all wolf, and its fur—though longer and shaggier than mine—was wolf fur with a thick coarse overcoat.

It looked like Hollywood's version of werewolves, post–Wolf Man era—a massive beastlike thing. But that wasn't what had stopped my attack dead. It was the eyes. Blue eyes as human as ours when we Changed. When I looked into them, I knew Lynn Nygard's tales of Ijiraat were right. Only this wasn't a man that shifted into either wolf or bear—it was a blend of all three at once.

The beast stopped a few steps short of me and curled his lip back in an experimental growl. Like the bear, he was curious yet wary. I met his gaze, neither backing down nor returning the growl, but doing the same as I had with Tesler—standing my ground and keeping eye contact.

The beast paced one way, then the other, his gaze still

locked with mine. He lumbered like a bear, but his movements were quicker. His shaggy fur made him look heavier than he was. He still had a good hundred pounds on me, though, and little of it was winter-stored fat. Though I could tell by scent it was the beast Clay attacked, the only signs of injury were a few patches of missing fur and already-healing wounds.

He stopped to get a better look at me. Our paths had crossed often enough that he wasn't confused by the sight of an oversized wolf draped with shredded clothing and reeking of human scents.

He leaned forward and sniffed me. When I didn't attack, he leaned forward some more. I moved and he fell back, but I only turned sideways and let him sniff me, the same way I would with a fellow werewolf. Because that's how I had to treat this. No matter how hard my heart pounded, I couldn't let the fear show.

As he sniffed, I gnawed—as casually as possible—on the rope holding my foreleg aloft.

He sniffed my flank. Then he sniffed my hindquarters. When he spent a little too long back there—and when his nose brushed where I didn't want to be brushed—I was so intent on the rope that I reacted the same way I did when a werewolf got a little too interested in that end of me. I spun, snarling and snapping.

The beast jerked back, grunting as if to say, *What'd I do?* I grunted back . . . then sat. He prodded my hindquarters. I stayed sitting. When he prodded harder, I growled.

He chuffed, his eyes narrowing, head tilting one way, then the other, considering. Another chuff and he turned his back on me and started walking away, grumbling as if thoroughly offended by my lack of interest.

I returned to my rope-gnawing, and the moment I did, I heard the thunder of running paws. Before I could turn, the beast leapt onto my back, hind paws still on the ground, forepaws cinched around me. Male mounting position.

I didn't panic. This wasn't the same as Tesler's rape attempts. To a wolf, this was simply a sexual overture, and had to be answered much the same as any unwelcome attention— with a very quick and firm "not interested."

I pitched forward, out from under him, and twisted around as far as the rope would allow, then threw in a few serious growls for good measure. His eyes lit up like a puppy that's been swatted and thinks it's an invitation to playtime.

He dove at me and nipped my front leg, then pranced back, jaws open in a very canine grin. When I didn't react, he chuffed in disappointment . . . and tried mounting me again.

I warned him off. He thought it was foreplay. I ignored him. He tried to mount me. I warned him off . . . and so the cycle went. I suppose I should have been a lot more concerned about this scenario, but he gave no sign of tiring of the game or forcing himself on me. So I kept playing . . . while sneaking nips at the rope on my foreleg, fraying it strand by strand.

Finally, with a yank, I was free. The beast backed off, but only to get a better look. Then he chuffed, as if pleased with this new development. When I pulled on the leg rope, he leapt in and, with one chomp, snapped it. And, ungrateful bitch that I am, I took off.

That didn't bother him in the least. He simply interpreted this as step two of the canine seduction game. First, she rebuffs you. Next, she runs away. Finally, you catch her. And then? Well, that's when the real fun starts.

So he chased me. I wasn't concerned. He may have had the muscle, but I had the speed. Only I didn't count on one thing. Okay, make that two things.

One, he was a little more invested in winning this chase than he'd been the night before. Two, I was battered and exhausted. I didn't make it far before he caught up and leapt onto my back. I let my legs give way, dropped and rolled, snarling and slashing. He yelped as my teeth sunk into a healing wound on his neck. Then a roar echoed through the night and I turned my head to see another beast—a bigger one—charging straight for me.

I scrambled up, stumbling out of the way, my legs skidding like a day-old fawn's. But the new beast wasn't running at me. He hit the smaller one in the side and knocked him flying.

My first instinct, naturally, was to get the hell out of the way while these two battled it out. When I'd lunged to the side, though, I'd twisted my already-tender, formerly bound foreleg. So when I tried to lope gracefully into the sunset, it gave way and I sprawled into the snow.

As I pushed up, I heard a yelp and looked back, not to see a roiling beast battle, but the smaller one cowering as the larger one cuffed him across the head, growling as if to say, *What the hell did you think you were doing?* Like a father swatting his misbehaving kid . . .

I gawked for another moment. Then the older one

looked my way and I realized I was staring when I should have been running like hell. So I took off.

Again, I only made it a few steps before the crunch of paws in the snow sounded behind me, now in stereo as they both gave chase. This time, though, two things let me pull into the lead. One, Junior knew he wasn't going to get any "reward" with his father around, so his heart was no longer in it. Two, with double the muscle pursuing me, I seemed to find a final reserve of strength.

When we'd gone half a mile and neither sped up nor slowed down, the huff of their steady breathing told me they weren't giving it their all, and I realized they were *letting* me pull ahead.

They were wearing me out, the same way we did with deer, letting that first panicked burst of energy drain them. Behind me, the bigger beast grunted and I looked back to see him stumble a little, as if his paw had caught a root. It didn't trip or slow him down, but it was a reminder of his position—at my left flank. And the young one was at my right. They weren't using the old run-your-prey-to-the-ground trick. They were using the old drive-your-prey—

Oh, shit.

I hit the brakes and made a hard right. I caught the younger one off guard and zoomed past him as he was still executing his own skid and twist maneuver. But the older one was better prepared and stayed right on my heels. From the crashing of bushes behind us I knew I'd narrowly avoided exactly the trap I'd anticipated—a third beast lying in wait ahead.

How many were there? Was it a pack? An extended family? Where did they live? Out here, dangerously close to civilization? How did—?

I shut off my brain and poured that energy into my legs. As I ran, I caught a whiff of a fourth beast, its scent blowing straight into my face, and I realized they'd boxed me in with a rear guard, too.

I tried to veer, this time plunging into the forest, hoping to escape that way, but the older one was too close behind and as soon as I slowed to turn, he grabbed my rear leg and wrenched.

I fought, all three legs scrabbling in the snow, scraping it away to dirt, desperately trying to find traction. But he had me tight, and from the pressure of his fangs, I knew I wasn't getting away . . . not with the bottom half of my leg intact.

When I stopped struggling, he gave a yank and my forelegs splayed out. I thumped belly-first to the ground. He dragged me back into the clearing. Then he let go.

I got up to find a beast at every compass point blocking my escape. They just stood there watching me, no expression in their matching blue eyes. Only the youngest moved, shuffling with youthful impatience, looking from one elder to the next, waiting for them to get on with it. After a moment, two of the older ones started casting the same looks at the third. He was the biggest, and also the oldest, judging by the gray spicing his dark fur. The Alpha.

After studying me, the Alpha grunted. Then he stretched his forelegs out, his back legs following, his head dropping between his shoulder blades. It was a position I knew well and when I saw it, my heart started hammering.

The beast began his Change. I should have expected

that. But I didn't. The bigger shock came when I saw what he Changed into.

I remembered my first-year anthropology course, when we'd been discussing Neanderthal man. The professor had taken a sketch of one and put him in a suit to prove that, despite the popular perception of them as inhumanly primitive, he could have walked down Wall Street without turning any heads. Sure, he might have gotten a few caveman jokes in his lifetime, but no one seeing him would scream, "Oh, my God, it's a Neanderthal" any more than people seeing us in wolf form scream, "Oh my God, it's a werewolf." We looked close enough to the norm to pass for it.

When this guy completed his Change, he reminded me of that sketch. Well, minus the suit. He was naked, of course, but in his case . . . let's just say that he had a *lot* of hair where men normally have hair, so nakedness wasn't really an issue.

He seemed slightly shorter than he had been in beast form, a few inches shy of seven feet. He had a thick beard and shaggy hair, a popular look among backwoodsmen everywhere. If someone bumped into him in the forest—presuming he didn't normally run around naked—he'd just look like the kind of guy who spent most of his life in these woods and ventured to town only for necessities.

He had the classic Neanderthal features—a heavy brow, sloping forehead, large nose and presumably a receding chin, though that last was hidden under his beard. The hair in general did a good job of masking the less gracile facial features. Despite his height he had an almost squat appearance, powerfully built with short legs and forearms. Something about Neanderthal adaptations to cold flitted through my brain—one of those stray bits of academia you study so hard that it never quite leaves.

"You come with us," he said.

His voice was gruff, almost a growl, and he spoke with the slightly halting inflection of someone whose first language wasn't English. When he spoke again, I thought it was a word in his native language—a barked command to the others. Then I realized it really was a bark, two quick guttural sounds with an inflection like speech.

The other two elders clearly understood, grunting and nodding. The younger one paid no attention. The Alpha turned his gaze on him and said what sounded like "Eli." The youngster grunted grudging agreement.

The Alpha crouched, then Changed back to beast with a speed and ease that left me sighing with envy. I guess a long and torturous transformation is the price we pay for Changing more completely between human and wolf form.

When the Alpha finished, I looked at him with fresh eyes and realized that what I'd mistaken for bearlike features were really human—his bulk, the longer fur, the rounded head, the ease with which he stood and walked on two legs. They didn't change into a wolf-bear hybrid, but a wolf-human one.

One of the elders nudged my flank hard, telling me to get moving. I set out behind the Alpha.

RESPECT

AS I LIMPED along, surrounded on all sides, I was struck by the stillness of the forest. When I ran as a wolf, I was accustomed to smaller creatures giving way, particularly if I was making no attempt to run quietly. Beyond that pocket of empty space, though, I could always hear, smell and sometimes see life deep in the forest. With the beasts, the dead zone seemed to extend as far as smell or sound could penetrate. It was as if every creature heard those thundering paws, screamed, "Oh, shit!" and scrambled for higher ground.

As a wolf, I was like the jackals in the African savannah—prey avoided me and predators paid me heed. These beasts were the lions—everything great and small cleared out when they came running.

The Alpha led us toward one of the small mountains dotting the wilderness. At first he cut a trail through unbroken snow, but deeper into the forest, we turned onto a well-traveled path that led through trees so dense we had to duck under branches. We reached snow-barren rock and began to climb. Finally, the Alpha disappeared behind what seemed like a solid stone wall. I followed and found the concealed entrance of a cave.

Almost no light penetrated the interior. Even my good night vision was useless. When I paused, though, the beast behind me gave me a nudge and grunted, as if exasperated by my ineptitude.

I followed the wall for a few feet, then sat on my haunches. My eyes had just begun to adjust when the *thwick* of a struck match made me jump. A kerosene lamp hissed. Light flared. I blinked and saw the figure of the Alpha holding the lantern. He was dressed now, in jeans and a flannel shirt. His thickly haired feet were bare, the cave floor covered in dried strawlike reeds.

Behind the Alpha was one of the elders, also Changed and dressed, lighting a fire. I couldn't see the third, but the youngest was off to my left, buttoning his shirt. He wasn't any older than Noah, which I supposed explained his hormone-fueled reaction earlier. He was more slender than the others, with light brown hair to his shoulders, his cheeks still smooth.

Looking over, the young one grunted and waved toward me. The Alpha grunted back. There was nothing overtly primitive about their communication—it sounded like a couple of guys who weren't much given to conversation, making do with gestures and noises instead, the younger one clearly pointing out that I was still in wolf form and the older saying, "Yes, I know."

The Alpha lit a second lantern, then turned to me. "Shift to human."

While that would certainly aid communication, right now, I was happy to keep my warm fur and sharp teeth.

When I made no move to start my Change, he said, "We would like you to shift to human."

He enunciated carefully, as one unaccustomed to such complete and formal communication, but wanting to accommodate a guest from a culture that valued such things. And that was how I think they were trying to treat me—as a guest. A captive guest to be sure, but they hadn't made any threatening moves. They weren't even blocking the exit, though I suspected if I bolted outside, I'd soon discover where the third elder had gone. Yet they seemed anxious to maintain the appearance of civility, and it seemed wise to go along with it for now.

"Over there." The Alpha pointed to the corner. "It is dark enough."

The young one—Eli—tried to follow me. A growl from the Alpha stopped him.

"I'm just going over here," he said, his speech surprisingly normal, like that of a second-generation immigrant. "To watch her."

The elder tending the fire chuckled and Eli blushed.

"To guard her, I mean," he said.

"Sit," the Alpha growled.

"Clothing?" the other elder said.

The Alpha grunted and nodded, then waved Eli toward a rough-hewn chest. I waited while Eli dropped clothes near me. When he'd retreated, I began my Change. Once finished, I pulled on the shirt and buttoned it, reached for pants ... and found none. The shirt fell to my knees, though, and the reed-covered floor kept the cold from my feet.

When I stepped forward, the Alpha took one look at me and growled. "Eli ..."

The boy only looked over, his face a study in wide-eyed innocence.

"Pants," the Alpha said.

"They're too big for her."

"Eli!"

He found me a pair of jeans. As he was bringing them over, he snuck a look at me.

"Eli ..." The Alpha's voice was a low growl now. "Respect."

I thought he meant for Eli to respect *him,* but when Eli kept staring, the elder—the one I suspected was his father—cuffed him as he had in the woods and growled, "Respect, Eli. She is werewolf."

The look the boy gave me said this wasn't, to him, cause for respect. But I already knew that. He'd been the one Clay and I had encountered in the forest, and judging by the way that mutt-who-runs-with-the-wolves had acted, we weren't the only werewolves Eli had been terrorizing.

The Alpha pulled out a chair made from bound branches and draped with an animal skin—bear by the smell—and he motioned for me to sit. As I did, I looked around. The cave was a jarring mix of primitive and modern—furs and twig furniture mingling with parkas, winter boots and, beside the fire pit, a steel pail of water. Not primitive, I suppose, just old-fashioned wherever modern wasn't necessary, no different from humans who'd decided to live off the land.

When the Alpha followed my gaze, though, he said quickly, "This is only a hunting camp. We live a distance away. In houses," he added emphatically, lest I mistake them for cave-dwelling savages.

"Is that where the women are?" I had no idea whether there *were* women, but I had a sneaking suspicion these guys weren't strolling into Anchorage, picking up chicks in the local bars.

He nodded. "They come sometimes. Not this time."

"And they're . . . like you? They can . . . shift into . . . what you do?"

He looked confused. I don't blame him—my question wasn't exactly clear, but I had no idea what they called themselves.

"The women," I said. "They're like you? They . . . shift form?"

"Of course." He frowned, then nodded. "Yes, there are not women among the werewolves. Or that is what I have heard, but clearly you are . . ." He thought this through a minute, then said, "You are a bitten one, then."

I nodded. "Is that what your women are? Bitten?"

"No, it is not the same. We cannot . . . do that. We are born Shifters. Our women are, too. But they are rare."

Behind him, Eli grumbled. Not a situation to his liking, I supposed.

I turned back to the Alpha. They hadn't invited me here to exchange notes on our species, so anything I wanted to know, I'd better ask fast.

"And you live deeper in the woods? In a community? Are there many of you?"

Typical questions, particularly for someone with an anthropologist husband who'd drill her for details. But from the look on the Alpha's face, he didn't care to give those details. He hid his unease by quickly glancing aside and muttering, "Not important."

"Sorry. I didn't mean to pry. I just—I've never met... Shifters before."

"There are many of us," Eli said. "More than you werewolves, and all bigger and stronger than your best. If you come, we'll fight." He met my gaze. "And we'll win."

"Respect!" the Alpha snarled, wheeling on him.

"Why? Look at her. She's no bigger than a human. And she shifts into a normal wolf. Why should we be afraid of—?"

His father cuffed him. "Respect!"

"It's okay." I tried for a wry smile. "I can see how my questions could have been misinterpreted, but it was only curiosity. Your territory is yours. We have our own, and we're happy with it."

"The werewolves like cities," the Alpha said, in a tone that implied he pitied our preference, but was trying to remain politely neutral on the subject. "They have never given us a problem. Until now. These werewolves in the valley. The ones in the cabin..."

"If you mean the two brothers and their friends, they aren't part of my Pack. In fact, I just escaped from them."

"We know this. We have been watching them. They are... trouble."

That was putting it mildly.

"Did the others in your Pack come with you?" the Alpha asked. "You are not alone, are you?"

Eli had seen me with Clay, but from the nervous looks he was tossing my way, the others knew nothing of those encounters. Given their carefully polite behavior now, I suspected they wouldn't be happy to hear that he'd tried to run us off "his" territory.

"I'm with my mate."

"Good. You will bring him. Then you will get rid of these werewolves."

"You mean kill them?"

The Alpha met my gaze with an inscrutable look, like the one I'd seen so often from Jeremy. I wondered if it came automatically with Alphahood. I hoped so, because otherwise, I doubted I'd ever develop it.

"If that is what you think best," he said, as if leaving the final call up to me. Not that I had any problem killing Tesler. Hell, I didn't plan to get on a plane out of Alaska until I had. But being commanded to do so wasn't something I took lightly.

I demanded—well, asked for, relatively nicely—an explanation. Getting one wasn't easy. The conversation proceeded slowly as the Alpha searched for the right words. Eli kept sighing and fidgeting, clearly wanting to take over. But in this, the Shifters were like a werewolf Pack. While they made some allowances for his youth, he couldn't speak for the Alpha. When the Alpha is present, he must speak for his pack.

As he'd said, this was one of the main hunting camps for his community, as well as a way station between it and the city, where they went for supplies. While Dennis's cabin had been here for years, he'd never caused any trouble, so the

Shifters treated him as a fellow predator—leaving him alone. Tesler and his boys were another matter.

If Dennis was the respected fellow hunter, the Teslers were like the rednecks who rent a cabin for the week just to get drunk and shoot stuff. They'd been running in wolf form not caring whether they were seen or heard, scaring the game for miles and preying on humans, then—worse yet—leaving their kills in the open.

Now, I'd already suspected the mutts of the killings, despite Dan's denials. When I expressed even the slightest skepticism, though, just a gentle "Are you sure it was them?" the Alpha got his back up.

"Yes, we are sure. Miles"—he gestured to Eli's father—"was at the cabin after the first man died. He heard them fighting. One had been seen by a human as he Shifted, so he killed him and the leaders were angry with him for not hiding the body before it was found. They sent him away."

That matched Dan's story. But if the Tesler brothers gave their lackey shit for leaving the corpse, and kicked his ass out because of it, why were two more bodies found later?

And here I discovered that the Shifters lacked a certain sophistication when it came to scheming and subterfuge. That's not to say they were stupid. They just weren't accustomed to the kind of political machinations the Pack dealt with every day. When I pointed out the fallacy of the Alpha's logic, he grew agitated.

"They did kill that man. And that is not the worst. They killed girls. Two of them. Maybe more. We found only two. They buried them, but not with respect. They threw them away. Like..." He waved his hand, searching for words. "Like garbage. They are monsters."

Agreed. And at confirmation of the girls' fate, my determination to kill Tesler only grew. But I noticed he'd shifted my attention from the question of the other two "wolf-killed" men. The Tesler gang hadn't killed them and the Alpha knew it. Another, less comfortable explanation slunk into the back of my mind.

"You say these pack leaders were upset with the body being left out and found," I said slowly. "Very upset. Maybe, if it continued, they'd get upset—and nervous—enough to leave."

"Yes, but they did not."

"Because they knew they weren't responsible and, being clueless about normal wolf behavior, they presumed it was wolves and ignored it. So your plan failed."

The Alpha nodded... then stopped, as he realized what he was admitting to. He blustered then, not denying it, but pointing out that the two men *they'd* killed were poachers and trappers, stealing animals meant for sustenance and taking only the skins.

"And animals aren't the only thing they kill," Eli muttered.

His father tried to shush him, but halfheartedly, his gaze averted, eyes filled with grief.

"Poachers killed one of you," I said. "In Shifted form. They mistook you—"

"They mistook him for nothing," Eli snarled, spittle flying. "He wasn't Shifted. The guy shot him and tried to hide his body, like he'd killed a deer out of season."

"My other son," Miles said. "Eli's litter mate."

Eli's twin brother, accidentally shot in human form. That would explain the animosity toward us—probably toward werewolves, wolves and humans alike, running them off his territory with all the single-minded rage of a grief-stricken teenage boy. Sure, he'd been trying something else in the grove a little while ago, but that was pure instinct. My scent at work on his teen hormones. Even now, when he slid glances my way, checking me out, contempt warred with attraction.

"But what we did, it was not revenge," the Alpha said.

Not consciously, I'm sure. But subconsciously, it would play a role. While Eli acted out his grief by chasing every predator off his turf, his elders found an excuse to do the same with poachers and trappers, men they would now consider a threat. To them, the killing of those two humans, while regrettable, could be justified by their actions and the necessity of stopping the greater threat: Tesler's mutts. And while I could strenuously argue the logic of this, it made perfect sense to them, and that I couldn't dispute.

But all that still didn't answer one question. There was another way to handle their problem. One that was far more reliable—and ethically justifiable—than framing them for murder.

"You want Tesler and his gang dead," I said. "So why not do it yourselves?"

"It is forbidden."

"Maybe, but—"

"No. Killing werewolves is *forbidden*."

His tone said this was an unbreakable and unquestionable law. So they could kill humans, but not werewolves? That made no sense.

Or maybe, to them, it did. They'd chastised Eli for disrespecting me. He'd hinted they feared us. Fear and respect. Feelings one might have toward, not a fellow supernatural, but a superior being. Even Eli, while he'd been quick to terrorize us, hadn't done more than smack us around, trying to scare us off without breaking that commandment.

"You will do this for us," the Alpha said. "You will kill them."

Before I could answer, he whistled. Tramping footsteps and muffled oaths sounded at the cave entrance. In walked the missing fourth Shifter, pushing before him a slight figure in an oversized parka, arms bound behind his back. The figure struggled and the hood fell back. It was Noah, gagged with a strip of leather, eyes blazing with fury and humiliation.

"He is yours?" the Alpha said.

"Yes," I said. "He's ours."

"Then do this for us and he is yours again."

CONTACT

THIRTY MINUTES LATER, I was tramping through the snow, ready to sell my soul for a snowmobile. What kind of Alaskan backwoodsmen—even shape-shifting wolf-beasts—didn't have snowmobiles?

I knew I shouldn't complain. At least they hadn't shoved me out right away, cold, exhausted and battered, to find my way back to civilization. They'd insisted I rest and eat, even when I'd argued I was fine. They'd served me a surprisingly good stew of venison and root vegetables, and a thick brick-like bread that hadn't been nearly as tasty, but I'd eaten it anyway.

I drank the tea they brewed, too, some herbal blend to ease my aches and pains. They'd said it was willow bark, but I suspected it contained something a lot stronger. It reminded me of the Tylenol 3 Jeremy made me take after bad fights. I was feeling no pain and a little light-headed.

One thing was for sure—this was a night I wouldn't forget. Life as a werewolf means a lot of fights and chases, and in the last few hours, I'd done more than my share of both, but with new twists. Falling through the ice. Fending off an eight-foot brown bear. Being taken captive by a werewolf precursor race. Someday, I'd be sitting in my rocking chair, telling my grandkids about this night. Right now, I just wanted to get through it.

The Shifters had given me all the clothing I needed, from a parka to boots to doubled-up work socks. But with size nine feet in size gazillion boots, I might as well have been wearing snowshoes. In fact, I'd have been better off wearing snowshoes. Worse, I could have been. They'd offered me a pair, but after a few awkward steps and a face-plant, I'd said boots were fine.

They'd escorted me to a road. At least, they said it was a road. But after twenty minutes hiking through boot-deep snow, seeing only a thin swatch of white ahead, winding through the trees, I was uncomfortably reminded of the last untraveled "road" I'd taken . . . the one that turned out to be a river.

The Shifters swore the highway was only three miles away. They'd even offered to have Eli escort me, though hadn't seemed surprised when I said no. I'd had enough of teenage lust to last me awhile.

I suppose I should be flattered—all that attention from guys half my age—and I would be . . . if I didn't know that without my unique scent, I wouldn't get a second glance. And, really, that would make me much happier. I knew now how Clay felt, getting checked out by twenty-year-old girls. Eww.

Even as I bitched about the situation, I knew I should be overjoyed just to be warm and rested and free. How many times tonight had I thought I'd never see morning? And there it was—the faintest streaks of red cresting the valley between two mountains behind me. I hadn't been killed, hadn't been raped, hadn't even been seriously injured. I should be dancing down the moonlit road, singing to the stars. But if I was, I'd know whatever was in that tea was more than a painkiller.

So I trudged. And I bitched. And I dreamed of a cozy bed, hot food and Travis Tesler's head on a pike... not necessarily in that order.

I was following that seemingly endless road when I heard the faint squeak of snow under a boot. I stopped. Everything around me was still. Then a figure stepped onto the road. I tensed, but he only lifted a hand in greeting and started toward me. He was tall and slender, dressed in one of those parkas with the long, tubelike hoods, his face lost within its shadows. As he approached, though, his smell hit me. And I didn't believe it. I inhaled more icy air so fast my brain reeled from the shock. The scent stayed the same. But it couldn't be. Couldn't possibly be.

The man pulled down his hood and I saw his wavy dark hair, big brown eyes, olive-skinned face, swoon-worthy grin... and still I couldn't believe it.

"See," he said. "Clay was worried we'd never find you out here, but all I had to do was follow the bitching and moaning, and here you are."

"Nick..." I said.

"You can't be too cold, then, if you remember my name. I swear, another hour out here and *I'd* have forgotten it. Love the clothes. Seems we shop at the same designer." He looked down at his parka with such disgust that, at any other time, I would have laughed.

"Wh-what are you doing here?" I stammered.

"Good to see you, too."

When he stepped toward me, I fell back.

He paused, frowning, then nodded. "Blaming snow blindness? Some funky mojo from these weird woods? Don't worry, I'm real. And just to prove it . . ."

He leapt forward before I could back away, snatched me up and kissed me. As usual, it wasn't the kind of kiss you should give your best friend's wife. As I gasped for air, I said, "Nick," and he grinned.

"I knew that'd work."

My eyes prickled, throat tightening. I'd been holding up so well, but now, seeing Nick, knowing I was safe, it was like popping the cushioning bubble that had kept me going.

He put his arms around me and pulled me against him, grip only strengthening when I murmured that I was okay and to put me down. After a moment, I gave up and let him hug me. A tear or two might have stained his parka, but we both pretended not to see it. When his arms loosened, I stepped away.

"How did you get here?" I asked.

"Hold on, let me try Clay again while I explain." He fumbled in his pocket. "Last night, when Joey drugged Clay—I can't believe he—" He shook his head. "Anyway, Jeremy knew something was wrong. You know Jeremy."

He stopped fumbling, yanked off a glove and pulled his cell phone from his pocket, checking it as he talked. "Jeremy called. No one answered in your room or on your phones.

So he talked the hotel staff into opening the door and checking. Having a stranger walk into his room woke Clay up better than any phone call." He shook his phone, cursing. "Still no reception. I bet the radio isn't working either."

He exchanged the cell phone for a walkie-talkie, still talking. "We knew you guys might need emergency help, so by the time Clay woke up, Antonio already had a buddy's company jet on standby. We were on the plane with Reese."

He tried the radio. Swore. Shoved it back into his pocket and kept talking. "Jeremy is on his way, but he didn't want us to wait for him. He's taking a regular flight and leaving the kids with Jaime. Karl's supposed to be coming, but I'll believe it when I see him. They'll be a while, though. We just got here ourselves. We managed to get in touch with Clay, who was already up here searching. We found him and split up—me with Clay, Antonio with Reese."

"So where's Clay?"

"Took off. I wasn't keeping up. Next thing I know, he's gone and I'm trudging through snow up to my knees, searching for a path, a road, anything. Then I heard you."

"In other words, you got lost in the woods. Again."

He shot me a mock scowl. "No, Clay *lost* me in the woods. Again. And he's probably lost himself by now, the way he was going. Do you want to hunt for him? Or keep going and hope for cell service?"

I wanted to find Clay. Even the thought that he was out here was enough to make my eyes prickle again. Nick was a decent substitute, but I needed Clay—to see him, know he was safe, show him I was safe, tell him everything, then get to work.

And I wanted a hug. A long one, inhaling his scent, proving to myself that everything really was okay. There was a time I wouldn't have admitted that, much less planned to act on the impulse. Today I would.

What I had to do, though, was option two: trust that Clay was okay and keep going until we could make radio contact. If both Clay and Antonio were out of range, then I'd contact Jeremy or Karl—maybe even Hope—and have someone keep trying Antonio and Clay for me while we headed back into the forest to search for them. That was the sensible plan, so that's the one I told Nick. He didn't argue; he never did.

So we walked. I took the radio and he kept the cell phone, and we continued checking for service as I explained everything that had happened in the last twenty-four hours.

Nick accepted the existence of Shifters with little comment. It interested him no more than any minutiae of the greater supernatural world. What did get his attention was the tremor in my voice each time I mentioned Travis Tesler.

"What did this Tesler guy—?" Nick stopped himself. "No, I think I know what he did. Or *tried* to do, because if he'd succeeded..."

"I'd be an emotional wreck?"

"No, I was thinking more 'covered in blood and bits of the bastard.' But, yeah, after that settled, you'd be in rough shape. You'd get through it, but I'm glad you don't have to."

He tucked his glove into his pocket, and slid his bare hand into the massive mitt over mine, taking my hand inside it, that last bit of chill vanishing as my fingers entwined with his warm ones. We walked in silence, hand-in-hand.

I've always liked this about Nick, a physical closeness I don't allow myself with anyone except Clay. It's a safe intimacy that some part of me craves.

It's not asexual—nothing is asexual with Nick—but it's completely nonthreatening. I'm his friend and his best friend's wife, and while that doesn't stop him from kissing me or slipping into our bed and getting friendlier than a friend should, he means nothing by it, would never push the boundaries. If Clay isn't threatened, then I know I don't need to be, because it's nothing more than it appears to be— another level of the physical play and intimacy that cement Pack bonds.

"Do you want to talk about it?" he said after a few minutes. "I know you'll talk to Clay but... maybe there are things you'd rather discuss with me?"

I nodded. "I might. And I probably will. Later. For now, I'm holding up. It just... It made me so..."

"Angry."

"Sure. It pissed me off. That's part of being a woman, I guess. If some son of a bitch wants to hurt us, he knows how to do it, and there's really nothing we can do in return, nothing on that scale."

"I don't mean you're mad at him. Of course you are, but you're more angry with yourself for letting it get to you. For not being perfect."

I didn't answer. I didn't need to. The Pack might tease Nick for not being the quickest on his mental feet, but there's more than one kind of intelligence, and when it comes to seeing through people, no one was better than Nick. It just wasn't an ability I liked him practicing on me...

"I'll be fine," I said.

"I know you will."

We checked our devices, then kept walking, the dark sky ahead now streaked with gray.

"Everyone has a button, Elena. This guy found yours."

"And, apparently, he's not the only one who sees it, meaning I'm doing a shitty job of hiding it."

He gave me a look. "I've known you for twenty years. If I hadn't figured it out, there'd be something wrong with me, especially considering I've brushed that button a few times myself."

"It's not the same."

His hand tightened around mine. "I know."

We walked some more. Checked again. Still nothing.

"You're allowed to have a soft spot, Elena."

"I'd rather not."

"I know."

More quiet walking. More futile checking.

"How far did you get before you lost the signal?" I asked.

"No idea. Clay had driven in as far as his rental truck would go, and we met him there. At that point, we had radio but no cell. After we split up, there wasn't any reason to call each other, so we didn't think to check."

"Any idea whether we're heading in the right direction?" I caught his look. "Okay, dumb question. But I know the highway is west, and the sun is coming up behind us, so we're at least heading into a cell phone area. I hope. Now let's just hope they—"

The howl of a wolf brought me up short. I followed the sound, then shook my head. It wasn't Clay or Antonio.

"Could be Reese," Nick said. "Maybe I'm not the only werewolf who gets lost in the woods."

A chorus of howls answered the question.

"Wild wolves?" he said.

I nodded. "But I'm sure even they get lost now and then . . . when they've taken a hard blow to the head."

He jostled me, threatening to send one of those hard blows my way. We goofed for a few steps, trading shoves and trying to trip each other, then we slowed to listen as the wolves broke out in full song.

"Something's got them going," I said.

"Those Shifter things?"

"Could be. I—"

The radio in my hand chirped, the sound so loud and unexpected I almost dropped it.

"Goddamn it, Nick," Clay's voice hissed. "Where the hell are you? I don't have time to be chasing you all over the fucking Alaskan wilderness. If you freeze to death—"

I pressed the button. "Nick's with me. We're okay."

Silence, then, "Who—? Is someone there?"

"It's a two-way radio," Nick said. "If you interrupt him, he can't hear you."

"Nick's with me," I repeated. "And we're fine."

More silence and I thought I'd screwed up the transmission again, then, faintly, "Elena?"

"Yes, unless Nick found a woman in the forest, which I suppose wouldn't be too surprising."

"Where are you? Stay right there. You said you're fine?

How fine? Are you hurt? What're you wearing? Tell Nick to give you his—"

"I'm battered, but fine," I said. "And if I needed a coat, Nick would have already given me his."

"What?"

"You can't interrupt him," Nick murmured. "As tempting as it might be. Tell him we're at . . ."

I glanced over to see him operating another handheld device.

"At least this has a signal," he said. "Too bad the screen isn't made for a hundred below. Give me a sec to clear the condensation and I'll have our coordinates."

"You got lost . . . with a GPS?"

"Elena?" Clay's voice crackled through the radio. "Are you there? What's going on? Talk to—"

I hit the call button, hoping *that* would cut him off, then said, "I'm still here. Nick's getting you our coordinates. He's having trouble reading— Oh, wait."

Nick passed over the unit. I squinted at the foggy display, then read off the numbers.

"How close is that to you?" I asked.

Silence.

I asked again. Still nothing. We tried the call button, but there was no answer.

"Lost him," I muttered. "And the question is: did it happen before or after he got the coordinates?"

The wolves howled again. They were closer now, on the move. A distant one answered.

"Now *that's* foolproof communication," Nick said. "Maybe if we Change and howl . . ."

"Possible. Though we might also alert the Teslers. But that does give me an idea."

I whistled. Then whistled again.

"I'm not sure Clay will be close enough to hear that," Nick said.

"No, but I'm hoping the wolves will. I want to talk to one."

"Um, okay." Nick studied my face for signs of hypothermic dementia. "I don't think wolves come when you whistle."

"This one might."

We stepped off the path to wait, getting behind a windbreak and hunkering down. Sure enough, the dark red mutt showed up. He didn't exactly come bounding over the snow. He drew close, then circled, as if making sure it was me before he answered... or maybe trying to decide whether he wanted to bother.

When I caught a whiff of him on the breeze, I slipped into his path.

"I need your help," I said.

He sighed, as if this was what he'd feared, and his gaze slid to the side, gauging the escape routes.

"Yes, I know, helping us probably isn't at the top of your priority list, but if you answered my whistle, you're at least curious to hear what I want. And don't worry, there's something in it for you... including getting us out of these woods and off your territory."

That made him look my way. Nick edged closer, sizing him up. The werewolf did the same.

"We're not the only trespassers you and your pack would like gone," I said. "In fact, I suspect we're the least of your worries right now. Heading the list is a group of thugs who think this 'unclaimed wilderness' is the perfect spot to set up illegal operations, while killing locals."

His green eyes shifted to the side again, just enough to tell me something.

"Ah, so you do know they aren't the ones who killed those men."

A growling grunt.

"Except the first, yes. I guess you know that. And you know who was responsible for the rest—the Shifters, who I'm going to assume haven't given you or the wolves much trouble until recently. That's another problem I can fix for you."

Another grunt, this one saying, "Yes, yes, now get on with it." I did. I told him that we planned to kill the Teslers, and that would quiet down the Shifters and end the killings. I'd also let the Shifter Alpha know that Eli had been playing "roust the wolves" with him and the pack.

"That'll put an end to his antics," I said. "But before I go after the Teslers, I'll need backup. And don't worry, I don't mean you. My mate is out here, along with two other were-wolves from my Pack looking for me. But I suspect you already know that, which is what has your pack nervous and what made you come running when I whistled."

A soft chuff of agreement.

"Find them and lead them to us. We'll be here for a bit, but then we're moving on. If you get them as far as our trail, they can take it from there. Deal?"

Another chuff and he loped off.

"That was interesting," Nick said.

"Out here, that's only the start of 'interesting.'"

WE'D BEEN WAITING five minutes when the buzz of an engine made my head jerk up.

"Snowmobiles," I said.

"Think Clay liberated one from a cottage?"

I shook my head. "Between the noise and the smell, it would be useless for tracking." The whine was getting louder. "And if it's not them..."

"We'd better get farther from the road."

We ducked behind a thick stand of bushes. As the first snowmobile approached, I peeked out. I saw only a figure and a shadowy face, but it was enough to start my heart pounding.

"That's him, isn't it?" Nick whispered. "Tesler Senior."

I nodded and pulled back as it passed. Then a second headlight crested a dip in the road.

"And Tesler Junior, I presume."

I nodded.

"Should we wait until that mutt finds Clay and my dad?"

I shook my head.

"That's what I thought."

REINFORCEMENTS

YES, WE *SHOULD* wait. But we couldn't, because if we did, we'd be combing these woods for days trying to find the Teslers' cabin again. And it would only be a few hours until they realized I must have made it to safety, and took off before I came back for vengeance...with my Pack in tow.

I needed to find that cabin, hide someplace safe, then hope the mutt brought Clay to me. The Shifters *had* told me where to find the cabin. I'd taken mental notes, but even at the time, I'd known it wouldn't help. Their idea of directions went something like this: take the road that crosses the river, then turn onto the one that heads toward sunrise, follow it past the fallen oak, turn toward the city, cut over the hill with the abandoned shack...

I'd figured I'd be able to find the place on my own, but it was like when someone offers directions to a house you've visited before. You think you'll remember your way there. But now I realized that hoping to find a specific cabin in all these miles of wilderness was like hoping to find a single house in a neighborhood of hundreds.

The best chance to fulfill my promise and get Noah back was to follow the Teslers now. We'd barely set out when they turned off the road and had to slow down. A brisk jog kept us close enough to track them.

We followed the sleds back to the cottage, which wasn't as far away as I'd thought, proving how screwed we would have been.

Once we neared the cabin, I remembered the territory down to the last tree. The snowmobile shed was on the other side of the cottage. We cut through the forest, staying downwind and coming out there, hidden in the bushes, too far for them to pick up our scent.

As soon as the engines died, the brothers started talking. We could only pick up snatches of the conversation, just enough to know they'd been looking for me, which I could have guessed. Tesler had gone back to the stakeout point to find broken ropes, paw prints and bloodied snow.

"Oh, come on," Eddie said as they came out of the shed. "You've got to admit, it is kind of funny. You stake her out, trying to scare her with stories of that beast thing...and it really does carry her off. What do you think it's doing with her?"

Tesler snarled something.

"Hey, don't give me that look," Eddie said. "If you'd kept your cool, you wouldn't have lost her. I told you to bring her back inside. But you had to push it. Time to focus on the consolation prize, which you gotta admit is a helluva score. Six months from now, you won't remember what Elena Michaels looked like. All that'll matter is that you get the credit for killing her...and for killing Clayton Danvers."

I didn't hear what Tesler said next. The next thing I knew I was facedown in the snow, rage and panic pumping through me, Nick's knee digging in my back, his voice at my ear telling me it was okay, Clay was okay, they hadn't found him, just lie still and listen.

". . . would have been easier if plan A worked out," Eddie was saying as their boots crunched across the snow. "Stillwell delivers Elena and tells us where her hubby's stashed. Now we have to wait for Danvers to show up. But he will. No doubt about that, not after the way he went after you the other day. He'll come for her, and we'll be waiting."

Their boots clomped up the cabin steps. Eddie kept talking, trying to lift his brother's mood.

"If we kill those two, we won't have to hide out in this godforsaken wilderness anymore. We can ply our trade anywhere in the country, because there's not going to be any Pack to worry about."

"Still got four more where they came from," Tesler grumbled.

"Who? Two old men and a jewel thief?"

A frown creased Nick's handsome face.

"Oh, wait," Eddie said. "We can't forget Nick Sorrentino."

Nick nodded.

"No, actually, I think we can," Eddie continued. "Unless we're competing for best-dressed pansy-ass. Muss up his hair and he'll run screaming for his stylist."

That got a chuckle from Tesler . . . and then it was my turn to hold Nick down.

"We have to figure out what we're going to do with

Danvers when he shows up," Eddie said as the door whooshed open. "It has to be good. And we need to take photos. That'll cement our reps. We'll have every mutt in the country begging us for jobs."

"Speaking of which," Tesler said, as they went inside. "We have to call the others. Tell them to get their asses back here…"

I waited until the door closed and lights turned on inside, tracking their passage through the cottage. Then I let Nick up.

"Pansy-ass," he muttered as he scooped snow from his hood.

"It's a front. Which he's about to find out."

"Damn right."

Nick's lips twitched in the faintest sardonic smile. He knew he wasn't the Pack's best fighter. His father and Clay never let him be—they'd always been quick to jump in and fend off any threats, as they did with Jeremy. But like Jeremy, Nick could hold his own, and unlike Jeremy, he enjoyed the chance to prove it.

"Junior is mine," he said as we rose and stretched.

"Good, because I own Senior. And no one better get in my way."

We brushed ourselves off, then I looked around for any sign that our local werewolf had found Clay or Antonio. Nothing.

"Do we wait?" Nick asked. "There's only two of them, and it sounds like there will be more soon."

"Not too soon. They're talking about their comrades, who are in the Lower 48 on business." I looked from the house to the gray woods. "As long as the Teslers stay put, we should wait."

AGAIN I TRIED to do the right thing and wait for backup. Again, an interruption made me rethink the wisdom of that. This time it wasn't a sound, but a scent.

When I lifted my face to catch it again, Nick inhaled, too.

"Mutt," he said. "Is that Joey's boy? Maybe he escaped."

For a moment, I hesitated. I don't know why—the scent clearly wasn't Noah's—yet something in it made me pause before shaking my head.

"Those Shifter things?"

"No, they smell different. And very distinct. Their cave was well appointed, but I don't think it included hot showers."

Nick made a face, then sniffed again. "So it's not the Shifters. It's not Joey or his boy. It's not Reese, not the Teslers, not the wolf-guy . . . Exactly how many werewolves and werewolf-like critters are running around out here?"

"Too many." I pushed to my feet and looked at the cabin. The lights were still on and I could hear the faint clatter of dishes, as if they were making breakfast. "Let's go see who's sniffing around."

MISSION

WHAT WE FOUND were two werewolves dressed in full winter walking garb, from boots to gloves to parkas that covered their faces. One whiff told me I'd never met these mutts before. I had, however, smelled them—or traces of them, earlier tonight, in the cottage.

When Tesler told Eddie they needed to call their men in, he didn't mean bring them back to Alaska. They were already here.

It's a testament to my exhaustion that even as we tracked the two mutts downwind, I held out hope that these weren't actually the rest of Tesler's gang. Even when we got close enough to hear them speaking English with thick Eastern European accents, I thought maybe Roman hadn't heeded my assurances that we didn't need help and sent some of his "Russian wolves" to help, and they'd been nosing around the cabin earlier. But why would they be speaking English? That only made sense if their leaders were English-speaking, and insisted on that as their common language. Their next words confirmed that suspicion.

"Fucking Eddie thinks he is such a fucking hotshot. Thinks he fucking runs this outfit."

"That is where you always get into trouble, Marko. You still think it is Travis in charge. It is Eddie...letting his brother think he is leading."

"Travis would have let us steal a snowmobile."

"And that is why he is not in charge. Eddie is careful. Two stolen snowmobiles are enough."

"Because it is enough for the two of them. *We* have to walk through the fucking snow, looking for some fucking werewolf girl they let escape."

"You can be sure it was not Eddie who let her get away. You are just angry because we did not find her, which is good, or you would be in more trouble than you were when you killed that hiker."

"I just wanted a poke."

"You think Travis would not notice? Would not smell you on her?"

"I have condoms."

The other man, whose accent sounded Ukrainian, snorted. "You think that would cover all the smell?"

We were crouched behind bushes, keeping our distance.

"If they get to the cabin..." Nick whispered.

"It doubles the odds in their favor. We should take them out."

I wasn't in top-notch shape, but still feeling no pain, and Nick was fresh and raring to go. With the element of surprise, we could take them. Nick slipped back to cut across behind them and come up on their left.

Marko was still complaining.

"I don't know why we had to come back from the city. We'd have found the hotel, caught this Danvers, brought him back..."

"If Eddie is right, which he usually is, Danvers is already here. You just wanted to stay in the city. You always want to stay in the city."

"Why not? It's warm. The beds are warm. The girls are warm. This—" He gestured at the surrounding forest and swore in Russian.

"Enough complaining. If you do not like it—"

"The money I like. Eddie, I don't. Always ordering us around. Come to Alaska. No, go back. No, come again. Back and forth, back and forth."

The Ukrainian told Marko to shut up before someone heard.

"That's why I'm talking so much," Marko said. "If this girl is out here, she is alone, afraid. If she hears a voice, she'll come running."

I signaled Nick, who swung out into their path. The Ukrainian leapt out of the way, whistling as he did, but Marko, caught in mid-rant, just stood there, mouth open until Nick shut it for him with a line-drive upper cut.

I caught Marko and slammed him to the ground, glancing back only long enough to check on Nick. He didn't have the Ukrainian yet, but he'd backed him into the thick bushes. The Ukrainian whistled again.

"That's not going to bring anyone running," I said. "Your buddies just sat down to breakfast."

Beneath me, Marko tried to twist and bite. So I broke his arm. I wasn't in the mood for threats. I would have killed him already, but if I needed information, he was more likely to give it than his friend. I could do without the shrieks of pain, though, so I shoved his face into the snow to stifle them.

When he shut up, I wrenched his head back and hissed in his ear, "I hear you like killing humans, Marko. You're on American Pack territory, and do you know how we treat man-eaters here?"

He swore at me in Russian. I smashed his face into the snow again.

Nick was sizing up the Ukrainian, knowing the mutt couldn't run, but that he'd fight as soon as Nick moved. And a cornered wolf fights hard.

"Tesler summoned you boys back the minute he got a whiff of trouble, didn't he? Figured he and his brother weren't enough to take on two Pack werewolves? Poor excuse for tough guys, if you ask me. Did you do any man-eating while you were in the Lower 48?"

"Is that where we were?" Marko turned his head and smiled up at me through the blood streaming from his nose.

"I don't really care where you were. I'm just making conversation."

"Oh, you'll care. You'll care very much soon."

Nick feinted left, preparing for engagement and takedown. Then he stopped short, gaze shooting behind me, lips parting.

"Elena!"

He twisted and lunged at me. The Ukrainian grabbed him. As I shot up off Marko, a shadow passed over me and

I caught a whiff of werewolf scent. I wheeled to see a strange mutt, with two more behind him.

"Now do you want to know what we were doing?" Marko said. "Bringing fake passports to the rest of our pack, and escorting them here."

It was a short fight.

DRAMA

MARKO KICKED OPEN the cabin door and shoved me through with his good hand.

"Anybody home?" he called. "We brought you a present, Travis."

"Two presents," said the Ukrainian, pushing Nick in. Two other mutts followed. "I don't know if you wanted this one alive, but I guessed you did."

"And if you don't, I'll take him," said one of the newcomers, a paunchy, graying brute with only traces of an accent. His grin was a picket fence of missing teeth. "He's pretty."

Nick ignored him, taking everything in, unperturbed. I could say he was putting on a brave show, but he just wasn't all that worried. I was with him, so all he had to do was pay attention and await orders. Sometimes it really sucks to be in charge.

Admittedly, I wasn't as worried as I should be either. The others were on their way and I didn't think the Teslers would kill us. Their endgame was killing Clay. What better bait than his mate plus his best friend?

As for what Tesler would do with me while passing the time, I was surprisingly unconcerned about that, too. I blamed the drugs. I was sure when they wore off, I'd blame them for this whole "captured again" mess. An Alpha-training lesson for me—never make field decisions while under the influence of painkillers.

Even when Tesler walked in from another room, saw me and grinned, my pulse barely jumped. He strode over, took both my hands and held me at arm's length for a once-over, like a groom checking out his arranged bride.

"All that and she still looks good. You hold up well, honey. Too bad you're not going to look so good when I'm done with you."

He pulled me closer and slid his hand under the parka, squeezing my ass. I heard a scuffle behind me, and I glanced back to see Nick struggling against his captor, glowering at Tesler. When I shot him a look, he stopped. I appreciated the sentiment, but if he didn't play good hostage, they might decide they didn't need two of us after all.

"They killed Andrej," the Ukrainian said.

When Tesler frowned, Eddie leaned over and whispered to him, "The big Romanian. Joined up just before we left."

Tesler's expression didn't change. He might remember the guy. He might not. Either way, he didn't really give a shit.

The Ukrainian was right. Eddie pretended his brother was in charge, but it was what Clay and I planned to do when I was Alpha—if mutts wanted to think the big scary guy was in charge, let them. Yet a pack is really no different from a human organization. While the strongest might make the best leader short-term, it took more than that for long-term success. In this case, though, even the pack members themselves couldn't agree who was their Alpha, meaning they wouldn't agree on who to protect. I could use that. I just wasn't sure how.

"Paul? Stefan? Tie him up," Eddie said. "Marko, let's get that arm set. Gavril—"

"Can I eat, please?" Gavril—the chubby guy with the bad teeth—whined. "I haven't had anything since the plane."

Eddie waved him to the kitchen. "Get something and come back. Danvers could show up any minute and I want to be ready. This is our big moment, guys."

"We're gonna wipe out the North American Pack," Tesler said.

"No, we're going to replace them. And *you* guys are getting in at the start." The others lit up like ground-floor investors about to watch their company go public. "You've worked hard and it's all going to pay off now. By summer, we'll be out of this godforsaken wasteland, living in California, Texas, Florida . . . We'll have a whole damn country to choose from."

They nodded, true believers at the revival, the Promised Land shimmering before them.

"Anyone who opposes us goes down. Anyone who wants to join up will be welcome, as long as he's willing to pull his weight and understands that you guys are at the top of the heap. You were here first. You'll get the best territory, the best girls and, most of all, the best-paying jobs in the operation."

As he preached, I plotted possible escape routes. I liked the big picture window a few feet from us. Of course, I'd like it even better if I could see some familiar werewolves slipping through the forest to surround the house...

"And remember who got you here," Tesler said. "Me and Eddie, we did all this for you guys."

"We have to give Marko credit, though," Eddie said. "As mad as I was about him killing that guy out here, he gave me an idea. Kill a few humans on Pack territory and look who comes running."

He waved at me. So he was taking credit for bringing us here? The guy had balls; I had to give him that. And brains, unfortunately. Which was more than I could say for his flunkies, who all nodded, convinced their brilliant leader— or their leader's little brother—had delivered the Pack right into their hands.

Now, if only the rest of that Pack would actually show up...

As long as Eddie was basking in the sound of his own voice, though, it was giving the others time to get here. Just keep yapping...

"Enough of that," Eddie said. "Time to get ready for our guest."

Damn.

"Paul, get Mr. Sorrentino tied up while Marko holds him still. Be careful, though. I'm sure those manicured nails are sharp. Gavril! How long does it take to grab food? Bring some for the rest of us. And, Travis, how about you take your prize into the bedroom and finish up with her? Do what you want. Just keep her alive."

Eddie tensed, ready for me to fight. I didn't. I had a better chance of beating Tesler alone. The challenge would be defeating Tesler *and* getting Nick free. As I pondered that, though, Tesler took a good look at me, noting my lack of mortal terror.

"I'll wait," he said.

"For what?" Eddie said. "No. Don't even suggest—"

"You want to rile up Danvers? What better way than for him to watch while—"

"No."

"Why not?"

Eddie leaned in, lowering his voice. "Because I *don't* want to rile him up. I'm holding hostages to keep him calm. Now take her in the bedroom or you're going to lose your chance again—"

"Too late," said a voice behind us.

We turned to see Antonio in the kitchen doorway.

"You guys really need to be more careful with security," he said. "The back door was unlocked, and I found a guy raiding your fridge. Don't worry, though, I took care of him for you." He glanced over his shoulder at the floor, presumably where Gavril lay. Then his gaze traveled over their faces. "Oh, was he one of yours? Damn. I'm really sorry about that."

While he spoke, the only person who moved was Eddie, backing up toward me, guarding the prize. Everyone else stared, as if trying to figure out what was going on. Finally the Ukrainian ran at Antonio. Antonio barreled forward, meeting his charge.

A figure slid from the opposite hall entrance, behind Nick, still held by Marko.

"Marko!" Eddie shouted.

Marko only frowned at Eddie, as if wondering why Eddie wanted him to go help fight Antonio when he only had one good arm. The other mutt figured it out, shouting a warning and gesturing at Reese, who'd slipped in, armed with a fireplace poker. He swung and hit Marko in the side of his head.

Tesler pulled me against him, arms pinned behind me with one hand, the other forearm at my throat. Any notion of fighting stopped—not with the choke hold, but with Eddie, backing up to us, protecting the booty as his soldiers did battle. I couldn't take them both on, and with Eddie staying out of the fight, the odds were in our favor anyway.

Antonio killed the other newcomer—I'd already forgotten what Eddie called him. That left the Ukrainian, pinned to the floor now by Nick, and Marko, easily held by Reese, who had only to twist his broken arm to keep him on his knees. I motioned for them to hold fast. Kill these two and we lost our negotiating power.

When Antonio stepped toward me, Eddie jerked one of my arms from Tesler's grasp. "Take another step and I break this. And that's just for starters."

Antonio stopped.

"I do believe this is what we call a standoff," Eddie said.

"Not much of one," I said. "I'm the only prize worth holding. Notice I'm not even asking for a trade? You'd never go for it—they're just cannon fodder."

Marko and the Ukrainian tensed, Marko looking to Tesler, the Ukrainian to Eddie.

"I'd like my men back," Eddie said quietly.

"But you won't turn me over to get them, will you? Two for one. That's quite a deal. I won't even ask you to walk away. You let me go. They let them go." I twisted to look at Eddie. "Game on."

Neither man moved.

"Guess not," I said. "Sorry, guys. You aren't worth it, apparently."

"No, I'm just not taking the offer seriously, considering where it's coming from." Eddie turned to Antonio. "You don't let a woman talk for you, do you?"

"Usually. They're better at it."

"Speak for yourself," Nick said.

Reese chuckled.

"I'd suggest you start taking this a little more seriously," Eddie said. "And tell me who I'm negotiating with. I know you don't let the Beta's mate speak for the Pack."

"No, we let the Alpha-elect speak for us," Nick said. "She just did."

I glanced at him. Had *everyone* in the Pack known before me?

"You think this is funny?" Eddie lifted one of my fingers. "Maybe you'll find this even funnier."

He snapped my finger. Nick winced. I didn't. I won't say I didn't feel it, only that I saw it coming and bit my cheek against the pain.

"Sure, you can do that," I said. "But a word of advice? The worse shape I'm in, the harder it'll be to get Clay to come to my rescue. He may be my mate, but he can always make himself another. And if I'm gone, he'd be next in line for Alpha."

"Not giving yourself much credit, are you?" Eddie said.

I shrugged. "I'm practical and so is he. He'll come for me as long as I'm reasonably healthy, but ultimately, I'm replaceable."

A shadow passed over the picture window behind us. Then it exploded, glass flying, as Clay leapt through. He landed on his feet with a thud and a grin.

"Nah, darling, you're definitely one of a kind."

I elbowed Eddie as Clay grabbed Tesler by the shirt and ripped him off me. Across the room, Nick and Reese struggled to hold their hostages, waiting for a sign from me before finishing them.

Eddie bounced back. I swung, dislodging a shard of glass from my shirt, which nearly caught me in the eye. Beside me, Clay was advancing on Tesler while wiping blood from a cut on his neck.

"That's what you get for insisting on a dramatic entrance," I called. "Next time, do us all a favor and use the front door."

"That wasn't drama, darling. That was the element of surprise."

I snorted and roundhouse kicked Eddie. Out of the corner of my eye, I could see Tesler, and I had to struggle to stay on target. Eddie was the bigger threat, and less of a fighter, meaning I had to leave Tesler for Clay.

Clay grabbed Tesler and pitched him into the wall

beside the broken window. As Clay bore down on him, Tesler scrambled up . . . and leapt right out the window.

When Clay grabbed the sill to vault it, he put all his weight on his bad arm. It didn't give way, but it gave enough to make him fumble the hurdle, landing hard in the snow and staggering a few steps. By then, Tesler was racing into the forest.

Clay glanced back at me.

"Go on," I said. "Take him."

My gaze only flickered from Eddie for a second, but it was enough. He followed his brother's lead and ran the other way. Antonio tried to cut him off, but he was too far away.

As I ran after Eddie, I waved Antonio back. "Finish them first."

The back door slammed. I grabbed my sneakers, then raced after him, kicking off the oversized boots as I went.

HITCHHIKER

AS I CHASED Eddie, I heard a distant yelp from Tesler, followed by a growl of frustration from Clay, meaning he'd caught and lost his prey. I instinctively started swerving that way, then stopped myself.

Yes, I wanted to be the one to kill Tesler. Part of me desperately needed to be. But to do so, I had to abandon the greater threat. The good of the Pack came first, and killing Eddie was in the Pack's best interests.

That didn't stop me from hoping Eddie would run toward his brother, but he was too smart for that. He was heading in the opposite direction, dividing Clay and me.

And as hard as I strained to hear signs that Antonio was on his way and could take over the chase, I knew that wouldn't happen either. It didn't matter how much killing experience Reese had, Antonio wouldn't leave him to do the job alone. And Nick's only experience was as part of a group, following someone else's lead. So his father would stay, trusting that Clay and I could handle our targets alone.

When I heard the sound of a motor, I smiled. We were

coming to a road. Once Eddie realized that, he'd change direction.

Instead, he picked up speed. Ahead, I saw a truck barreling down a road, snow sluicing up chest high on both sides. It passed before Eddie reached the edge, so he didn't need to check his speed to cross.

By the time I reached one edge, he was past the other and zipping back into the endless forest. The road was empty, but pitted with enough tracks to suggest it was what passed for a major artery out here, probably the road that linked to the highway.

I crossed and followed Eddie into the forest. Before long, I caught the faint whiff of exhaust. Sure enough, we'd circled around and were heading back to the same road.

Had he decided to return to the cottage? Or try to find his brother? God, I hoped so, because at this rate, I wasn't catching him unless he tripped.

Eddie ran less than twenty paces past the road, then circled through the woods and headed back toward it.

What the hell was he doing?

The answer hit with the buzz of another motor. Eddie was trapped. Eddie was smart. Eddie had no intention of risking his life to fight me—he was interested in survival, not belt notches. So what would he do? The same thing Reese had done in Pittsburgh: take refuge with humans.

But again he dashed onto the road in front of the car, then made no effort to stop it, just disappeared into the forest. Was he trying to use the traffic to slow me down? If so, it wasn't working. The car was a compact, grinding along, spitting up snow, moving at the pace of a fast walk. I easily crossed in front of it, and the driver didn't even seem to see me, too intent on staring at the road right in front of him, struggling to get through the snow.

Eddie continued running into the woods. And as could be predicted by this point, he didn't stay there, instead circling wide and heading back for that road. I was sorely tempted to just stand in the middle of it and wait for him.

It was then that I finally figured out what he was doing. I had only a split second to realize it before we heard another vehicle—a pickup truck this time—and, as I expected, Eddie looped around, coming out right behind the passing truck.

He'd been crisscrossing the road waiting for the right vehicle, pulling a version of his brother's "hop on the train" trick. Now, admittedly, over the last few days my brain hadn't been running on all cylinders, courtesy of Eddie's rapist thug brother, but I wasn't completely brain dead yet. I'd realized his ruse just in time, and when he tore out behind that passing truck, he didn't find an open pickup bed in his path. He found a werewolf who was a little tired of letting her prey escape.

He tried to race around me. I grabbed him and hauled him into the forest. We fought. Spurred on by the boost of actually catching him—and the potential humiliation of losing him—I won. I snapped his neck. A short fight and a quick death, neither worth much comment. I dragged his body a little deeper into the woods, covered him in brush, made a note of the spot to bury him later, then ran back to find Clay and Tesler.

• • •

ONCE I WAS back in the forest, locating Clay was easy—just follow the sounds of battle. As I drew closer, I realized it was more a struggle than a battle—one struggling to start a fight and the other struggling to avoid it. First came the thump of a blow. Then a grunt. Then a scuffle and a curse. Then the pounding of running footsteps. Another thump, grunt, scuffle, curse.

Sure enough, I found Clay hot on Tesler's heels. He'd catch up enough to punch him, maybe grab a fold of his shirt, but Tesler always scrambled free and started running again. Or he did, until he found me standing in his path.

Clay pulled up short behind him and grinned a greeting.

"Looking for a little more action, darling?"

"Doesn't seem like you're getting any. What's the matter, Travis? I thought you were just itching for this. Eddie's plan worked. Clay's right there. Go ahead. Have some fun. Or did you forget your camera?"

"Was that the plan?" Clay said. "Let me guess. Lure me in. Carve me up. Take photos. Pass them around to prove what badass motherfuckers you are." He shook his head. "Mutts. Not an original idea in their thick skulls. But sure, we can do that, Travis. I'll even send Elena back to get your camera. Just step on over here and we'll get started."

Tesler's gaze shot to the side, checking and rejecting escape routes. Then he looked over my head.

"Your brother isn't coming," I said.

"Well, you sure as hell didn't kill him," Travis said. "He'd have left a mark, and I don't see any, except that broken finger from earlier."

"They broke your finger?" Clay said.

"Yes, while you were outside preparing your dramatic entrance."

"Shit. Sorry, darling. You want to take one of his?"

"Your brother *is* dead," I said. "The only marks he left were bruises, and I've got enough of those that a few more don't matter."

He eyed me, as if he didn't quite believe this. Too bad. If he thought Eddie was coming to his rescue, all the better for us when he found out otherwise.

"So you're going to team up against me?" he said finally. "That's not fair."

"No? All right, then. Choose your opponent."

He looked from Clay to me, and sneered. "You think I'm falling for that? If I even come close to taking out one of you, the other will jump in."

"And that's not fair. Because you're all about fair, aren't you, Travis? Pump yourself full of steroids to get that extra advantage. Just as cowardly as using a gun, which I'm sure you'd do, too, if you'd thought to grab one."

"I've *never* used a gun—"

"And you've never had backup either, have you? When you fought me, your little brother didn't jump in and save your ass. I was hallucinating."

He glowered. "That was different. You were our captive. We had a plan."

"And right now, you're our captive." I smiled. "And guess what? We have a plan, too. It's almost a carbon copy of yours. Only in ours, you're the one who dies and gets his picture taken, shoring up *our* reputations. Now pick your poison."

He looked from me to Clay and back again. I was the obvious choice—smaller, less experienced and already battered from earlier. But he kept looking, kept thinking.

"I choose..."

Another slow look from me to Clay, then he wheeled, snapping off the nearest branch and lunging at Clay. I leapt forward. Clay leapt back. Neither of us was fast enough. Tesler plunged the jagged stick into Clay's chest. Then he ran.

I raced over to Clay as he staggered back.

"Go after him," he said, as I dropped in front of him.

"No."

"Elena."

"No!" I snarled the word. That shut him up. The branch still protruded from his chest. It wasn't as big as I thought, less than an inch diameter. If anything, though, that made it worse—thinner and sharper, like an arrow. As I fumbled with his jacket, he reached up to pull the branch out.

"Don't," I said.

"Darling, it's not—"

"Don't!"

"I'm fine. Go after him. This is what he wanted."

"Then I guess it's what he's going to get."

My voice quavered as badly as my hands now. I'd been so afraid of being raped by Tesler. Did I think that was the worst he could do to me? No. There was something far worse, and I'd been such a fool, working myself up over that, letting him scare me, letting fear slow me down, when I could have killed him, and I wouldn't be here now, shaking so bad I couldn't get Clay's jacket undone.

"Elena, I'm okay."

He tried grabbing my hands. I knocked his away with a mumbled apology, telling him to stay still, don't move, don't do anything.

The branch had gone through the jacket, meaning I couldn't easily get it off without dislodging the stick. Rule one of dealing with impalements—don't pull out the object because it might be the only thing keeping you from bleeding to death.

I worked his jacket and bloodied shirt off enough to see the wound. Then I let out a long, shuddering sigh. My eyes filled and I swiped at them. The second time in one night I'd come close to crying. A record for me. But even as I blinked angrily, a tear rolled down my cheek. Clay tugged off his glove and wiped it away.

"Did I say I was okay?" he murmured.

I nodded.

"Still don't trust me, huh?"

I choked a laugh. He was right—at least the part about being okay. The down-filled jacket stopped most of Tesler's thrust, knocking Clay over, but otherwise doing little damage. The stick had only penetrated about a half inch, and in the fleshy part of his shoulder.

"Can I pull it out now?" he asked.

I did it for him, carefully, so I wouldn't leave any splinters. Blood gushed. I pressed his glove to it and the flow slowed to a trickle. Clay peeled my fingers from the glove, taking over.

"Now will you go after that bastard? Before he gets away? I'm right behind you."

I nodded, pushed to my feet, gave him one last look, then took off.

I CAUGHT UP with Tesler. It wasn't hard. He figured I was busy saving Clay's life, so he ran straight for the nearest snowmobile shed. I found him trying to hot-wire his getaway vehicle. We fought. Again, it wasn't hard. If I was in rough shape, he was just as bad, and I had fear on my side—his fear. His gang was dead, his brother was dead and he was on his own. Travis Tesler wasn't accustomed to being alone.

As for my own fear, the last traces of it had evaporated when Clay had been stabbed. Rape I could survive. I'd do almost anything in my power to avoid it. *Almost* anything. The one thing I wouldn't do was put my family at risk.

Nick had said I was allowed to have a soft spot. I'd been certain I had only one, and Tesler had found it. But there were more ways to hurt me. Come after Clay. Come after my children. Come after my Pack.

Those were weaknesses I couldn't overcome. I shouldn't. I'd thought an Alpha should be invulnerable, but that was ridiculous. What kind of Alpha would Jeremy be if he didn't care what happened to his Pack?

I had soft spots. Mutts would always target them. All I could do was shore up my defenses. Protect my Pack. Protect my children. Protect my mate. And, yes, protect myself.

Now I had in my sights a man who'd threatened all of that. This time, though, he was afraid and I wasn't, and that made all the difference. Having a broken finger didn't help—he wasn't the only one who felt pain when my punches connected—but finally I hauled him out of the snowmobile shed. He broke free just as Clay caught up.

Tesler charged me, and charged me again, not even bothering to change angle, let alone tactic. I sidestepped and wiped blood from my nose, the droplets spraying the snow. As Tesler recovered and wheeled, I glanced at Clay. He had his arms crossed, face immobile, only his eyes betraying his concern.

"I've got him," I said.

"I know."

Tesler charged again. I sidestepped. This time, though, my left foot slipped and, had Tesler been quicker, he would have spun and taken me down. As it was, he tried, but I managed to dance out of the way.

My heart thumped. Not fear. Exhilaration. Tesler was still standing, but I had him, and he knew it. I could tell by the set of his jaw. The wild look in his eyes. The desperation in each charge. He was a wounded bull making his last stand.

Clay crossed and uncrossed his arms, holding himself in check. I knew what it must be like for him, watching me, knowing how tired I was, how every muscle ached. He was still fresh and spoiling for a fight, and he longed to take over this one for me.

Yes, this felt good. It felt so damned good. But Clay was right. I was taking chances, and it was time to end this.

When Tesler charged again, I started to dance out of the way, then shot out my foot and tripped him. I jumped onto his back, grabbed his hair and ground his face into the dirt and blood-streaked snow.

Then I thought of all the ways I could kill him.

Clay had killed that mutt thirty years ago to cement his reputation. If I was worried about being accepted as Alpha, here was a way to solve the problem. Prove I was just as crazy, just as sadistic and just as dangerous as Clay.

If that was my entire purpose in making Tesler suffer, then I could have done it. But Clay hadn't made that mutt suffer. He'd knocked him out with anesthetic before he even knew what was happening. He wasn't crazy. He wasn't sadistic. Dangerous, yes, but not in the way they thought.

Clay wasn't a monster. But if I tortured Tesler because I wanted him to die horribly, that would make me one.

I glanced over at Clay. "Do you want him? You did want to make an example of a mutt again."

That got Tesler's attention. Until now, he'd been still. Not surrendering, I was sure. Just resting as I contemplated my next move. Now he bucked. But I saw that one coming, and easily kept him pinned, grinding his face into the ground again for good measure.

When I glanced at Clay, though, he said, "Nah, too much bother. I just want to go home."

"So do I."

I grabbed Tesler's hair, ready to snap his neck.

"Wait!" he said.

I leaned over him. "Got a few last words, Travis? Unless they're 'I'm sorry,' I don't really want to hear them."

"Sorry?" He sneered. "Is that what you want from me? An apology for hurting you?"

"No, not particularly. I've had those. They don't do much good."

I thought of the letter and, for the first time since it arrived, the memory didn't make my stomach clench. I didn't accept that apology and I damned well wasn't going to feel guilty about it. But I wouldn't send a nasty letter back. Just silence, and in that, he'd know he wasn't forgiven. And if he suffered more guilt for what he'd done? That was fine by me.

"What I'd like an apology for is the others," I said. "For Dennis, who never did a damned thing to you. For those girls, whose only mistake was looking for a little fun. And for all the other girls you raped and murdered before you came here. I'd like to hear an apology for them, but I know you won't give it and I know they wouldn't want it. So we're going to skip those final words—"

"I'll join the Pack."

"What?"

"You need recruits. I heard that. I'll join."

I couldn't help laughing. "And what makes you think we'd let—"

"I'm a damned fine fighter. I'll fight for the Pack and you'll own my ass. That's the price I'll pay for my life."

"How...noble. Really. Only one problem. That damned fine fighter part. You're good, I'll give you that. But I still beat you."

"You had help. I could have taken you. Back in the cabin, I had you beat until *he* showed up."

"No, you and Eddie had me. Without Eddie, you'd have

been screwed. So we both had help. But in the end? You were outsmarted, outlasted and outfought. As much crap as you pumped into your body, it didn't change the fact that at heart you're a coward who likes to beat up helpless humans."

He bucked and snarled. "That's not about fighting. It's—"

"About sex? Hell, no. It's not about sex, Travis. It's about dominance. And, apparently, the only women you can dominate are helpless ones. Put you up against a female of your own species and look what happened. Outmatched." I leaned down, and lowered my voice. "And outclassed."

I snapped his neck.

SURVIVOR

NICK HAD TAKEN cell phone shots of the mutts from the house, then some of Tesler before we buried him. He figured the Shifters might demand proof before returning Noah. I was sure pictures from a cell phone weren't what they'd have in mind, but I didn't stop Nick.

The Russian Pack might expect proof, too, and this *would* be what they wanted. Plus, having pictures showing an entire upstart pack wiped out by us in a few hours might be something to have on hand if there were any questions about the Pack's power after my ascension was announced. So I let Nick take photos, and just warned him to upload them and get them wiped off his camera before we went through airport security.

After I assured them I was fine and Clay set my finger with a makeshift splint, Clay and Nick buried Tesler. While they were doing that, I took his clothing and ID back to the cottage, where Antonio was burning everything in the fireplace. I got about halfway there when a familiar scent wafted past. I turned to see a shape hidden in a thick patch of trees, silently watching me. Our wolf friend.

"Come by to make sure we kept up our end of the deal?" I called as I walked over. "We did. They're all dead except one, and he won't be coming back. Thanks for helping find the others. I appreciate that."

"You're welcome."

The voice startled me. I'd figured he was still in wolf form. As the figure rose, I had to sniff again, making sure it was the same werewolf. If I'd been asked to picture him, I'd have guessed he'd be older, living out a midlife crisis by exploring that other side of himself, as Dennis had been. He was younger than me, though. Late twenties. Dark reddish-brown hair to his shoulders, lean with a narrow face, high cheekbones and piercing green eyes. Native blood, I guessed. And he was dressed. To be honest, that surprised me, too. I didn't expect him naked, but maybe just wearing a fur thrown around him or clothing stolen from a nearby cabin. The clothes were clearly his, though—a leather jacket, jeans, T-shirt, Doc Marten boots...

"Not what you expected?" he said.

"No," I lied. "I'm just trying to place the accent." Actually, I didn't need to place it at all—that singsong mishmash of British, Irish and Canadian was unmistakable. "Newfoundland or Labrador?"

That made him smile, if briefly. "Both, now and again," he said. "They both have their charms."

"I'll bet. I've only been out there once, but—"

A low growl cut me short. I glanced over to see a gray wolf peering around a tree. It was the one I'd seen earlier with him. She growled again, lips fluttering over sharp white teeth.

"I'm okay," he said, drawing it out, more reassuring growl than words. "Go on now."

She backed up, but only to sit down, death stare fixed on me.

"She thinks you're checking out a new mate," I said.

"New...?" He stared, then sputtered a laugh. "Exactly how native do you think I've gone? Or maybe you just answered my question."

"I just thought— Well, I mean, if you prefer wolf form... Anyway, I think she considers *you* her mate."

"That she does, but I've not been encouraging her. She's a very nice girl, but it just wouldn't work out."

"That's a relief." I extended a hand. "Elena Michaels."

"Oh, I know who you are. We aren't as isolated on the Rock as you might think."

"Are there more of you out there? More werewolves?"

He shook my hand. "Morgan Walsh."

"In other words, if you do have family there, you aren't telling me. If they've been living there awhile and the Pack doesn't know it, then they're flying far enough below the radar that we'll keep pretending we don't know. So to change the subject, how long have you been...?" I glanced at the gray wolf.

"Running with the wolves? Well, it was the strangest thing. One day I came out to Alaska on a trip, I went for a run and totally forgot I could Change back. Luckily this wolf pack took pity on the poor dumb Newfie and took him in."

"Uh-huh."

He smiled. "All right, then. What do you think I'm doing out here? No, wait, let me guess. Wounded and scarred by life, I've decided to turn my back on the world and retreat into the forest, embracing my purer, simpler half."

"You don't look particularly scarred to me."

"Oh, I have my share. I'd show you, but I know that mate of yours can't be far behind, and I'd better not be taking off my clothes when he comes by."

"Actually, I'm more worried about *her* taking offense." I nodded to the wolf, who growled as our eyes met. "So *are* you going to tell me why you're running with the wolves? Or was that another polite brush-off?"

He leaned back against a tree, hands going into his pockets, looking out at the forest before answering. "Have you ever wondered what it would be like to switch? Live as wolf, Change to human only when you need to?"

"Sure."

"I finished college a few years ago. Got a job. Hated it. Quit. I'm young. No ties. Other guys, they'd backpack through Asia, bum around for a while until they got their shit together."

"Instead, you did this. How long have you been out here?"

"Since summer. I figure I'll give it a year."

"And how did you get the wolves to take you in?"

"Food," said a voice behind me.

As Clay stepped into view, Morgan jumped. He quickly recovered, retreating behind an impassive expression, but his eyes stayed wary, watching Clay's approach.

"Food, wasn't it?" Clay repeated.

Morgan found a smile for him, if only a small one. "It was. I'm a good hunter. It took some time, but if you leave enough offerings, they'll overcome their prejudices. There weren't many prejudices to be overcome before those knuckle-draggers set up camp. And I don't mean the beast-shifters. Yeah, that young one has been throwing his weight around this winter, but we just stay out of his way. Things got a lot worse when *they* showed up." He pointed at the clothing in my hands. "Before them, the only werewolves the wolves knew were the old guy and his grandson, and neither of them ever caused any problems." He glanced at Clay. "The old man was a friend of yours?"

"A Pack mate, once upon a time."

"Sorry for your loss, then. I didn't know him myself, but he seemed a decent guy. And, before you ask, no, I didn't know they'd gone to kill him. I was off hunting at the time. When I came back, the rest of the pack had found him— you probably saw their tracks at the cabin."

"We did."

"They..." He rubbed his chin. "It upset them. Confused them. It was as if they'd known your friend, even if they never made contact. They mourned for him. Anyway, I wasn't around at the time or—Well, as you can tell, I don't like getting involved. I've learned not to. But I'd have done something. And probably gotten myself killed. I'm a whiz at catching dinner, but I don't do so well with the predators." He glanced at me. "I mentioned the scars?"

"You did, and I appreciate what you *did* do, bringing the others to us."

"Tracking and hunting, those are my specialties. That means, though, that I usually arrive after the damage is done, like with your friend. But there's a reason I Changed back, and it's not just to say hello. I found something the other day you'll want to take care of before you leave. The beast-shifters buried the two girls that big son of a bitch killed. Only I kept finding traces of a third."

My head jerked up. "There *was* a third missing girl. You found her body?"

"No, I found her."

"What? She's alive?" I wheeled on Clay. "Travis must have been keeping her locked up. We need to—"

"Whoa, slow down," Morgan said. "He wasn't the one keeping her. The way I figure it, he left her for dead. Someone else found her. She's recovering. But . . . Well, I think you'd better just come along and have a look. It's . . . a bit of a situation."

I glanced at Clay. He took Tesler's clothing from me. "You go on. I'll catch up."

THE FIRST HALF of the walk was nearly silent. I could say that Morgan had just been uncharacteristically chatty earlier, after months talking to no one, but I got the impression he was, by nature, the kind of guy who talks a lot to cover the fact that he doesn't say very much.

It was a trait I recognized well. Not so much the chatty part—I've never been the type—but I've always been quick to join a conversation and hold up my end, which usually hides the fact that I'm not giving away anything of myself.

Act friendly and sociable, and people won't realize that you're keeping them firmly on the other side of your comfort zone.

I think what quieted Morgan down was Clay sending me off with him alone. Morgan was not only a stranger, but a younger, good-looking mutt. For Clay to casually allow me to go off with him must have seemed suspicious. Maybe he took offense at the suggestion that he didn't pose a threat. But if I had to hazard a guess, I'd say he suspected he was being tested . . . or set up.

After we'd walked for a while, with no sign of Clay or the others lurking in the trees, he relaxed and maybe understood the simple truth—Clay trusted me, trusted I could take care of myself, and trusted I wasn't the least bit susceptible to cute younger werewolves, which on this trip was proving to be a good thing.

So he finally started to talk again. He'd heard I was Canadian and asked where I was from, tossing in a few barbs about Toronto, which is our version of New York— everyone who doesn't live there has nothing but contempt for everyone who does. When he found out I reported on Canadian affairs, he asked for news of his home province— the ongoing sad state of the fisheries, the new offshore oil projects.

Wherever we were going, it was a long trudge through difficult landscape. But Morgan didn't have a problem traversing it, a fact he liked to point out every time he had to slow for me.

"Do you hear that?" I asked when a low moan set the hairs on my neck rising.

"Wind."

"No, I've heard wind, and that's not—"

"Trust me, up here, the wind does things you've never heard before. Sometimes I swear I hear voices. Entire conversations. I go to check it out, and there's no one there. I tell myself it's the wind, but . . ." He shrugged.

"There's something out here, isn't there?"

He hopped a fallen log buried under the snow. "There are a lot of somethings out here. Those beast-shifters are just the beginning. Voices, lights . . ."

"I've seen the lights. They led me onto a frozen river last night—one that wasn't frozen nearly well enough."

"I don't doubt it. I've had them lead me nearly over a cliff, and I've had them light my way back to the wolf pack. Capricious little buggers. I find tracks I don't recognize, scents I can't place, catch glimpses of shadows. Alaska's the last frontier—for man, beast and spirit alike. Now we'd better pipe down. The cabin's just ahead."

"Are you going to tell me who's responsible?"

A flashed grin. "No, I'll leave that up to your nose. See how long it takes you to figure it out."

As trustworthy as Morgan seemed, I couldn't help feeling those niggling pricks of paranoia. But now it took only one strong sniff to know he was playing me fair.

"Eli," I said.

"Is that his name? The young beast-shifter?"

I nodded. I glanced quickly at Morgan. "The girl. He didn't—"

"Rape her? No. Nothing like that, or I would have interfered. He found her and took care of her. She's not his prisoner, though she's probably not in any shape yet to think about leaving. But I suspect teenage infatuation—and teenage hormones—are at the root of this particular act of altruism."

"Damn." I sighed. "You were right then. This is a situation. I guess the first thing to do is get a look at the girl." I checked the wind. "No sign that Eli's still here."

"I've got your back."

"Thanks."

I moved forward, straining to see a building in the distance, and suddenly there it was right in front of me—a tiny wood log cabin, nestled among the trees.

I pulled back and took a good sniff. Still no sign of Eli. The scent of wood smoke lingered in the air, but none came from the chimney. All the windows were dark. I crept forward, Morgan at my heels. As quietly as I moved, though, he was quieter. I hesitated, then motioned him forward. I hated giving up the front spot, but the quietest tracker should lead.

Morgan took no more than a half-dozen steps before he stopped, swore and strode forward.

"Wait!" I called. "If you spook her—"

"Can't spook her when she's not here."

He wrenched open the cabin door. I peered around him into the dark, dank depths of the cottage. The empty depths.

Morgan swore again. I joined him. "If she escaped and she's out here alone . . ."

Morgan was already crouched, checking out the trail.

He brushed past me and hunkered down outside, moving about until he'd covered the area.

"She's not alone," he said. "Eli relocated her. In the last hour, too. I tried not to get too close, but I wanted to get a look at her, make sure she hadn't been bitten."

My stomach twisted. "Had she?"

"Nah. That guy used his fists, not his teeth, thankfully. But Eli must have found my trail, and knew I was coming around, checking up on her."

Snow crunched in the distance. Morgan wheeled, straightening and stiffening as he lifted his head to catch the breeze.

"Did our situation turn into a problem?" Clay called as he stepped from the thick trees with Antonio, Nick and Reese close behind.

"A small one, I hope," I said.

As I explained, Morgan followed the trail, then came back to say it led into the nearest creek . . . and disappeared.

"He waded through it. So what I'd suggest . . ." Morgan began, then looked at the faces of the others, all turned toward me. "Or maybe not . . ."

"We split into pairs," I said. "If anyone other than me finds him, call for backup. I've talked to him, so I know how to handle it. If you bump into the other Shifters, tell them you're with me and we've done as they asked. Now, for pairings . . ." I turned to Reese. "How's your tracking?"

He opened his mouth, chin lifting a fraction, clearly ready to say his tracking skills were top-notch. Then he glanced at Nick, and said, "Not bad."

"All right then, you come with me. Nick goes with Antonio. Clay? You and Morgan?"

Clay nodded. Morgan slanted a wary look his way.

"Um, I'd really rather pair up with..." Morgan began, then glanced around at everyone else getting ready to go. "Or, I suppose it doesn't really matter what I want, does it?"

"Sorry," I said. "This works best. You concentrate on tracking; he'll have your back."

And we split up.

CHOICES

I'D BE LYING if I didn't say I picked Reese more for his company than for his skills. He hadn't said much since arriving. Under the circumstances, that wasn't surprising. But I wanted to make sure he was okay. I felt...I don't know, responsible, I guess, having been the one to send him to the Sorrentinos.

"How are your fingers?" I asked as we walked along the creekbank, trying to pick up Eli's trail.

"Still gone," he said. "Jeremy stitched me up good and gave me painkillers, so it's just a matter of getting used to not having them. I keep fumbling stuff. It'd be worse if I'd lost the whole fingers, though. And if I have to lose part of two, better those ones than the thumb and index. And better fingers than my hand. Better part of my hand than my life..." A wry smile. "I'm trying to look on the bright side."

"I'm sorry it happened. If we'd known there were other mutts in Anchorage—"

"And if I had stopped long enough to hear you out... Or if I'd tried to contact the Pack and explain instead of running... Or if I hadn't hooked up with those losers in the first place... I'm pretty sure the blame falls squarely at my feet on this one. You guys have been great to me." He looked over, meeting my gaze. "Really."

I bent to sniff a scent, but it was only a bear. "Nick tells me you still don't want to go back to Australia."

Reese stiffened, and I knew I wasn't getting anything more out of him on that count. Not for a while, I suspected.

"No," he said. "I'm staying."

"Any thoughts on the future?"

"Antonio offered me a job." He bent to sniff something, then wrinkled his nose and shook his head. "It's student work—the kind of thing he hires college kids for during the summer. I'm thinking of taking it." A glance at me, gauging my reaction.

"Sounds good."

"It's temporary," he added, as if starting to hope maybe it wouldn't be. "Antonio said I can stay with them, take over some yard work, maybe move into the guest house. They've been great. Antonio's fair, and Nick's—" He smiled. "Nick's cool. It's not what I expected. The Pack."

"That's good," I said.

And it was. I'd already started thinking Reese fit in well—obeyed orders, pulled his weight, was still young enough to assimilate. The kind of recruit the Pack could use. I didn't suggest that, though. It was too soon, and he wasn't going anywhere. Let him settle in and, maybe, stay settled.

When I found the trail, I whistled for the others. Sure, I'd said I could handle this alone, but that only meant I wouldn't waste time hunting for them. A whistle or two, I could do. When no one answered, though, Reese and I set out on the trail.

We hadn't gone far when a blast of icy air whipped past, laden with that thick musky scent.

"What the hell is that?" Reese asked, rubbing his nose.

Before I could answer, a massive form lumbered from the woods, stopping twenty feet away and turning to look at us.

"What the hell—?" Reese said.

The beast reared up, casting a shadow that reached to our boots.

"Holy shit!"

The beast dropped and charged. Reese grabbed my sleeve and tried to yank me to safety. When I wouldn't budge, he gave me a shove off the trail and raced past me into the forest. I calmly walked back to the path.

The beast roared...and ran around me. Then he turned, pawing the path, breath streaming from his nostrils.

"Eli," I said. "Cut it out."

"That's—" Reese said from his spot in the woods. "That's Eli? The Shifter guy?"

"Shifter *kid*. He's a teenager."

"I don't care how young he is. He's fucking huge. And fucking pissed off."

"No, he's just putting on a show, trying to warn us off. Do you want us to leave, Eli?"

He snorted, still pawing the ground like a bull, head down, eyes blazing.

"Okay, we'll do that," I said. "We'll go pick up Noah, and let your Alpha and your father handle this."

Eli growled. He lunged. When I stood my ground, he stopped short, snow flying from his massive paws.

"Go Change back so we can talk about this."

"SHIT, THAT WAS fast," Reese said as Eli lumbered out of the thicket where he'd Changed.

"That's one advantage they get," I murmured.

"Nice, but I don't think I'd trade," Reese said as he took a better look at Eli.

Reese quickly hid his reaction to the young Shifter, but Eli couldn't disguise his own response to the young werewolf, shoulders and jaw lifting as he drew nearer, eyeing Reese with the barely disguised envy of an awkward sophomore in the presence of the high school quarterback. I felt sorry for Eli, then. He wasn't an ugly kid, but at that age, no one—supernatural or human—needs to be reminded of his shortcomings.

He turned his back on Reese and talked to me. "She doesn't want to go back."

"Good. Then she can tell me that."

He hesitated, big jaw working. Then he pushed back his hair and scanned the forest, and I thought he was working on an excuse, but instead he said, "Fine. She won't like it, though."

He led me along the path.

"She does want to stay," he said as we walked. "She *asked* me to move her."

"All right."

"You don't believe me."

I glanced over at him. "Do you really expect me to take your word for it?"

He didn't answer, and we walked the rest of the way in silence.

WE REACHED THE cabin, another small backwoods, off-the-grid one probably used by anyone needing shelter.

When we arrived, Eli insisted Reese stay outside—apparently, he didn't want the cute, blond Aussie getting too close to his girl. That was fine, but I made Eli wait, too. If this girl was as set on staying as he said, then she needed to tell me that herself.

I opened the door. Inside, it was dark, the light having flicked off the moment we drew within sight of the cottage.

"I won't go," said a voice from deep in the shadows. "You can turn around right now. I'm eighteen, so I can make my own decisions."

Of the three missing girls, two had been twenty, which gave me a good idea who I was talking to. The one who'd been living on the streets, trying to escape a life of abuse and neglect.

"You're seventeen, Adine."

"Eighteen next month. Better off saving yourself the paperwork and pretending you never found me."

"I'm not from social services. I'm just someone who wants to make sure you're okay."

I turned on the nearest lantern. A wavering light filled

the cabin. Adine sat on a cot in the corner, her face set, her expression saying if I was going to take her out of here, I'd damned well better have brought an army to do it.

"I know what happened to you," I said.

"Yeah? Same shit, different day."

I met her gaze and recognized that haunted, hunted animal look. I'd never been this tough, though, as much as I'd wanted to be.

"What happened to you is—" I began.

"Gonna leave scars. Scars no one can see. Yeah, I've done the sessions. If you're expecting me to say I'm fine, you're wrong. But I'm sure as hell going to get back to fine. And Eli's going to help me."

"He—"

"He's just a kid, I know. And something...something's not quite right about him. I know that, too. But I don't care. He rescued me and he took care of me, and he doesn't want anything in return, just to be with me, talk to me." She met my gaze. "You know what that's like?"

Actually, I did, but I knew she wouldn't believe me. And as I looked in her face, I knew she wasn't kidding herself. Eli wasn't her knight in shining armor. She didn't expect happily ever after. But whatever it was, it's what she wanted. What she needed.

"If she wants to join us, she may," rumbled a voice behind me.

I turned to see the Shifter Alpha in the doorway. Behind him, Eli's father had his son by the scruff of the neck. The Alpha stepped in and shut the door.

"This is not our way," he said. "But if the girl wants to come..." He looked at me. "We should not argue."

In other words, sending this girl back to civilization, angry and unhappy, really wasn't the best idea. She was likely to start talking about the Shifters. That might only land her a bed in the psych ward, but they couldn't take the chance.

He turned to Adine. "We live far away. You will not be able to visit your people."

"Fine by me," she said, chin lifted, defiant.

"We have a village, but we are hunters. We do not come to the city."

"I can hunt and I can fish, and I'm a damned fine cook—though I like the hunting and fishing part better. I've had enough of the city. It wasn't..." A look passed over her face, disappointment and regret. "It wasn't what I thought it would be. I'm ready to go back inland." She straightened and met his gaze. "I'll do my share. You won't regret it."

The Alpha's expression said he was pretty sure he would, but he only nodded.

I turned to him. "She might want to go now, but after a while..."

"She may change her mind," he murmured. "If she does, we will bring her back. You have our word."

As I looked at Adine, I realized I had no right to make this choice for her. No one had that right, because no one was her, no one else lived her life and knew what was best.

What would I have done if someone told me to stop seeing Clay when we were dating? They couldn't have told me anything I didn't already know. I'd spent years telling myself that Clay tricked me, deceived me, but he hadn't. I'd seen the warning signs and I'd worried about them and, in the end, I'd decided to do what was best for me—stay with him.

I'd spent years dealing with my choice, and the consequences, and went right back to where I'd been. Did that make me weak? No. I'd realized that what I needed wasn't necessarily what the world thought was right.

For me, this worked, and no one had the right to interfere. No more than I had the right to interfere with Adine now.

So I gave them my blessing. If this was the life she chose, if it made her happy, that was what mattered.

INITIATION

THE SHIFTER ALPHA and I stepped from the cabin, leaving Eli and his father inside with Adine. Reese stood beside the window, where he must have been peering in. As I came out, he heaved a sigh of relief.

"Everything okay?" he asked. "I wanted to go inside, but they—"

"I'm fine."

"I whistled for the others," he said, as much to the Alpha as to me, as if warning him. "Someone whistled back, so they're coming."

"Good, thanks."

I turned to the Alpha and told him that I'd taken care of Tesler's pack, as per our deal. I'm sure he already knew, but he listened politely. Reese hovered at my elbow, playing bodyguard, which would have been just fine except for the awkward glances he kept shooting at the Alpha. He was trying so hard not to stare it would have been better if he'd just taken a good, hard look and gotten it out of his system.

"Reese? I think I hear the guys coming. Can you run

and warn them, so they don't come barreling in, ready for trouble?"

He hesitated, gaze shunting again to the Alpha.

"I'm fine," I said. "Go."

And he did, but slowly, shuffling off with plenty of checks over his shoulder, making sure I wasn't in imminent danger of being devoured. A week ago, the guy ran every time I came near. Now I couldn't get rid of him.

At a noise, Reese whirled, fists raised. It was Noah, rounding a corner in the path, walking a few steps ahead of his captor.

"He is yours now," the Alpha said.

"Hey there," I said.

Noah smiled weakly. Reese pulled off his glove, extended his hand and introduced himself. I could see the wheels turning in Noah's brain, running through the names he'd probably heard from Dennis—Pack names—and not recognizing this one. I was about to explain when he took Reese's hand in an awkward shake, and felt the bandages.

"Oh, you're the guy..." Noah said. "Travis told us. Sadistic bastard."

Reese gave a wry smile. "Yeah. But he's worse off now than I am, so that's some consolation." He thumped Noah on the back. "Elena's got some business here, and I can smell Nick coming. Let's go see if we can sneak up on him."

Terror flicked across Noah's face. Obviously he didn't consider scaring the crap out of a senior Pack member a good way to make a first impression. I sent Reese on his way and motioned Noah over, stepping from the Alpha and lowering my voice. The Alpha nodded and went back into the cabin.

"Are you okay?" I asked.

He nodded. "I went back for you, but they grabbed me. I tried to fight, but..." His face reddened and I could see a bruise along his jaw, probably only one of many hidden by the oversized parka they'd given him.

"You weren't the only one who got captured. And I *didn't* fight. Took one look at them and didn't dare."

A shout to our left. I glanced up as Clay loped through the trees, Reese on his heels. I don't know who looked more worried—Clay hoping I was okay or Reese thinking of how Clay would react if I wasn't.

"Everything's good," I called as Nick, Antonio and Morgan jogged up behind Reese. "Guys, this is Noah."

When Noah didn't budge, I took his arm with my uninjured hand and pulled him forward. I could feel him trembling through the parka, and the mother in me wanted to let him hang back, not push too hard. But the Alpha-to-be knew how important this was. So I only held him steady when it seemed his knees might give way.

"This is Noah," I said again. "Joey's son."

Clay stepped within inches of Noah, towering over him. I can only imagine what stories the Teslers had told him about Clay, what stories even Dennis might have told. I can only imagine what fate Noah thought might lie in store for him now, after joining the enemy in his misguided attempts to protect his father. So I can only give him full credit for not turning tail, but standing firm, even if he was shaking so hard his teeth chattered.

Clay's nostrils flared, taking in Noah's scent as he surveyed him head to foot. When he reached forward, Noah flinched, but didn't fall back. Clay took his arm and drew him over to the others.

"Noah, this is Antonio Sorrentino..."

PACK

TWENTY-FOUR HOURS LATER, I was still in Alaska, back in those woods, in a huge clearing, watching the rest of the Pack play touch football in the snow with the twins. My bruised and battered body—and broken finger—kept me sidelined, but I was enjoying the rest and peace.

There'd been little rest and peace in the last day. Less than Clay and Jeremy wanted for me, anyway.

Joey was gone. He *had* returned to the hotel; I gave him credit for that. He'd left a message with a hotel clerk, saying it was urgent and Clay had to get it right away. That was about the same time that Jeremy convinced someone to wake Clay. They gave him the note, which explained what had happened, and provided a map to the last place Joey had seen me. Then he asked for forgiveness and promised he wouldn't trouble us again. When Noah took us to Joey's condo, we found it empty.

While a happy ending, full of forgiveness and mercy, would be wonderful, I think this was the best solution for all. At least for now. If anyone remained of the Tesler pack—

some lackey who hadn't come to Alaska but knew the story—and spread the word that Joey betrayed us and Clay had done nothing... Clay would have had to make an example of his old friend. Maybe Joey knew that. Maybe that's why he ran.

I looked out at the field. Logan was at Jeremy's side as they tried to get Antonio to pass them the ball.

Jeremy was concerned about any Tesler pack members still at large, so he'd had Jaime and the twins take the next plane out. I'm sure a long plane ride with toddlers wasn't her idea of heaven, but she didn't complain. Arriving to find that Jeremy had booked her a day at the spa helped. That's where she was now, Jeremy having suggested it, knowing that an afternoon in the Alaskan wilderness really wasn't her idea of a good time.

Karl was here, too, with Hope. They were off on the sidelines, Hope sitting on a tree stump, leaning back against Karl as she tried to persuade him to join the game. He'd insisted Hope come to Alaska, in case we needed her trouble-sensing skills. She wasn't entirely comfortable with that, no matter how many times I told her she was welcome.

Hope and I were going to visit Lynn Nygard later. That was a contact I wanted to keep, in case Adine decided Shifter life wasn't for her. After her experience, handing her over to a paranormal enthusiast might not seem wise, but at least she'd find support and a sympathetic ear. No one else would listen to those stories, and Lynn would be the first to tell her so.

Karl finally gave in and joined the game, dragging a protesting Hope behind him. He stole the ball. When he passed it to Hope, she stared down at it, a tiny figure swallowed by an oversized parka. Then she noticed the half-dozen big guys bearing down on her and took off running, ball in hand.

Nick, Reese and Noah pulled a fast surround maneuver. Nick got the ball, and the three of them raced down the field, passing it back and forth. Yes, it seemed Noah was staying with us. Whisking him out of the state while on parole was far from ideal, but he couldn't exactly go to the authorities and explain why he'd broken parole... and why his newfound father and grandfather had disappeared. So he'd disappear, too, and the authorities would presume all three had gone into the forest and met some mysterious fate. Out here, there were a lot of mysterious fates to be met.

Noah was going home with the Sorrentinos. That was Nick's idea. He joked that they were opening a home for wayward young werewolves. I watched him, now huddled with two young men, figuring out a way to get the ball back. Nick had realized that having kids of his own wasn't in the picture, but he'd still needed something, still seemed to be looking for a way to fill that void. Maybe this would do it.

So the Pack had a new member. Maybe two, if Reese stayed. There was even the chance of a third. Morgan had hung around yesterday, helping out, meeting Jeremy and asking questions about the Pack. He'd expressed nothing I could interpret as obvious interest, but agreed that when he was done with his experiment, he'd come by Syracuse for a few beers.

At a shriek, I looked out to see Kate with the ball, tearing toward the goal, little legs pumping. Clay ran backup, shouldering Nick and Reese aside when they tried to get close. Noah raced over, glanced at Clay, then backed off. As Antonio snuck up, I leaned forward to shout a warning to Kate. My ribs protested and I grimaced.

"Are you all right?"

I looked down to see Logan beside me.

"I'm fine," I said. "Just a little sore."

He studied my face, then nodded. He started to settle in at my feet, ready to take up the task of keeping his invalid mother company.

"Go on," I said. "I'm fine."

He checked my face again, uncertain.

"A jelly doughnut says you can't get that ball from your sister."

Like his father, Logan can never resist a challenge. With a grin, he raced off. Kate was almost at the goal line, but Antonio had leapt into her way.

"Kate!" Logan shouted, racing toward her.

He held his hands out for the ball. She threw it, a pitch-perfect toss. He caught it . . . and started running toward the other goal. Kate howled and tore after him. So did Clay, keeping right on his heels as Logan's giggles rang out, cheeks rosy, snowpants swishing, snow flying up around him. At the last second, he veered, ran back and threw the ball to his sister. They took off, tossing it back and forth as the adults pretended to try getting it back.

"So," said a voice beside me. "What do you think of your Pack?"

I turned to Jeremy as he stepped up beside me.

"Not mine yet," I said.

"But it will be." His dark eyes danced. "Think you're up to it?"

Someone shouted and I turned to look at them all, playing in the field.

I smiled. "Not yet. But I'm working on it."